Praise for Nisha Minhas's novels,
Chapatti or Chips? and *Sari & Sins:*

'Wonderfully vibrant characters . . . beautifully (and sometimes painfully) observed' Chris Manby

'That old dilemma of sex and passion versus prudence and a healthy bank balance is given an entertaining Eastern spin' *Marie Claire*

'An entertaining read with characters you can easily warm to' *Asian Woman*

'A funny look at the East-West culture clash' *Heat*

'Minhas conquers the touchy subject of arranged meetings in the UK with her witty novel' *OK Magazine*

'Tradition and family loyalty collides with desire, resulting in a story that is interesting, funny and insightful . . . The characters are outrageous but also so real' Faith Bleasdale

'A fun read which raises important issues about two very different cultures, filled with vibrant characters and some painful observations about life' *Newcastle Journal*

Also by Nisha Minhas
Sari & Sins
Chapatti or Chips?

In her early thirties, Nisha Minhas lives in Milton Keynes with her partner and two cats. *Passion & Poppadoms* is her third novel.

Visit www.nishaminhas.co.uk

Passion & Poppadoms

NISHA MINHAS

LONDON • SYDNEY • NEW YORK • TORONTO

First published in Great Britain by Simon & Schuster, 2004
This edition first published by Pocket Books, 2004
An imprint of Simon & Schuster UK
A Viacom company

1 3 5 7 9 10 8 6 4 2

Simon & Schuster UK Ltd
Africa House
64-78 Kingsway
London WC2B 6AH

www.simonsays.co.uk

Simon & Schuster Australia
Sydney

A CIP catalogue record for this book is available from the British Library

ISBN 0 7434 6880 5

Typeset by SX Composing DTP, Rayleigh, Essex
Printed and bound in Great Britain by
Cox & Wyman Ltd, Reading, Berkshire

For the love of my life, Dave.
∞0X9!

In loving memory of my dad,
Gurmit Singh Minhas.
You are always in my thoughts and
will never leave my heart.

Acknowledgements

My wonderful partner, Dave – who helps make my writing so much fun, who encourages me to write even when I think I can't. Thanks for everything, the help, the ideas, the poems, and especially the laughs. You are so sturdy and sweet – you are my rock, my stick of rock.

Kate Lyall Grant, my editor – many thanks once again for your brilliant skills and professionalism. At times I feel my books are like spoilt children, they swear too much, don't make sense sometimes and are too crude and rude. Thankfully you are there to sort the spoilt brats out. So thank you, Aunt Kate.

Lorella Belli, my agent – thanks for the hard work you do behind the scenes and everything you do to make my life easier. Also *molto grazie* for the Italian in the book.

To everyone at Simon & Schuster who I don't get to see but I know work so hard – thank you. And a special thank you to Nigel Stoneman, in publicity; I know I'm not as glamorous as Jackie Collins but it's fun working with you. Cheers. Also I'd like to thank the cover designer and artist for the excellent jackets.

Rob Bell – thank you for your kind help that time (it will always be remembered), and thanks for showing a genuine interest in the books.

My parents and family – whom I love with all my heart. Writing these books has made me realise the difficulties of moving to another country while trying to tow your homeland behind you. You are so brave.

The Dichotomy of a British-born Asian

To thirst for India
when India thirsts.
To know you're free
when freedom hurts.
To be proud of brown
and yet be cursed.
To be British-born
but Indian first.

by Dave Bell Carney

Chapter One

It came as no surprise to the people who knew Thomas Harding that he would end up living with more than one woman at the same time. Some nights he would have over twenty women under his roof, all satisfied, all completely amazed at the service that he provided. Single, married, engaged, Thomas did not care, just as long as they went away with a smile on their face.

Today, on this sweltering Friday in August, as he sat alone on a king-sized bed, with the air-conditioning on full, Thomas was far from smiling. The big Three-O had never really bothered him before. Until this morning that is, when his thirtieth birthday cards came through the letterbox. Normally his birthday went unnoticed, a couple of cards, a couple of presents and it was over. Another year gone by. Today, half of Clintons was on the mat. Everyone wanted to make sure Thomas knew he was thirty; his twenties were gone. He had now crossed the thirty threshold. Even going downhill nowadays would be an uphill battle.

Thomas jumped out of bed and walked to the window. His garden was a Titchmarsh wet dream. Or 'a handful of heaven' as one of Thomas's customers had commented. A barrier of thick-set oak trees guarded the rear of the garden, hemming the grounds in from the Oxfordshire countryside. Colourful flowers and exotic plants wove across a perfect lawn, which was dotted with wooden benches and the odd outhouse. A huge black and gold speckled marble gravestone protruded from the grass near one of the gardener's sheds in the distance, and Thomas stared towards it, drawn to the comfort it brought on depressing days like this.

He kicked himself. Millionaires shouldn't get depressed. Millionaires who owned successful four-star hotels, who drove top-of-the-range Porsches, who wore designer clothes, who owned a multitude of stocks and shares, who lived in an apartment fit for Beverly Hills, who had a first-class honours degree in English from Oxford University, who could speak fluent Italian, French, German, Japanese and get by in most European languages, who had a loving family, who were born with fantastic looks, a wicked sense of humour and an unbelievable personality to boot. Depressed – most people who knew *him* were. But why was he?

Sitting inconspicuously on Thomas's duvet was the cause. A letter scrawled in the scribble of a teenager: the letter he wrote to himself when he was just fourteen. Thomas could remember giving his mother the sealed envelope and asking her to make sure he received it on his thirtieth birthday. And, as promised, she delivered. Until today he'd forgotten all about it. Now, it was going to change his life. Thomas picked up the letter and read it through one more time.

Thomas,

Happy thirtieth birthday. I bet you've grown up to be quite a stud by now. If I've guessed correctly, you are with a beautiful, leggy blonde, who turns heads wherever she goes. I've dreamt about her many times, with tissues beside my bed. I expect you to have achieved great wealth, to drive a sports car, to demand respect, to live the life. I've dreamt about him too, many times (without tissues, mind you).

From the outside, I expect you seem a success. I expect when people see your packaging they see a man who has it all.

Now for some depressing news. I know you. *I know what forces spin your mind in your skull. I know that you don't love the woman who you are with. I know that you have only picked her for her packaging.*

DUMP HER!

DUMP THE LEGGY BLONDE! . . .

Noises outside the bedroom pulled Thomas's eyes away from the partly read letter. He now had three seconds to cover his willy. Three . . . two . . . Thomas grabbed the duvet. One.

His bedroom door banged open. 'Oh, Mr Harding.' It was Josephine, the head chambermaid, metal bucket and mop in hand, an embarrassed red rash crawling up her neck. 'Sorry, I didn't realize you were here. You forget to hang the "Do Not Disturb" sign on your knob, again.' She stared at the ceiling.

Thomas nodded to himself, then in his upper-class voice replied, 'Yes, Josie. My mistake, sorry about that. Would it be possible to clean the apartment later? I will endeavour to make sure I make full use of my knob next time. Two o'clock okay?'

She agreed, then scurried away into the bowels of the eighty-room four-star hotel. Josephine had been with Thomas since the beginning and watched at first-hand how a man could become a success. It had taken him five years of sweat and graft to build up. From a small homely guest house with barely four guests a week, Thomas had built the business like a termite nest. Extensions created more extensions. Word-of-mouth created more word-of-mouth. Until finally, one fine summer's day, Thomas stood with his back to his huge car park, facing the built-up, lit-up building and declared: 'It's finished.' The Regency Hotel had been born. Suspicion that he was doing well for himself arose when his bank manager sent him a Christmas present. And more guests had been turned away than had stayed. *Fully Booked* was the Regency's slogan.

But even though fully booked, Thomas always seemed to find room to stay there. In fact, he lived there. A huge open-plan luxury apartment built into the structure on the second floor. A futuristic, gadget-filled, airy home which encouraged great laziness. He even had a voice-activated computer, called Hal, who adjusted lights, curtains, stereo, TV and heating.

About to return to the letter, Thomas was disturbed yet again, this time by the noise of stilettos on the wooden floor, and he wedged the pages under the mattress. Nicole, his girlfriend of three years, might take offence at the words 'Dump the leggy blonde.'

After all, she was one.

She appeared at the bedroom entrance and smiled. 'Mummy's twisted Daddy's arm and if you wish to, Tom, Daddy will take you on a shoot this weekend. It will be his present to you.' Nicole jumped into bed beside him with a bottle of champagne in her hand. 'Happy birthday.' And she kissed him on the lips.

'Am I allowed to shoot him? No, I think I can find better ways to spend my time than assassinating wild-life. Besides, I have a wedding to host this weekend.'

Nicole's mouth twisted slightly. 'I see. How do you expect my father to ever like you when you snub him at every turn? Can't you at least try for me? Shoot at their legs or something. You don't *have* to kill them.'

'I am not maiming a bunny just so your father likes me,' he said, ripping open another birthday card. 'Anyway, you can't bear the suffering of animals. No matter how tiny. You even cried when the scientists said they might be eradicating smallpox. "A whole civilization wiped out," you said, if I remember correctly.'

She huffed. 'I just want Daddy to like you.'

But Daddy didn't like many people. He was a powerful man named Edmond Newton-Harrington, rumoured to be a billionaire and held in high regard amongst the elevated echelons of propriety society, the upper crusts. Any kindness he did show was showered on his daughters, the three beautiful, blonde spoiltlings. Arabella, Holly and the baby of the bunch, twenty-eight-year-old Nicole. Edmond was surrounded by the colour brown. Most people who came into contact with him had their noses so far up his backside that by the time they resurfaced for air their lives had been ruined. Thomas refused to go anywhere near Edmond's back passage, and therefore Edmond had taken an instant dislike to him from day one. Thomas was never far from Edmond's gun sight. One step out of line with his youngest daughter and he would be squashed like a soggy pea.

And Nicole was used to being protected. It came with the territory of being born into money. Ask and thou shalt get, was her motto. And cry if denied. Money was just paper. So much so that Nicole and her two sisters found great pleasure in wrapping the hired help's birthday presents in £50 notes. It didn't take long for the staff to begin requesting huge presents. One even asked for an inflated bouncy castle – and never had to work again.

Undressing beneath the duvet, Nicole tossed her clothes on to the wooden floor, and pressed herself up to Thomas. There was definitely not a 'Do Not Disturb' sign on this knob, and if Nicole didn't have £200 lipstick on, she would have licked her lips. Sex was right up there with shopping when it came to excitement, as far as she was concerned. Although, after shopping, no one rolled her over to the cold side of the bed and fell asleep, muttering the words, 'Probably the best hotel in Oxfordshire.'

Caught up in the sounds of their passion, Nicole couldn't help but hear the tinkling of her gold bracelet. The immensely expensive piece of jewellery, clustered with diamonds, was a symbol of Thomas's love for her and was engraved with the words: *Light My Flame. End This Pain.* She wondered if she could bear to take it off.

Thomas saw fear in Nicole's light-blue eyes as she studied her bracelet. He gently spoke. 'Nicole, babe, now is not the time.'

'It is the time. It's your birthday and you said yourself the longer I leave it, the harder it will become.' She forced a smile. 'Don't you want to see me completely naked again? Are you afraid?'

'I just don't want you becoming depressed. That's all.'

Somewhat relieved, Nicole threw herself back to work. She loved sitting on top and gawping down. His fantastic looks had caught her off guard many a time. Shouldn't men this good looking be bastards? And not just in her eyes. He left a wake of turned female heads wherever his perfectly formed body sailed. Thomas was prime hunk. In fact, even though he didn't know it, Thomas was Brad Pitt's worst nightmare (that's Brad Pitt without the four-foot-long matted beard and hill-billy accent). His dark-blue eyes were temptation itself, his hair was Bournville brown, in need of a comb – or maybe it was meant to be that way, it didn't really matter, he was simply gorgeous. And women loved him.

Nicole had to smile sometimes, though. With all Thomas's wealth and upbringing, even he had a tacky taste that defied imagination. How many men, normal men, had condom vending machines by their bed? Taking coins from a pile beside the machine she slotted them in and waited for the Durex to drop.

Rattling the box as if she'd won a prize, Nicole was frustrated to hear his mobile ring.

'Don't you dare answer that, Tom. Don't you dare pick it up. The hotel can live without you for one minute.'

His hand hovered. He sheepishly glanced her way; but he wasn't going to let a woman's orgasm get in the way of his hotel. 'Hello.'

Smack! Nicole's palm went across his head. No visual response from Thomas, which was most annoying. In 'room booking' mode, Thomas was like a Buddhist monk, feeling no pain, hearing no outside interference. She jumped off the bed in a huff, threw the condom box at his face, grabbed her clothes, then stormed out of the bedroom, slamming the door behind her. How dare he treat her like this on her birthday? How bloody . . . She stopped in her tracks. On no, she suddenly remembered, it was *his* birthday. Shame on her. Cringing back into her Jean Paul Gaultier dress and high-heeled strappy sandals, she crept back in. Thomas, by now, was finished on the phone.

'Sorry about that episode, Tom. I come from a family genetically handicapped, without the ability to hold in their frustrations.'

'You mean you are spoilt?'

'Yes.' She sat beside him on the bed. 'I just want to spend some quality time with you, without this bloody hotel interfering. Which is quite ironic really, considering the only way that I'll get to spend this quality time with you is if we book into another hotel.' She paused. 'Then again, you'll most likely end up comparing prices and standard of service.' Nicole grabbed his hand. 'What is the point in having a hunk of a man, when I don't get to show him off sometimes, hey? The only women who get to see the quality of man that I can attract are your precious guests. It's so unfair. I'm sick of showing people that photograph I've got of you, I want them to see the real you, the one without the red eye. I'm taking you out for dinner tonight, and no buts.'

They arranged to meet that evening, kissed and cuddled, then Nicole left for her other home in the country. The vast, stretching mansion of Castle Cliff Manor was the family estate. Her two sisters, Holly and Arabella, lived there full time with her parents, pet dogs, horses and servants, whilst Nicole spread her time between Thomas's apartment and the Manor, not willing to take the full plunge until they were married.

And marriage could be a stumbling block. Thomas had been through all that before. The going down on one knee, the hopeful smile, the perfect moment. Always he told the women to get up off the floor, wipe their eyes, and think of a more sensible question to ask him. They were dumped soon afterwards. Only to be replaced by a replica. His twenties, before he met Nicole, had been one long party. A woman in tow wherever he may go. The dances and clubs, the parties and stag nights. The masked balls, the yacht trips, the chartered flights to New York. Rich boys with just one ploy: enjoyment at all costs. Everything a man of his age should have done was done, and more besides. His life so far had been devoid of regret. And he wished it to stay that way. Hence the reluctance to jump into the minefield of marriage.

Dressed in his Valentino suit, Thomas smiled as he read the message on the birthday card his mother had sent him.

Happy Birthday, Son,

As you know, you have always been my favourite, a cut above the rest. Out of all my children I love you the most, even though you are my only child. I say this with a heavy heart, but, if your father and I had had another child, I think that you would not have been our favourite. But, you are our favourite, and with that favouritism comes the burden of high expectations. You have made us proud. Age thirty and you are not a junkie. Enjoy yourself.

Love,

Mom and Grumpy Pops

PS Text me and let me know what you think of your present. Love you from all four chambers of my heart. X X X

There used to be a time when Thomas had wished for a normal set of parents. Like when his school mates were being waved off on school skiing trips by normal mums and dads, and Thomas would be waving to a set of parents who thought it highly amusing to dress up as gorillas. Or the time Mom came to a school sports day dressed in a nurse's uniform, pretending she needed urine samples from the winners in case they were using steroids. The headmaster was offended that anyone would think his private school would have cheats, although even he was slightly suspicious of ten-year-old Matthew

Tobias Jarvis's shaving rash and receding hairline.

But as Thomas grew through his teenage years, he began to appreciate the value of originality. Of difference. Of humanity. Why try to be like everyone else? He wouldn't swap his parents and their quirky behaviour for anything. And they made him appreciate where he came from. How not all children were as well off as he was. Not all children had the luxury of a private education. Not all children owned their first Mercedes convertible at seventeen. Money was never short in his house, but nor was love. And the value of recreation was never underestimated. But what sport would Thomas excel in?

Mom's mind was made up when she saw a programme on the television about Russia. How the quickest way to teach someone to swim was to throw them in the water. At just eleven months old, Thomas was hurled into the family swimming pool and encouraged to swim for glory. She would never listen to the Russians again (Pops insisted that Thomas would have stood more of a chance in reaching the other side without the nappy on). But somehow Thomas grew fond of the water, his mother encouraging him to join a club at an early age. Training, training, training. And then came the medals.

In some ways Thomas's first love was the water. A genuine water baby. He still swam a couple of hundred lengths per week, enjoying the weightlessness, immersing himself in the freedom that only water could bring. Maybe he was a dolphin in a former life, or the man from Atlantis.

Thomas unwrapped the present. Mom's wrapping

paper was slightly unnerving – a hospital sick bag. Inside was a blank DVD disc with one instruction: *Play Me In Private.* This was an ominous sign.

'Living room. TV on, Hal, thank you,' Thomas said clearly, always polite to his machines.

The enormous plasma television flashed to life as ordered. The surround-sound speakers made a quick sound check as Thomas loaded the DVD into the player. Thomas was beyond surprise with Mom. This could be the very film of Lee Harvey Oswald shooting JFK and he wouldn't bat an eyelid. He slouched into the gargantuan sofa and waited for the DVD to begin.

Thomas watched with an open mouth; what he was witnessing was beyond his pain threshold. By the sounds coming from the speakers it was beyond his mother's pain threshold too. A gagging sensation crept steadily up from Thomas's stomach, tickled his tonsils, then barged into his mouth. He grabbed for the sick bag as his mother screamed louder. He retched noisily.

'Living room. TV off, Hal . . . thank . . . you.' Thomas turned his head away. What mother sends her son a copy of his own birth? What son really wants to watch his mother's legs jammed apart as his own head emerges into this world? SICK!

Chapter Two

The two twenty-something flatmates sat across the small table in their kitchen contemplating how awful they had been to people over the years. The 'something' depended on whether they were after an older man or a younger one. It was time they sorted out the yin from the yang in their lives – before it sorted them out.

Marina sipped her Horlicks. 'Remember, Emily, the people we *were* are not the people we *are*. Think of it as apologizing for the bad deeds of someone else.'

Emily folded her arms. 'And by wiping the slate clean, you are guaranteeing that we will find ourselves dream men?' She laughed.

'Not only dream men, but dream husbands who will cherish all our womanly assets. We will become the women that other women hate. I'm reluctant to say it, Emily, but within a few weeks we are going to be despised.'

'Despised?' Emily slipped her feet into her heels.

Marina smiled smugly. 'Deeeespised!'

The problem was, they already were.

Just downstairs, through the damp wooden floorboards, the landlady, who was called various names, but christened Hilda, waited for the two layabout occupants above to become boisterous. They were late paying rent, late coming through the front door, late getting up in the morning, but never were they late with Friday nights. And Friday nights always started – Hilda checked the wall clock: 10.00 – about now!

Boom Boom BOOM BOOM BOOM! The music rattled the picture of Hilda's late mother, who was also once called various names, but christened Mavis. The picture was surely one day going to drop to the floor – just like poor Mavis had that awful day on her first and only visit to sprawling London. Her words when she arrived were: 'My goodness it's busy,' and then she was hit by a truck. The loss was terrible but cushioned by the fact that Hilda could now rent out the space that her mother used to occupy. Hence the two layabouts above.

The front door slammed shut: the two layabouts on the way to do 'unladylike' things. Hilda quickly switched off the light and squatted by the front window waiting for the girls to pass by in the dimly lit street outside. In her day even a whore would be ashamed to wear what these girls wore. But would the modern-day woman listen to an old lady? Would she heck.

As the girls disappeared up Fairground Road, Hilda did what she always did come Friday night: Hilda snooped in the girls' flat. She'd only been caught the once; quite surprised to find classical music amongst Marina's, the Indian girl's, collection, she'd lain back on the bed and fallen asleep in the middle of Holst's 'Mars'. The God of War. She'd needed the God of Peace to talk her way out of it, as she lay there snoring and dribbling on the pillow when the two drunk girls had returned from the pub. Her excuse was short and simple: 'Senile.' And she then went on to explain that sometimes she still thought she could hear her mother up there crying for help, which totally spooked the girls out. The two fools fell for it. Senile? Pher! Her 125-year-old mother still religiously played bingo at Mecca on Fridays anyway.

Hilda bolted the front door and climbed the stairs to the flat. From her apron pocket she pulled out a green surgical mask and placed it over her face. God, she hated the smell of Indian food! She entered the flat with trepidation, talking to herself as usual, knowing that the talking would soon stop. For always the girls would have left out something that would leave her lost for words. And today – she spotted the long list – was no exception. Written neatly on the back of a film poster (*Barbarella*) was a register of people's names, titled *Marina's & Emily's Hit List*, followed by the people's names (she presumed they were still alive at present) and at the bottom, the worrying message, *Deal with these living souls and we will be given a Sex God, each.*

Hilda imagined the worst.

The stink of kebabs, the shrill of sirens, the dirty laughter. Friday night down the High Street, with its multitude of pubs and clubs, sluts and slobs, grins and groans. A half-mile stretch of action that slowly becomes more yellow throughout the night as vomit paints the pavements. Welcome to Fenworth, in Oxfordshire. Only a couple of miles away from Britain's brightest brainboxes, or as Marina would say, 'the gifted ones', Fenworth is a mapless town without reference in most atlases and unfortunately without reference to sophistication. Most people refuse to pay their poll tax here on the grounds that they are not Polish. A bit fick. A bit soft in the head. A bit of a dump.

'He's a bit of all right,' Emily said, laughing, pointing to a poster of Bernard Manning glued to a boarded-up shop.

Marina plucked off her *bindi* and thumped it down on Bernard's head. 'There's a bit of India for you, my precious.'

They continued up the road, both enjoying the mild heat of August, with many male eyes enjoying the little clothes they wore. Before any headway could be made into the inner sanctum of Fenworth, a rendezvous with Knotty Cuts hairdresser's window was essential.

Directly under a street lamp, the girls stood staring at their appearance in the shop front. The view returned to their eyes was both honest and complimentary, it was also the only place which hadn't been donned with ram-raid-proof shutters where they could get a final check on their appearance.

'Reflections to give men erections,' they both said in unison, and then sneered at the picture of Kate Moss hanging at the back of the shop.

'I hope they nailed Kate's picture up with super-strong nails. I mean, she must weigh – what? – all of three ounces. Wouldn't want her bringing the wall down, would we?' Marina covered her mouth. 'God, Emily, I'm being bitchy again, aren't I? Must resist. Now, I will give you three compliments and you give me three in return.'

They faced each other. Marina was Bollywood beautiful with a body that broke the rules. Cakes and biscuits begrudged being eaten by her as she refused to get fat. Her long legs declined the offer of orange peel, her bum was still referred to as a bottom and not a bag of potatoes, her bust didn't need a burst of helium to keep it upright. She was a stunner. A bit of a late bloomer by Emily's standards, who was voted sexiest girl in Florence Nightingale School (even ousting Ms Madding, the French teacher, into second place), but a bloomer all the same. Emily was a blonde whose beauty was legendary; and even today there were two public toilet walls totally dedicated to Emily and her fabulous breasts. And although she had the fairest of complexions, her skin took to the sun swimmingly. Well, that's what she told people. The fact of the matter was she used a bottle tan.

So, with two twenty-eight-year-old babes, one might wonder why the need for compliments . . . because a girl could never get enough.

The waning moon, with its craters bold like acne, shone clear and bright, playing hide 'n' seek in the puffed-up clouds. Like a blinking eye in the sky, it followed the two girls as they walked up the street dodging drunks, speaking to acquaintances here and there, laughing at the odd comment. A small queue of people waited patiently behind a huge bearded man swearing into a cash machine.

'Me focking overtime, where the fock is it?' His accent was a mixture of Scottish and gibberish; his breath a mixture of whisky and onions. 'Aye, that's roit, I'm a talking to you, pal.' His fist thumped the machine.

The girls giggled. They knew all about money worries. Filling sandwiches for a living wasn't the best job, but it paid the bills . . . Actually it didn't even do that, it just about paid for their make-up. The bearded man, now quite aware of the crowd of people behind him, decided to show off some more and gave the machine a mighty head butt. He then casually removed his Sainsbury's Nectar card from the Halifax machine, and stumbled down the road trying to stem the blood oozing from his gaping wound. His kids would just have to go hungry, they got skool dinners, wot more do they want?

Since moving down this end of town four years ago, Marina and Emily had borne witness to seven muggings, one pram snatch, weekly police chases, two student march revolts, one university teacher revolt, and an ongoing territory feud between Pete's Kebabs and Peter's Kebabs. A heavily bearded man head butting a cash machine was child's play to them and they sauntered up the road desperate for some real action. Even if it turned out to be the pub.

A voice shouted from across the street, 'Oi, you should be ashamed of yourself. You should be at home cooking *samosas* for us men.'

Emily had a few choice words ready to hand for high-street hecklers, but they normally ended in a fight, and they were normally directed at women. Knowing what to say to three Asian men was Marina's responsibility and she nudged Marina to stick up for their women's rights.

But Marina refused eye contact with the Asian men and whispered in Emily's ear, 'Come on, let's go. You can never win with them.'

'Taboo?' Emily said, raising eyebrows.

'Yeah, taboo.'

And many things were between Marina and Emily. Especially when it came to Marina's family and upbringing. But roll a huge spliff, turn the lights down low, and she would tell you everything you needed to know. Well, more or less everything. How dare these Asian men judge her just because they had the same colour skin? What did they know of her life? Nothing. Even she didn't understand why or how she came to be the Marina she was. She certainly wasn't the Marina her grandparents had expected her to be. But they were far far away in New Delhi.

Far far away in a different world.

New Delhi, home of the India Gate, home of the *chapatti*, home of the turban and home to 320,149 Indians (and counting). Marina's homeland. The country to which she owed so much. And yet? Yet it seemed like such a strange place, strange people and even stranger customs. And yet? Yet she was born there. Born in another world; and sometimes alien to this one.

Mum was adamant, even though she lived in Watford, England, that all children taken from her womb would be taken in India where her family's roots lay deeply buried. Alas, in mid-flight, without a midwife, epidural, gas or morphine, her waters broke early, sending Dad to his knees praying to turbo the plane towards New Delhi. This was a mile-high club her parents were keen to avoid. Mum's moans began to drown out the engine. Dad's moans began to drown out Mum's. Panic spread all the way to non-smoking. Giving birth at twenty thousand feet was never practised at pre-natal classes. Where were the hot flannels? Dad worriedly asked an air hostess whether they would be charged an extra fare if the baby was delivered en route. And what would be written on the birth certificate? Born en route to India? It was a disgrace. Air India would be held to account if their baby was born without a country to its name.

Luckily, all ended well and Marina arrived in Arrivals. The First Aid room in Indira Gandhi Airport was officially her place of birth. And because her mother went into labour over the Mediterranean her name was officially Marina.

The girls continued up the High Street in silence until Emily sensed Marina's anger had subsided.

'You okay?' Emily asked.

'Hunky-dory, that's my story.' Marina paused. 'Anyway, I think we should pay particular attention to this evening, Emily,' she said, parting a crowd of young teenage boys with a firm shove. 'It's the very last one of its kind. Once we begin working on our Hit List, then our karma will improve. You'll see.'

Emily thought back to the Hit List that she had compiled so far; it read like a telephone directory. Marina had made the rules absolutely clear: it was only worth apologizing(1) to people who truly did not deserve the treatment that they had received, and (2) if the apology would do some good (i.e. not open up old wounds).

An ambulance rushed past, wailing up the road. Emily nodded her head woefully. 'You're right. We sort out our karma and our luck has got to improve. I don't care if I have to grovel to be forgiven by some of those stupid cows on my list, but it can't be right for two girls, of our age, to be living in a grotty hole like Fenworth. It can't be. It must be punishment for the bad we've done.'

Marina placed a consoling arm round her friend, the cooling evening air beginning to take its toll on her goosing flesh. 'Before you know it, and picture this if you will' – Marina made a waving motion with her arm, pointing to the moon – 'us, you and me, a fairy tale come to life. Two princesses with a palace each. New interesting jobs, no spreading of margarine on bread any more, no bloody coronation chicken.' She made a gagging noise. 'And, most importantly of all, no more worthless, penniless Fenworth men.'

'Sounds too good to be true!'

A roar of a car engine interrupted any chit-chat down this stretch of road. All eyes trained quickly on the culpable exhaust. All eyes aimed enviously at the brand new flame-red Porsche hurtling up the road like a bat out of hell. But it wasn't leaving hell, just entering into it. Fenworth – the poor man's hell. Marina and Emily licked their lips. Now, men with Porsches were brilliant in bed, they decided that one year ago. Oh, to have the man of your dreams.

If only.

*

'Slow down, Tom, please, you know how much this scares me. Please slow down. Just because it's a Porsche, you don't need to thrash it. You don't want to kill us both on your thirtieth birthday now, do you?'

Thomas ignored Nicole, revving the engine harder. 'This is Fenworth, slow down? Are you a loon? Now, hold tight, I'm going to try and overtake the ambulance.'

The Porsche burned ahead, swerving past the flashing ambulance, just missing a large, bearded man stumbling across the road, and then onwards, away from Fenworth. As far away from Fenworth as possible. As far away from the only town in which Thomas had been threatened with a knife. He'd come away with his life, but had been forced to relinquish his spanking new leather jacket. Statistically he should have been safe that day. Fenworth normally had just the one mugging a week and he'd already heard about what happened to poor Mrs Blanders. Apparently, two lads had threatened they were going to electrocute her ear lobes with a car battery if she didn't hand over her catalogue money. Mrs Blanders was a fighter, though, not letting go of her £5.62 until she'd nearly drained the battery dry.

Colour returned to Thomas's face, as Fenworth became more distant and his hotel grew nearer. The Regency Hotel, although only fifteen miles away from dumpy Fenworth, seemed a world apart. Based in quaint, little old St Meridians, where the winding roads and open fields were so still and uplifting that even the meanest axe-murderer would take up knitting once he'd paid a visit. The suicide rate for St

Meridians was currently nil and the inhabitants wanted to keep it that way. Driving at 100 m.p.h. around tight corners, where families of bunnies hopped across, might not be the best way to keep the rate down. Thomas applied the brakes, easing down the speed. He checked the windscreen for bunny brains.

'Sorry about that, Nicole, babe.'

Nicole took her hands away from her eyes. 'I'm sorry, too. If I had known we had to go through Fenworth, I would have booked somewhere else. You know how hard it is to get a decent table in that restaurant.' She stroked his arm.

The car drove smoothly back to the hotel. His troubled thoughts returned to the issue of what significance to read into the letter he had written himself. Could it be true? Was it possible for the younger you to know the older you better? Wouldn't it have been more appropriate for a younger him to send the older him some porn rather than some philosophy? Like a normal healthy lad would have done.

God, he hated that fourteen-year-old self. Most children wrote diaries about the past, about what *has* happened. Oh no, not him; Thomas the younger Harding decided to write about what *will* happen. First there was Nostradamus, then Mystic Meg and now . . . Thomas Harding. He changed down gears, crawled through the hotel gates and up the long drive. Maybe he'd make a minor prediction about tonight.

Tonight he was going to get pissed.

Chapter Three

Rainbow Radio rabbited in the background, trying to prise open Thomas's clam-like eyelids, trying to wake the dead.

The DJ (whose name was Derrick Jones, which was quite handy) made love to the microphone with his early morning voice. 'So, last week we discussed the topic, "If you had a choice, which star would you have been a Siamese twin with?" Today, we lower the tone,' he said, lowering his vocals accordingly. 'Today's topic is . . . Do you believe this, folks? We actually had a caller ring in saying he had smeared super-glue over his stomach and was willing to stick himself to Courtney Cox Arquette so that he could be her Siamese *friend* . . . Anyway, I'm losing the plot and probably I'm losing you, my lovely, lovely listeners. Today, the topic is, "What is the most important day of your life?" Ring in, you know the number, but I'll remind you anyway, 3383 279502.

Now here's Red Hot HOT **HOT** Chili Peppers "I Could Die For You".'

'I wish you bloody well would.' Thomas summoned the energy to remain conscious. Nicole had been gone an hour, no doubt back to Castle Cliff Manor, and left him with this joke of a DJ. Spiteful. He was surprised the station still employed DJ after his April Fool's motorway pile-up prank when he announced, as a joke, twenty dead, fifteen critical, blood everywhere, many orphans expected.

Falling out of bed, Thomas chuckled at the note Nicole had placed on his pillow: *Nil by Mouth*, and made his legs walk him to the shower, the drink from last night still swishing in his brain. 'What's the most important day of my life?' He pressed a few buttons on his top-of-the-range power-shower, turned a few dials, squirted a few gels, and stepped inside the mist. 'Who cares!'

But he did care. More than most.

Ever since buying his first hotel at the age of twelve, Thomas had loved the idea of owning his own establishment, of directing his destiny. But the rules of real-life hotels as opposed to plastic red Monopoly hotels were streets apart – stealing from the banker when one needed a little collateral was a lot harder in the real world. And so, by all accounts, was directing your own destiny. Taking real-life risks was sometimes the only difference between the dreamers and the achievers. And ever since he was in nappies, Thomas wanted to be the achiever. The achiever of his dreams.

And that's how the Regency Hotel came into existence. Eighty lavish rooms individually decorated, all unique, each with its own personality. 'The hallmark,' Thomas boasted, 'of a great hotel.' The builders had said he was out of his mind, the architect had said he was out of his mind, and even his parents had said he was out of his mind, but the AA book of hotels said, 'Unparalleled. To stay at the Regency Hotel, one never wants to leave.' Its list of happy guests continued to grow and his bank manager continued to smile. Not quite so out of his mind after all.

Or maybe he was.

Thomas gargled the shower water, the tattered memory of last night beginning to restore itself. And starting with a few mild cusses, he ended with quite a ferocious verbal attack on himself, cursing himself for a bad business decision that could cost him dearly. Last night, in a buoyant state of birthday drunkenness, he had agreed to the worst, most irresponsible thing he'd ever agreed to in his entire life. He had agreed to marry Nicole.

Totally rebelling against the words of his youth, trying to show that fourteen-year-old know-it-all kid to keep his nose out of adult life, he'd . . . agreed to marry Nicole Newton-Harrington. If memory served him correctly – and it's a good job that he didn't have a soap-on-a-rope in the shower or he'd be strangling himself with the cord right now – he'd also agreed to father a couple of children, to feed and clothe them, and even send them to those poshford Oxford colleges up the road, one of which he had attended himself. With a towel wrapped tightly round his trim waist, Thomas skidded out to the bedroom, his head full of shampoo. He'd never been so keen to find a used condom in all his life. He began his search, as the gooey lather settled like mousse on top of his brown hair. DJ Derrick Jones was in the midst of a discussion with a listener.

'I think the most important day in my life was when I was born,' said the caller, on Rainbow Radio. His voice was coated in smug.

'Do you now?' DJ remarked. 'So everything after that is downhill, I take it? Nothing is going to live up to the day you were born? I want some originality here, folks, none of this cliché rubbish. Next caller, please.'

A nervous cough, then a female voice: 'The most important day in my life was the birth of my child, Joshua. He means the world to me.'

'Kids kids kids, it's all about kids these days. Forget about those horrible little tykes for one second, I want to hear something of interest. The day you received a heart and lung transplant, or the day Kofi Annan texted you for advice, that sort of thing, even . . .'

The radio became background noise again as Thomas rested his head on his hands and concluded the inevitable: he'd had intercourse without a condom. Worse than that, his eyes, now red and weeping from the shampoo, stared at Nicole's 'ovulation chart' on the wall. It was egg time. After all these years of being so careful, and now the sperm had turned. This could well be the most important day of Thomas's life and he could feel his hotel slipping from his grasp already.

He could almost hear the wedding vows: to love, honour and cherish all the way to bankruptcy. Nicole was never meant to be a marriage item, she was just supposed to look good on his arm. Eye candy for his guests and bed candy for his willy. But with the sweet sometimes comes the sour, and nothing was more tart on his palette than a future filled with kiddies. His life would become drained like an octopus's ink sac.

Returning to the shower, he rinsed off the shampoo. Both Nicole and the Regency Hotel were equally demanding. Always at loggerheads with each other over who deserved the extra attention. Should he continue to massage Nicole's back or should he help out in the kitchen because the chef's come down with food poisoning? Should he comfort Nicole from her tears on a stormy day, or should he stand out in the car park to prevent the wedding party guests from double parking? Thomas stepped out of the shower and began drying. And what about the future that married life would bring? How would that affect him? Would he miss the birth of his own child because the Regency demanded he should? The words 'more staff' echoed inside a very hung-over head. But the words 'more trust' echoed even louder. He hadn't skimmed off most of his twenties and worked like a shire horse just to settle down in the prime of his life, married, with kids, so his staff could wreck all he'd strived for. No way! Neigh.

From the huge apartment window, Thomas looked out to the greens of the country, the English jungle. Many church steeples stood erect, poking through the dense trees in the far distance. Each Sunday the ghostly chimes from the church towers impressed upon the land – *Tubular Bells* revisited via Oxford – and only when the bells were truly quiet could Sunday begin. It would take a seriously stretched imagination to think of this beautiful place of solitude as a place of future gloom. He breathed condensation on to the window-pane and wrote the words: *what will be will be,* and then changed into a Lacroix suit and tie. A wedding-do beckoned, and, judging by the Cockney voice of the man who had booked it, it had 'trouble' written all over it. 'Don't worry 'bout me, guvner,' the bloke had said, 'nothing too flash, jellied eels, pie 'n' mash, that sort of grub. We ain't into this fancy foreign muck. My Tracy 'ates that stuff. Can't risk puke down her wedding dress, got to take it back after she's made an innocent man of me. One more fing, I take it the love suite is soundproof? We Jenkinses tend to be a bit noisy in the ol' bed department. Get my drift? *Very* noisy.' Thomas blamed Camelot for guests like this. Only the lottery would have given them enough money to have been able to afford the Regency Hotel. And he blamed Southend-on-Sea for their taste in food. Jellied eels? Yuck! But money was money – and he made lots of it.

Which was just as well. In walked Nicole, weighed down with designer bags, her four-inch heels squashed to two inches.

'I have just spent £8000!' said Nicole, kissing him on the cheek.

'What didn't you buy?'

She giggled. 'You are going to just die when you see what I have bought. Now close your eyes.'

Thomas closed his eyes, unsure whether he ever wanted to open them again. Rustling noises filled the air, overpowering the radio. The excitable squeaking coming from Nicole's mouth sounded like a family of mice debating Dairylea cheese's worthiness. The only thought calming Thomas's otherwise turbulent mind was the fact that Nicole did not show the characteristics of someone with morning sickness. *He* did, though, as soon as he opened his eyes.

'My God,' he remarked, feeling giddy and in desperate need of a chair.

'So cute, isn't it? Feel the fabric – dare I say, baby soft.' She ran her French-manicured fingers over the £560 baby romper suit. 'It's designer, only the best for our children.'

Thomas now had a topping of sweat all over his body. His forehead glistened and without thinking he made a grab for the romper suit to wipe his face down.

Nicole backed away, disgusted at his actions. 'What is wrong with you?'

'I feel ill.'

'You're hung-over, that's all. I'll just have to wait until later to show you the other items.' She snatched the romper suit from his trembling hands. 'You should see the dinky little cowboy boots they do. So cute.' And her squeaking started up again.

Thomas felt an urgent need to yell something. Anything. 'Three's a bloody crowd!' he shouted and stormed towards the door, slamming it shut behind him.

Nicole sat on the sofa, ignoring her grouchy, hung-over man, and poured out the contents of her bags. Nothing was going to wreck her day. The radio eased its way into her hearing.

A lady caller spoke, her Welsh accent almost singing, 'The most important day of my life, ooh, that's a difficult one, now, isn't it? *The* most important day. My, I can't think—'

DJ interrupted, 'Well, what the F-ing hell did you phone in for then? What about when they said Wales was foot-and-mouth free? Surely that ranks quite high? You must have missed the sheep. Remember, folks, we're asking you what's the most important day of your life. And I want originality. Next.' And then he made a sheep's 'bahh bahh' bleating noise down the microphone.

Nicole held up the hand-stitched leather-soled baby bootees. 'That's easy. The most important day of my life will be when I give birth to you.' And she snuggled up to the baby clothes, a gleaming smile on her beautiful face, unaware at this moment that it was beginning to rain outside.

Unaware that, soon, the last thing in the world she would be wanting would be a baby.

You can't pay for beauty. But you can pay to improve your beauty. Marina and Emily sat cross-legged on the worn carpet, worshipping the huge, plastic Pepsi bottle in front of them. Every year the two girls would save their pennies, putting in spare change when they could spare it. Traditionally the bottle opening ceremony would be held at the beginning of October, after the holiday season had ended, to cheer themselves up for the grim reality of the long winter ahead. Today, with the Hit List sitting beside them, it was decided they needed the money early this year. If they were going to be improving their karma, they must look their most beautiful – and besides, with the battalions of men who would soon be fighting for a piece of action, they had to be ready. The logic was slightly flawed, but so was Emily's skin at the moment, threatening to sprout a few spots if steps weren't taken swiftly. It was impossible to be considered seriously with a face full of zits, they presumed. Unless you were a member of AA. Acne Anonymous.

'Our beauty is apparent. Our beauty is apparent,' began Marina, chanting the mantra.

Emily joined in. 'Our beauty is a parrot. Our beauty is a parrot.'

'If you're not taking this seriously, then you can stay in Fenworth all your life. I mean it, Emily. You can marry a Fenny man, not me. I'm going places.' She paused, took hold of Emily's hand and they both closed their eyes.

'Our beauty is apparent,' they recited.

Fifteen minutes later, with the mantra maxed out, the money all counted and bagged up, it was time to book the beauty treatment. Marina picked up her mobile and dialled the once-yearly number.

A receptionist answered, 'The Regency Hotel, beauty salon. Gabby speaking.'

'Good morning, Gabby. First question, do you take cheques *without* guarantee cards?'

'No, I'm afraid we don't, madam.'

'Okay. Do you take money bagged up in cellophane bags? Last year there was a problem and I thought I'd better check first.'

'Well, usually our guests pay with a credit card. We take most.' She paused. 'I know Lloyds Bank is still open, I'm sure they would be willing to exchange your pennies for notes.'

Marina tutted. 'Will do. Thanks awfully. Back to beauty talk: do you still do the Regency Special? And if so, is it available today?'

It was, and it was booked for later that evening.

The previous year the Regency Special had included one all-over body massage, facial, bikini-line wax, mudpacks, manicure, pedicure, Indian head massage, sauna and cocktails between treatments.

But that was last year.

It pays to ask.

Although they had been best friends since school, there were still occasions when two was a crowd. Or, to put it bluntly, 'they were in each other's face'. Emily retired to her room, to pick out her best outfit, leaving Marina alone in hers. And Marina loved her room. Even though it had various six-legged and eight-legged visitors from time to time. Hilda had granted permission for the girls to decorate as they pleased; not taking too kindly to Emily's joke that she would be decorating in the style of serial killers. Whatever style that might be. Marina's choice was an easy one: India. A huge country with many manifestations of what constituted Indian. Marina's room was decorated in bold bright colours with tandoori orange walls, yellow and gold curtains made from sari material, and filled with various Indian artefacts given to her by various relatives when they visited damp, cold England, from dry, hot India. The room was a hybrid of East and West. Emily stated that Marina's decor was not so much a culture clash as a culture rash, with colours that pierced the eyes and joss-stick smells that cleared the sinuses. In the corner, a dinky shrine was set up for prayer. A small bronze statue of Shiva greeted you from a tiny table, a welcoming face in times of strife. On either side of Shiva, Marina had placed vases of yellow marigolds, softening the sometimes solemn image that her Hindu God projected. And not only was Shiva her God of protection, he was also her guard and secret keeper. Behind his many arms, out of view, stood a large sealed copper bottle. Inside the bottle, caught in a vacuum of time from eighteen years back, the sacred water from the Ganges waited patiently for *the day*. And in front of the shrine was placed a cushioned mat for *puja*, worship. Any personality in the room stemmed from this corner and it was here that Marina was now kneeling. Doing her usual, asking for forgiveness. Her favourite quote from a film was, 'Nothing to forgive', from *The Killing Fields*.

She just wished her God would say it to her sometimes: 'Nothing to forgive, Marina, nothing to forgive.'

Chapter Four

Even though it was daytime, the sky was night. Moody storm clouds had gatecrashed the heavens, and in some ways gatecrashed the wedding reception preparations being made inside the Regency Hotel. One might hope that the bad-tempered weather would be the only uninvited guest tonight. One could but hope.

And while outside it was foreboding, inside a hurricane brewed.

The banquet room with its fairly large dance floor and raised platform stage had seen many a happy couple toast their future – totally ignoring that, statistically, two-thirds of them would be divorced within the year. Quite a shame for the parents who had remortgaged their homes to pay for the wedding, but, hey, that's life. Today, balloons, silk ribbons and banners decorated the ceiling in multicolour, and a heart-warming message sat directly over the DJ's decks.

Now's The Time To Mend Regrets
Feuding Families Forgive And Forget.

Six pretty, young waitresses in their black skirts and white shirts prepared the banquet tables for the two hundred and fifty or so guests due within the hour. Thomas called them his 'special wedding staff'. He expected them to be efficient, polite, dextrous and most importantly FAST. Because fast was an anagram of staff, he told them:

'But *staff* has got two Fs, Mr Harding, it can't be an anagram of fast,' pointed out one of the special wedding staff one day.

'The extra F in limbo stands for "fucking". Fucking fast staff,' Thomas had replied. 'And it can also be F for "fired". So I suggest you watch it.' He'd then walked off, smiling to himself.

The cosy lights of the chandeliers washed over the banquet room while Mozart's 'Ave Verum Corpus, K618', performed by the New College Choir Oxford, soothed the air. Tranquil sounds soon to be destroyed by the wedding couple's requested tunes. The staff worked in virtual silence, while every now and again the bulbs flickered from the thunder outside.

Emma, the least experienced of the waitresses, glanced nervously down to the sole of her left shoe on which was written the word 'left'. She then picked up a fork with her 'left' hand and placed it on the left-hand side of the place mat. She now had her key fork in place and setting out the rest of the table should be easy. Wouldn't it be nice if these wedding feasts served only soup, she'd often thought, then Mr Harding, Thomas, would never discover her – as her sister called it – 'disability'. When joining the Regency she was sure she could see written in the small print of Mr Harding's welcoming smile the skyscraper-high expectations for his staff: Don't let me down, and I won't let you down. His interview technique was simple; he smiled at the girls, they fell in love with him and, after that, anything was possible.

Well, not quite.

Thomas was a rare species of man. No matter how pretty the woman, how flirtatious, how perfect, he would never succumb to an affair. Countless red-faced women had been told, 'No!' From up-market career girl to market-trader scrubber, 'No!' 'No!' and 'NO!' Loyalty began and ended with Nicole. You could have stuck him on a desert island filled with naked bunny girls and still it would be NO and still it would be Nicole. Nicole, the blonde goddess seen from time to time in her designer clothes, Nicole, the woman whose immaculate looks made other women want to scratch her eyes out, Nicole, the woman who floated through the hotel premises on a chariot of beauty. Nicole, the only woman who Thomas had eyes for. And Emma? She sometimes wished she was Nicole. She continued to lay the forks.

Standing at the double-door entrance clutching a carving knife dripping with lamb's blood was Stuart, the commis chef, who'd been inspired to be a chef watching David Attenborough's *Life On Earth*. He waited to be noticed. He fancied all six of the waitresses. While they were alive.

'Ignore him,' Lauren whispered across the tables. 'He thinks women go for men in uniform.'

All six sets of eyes looked across and sniggered at

his gravy-stained apron. Some uniform. It wasn't a secret in the hotel that Stuart rinsed his condoms for re-use. It's just a pity he never rinsed his pants. One of the waitresses could not believe her eyes one morning after waking up next to him and spotting his dirty brown kecks on the floor. Deeeesgusting. But, amazingly, he was cute, in a boyish kind of way. And, amazingly, he could cook, in a girlish kind of way.

A crack of thunder slapped the hotel, causing the waitresses to jump. Stuart tucked the knife away in his apron pocket and came in to protect the girls, and, of greater importance, to make it up to Emma. He'd already upset her earlier by telling her not to bother setting all the tables: the chances were that quite a few of the guests would not make it to the reception that night and possibly may even die trying – due to the bad weather. 'Wouldn't it be awful if the bride and groom had a car crash? Big ball of flame, their lives snuffed out. You could say that the drive up here would be their last dance, funny hey?' he'd said, prompting Emma's tears to form. 'I suppose the party would still go ahead, though, they'd want that. Couldn't let those jellied eels go to waste. Anyway, must get on. Catch you later, Emm, my beautiful gem.'

And this was later. Angry storms battering outside, a commis chef coated in blood, a mob of Cockney guests on their way and the news of the day about to be spread to the waitresses.

Stuart hushed the girls down for his important announcement. It would do well for the girls to listen to what he was about to tell them. It would serve their interests immensely for the girls to make notes of all that was about to be uttered. It would make a lot of sense if the girls would . . .

'Just bloody well tell us, Stu-pot, we've got tables to lay,' blurted out Stephanie.

'It's bad. Big time.' For effect he drew his knife from the pocket, watching the glint of the chandelier bulbs catch its jagged edge. He smiled into the blade. 'Time's running out, for all of us. I guarantee that one of us will be fired today!'

All the waitresses eyed each other. Wondering. Wondering whether this was another of Stuart's sick little jokes, aimed at trying to get one of them into bed again.

Stuart continued, 'And before any of you even think it, this is not so that I can stick my meat in any of you. I say this for one reason and one reason only.' He slid the knife back in his pocket dramatically, obviously well practised. 'I say this as a friend.'

He went on to explain the situation, calling it 'The Regency Meltdown'. Within the last two hours a disturbing sequence of events had taken place. Overhearing Thomas and Nicole arguing in the closed main bar about babies, then weddings, and finally the weather, he'd been spotted by Thomas and asked what he was doing crouching behind the potted palm tree. 'Digging for root ginger' did not go down too well. Even from outside the bar, the argument was clearly audible and each shout was replaced by a louder one, until Nicole stormed out of the eye of the storm, crying noisily, and headed to the lifts. Thomas appeared shortly afterwards with the words, 'What is fucking wrong with her? I cannot control the fucking rain.' Stuart's explanation of what had happened didn't have a punch line so he decided to make one up.

'So,' he rubbed his chin, lying, 'Thomas runs into the kitchen and never guess what he does next? He tells me to open my hand and drops some root ginger in it. And then he says, "You're the best we've got in here, Stu. The *very* best. You are as good as it gets."'

Nothing was said until the laughing had stopped. Stu? The best? Likely story. He wasn't even a good broth, let alone a good stew.

Stephanie appeared confused. 'So they had an argument, so it's raining, so what? Get a life, Stu.'

'The point is . . . drum roll please . . . Nicole is staying over tonight. Here, in the Regency. And the weather forecast is not looking too promising. Gales, downpours, floods. The works. I'm telling you, this is going to be one of the worst nights ever.' He paused. 'You must know what she gets like when it rains.'

Nicole's tantrums were legendary. But Nicole wasn't their boss. Thomas was. And in he walked. His face a mixture of expressions, none friendly though.

'What's this? Staff meeting? Funny that, I was under the impression that we had a wedding reception to organize.' Thomas stared towards Stuart, the very best. 'And since when was this the kitchen?' He stepped a foot in, almost slipping on the lamb's blood spilt by Stuart's knife. By the time he looked back up, his eyes were nearly as bloodshot as the carpet. 'Explanation!'

Stuart ran across as quick as he could and whispered in Thomas's ear. 'Don't make a big deal of this, but Emma's on her period. I'll clear it up for you, Mr Harding. No harm done.'

Thomas gave them all equal looks of displeasure and headed out to Reception, pondering the worrisome thought of the next few hours. He would lay a good amount of money on Nicole's behaviour tonight being as erratic as it would be unpredictable.

He prayed the guests would be in a forgiving mood.

Ironically, Marina and Emily were sweating buckets arguing as to why a sauna was not included in the Regency Special this year. Dressed like Caesar's concubines in white, luxurious robes, they attempted to reduce rude Gabby, the beauty salon manager, to tears. Gabby hadn't cried since Bros split. She was as tough as her fibreglass nails and twice as sharp.

'I bet if we wore Tiffany rings you'd let us use the sauna,' said Marina, leaning on the marble counter and staring straight into Gabby's eyes. 'J-Lo get these problems, does she?'

'Look, you're making a scene.' Gabby sighed. 'Or, in your sweet language, you're making arses of yourselves. As I've already explained, the sauna is not currently included in the special. I'll try to put it in plain English. Kentucky Fried Chicken used to give away free bread rolls. Now they don't. Understand now?'

Emily nearly jumped on the counter. 'Are you speaking down to us like people who sleep on the street or crack-cocaine users?'

Gabby smirked. Since the day she gave Ms Wilkins a pedicure, on her twelve hairy toes, nothing fazed her. 'I thought Fen . . . worth girls would be used to being spoken down to by now.' She slid off her stool and retreated to the till. On a back shelf stood twenty different varieties of bottle tan. Gabby looked like she used all twenty. A noisy orange-juice machine gurgled beside the health food bars, and a neat pile of laundered white Regency towels stood on the edge waiting to be dirtied. Unhappy customers were a rarity in here. Which made the experience all the more pleasurable for Gabby.

She held out the receipt to yet another perfectly manicured set of nails, this time Marina's. 'I must insist that you leave me no tip. And off the record, those robes cost a small fortune, please don't steal them on the way out. And by the way, in this place the customer is *never* right. Ta ra.'

Marina snatched the receipt and leant in real close. 'We used to be nasty like you once. There was a time when I would have stood here and called you a horrible leach of a worm, but I'm nice now. Instead I would like to see the owner of this establishment and explain to him what a horrible leach of a worm you are. Ta ra.'

Gabby's smile lost its shine. Fifteen minutes of bartering with Marina and Emily wouldn't change their minds. They wanted the owner, they wanted their sauna and they wouldn't leave without seeing him or without getting hot and sweaty. It was at times like this that Thomas wished the mobile phone hadn't been invented.

The spa's lobby was set out like a miniature rain forest. A few tables and chairs were set amongst the fresh green plants and trees. Calming music drifted down from the ceiling and the gentle trickle of water from the numerous water features brought the heart rate down instantly. Marina and Emily sat next to a huge aquarium sparkling with light and busy with tropical fish. With one eye they waited for the owner, with the other they checked for snakes.

Through the brush, Thomas appeared, dressed in his best suit, armed with his false smile. He was not in the mood to pamper guests – the Cockneys woz 'ere. But the two girls in robes looked harmless enough.

Emily whispered excitedly in Marina's ear, 'Don't turn round, Marina, but I'll give you a clue how gorgeous he is. If I had a willy I'd be sitting here with a stiffy.'

Unfortunately Emily's whisper wasn't whispered whispery enough. Thomas heard. And through a narrow gap in his wall of seriousness shone the girl's humour, lightening up a mood dark with anger. Nicole could turn a bad day good but she could also turn a good day shit. And at this precise moment, while the wedding guests were in the middle of 'Knees Up Mother Brown', Thomas was in the midst of a shitty day. The shittiest. After the mega argument earlier with Nicole, he had wanted to jump in the Porsche and escape. Cast away all those hurtful things she'd said and find the peace of an empty road. Living in the present with a woman who often escaped to the past didn't look too promising for a healthy, rosy future. But watching these two girls with their contagious giggles somehow lifted his spirits – a tiny bit.

He joined them at the table.

'I'm the owner, Mr Harding. Gabby has told me that you are unhappy with the Regency Special. You were expecting to have a sauna? Because last year you had one.' He smiled. 'Well, please, have your sauna.' He got up to leave.

The girls looked at each other. Marina spoke quickly. 'What if we get the same problem next year?' They'd never seen a man this good looking this close before and letting him go this soon would be a complete waste. She continued, spurred on by the nodding of Emily, 'I hate to dramatize, but what if next year your special has shrunk so that all we see for our money is our bikini-line being waxed?'

Thomas, bemused, answered without thinking, 'Well, it would make sense to let it grow really bushy then, to get your full money's worth . . .' He stared at their open mouths, realizing he'd lost his cool edge. Flustered now. 'Sorry, I am at a loss to know where that came from. I can assure you that next year the Regency Special will still be a cause for celebration.'

The CD music changed from monks chanting to birds singing. Two fat sisters, Maisy and Daisy, waddled through the jungle wearing Lycra swimsuits stretched to the max. They waved to Thomas, who waved back. Perks of the job. Stu called them Gorillas in the Mist – and talk of *their* bikini-lines was a topic banned from the kitchen.

Emily didn't believe in love at first sight. She turned her head away from Thomas, counted to three, and then swivelled her head back. Emily was now in love. Her body filled with hormones and her mouth filled with gibberish.

'Thank you, Mr Harding, for the lovely, sexual gesture of a hot, sticky sauna. We really appreciate it. Taking time out to see to our needs shows great character for a man as busy as you must be. And . . .' She wet her lips with the tip of her tongue. 'And, we especially enjoyed sucking on our *cock*-tails earlier.

Didn't we, Marina? All that liquid shooting up the straw. I gobbled it all . . .'

Marina felt for Emily's third rib with her elbow. 'Don't pay her any attention; she's always trying to embarrass people. Last week this bloke . . .'

Thomas clapped his hands suddenly. 'Right, I think that's my cue to go. I think we have all embarrassed ourselves quite enough.' He stepped backwards quickly. 'Saunas and *cock*-tails are on me. I will let Gabby know.'

'Before you go, Mr Harding,' Marina scrambled to her feet, 'do you mind if I stand next to you and see how tall you are?'

He stood confused as Marina sidled up next to him, staring at him side on. He spoke uncomfortably. 'Can I ask why you wish to know? I am six foot one if it helps.'

'I'll tell you why; if you were to suddenly go missing I will be able to describe you better to the police, that's all.' Marina ignored Emily's giggles. 'Six foot one, extremely handsome, sexy, blue eyes, posh voice, erm—'

'I'm off!'

'Wait.' Marina went to grab his arm, slipped, then fell to the floor.

Emily was in hysterics by now as Thomas felt obliged to help Marina to her feet; the premium on his insurance was low at present and he could well do without an accident claim. He heaved her up by her hand, their eyes connecting briefly, the subtlest of liaisons, then Thomas let go.

'Goodbye, ladies.' And he was gone.

But he would be remembered. After the giggles had

ceased, Emily scolded Marina for using such a cheap trick with a hunky man. Falling to the ground was an ancient pulling tactic. With someone like Mr Harding, a higher level of sophistication might have to be incorporated to obtain the required results. Marina's Plan Two of faking an epileptic fit, foaming at the mouth and throwing furniture would have to wait for a thicker man.

Marina touched the place where Thomas had gripped her hand and she tingled inside. There was no denying the way he had stared into her eyes, either. Full on. I want you, do you want me? Love-struck. Well, sort of.

Emily was as red as an embarrassed flamingo. 'For fuck's sake, Marina, he was gorgeous. I've never felt so hot in all my life.'

'Hot? I'll show you hot. Follow me.' Marina ushered Emily along the footpath towards the sauna suite. 'Let me take you to India.'

Chapter Five

In the dusky light of the wooden steam box, Marina and Emily sat, draped in towels, beads of sweat coating their skin. They could get quite used to this lifestyle.

'Close your eyes, Emily.' Emily obeyed. 'This would be Bombay.'

'Ahh.'

'Keep your eyes shut.' Marina poured a ladle of water on the hot rocks, and the steam hissed angrily. 'And this would be Madras.'

'Ahhhh, lovely.'

'And this,' Marina giggled as she gingerly lifted the wooden bucket and tipped the remaining water down, 'is the heat of New Delhi. My homeland.'

'Hellish.'

The girls became quiet as the steam swum around them. Clearing the pores, and in some ways clearing the mind. But, unfortunately in Marina's case, not clearing the guilt. Silences between the two friends were uncommon and when they occurred the dreaded thoughts of yesteryear always came seeping back to Marina. If her family were to know what evil deed she had done, then she would be cast into the oblivion of loneliness. What seemed so innocent all those years ago to a young girl by the banks of the Ganges would be deemed deplorable now. Worse than going against traditions. Worse than sleeping around. Worse than drink and drugs. She looked towards Emily, the best friend she'd ever had. She couldn't talk about this even with her. This was nearly as low as any human being could stoop. But the truth always outs itself in the end, she only hoped that when it did, she would be ready with an answer. A good one.

With seconds to spare, the girls left the sauna before severe dehydration set in and they reappeared as chicken jerky. Gabby seemed to have been gagged – ha! Shouldn't mess with the Fenworth girls. Sipping their sunset-orange cocktails idly, Marina and Emily rehydrated as they relaxed on the deluxe sofa, flicking noisily, annoyingly, through the pile of *Vogue* magazines, both desperate to think of complaints that would bring the dishy owner running back down to them once again. The hot and flushed feeling they were experiencing had nothing to do with the sauna. And neither wanted to let the other know that from just one five-minute chat with Mr Harding they were both willing to strip naked and perform all sorts of shallow deeds. Good grief, were hotel owners really allowed to be this gorgeous? Basil Fawlty excluded, of course.

'I know what I said when I first saw him but he was quite ugly close up, really, don't you think?' said Emily admiring her newly done nails. 'The hotel owner?'

Marina put a finger in her mouth, imitating puking. 'No class, and that posh voice, what a *complete* turn off,' she said, tingling at the thought of him whispering all 'posh-like' in her ear. 'I bet he's called Rupert or Hugo, even Sebastian.'

'Undoubtedly.' Emily toyed with her long blonde hair, tossing the curls this way and that. 'And when was the last time you heard of a Rupert being good in bed? I bet he's a complete disaster.' Her eyes glazed over. The crystal-clear image of ripping his suit off and working her hands like magic over his . . . She shivered with delight. 'Err, yuck yuck yuck. The thought of having to sleep with him is giving me the creeps.'

'Well, don't think about it, then.'

'I'm not.'

The conversation deteriorated.

'I can't believe you couldn't see it in his unusual dark-blue eyes, Marina, shame on you. Men like Mr Rupert Harding would tie you up and perform all sorts, they're known for it. Their lust is animal-like and they have no respect for women. You would be his sex slave. That's all. Nothing but a sex slave!'

The girls sighed in harmony. Sex 24–7. Heaven.

The advantage of living in Fenworth was that one's imagination tried to keep up with one's surroundings. Fenworth was a filthy hole. As such, the girls' imaginations were . . .

'Filthy!' Marina shook her head in mock disgust. 'I

bet he does filthy things with women. We're the idiots if we sit here and think of him as a perfect gentleman. The joke will be on us. We'll be laughing stocks. I'm not fooled by a suit and a winning smile. He did smell nice, though, I must admit. Filthy man!'

Emily slurped up the last of her cocktail and burped out the last of her wind. 'Mmm. What a humdinger of a drink. You know what, Marina? I've got a sneaky feeling that I used Mr Harding for a masturbation session once. Remember that magazine with the fifty most eligible bachelors? He was on it, definitely. If he was in the top twenty-five men, then I used him, I'm still working my way through the others.' She began chewing on the umbrella stick, then changed the tempo. 'It was so obvious that he wanted to take the sauna with us, wasn't it? Men! No control over their dicks. I mean, it is his hotel and all and if he wanted to, then I suppose we would have had to have let him. I'm not bashful, he could look at me naked if he wanted to.' She paused. 'Do you reckon he's got a big one?'

Marina went through a catalogue of willies in her head. 'Tiny. He's overcompensating with this huge, overpriced hotel.' She directed her gaze towards Gabby. 'And the staff here are so obviously under-qualified. How he gets away with it, I'll never know. But he does.' She zipped up her pink *Charlie's Angels* bag and rose up, smoothing down her dress. 'People like Mr Rupert Harding with their rich parents and Oxford degrees get away with anything.' She put on her small child's voice. 'Oh, Mummy, oh, Daddy, Rupert Harding, your precious Little Lord Fauntleroy son, needs skis for his skiing holi—' Marina stopped in mid-sentence. Her face turned from raspberry pink to strawberry red. And if she still had tonsils they would have rung inside her head like a bell. At times like these the burka seemed a good idea.

Thomas wasn't smiling. Unless, thought Emily, he saved his best Cujo smile, the one that looked like a dog snarling, for his favourite guests. She contemplated flashing a boob to calm the situation down a little. HOW UTTERLY EMBARRASSING! Maybe both boobs.

Within earshot, Thomas had been busy working on this evening's wedding speech. Normally he threw in the speech for free but the Cockneys had insisted on paying extra so he was intent on making it a good 'un. However, a good speech needs a good writer, and it was damn hard writing good when two Fenworth girls were discussing him just three feet away. And it hadn't taken much effort to listen in, either, as the girls didn't understand the principle of 'quiet'. He wondered if they would understand the principle of 'shamed'.

He spoke to the beetroot-faced halfwits. 'We all say regrettable things. Some we can live down, others haunt us for ever. Sorry, ladies, I couldn't help but listen in to your conversation. And I found your impression of me, dare I say, most illuminating, considering the fact that you have met me for only one, single, solitary minute. Most illuminating. How I want all my women to be sex slaves? How I wish to tie them up and perform all sorts of filth on their unwilling bodies? How I—'

Marina cut in. 'We didn't say *unwilling*, Mr Harding.'

He concentrated on trying not to smile, realizing that the aim to shame them was futile. Women like these two revelled in the blush and there would only be one loser if the conversation swung back round to cocktail sucking again. Him. Before he had time to regret talking to them once more, he was rescued by the ring from his Nokia. His saviour. It was at times like this that Thomas was grateful for the invention of the mobile phone. He took the call: emergency in Room 42. Bloody mobile phones!

Emily and Marina stared at Mr Harding. He was obviously humouring them. They may not have the same education as him but he didn't have to try and belittle them. Using all fancy words like 'illuminating'. Cheek. After a few seconds admiring how sexy he looked talking on the phone, they decided to tear themselves away and use the rest of the evening hunting down more freebies within the hotel. They pecked him on the cheek and left.

Left Thomas dumbfounded.

Pissed and pissed off in the pissing rain, Nicole roamed the corridor on the second floor. Her red velvet dress was designer. Along with her designer knickers, designer shoes, designer stockings and designer upbringing. Born into the jigsaw world of snobbery, she sometimes felt like she was the piece that didn't fit. Not quite the black sheep of the flock, somewhere between grey and white. Mummy's stiff upper lip was straighter than a workman's spirit-level, and her method of dealing with life and its problems was summed up in one sentence: 'Go and spend some money, make yourself feel better, darling.' But spending money couldn't make Thomas the man she wanted him to be right now. And spending money couldn't give her the family that she so desperately ached for.

Doors opened at the end of the corridor and a laughing gaggle of people headed through to wait for the lift. A huge crack of thunder shuddered the building and two or three of the guests yelped in excitement. Nicole felt for the wall with one hand and slowly sunk to her knees, a heart-wrenching feeling forcing her legs to become weak. She wished she could overcome this fear. Sometimes there was nothing more lonely than the scared feeling she had right now. She cried painful tears into her hands. Only Thomas could make her feel better. Only Thomas could take away the sadness. But not tonight. Thomas had other priorities tonight. Nothing was allowed to interfere with his wedding guests' enjoyment.

Snivelling quietly, Nicole wished she'd headed back to Castle Cliff Manor before the weather had turned bad. Other people's weddings and her never got on. Sparks would always fly. And now the storm was here, her sparks were likely to match the lightning outside.

With an effort, she struggled down the corridor, descended the two flights of stairs, and out into Reception. A porter mopped up water by the entrance and the receptionist was busy on the computer. The din from inside the banquet room poached any silence she was expecting to find here and with the booze beginning to mix with her depression she slumped in an armchair, faced the rain belting against the windows, and cursed the sky for the murderer it was.

The grandfather clock in the far corner, a family heirloom of Thomas's, struck 7.00 p.m. and Nicole watched with amusement as the porter shoved the mop back in the bucket, spilling more water than he had cleared up, barged out of Reception whistling, returned with a yellow 'Be Careful Wet Floor' sign and thumped it on the still-drenched floor. His shift finished at seven. Not a second before and not a second after. Sod the guests if they slipped now – he heard BUPA were doing a good deal on hip replacements anyway – not his problem! He was going home.

And so would Nicole if the sun decided to make an appearance. She searched the gloomy clouds for any sign of rays. They say there are more stars than there are grains of sand. Enough grains in one bucket to fill the sky. Enough grains on one beach to fill a galaxy. And yet, thought Nicole, our star, the Sun, hides like a coward.

'Messy business, weddings, hey?' A Cockney skinhead in a suit pointed to the spilt confetti on the floor by Nicole's red stilettos. A spider's web tattoo peeped from beneath his dazzling white shirt collar. 'Messy and full of fakes. Tracy's too cheap for our Phil. But would he listen? No, he goes and marries the stupid fat cow. I wish I'd never introduced him to my sister.' He sat opposite Nicole, smiled, lit a roll-up, and stared at the posh bird. 'I know what you're thinking.' He turned his head to the side, offering his right profile. 'Spitting image, hey? A younger Ronnie Biggs. Well, between you and me, darling, no word of a lie, me dad, God bless his soul, used to work for the Krays.' He winked, wondering why a beautiful face like hers had been crying. 'Sad day when they died.

Sad day when any mobster dies. Very sad. London seems so quiet nowadays. It's lost its sparkle.' He put out his hand, the knuckles tattooed with H A T E. 'Marlon's the name, as in Brando. Me dear mum, God bless her soul, loved him. I would offer me other hand, with L O V E written on it, but me trigger finger's sore, get me drift?' He was about to explain the words tattooed on his bottom – *I'll make you an offer you can't refuse* – then he remembered the rules: Posh Do means Poshest Behaviour.

Standing up, Nicole gave him a feeble smile, then walked away. Conversing with yobbos was hard enough when sober, let alone after a glass of champers. She might say something that upset him and most likely he would get his flick-knife out and stab her. Mummy had always warned her to stay clear of skinheads. Especially the ones with eighteen-holed Doc Martens. On nights like this Nicole wished her loyal muscle-mountain bodyguard, Ramone, was here. But she rarely asked him to accompany her to Thomas's hotel. This was a place she should feel safe.

Bonnie Tyler's 'Holding Out for a Hero' croaked faintly from inside the hall and Marlon sang along with the lyrics of 'Total Eclipse of the Heart'. As Nicole risked a glance his way, he winked and blew a kiss. Loving him was a dirty job but somebody would have to do it, she thought, making her way from Juke Box Jury Marlon and along the thickly carpeted corridor that passed the noisy banquet room. Inside were two hundred and fifty people wanting a day to remember. Outside was one person just wanting to forget.

Who was joined by another person who wanted to forgive. Thomas. He'd watched half amused and half concerned as she'd zigzagged down the corridor towards him. Imagining Nicole roaming the Regency while he doted over his guests filled him with guilt. Today, with the weather so fierce, he should be with her, comforting and reassuring her.

Thomas spoke, his arm creeping round her shoulder. 'I know you didn't mean what you said earlier.' He hoped so, because the coffin she was planning on putting him in would cost a small fortune. 'I detest seeing you this way.'

She shrugged his arm away. 'I think I should let you know, Mr Hotel Owner, I am going to make a real effort to fall completely out of love with you. Shouldn't be too hard. I've already thought of some things to help sway me. It's not looking too good for you, I can tell you. Don't be surprised if, by tomorrow morning, I'm completely out of love with you. Over! Finished. We two never to be an item ever again. No babies. No wedding. No family tree.' She began to cry. 'Are you satisfied now? Is this what you wanted?'

Leading her by the wrist, he pulled her into the empty conference room, locking the door behind him. A long wooden table and chairs stood with that all-important jug of water. A Klix coffee machine hid in the corner, its red light blinking neon on to the framed paintings of Oxford landscapes. On the flip chart, in thick blue marker pen, was a flowchart, explaining nothing, achieving nothing, but boy did those marker pens smell good. Mmm.

Thomas switched on two of the sixteen lights, hung his suit jacket over the back of a chair and sat down opposite Nicole. No distractions. No interruptions. Just their problem to sort out. The flowchart title,

Intimidation Breeds Appreciation: Bully Your Employees For Greater Success, had been written by a local entrepreneur, Mr Brimstone, and would be of little help to him today – as it was of little help yesterday to the five non-English-speaking asylum-seekers newly recruited to Flash Bang Wallop, the local fireworks company. Explaining to the new recruits that it was Guy Fawkes, and not Guy Fucks, had been hard enough.

'Please, Nicole, I am having a very perplexing time of all this. One minute you're buying up Mothercare, the next you're slicing the clothes to shreds with a pair of scissors and then phoning up a Harley Street clinic and asking them if it would be possible to have your ovaries removed. It's nonsensical behaviour, really it is.' He tried to take her hand, but she moved it to her lap.

'How dare you. Mothercare? Do you honestly believe I would stoop to Mothercare?'

He ignored her comment. 'I know the storm is having a negative effect, making you all uppity and depressed, even hateful. I understand. But I am on your side. And—' The lights flashed off for a second. Thomas found her eyes sadly staring into his. 'Nicole, about earlier, about this baby, the way I acted was shameful.'

Silence while she looked at a picture of the River Thames, two punters on the water. Straw hats and stripes. Silence while she tried to get the image of Thomas kicking the baby across the room out of her head.

'I would love to know what having a baby with me would mean to you,' she said. 'To me, having a baby would be like the best thing ever.' She paused. 'I'm not going to help you out here. You tell me.'

What would having a baby mean to me? Thomas thought back to earlier and how easily the argument had started.

He'd walked into his apartment and he'd heard her say, 'Catch!' Flying across the room was a baby romper suit stuffed with tissue paper, made to look like a baby. Unfortunately he'd dropped the baby. Their baby. Thomas had failed the baby-catching test. He'd tried to explain that with a real baby he would have been more careful and, anyway, would she have lobbed their baby halfway across the room if it was a real one? What kind of mother would she be if she threw babies? They were so very fragile at such a young age. With the joking over, Nicole had sat next to Thomas on the bed. She had wanted him to repeat what he had promised the night before, but she needed to hear him say it sober.

Nicole had spoken nervously. 'You said yourself that we'd better hurry and start a family. Before your sperm start requisitioning Zimmer frames.'

He'd chuckled. 'I sincerely meant it. That's why when we arrived back here last night I ripped off your clothes and made mad love to you *without* a condom. Hardly the behaviour of one petrified of the egg and sperm race, do you think? And I would like to add, making love to you without a condom was truly liberating. I felt so free.'

'Don't be so sarcastic. I don't know who you made love to last night, Thomas, but it wasn't me. You fell asleep. Or, as Mummy would say, "Rip Van Winkle got your tinkle."'

'So, we didn't fornicate?'

'No!'

Thomas had not been able to contain his smile. Most blokes who had just been told by a beautiful leggy blonde that sex 'didn't happen' might be depressed. And if depression meant running around the room yelping at the top of his voice, 'She can't be pregnant, yippee, she can't be pregnant,' then maybe Thomas was depressed after all. He just had a funny way of showing it. Nicole had watched, horrified, as he took a small run up, kicked the tissue-filled baby and sent it flying through the air, shouting, 'Take cover, Patriot Missile Baby alert.' It was at this moment the major row had started.

Nicole had shot across the floor and returned with the baby clothes and a pair of huge yellow scissors. Snipping away at the designer garments right under his nose, she had cursed him bitterly. 'I'm never going to have a baby with you. Never!' The ribbons of material had fallen to his feet, her tears falling shortly afterwards. To her, things had never been so clear: Thomas had never wanted the baby. He had *never* wanted to get married. He had never really cared about her at all. It was all the talk of a man boozed up on his birthday. As she cut the last of the baby bootees, she had screamed how she hoped he never got to see his next birthday, and flew out of the room to find solace in the empty bar downstairs. Unbeknown to her, Stuart, the commis chef, was in the middle of hiding his skunk in the palm tree pot located in the bar. A good batch. A top-notch snappy of wacky tobacky. Stuart's best bet was to stay hidden. And hidden people often hear the most outrageous things.

Thomas had joined her shortly afterwards and that's where the fight continued. Rows could be graded on a scale. This row topped any scale they had reached before. Nicole wished death on Thomas and his family. She prayed for an eternity of sorrow to come his way. She even wanted his pet collie dog, Scrappy, to come back from the dead, learn to speak English and tell Thomas what a lousy owner he had been and how when they went for walks he always wished he belonged to somebody else.

It hadn't been the best of mornings.

Now, while sitting together in the conference room, Thomas tried to find the words that a good spin doctor might produce to describe what having a baby would mean to him. Maybe if he acted like a complete child, then she might not want a real one. He'd give it a shot. He just wasn't ready to be a father – yet.

'With the state of the National Health and the low income for nurses, I think rushing into a pregnancy might be ill-timed. I would love to have a baby with you, Nicole, but only when we are both ready. And what does a baby mean to me?' He jumped out of the seat, flipped over a sheet on the flip chart and began to draw with the squeaky marker. Mmm, that smell.

Nicole watched patiently, she knew he was playing for time, desperate to think up lies. And how Thomas could even contemplate that she would have their baby in a National Health hospital bed was beyond her. Would Thomas take his beloved Porsche to Kwik Fit? She thought not.

'What is that?' The picture was now finished and Nicole pointed to the result.

'A baby. Our baby. Poor little mite.'

She asked him to wheel the chart over. 'And what's that "our baby" is holding in his oversized hand?'

He smiled. 'It's a ballot box. I think that both parents should agree on whether he or she is born. Have a vote. So hands up if you don't want the baby.' Thomas put his hand up instantly. 'Hands up if you don't, hands down if you do. Nicole, this is one of the most important decisions of your life so I suggest you treat this very seriously. Put your hand up like me if you don't want a baby that could ruin our lives, and as a bonus I will buy you a grotesque amount of diamonds. Or, keep your hand down and look forward to having a horrible figure. Your choice. If it's a tie then we do stone, paper, scissors for a decider.'

Nicole stood up. 'Thomas, seek help. I suggest you get back to your wedding. It's so obvious that we are not going to have a wedding of our own. I knew men were childish but you . . . Oh, never mind.'

The volume of the music was deafening now and even down the corridor and through a set of fire doors 'Hit Me With Your Rhythm Stick' could be clearly heard. Thomas pecked Nicole on the cheek.

'I never thought being thirty would knock the wind out of me this way, Nicole. It truly is one of life's low blows. But fear not, like a warrior, I will come back stronger. And then there will be no stopping me. We could have a baby a year, one in winter, one in summer, one in spring and one in autumn. We'll call them our Four Little Seasons.' He tickled her for a laugh and headed out into the corridor now populated with drunks popping party poppers. At the door near Reception a trio of men on all fours were singing 'hit me' at full pelt, while a scantily dressed woman slapped their bare buttocks with the sole of her shoe.

Cockneys!

Chapter Six

Every woman who lives with a man also lives with a quote from Gollum in her head: 'What has it got in its pocketses?'

Under the dim light in the conference room, Nicole studied the picture Thomas had drawn of the baby. The three Michelin stars on the forehead and the 'Hotelier Of The Year' written on the bib gave clues as to where the baby's future lay. In fact, she was so sure of Thomas's passion for his hotel that on a romantic evening even his sperm would most likely ask if there were any vacancies at the Ovary Hotel. And if the baby was born early, no doubt Thomas would arrange for an en suite incubator with a full English breakfast mushed up in the bottle. Nicole gave a vague smile and checked her diamond-encrusted Cartier watch. Thomas had left her alone in the room for gone ten minutes.

Well, not quite alone. A woman with her curiosity is quite a crowd.

She circled his suit jacket hanging on the back of the chair, knowing that time was running out. Knowing he would return to collect it soon.

What has it got in its pocketses? Nicole's heart bounced heartily as her slim fingers felt for lumps and bumps through the fine material. If she proceeded any further, it would mean she didn't trust him. He had never given her any reason not to trust him, which, in her mind, was reason enough.

She proceeded, with Gollum coaxing her on, emptying the pockets out onto the table. Business cards, Regency pens, a set of Duracell batteries, mobile phone, a Swan matchbox, a folded piece of paper and . . . hang on a minute, matches? He didn't even smoke. More to the point, she gave the matchbox a shake; they didn't even rattle. They thudded.

Inside the box she found a small Hobbs key. Already it had opened the box of her suspicion, but what else did the key open? What was he hiding? Keys go on key rings and matches go in matchboxes. In some ways she wanted to find a skeleton in his past. Had she now found the skeleton key?

She placed the box to one side and continued with her hunt, keeping her ear aimed at the door to the corridor outside, which was now ominously quiet. She remembered as a child helping Mummy hunt the mansion for hidden stashes of booze when Daddy was at work. It was all so exciting. Daddy had sworn he was dry, but Nicole and Mummy found him to be a liar. It was her first experience of men and their lies. She had always looked upon her father as an intelligent man until she discovered that he hid his vodka in the Tizer bottles. No wonder she hadn't been able to recall her twelfth birthday party, she was most likely too boozed-up on his Tizer to remember.

It was tempting to check through Thomas's mobile phone, text messages, incoming, outgoing, but something was urging her to open up the folded paper she had found in his pocket and read the words. It was hard to ignore an urge.

> *Mr & Mrs Phil Jenkins Wedding Speech.* (*Cockneys!*)
> *This! Me standing up here looking down upon a happy couple is what it's all about. Seeing love blossom under the roof of the Regency is worth much more than money. It's not about staying in the best hotel in Oxfordshire, it's not about receiving the best in hotel service that money can buy, and it's not about the fabulous food we dish up in our silver-service eighty-seat restaurant. It's not about any of that. It's about you . . . Phil and Tracy. I toast you, and wish you all the happiness in the world. Mr and Mrs Jenkins.*
>
> *Pause for applause.*
>
> *I have seen many couples get married at the Regency. Not because it's the best hotel from here to London, and not because its generous-sized rooms with twenty-four-hour room service are . . .*

Nicole scanned down until she found words that

weren't an advert for the Regency. At the bottom of the page were a few lines that turned her already moody mood nasty nasty.

Phil and Tracy. Or should I say Mr and Mrs Jenkins, ha ha ha. I have searched the high ridges and travelled the deepest ravines, but in all honesty, I have never found love. True love is so precious and when I see Phil and Tracy together, they are bonded by that priceless aura of love that I have been searching for . . .

She dropped Thomas's mobile in the jug of water. Was this the best speech that Thomas could muster? Surely privately educated Thomas had a fairer grasp of delivering warmer speeches than this bundle of tripe? And even though Nicole had lost sight of the real value of money years ago, £250 for this trash seemed like a rip-off.

Nicole quickly bundled up the contents of his pockets and replaced them carefully. Tonight was turning into a migraine. Shooting lights behind her eyelids wreaking havoc on a mind already half fucked. She needed stability in her life right now, and yet her life was one big wobbly jelly. How dare Thomas treat love with such little respect! How infantile to turn Phil and Tracy's wedding speech into an advert for his hotel. They deserved more than the scrawl written on this piece of paper, she thought, clutching at the speech. And *more* was exactly what they would be getting. Much much more.

Heading out of the door and down the corridor, Nicole made her way towards the noisy banquet room. *She* would be making tonight's speech. And it would be delivered with love and meaning, not in the greedy fashion that Thomas would have done it.

Just inside the banquet room was the self-appointed twenty-four-stone bouncer called Truck, only letting in guests who uttered the magic password 'Barbara Windsor, London's Own East End Darling'. As the evening drew on the password shortened to 'Blonde Bird Big Bazookas'. Until finally it was plain old 'Babs' Baps.'

Marina and Emily had gained entrance to the exclusive party by way of humming the theme to *EastEnders*. Truck was 'Well impressed!' and let the two gatecrashers in without an invite. Two hours later, four 'Can Cans', three 'Hokey Cokeys', one 'Knees Up Mother Brown', one slow dance with nimble Truck, and they were now part of the family. The day was turning into a sensation.

A rainbow of strobe lights danced amongst the dancers while an ever-increasing volume of music hammered from the monster speakers. It was quite clear to all that the DJ would not be satisfied unless every guest left with bleeding eardrums and burned cataracts. The only break from the noise was when, every so often, the DJ muted the music and said, 'Shabba' into the mike. No one seemed to know why.

The dance floor was full but somehow room was made for the old lady in the wheelchair who was wheeled over and parked in the middle, leaving her to wave her arms enthusiastically in the air. A huge cheer erupted when she appeared to attempt 'body popping'. In time someone realized that she was in actual fact having a fit, nerves most probably, and she was hastily wheeled back to the table from whence she came, knocking back champagne, pinching men's bottoms en route.

The wedding was a lesson in misconception. If one concentrated on the dresses, handbags and shoes, and the suits, gold watches and jewellery, the generalization might be that these guests were from a privileged background, born rich, the lucky one per cent of Britain. On closer inspection, the generalization was wrong. You would be hard pushed to find one person here who was born rich. You would be hard pushed to find anyone here who *knew* someone born rich. But almost everyone in this room would be thankful for the rich who were born rich, the lucky one per cent of this country. And they would be.

They stole from them.

Thomas was playing host to the biggest crowd of criminals Oxfordshire had ever seen. And Marina and Emily had gatecrashed their party, which was almost a crime.

Hidden away in the corner, the girls sipped expensive champagne, careful, as always, not to spill liquid on their designer dresses. And the dresses! Phew! Knockout garments that cost a small fortune when new, but when bought from Oxfam on a freaky, lucky day last year cost only three pounds each. Emily had made Marina frown when she purchased her little lilac number, as she said that she would not bother washing the dress until the smell of Chanel no. 5 had worn away. A classy smell indeed, thought Marina, when not mixed with the prior owner's BO. And Marina's dress, black satin, Versace, meant for a woman who was born to thrill and designed by a man who was born to be killed, was breathtaking. The extra sparkly market sequins that she'd hand-sewn on the garment, to give it that 'Eastern feel', would have the designer turning in his grave. As it was, it had living men falling off their feet. And the dresses made the girls feel good too; made them feel rich. The dresses also made them feel pretty crap when they had to take them off. They often discussed how fantastic it would be to own more than one quality item. They were sick of digging up the only designer garment they had every time they visited the hairdressers or bank or even the fucking gynaecologist. It's not like the nurse appreciated the effort anyway. She didn't even bat an eyelid when the girls decided to wear matching crotchless knickers to save on time. Not an eyelid.

For such a busy party, the service here was excellent, almost military in its competence. And, ironically, there was no mess. The waitresses, virtually invisible, but highly skilled at clearing away the rubbish, were in and out before you could say 'My old man's a dustman.'

Marina handed her empty long-stemmed glass to a passing waitress and grabbed a handful of canapés. 'Thanks ever so,' she said in her pretend posh voice.

'Yes, thanks ever so,' repeated Emily, who then continued with her fake conversation to Marina. 'Yes, I was saying about the indoor swimming pool we just had built? Tristan, my eldest, is going to have a pool party when he returns from boarding school.' The waitress was now out of earshot. 'Did you see her wrists, Marina? The bruising? I'm sure Mr Rupert Harding has had his wicked way with her. Tied her up and whipped her raw. Sex slaves. The Regency house of porn.'

They both giggled. Their smiles not out of place amongst the beaming half-drunk, three-quarter-drunk and plain old pissed guests. One face, however, was not smiling. Like a tumour in the celebration. A look from across the floor that caught both Emily, and especially Marina, off guard. This unknown face staring directly into Marina's eyes stared with an amount of superiority. In fact she didn't stare, she glared.

'Do you know her?' Emily shouted above the voice of the DJ.

'Just because she's Asian, doesn't mean I know her, Emily,' Marina replied, while keeping her eyes fixed on the pretty Indian woman who looked to be in her late twenties. 'She's got attitude, though.'

And when the two of them received attitude they often felt obliged to return it.

'Leave it,' scolded Marina to Emily, who was about to gesture across the room with her hand. 'It's an Indian thing.' She grabbed Emily's middle finger and lowered it. 'Anyway, remember our karma. We're not the girls we were.'

Emily sniggered. 'Our beauty is a parrot.'

'I'm not going to let an Indian girl wreck my evening. It's not too often that you and I—' Marina stopped in mid-sentence as she watched the scariest-looking skinhead in the room thunder across the floor and launch himself into the Indian girl's mouth with his tongue. There was no resistance. Leading to one conclusion: the scary-looking skinhead was the pretty Indian girl's partner. And very proud of him she was too, thought Marina, watching the skinhead munch on her face. It wasn't the munching that was so off-putting, or the swastika tattoo on his neck, or even the way they swapped jellied eels from mouth to mouth. What was so off-putting was the way the Indian girl continued to stare smugly across at Marina while all this took place.

It *definitely* was an Indian thing.

And it was so terribly hard to explain. Because it was so terribly hard to understand.

Marina had often tried to educate Emily in the etiquette of the Indian runaway. How it is that many Indian girls who have gone against tradition sometimes walk around with a *chapatti* on their shoulder. The Indian equivalent of a chip. Because they have made the break, broken with family values, become a martyr, they look down upon the Indian girls who have not made that break. The weak ones. They stare with a pitiful eye and snigger with superiority. They see the Indian girls waiting for an arranged marriage as 'the unfortunates'. And it is unfortunate. Unfortunate that they act this way, like the Indian girl on the other side of the dance floor. Maybe she should eat her *chapattis*.

That's if she's got enough room left after eating the scary-looking skinhead, thought Marina, almost shocked at the tongue wrestling competition across the floor. And then she had a strange, almost racist thought. Wouldn't it be great, brilliant even, if the Indian girl's parents could see their rebellious daughter kissing Hitler's Shoeshine Boy. What would they make of Miss Superiority now? He certainly wouldn't have been the type of boy that they would have picked. Even his own parents probably had reservations about loving him. But he was obviously the type of man the Indian girl wanted. And that was all that mattered, wasn't it?

Marina felt the urge to smirk back herself. Fancy having to wake up to a swastika. Imagine having to iron his Union Jack T-shirts while he pogoed around the council bedsit to The Sex Pistols singing 'I am an Antichrist'. Imagine his mates, Toothy, Fats, Lucky and Mash. All taking turns crashing on the bedsit floor until hostel rooms became available. Bins full of syringes, foil on the sideboard, blood on the walls. Skinhead heaven. Imagine it all. Marina shivered.

It was here that her conscience politely tapped her on the shoulder just before her guilt kicked her up the arse. She was becoming her father. Judge and jury. Condemning before trial. She didn't like this side to anyone's character, especially her own. Many times she'd thrown wobblies at people for judging her. Making up their minds about her, her ways, her culture, before they even knew one per cent of her personality. How dare they? And how dare she?

She aimed another look towards the scary-looking skinhead, who was now being lap-danced by the Indian girl. Talk about taking this runaway theme too far. Next she'd be in her undies and he'd be waving his jellied eel about. But if the couple wanted to go and make a few lightly tanned Naziette babies, then that was their prerogative. It was none of Marina's business. Most babies come out as skinheads anyway – apart from Don King, who came out with a garden hedge on his head. Mummy King said it was a very prickly birth. But Don was a knockout baby all the same.

The music abruptly stopped. 'Shabba!' echoed in the room and then the lights switched on. Someone shouted out, 'It's the lady in red.' And all eyes turned to the small raised stage near the DJ's decks. There, standing on her lonesome, was Nicole. She seemed quite relaxed holding the microphone.

'Testing, testing, one, two, one, two,' she said, all prim and proper, tapping the mike with her fingers.

Marina and Emily clapped eyes on Nicole's fabulous figure and it hurt. They'd heard a few of the blokes talking about this 'stunning, blonde posh bird in a red dress', and how they wanted to 'do 'er'. No one is *that* gorgeous, the girls had convinced each other. But the men were right and Marina had to hold Emily back from making a wolf whistle.

'I'll do 'er myself, she's that gorgeous,' said Emily.

'Ladies and gentlemen, may I please have your undivided attention?' Nicole announced with the easy air of someone comfortable in giving speeches.

'Get your macaroons out,' shouted a kid, who quickly piped down when his mother clipped him round the ear and threatened him with the words 'foster home'.

Nicole, unfazed, continued, 'I know you were expecting to hear a speech by the owner, Thomas Harding. But, unfortunately, an emergency in Room 42 has arisen. I, therefore, Nicole Newton-Harrington, his girlfriend, will be making a short and sweet speech on his behalf.' She made a quick sweep of the room with her eyes. 'It comes as a pleasant surprise to see you have all made the effort and not come as scruffs as Thomas had predicted you might.' She smiled – Daddy had told her 'Always begin a speech with an insult to gain their attention.' So with the insult out of the way, Nicole proceeded. 'But what does Thomas know? Not much. And unlike Thomas I will not be mentioning money. And unlike Thomas I will not stand here and calculate how much profit per head I have made this evening. Because this evening is not about money, it's about another kind of profit. Love.' She waited for the expected applause . . . Oh well, she carried on. 'The Regency Hotel has been the spectator of many weddings. It has seen many happy couples become happier as they are united. And it will surely witness the happy coupling of many more.' She looked up. 'But unfortunately it will never see the wedding of Thomas and me. We will never even get the chance to divorce because we will never be married. There will be no fights over who gets the children because we won't be having any together. There will be no family Christmases because . . .'

The guests were enthralled.

Chapter Seven

From just outside Room 42 Thomas looked down the corridor as the Regency porter kicked the last of the tapestry suitcases into Room 49, muttering the words, 'Take your own fucking cases up, you snobby dirt bags.' He entered the room, slamming the door shut behind him and continued to lay into the cases with his boots, his voice raised. 'You snobby fucking bastards. I was about to have a fag break.'

From a spare bunch, Thomas quickly found Room 49's key and opened the door to see the young porter, dressed immaculately in his standard-issue burgundy and bottle-green waistcoat and crisp-pressed trousers, in the middle of what looked like the Haka, dancing angrily round the suitcases. Which, in some ways, was appropriate, for right now Thomas's mood was all black.

'You just couldn't give a shit, could you?' Thomas

shut the door behind him and closed in on a surprised-looking Antony.

Antony scoffed. 'Hardly keeping rare bird eggs in there, are they? It's not like they've got the AIDS cure in there, is it? Sorry, Mr Harding, but smelly under-pants don't qualify as valuables in my book.' He scrutinized Thomas's face – something was telling Antony that he could be sacked. He gave the case a severe last kick across the carpet. 'It was rumoured that you were going to sack someone today, that you were on the warpath because your girlfriend is having one of her rain fits. You always take it out on us. So, I resign. Tough! I got in first. Who's the idiot now then, hey, Mr Harding?' he said, wondering how the hell he was going to pay the mortgage. 'Who's the idiot now?'

Thomas frowned, he'd had enough of this cretin. 'You are. Because you resigned, Antony, it will be six full weeks before you can claim unemployment benefit, and, as you left me in the lurch without any notice, I keep your last month's wages. TOUGH! Now, will you leave my hotel.'

Telling people to leave went against the grain. But bad staff were like Dutch Elm disease and needed eradicating: a business could only thrive without rot inside.

Thomas walked the rot to the hotel's main entrance, metaphorically booting him out of the front door, and in passing the banquet room noticed how disquietingly quiet it was within. Surely the Cockneys had not succumbed to silence. How could two hundred and fifty drunk mouths be kept in suspended animation, he wondered, edging open the banquet door. He'd never known a wedding party so deathly still. Unless, perish the thought, he thought, the wedding had morphed into a funeral. His eyes quickly located the ancient woman in the wheelchair – no, she was still alive – just. So, what then? And then the noise siphoned through his ears. The penetrating voice of Nicole all souped-up with the help of loud speakers. Oh no, what on earth . . .

'I don't even turn the television on before 5 p.m. any more, in case it's children's T.V., it reminds me of how incomplete my life is without a child. So empty, so undernourished. Five o'clock is my watershed. It's when I shed my tears. I desperately want a baby but Thomas fails to see the importance. This, this hotel is Thomas's baby and he spoils it. Everything his baby needs it gets. And I put up with so much. Everyone else is allowed to be happy except me.'

Thomas stared at the audience, amazed how engrossed they all were. Some giggled, some cringed, some wiped tears from their eyes (what *had* she been telling them?) and some heckled.

'Leave him!' a woman shouted.

'You deserve better than him,' another woman.

'Marry me,' a rough, gruff male voice, 'I'll father your children.'

'Get your macaroons out.' And this time the kid was led away by his mother.

Clearing her throat, Nicole spoke. 'All I'm trying to say is how lucky Phil and Tracy are to have found each other. Man and wife. They can now be free and not weighed down by constraints.'

'Weighed down by Tracy's belly, more like,' said a voice. Then, 'Sorry, sis, I didn't mean it.' Marlon turned his attention back to Nicole. 'You carry on, darling. Spill your guts. Don't hold back on account of us. It ain't healthy. We all want to hear more about this bastard Thomas.'

Nicole's face jolted at the word 'bastard' but soon continued, the microphone crackling as she spoke. 'Even today when I broke down in tears to discuss marriage and babies, he said we should decide whether we had a baby by stone, scissors and paper.' The Cockneys gasped. 'Yes, it's true. His hotel always takes precedence. One time, we were late for a function being held here and we trailed a funeral hearse for three miles in his beloved Porsche. And for all three miles of the journey Thomas angrily hooted on his horn for them to get out of the way.' The Cockneys gasped again. 'Another time . . .'

Alarm bells rang in Thomas's head. He remembered sitting at lunch with Nicole one rainy day, in front of his entire family. She had stood up, blurting out a number – 0345 909090 – and asked if any one knew what it was. She then burst out crying explaining that she knew it, and she knew it by heart: it was the number to the Samaritans. Allegedly, Thomas had pushed her into such a dark corner that she had nowhere else to go, forcing her to phone the number often enough to put it on her Friends and Family list. He did *not* want that story being dug up tonight. Tonight was supposed to be a happy occasion. He shot across the wooden floor, jumped the small platform, and snatched the mike from her hand. He looked like a desperate man.

'Time to party everyone! Time . . . to . . . party.' Thomas turned to the DJ, and pointed. 'Hit it!'

'The Birdy Song' lamely competed with the booing crowd. The hostility towards Thomas only fizzling out after three laps of 'The Locomotion'. And while Thomas watched the guests dance around their track, he wondered about his own. Where the bloody hell was he heading with his life? If only this night would end.

With the persuasive qualities of alcohol in the blood, the Cockneys mellowed as the evening slowed. As Thomas held Nicole tight on the dance floor, he felt the entire weight of her expectations press against him. She was expecting certain things from him. He knew she was giving him one hundred per cent. And he knew he couldn't give the Regency the full one hundred per cent it deserved with her hanging around. Something would have to give.

'Look at me, Nicole,' Thomas whispered as they slow-danced to 'Torn' by Natalie Imbruglia. She peeped up, her blue eyes glossy with tears. '*Que sera sera*.'

She took a deep breath and with a husky voice said, 'What will be will be.'

And the funny thing was, they looked so good together.

Marina and Emily had been watching Thomas and Nicole, transfixed.

'She's taking it well,' Emily stated. 'It's so completely obvious that he's going to dump her. I mean, come on, but slow-dancing to "Torn"? He has to be dumping her.'

'She's unstable if you ask me,' Marina said, sipping her Martini, 'and a total embarrassment. No one, especially you and I, likes to watch when a couple splits up. Particularly when the woman is so beautiful.' They grinned. 'I'd lay a good few pounds that within a few weeks poor Mr Harding will have got over Miss World and will have found the real woman of his dreams. The woman chosen by destiny.'

Emily raised her pint glass. 'To the woman of destiny.' No doubt me, she thought, smiling.

Marina clinked her glass against Emily's. 'To the woman of destiny.' Hopefully, if I play my cards right, that will be me, she thought, returning the smile – especially after she and Thomas had shared that 'look' earlier.

They both stood up to leave. Not ones to outstay their welcome.

Marina glanced back to the smoky dance floor. A glitter ball dazzled lights above Thomas's head, green and blue lasers swept across his face, party popper paper tangled in his hair. And through the celebration mayhem she was sure she saw a smile. Her heart crashed like a computer. Please, she thought, please let that smile be aimed at me.

With difficulty, Marina ignored how intimate the so-called 'splitting couple' were on the dance floor. Most people, even half cut, could tell that Thomas and Nicole had a strong hold on each other. The softly-softly whispers in her ear, the ignited passion in their eyes, and the clutching of bodies as though it really was their last dance. It would take someone pretty stupid or someone pretty desperate to believe they had a chance with him.

Two pretty stupid desperate girls left the party.

*

'Open the letterbox and meow,' Marina said, irritably, sheltering under the porch from the rain. Hilda had locked them out. Her rules were clearly marked in the rental agreement. Anyone not back before 1.00 a.m. would not be let in. It was 1.05 a.m. 'And make it sound like it's dying.'

Emily knelt down on the worn un-welcome mat. 'I'm not doing a dying cat. I'll do a starving cat.' She flipped the lid open and pressed her mouth to the rusty edge. 'Meooow, ow ow ow, meow ow ow.' She scraped her newly manicured nails up and down the door. 'Me ow ow.'

Three bolts, two chains and one huge 'tut tut tut', and they were in. And boy, what a treat it was to see Hilda in her nightie. She'd been wearing the same one since 1942. If it was good enough to wear making love to her late husband, then it was good enough to answer the door to her late lodgers. The girls giggled out an apology and ran up the stairs to their flat. Hilda, in her increasingly wet nightie, searched up and down the dimly lit road for the moggy. Pinstripes, her fat ginger Tom, had been missing for weeks.

Upstairs, in the groggy gloom of a mangy flat, was where fantasy dismantled and reality revived. Any leftover feelings from a good night out were dissolved as soon as one heard the delicate but oh-so-annoying flap flapping of moth wings on the hot light bulbs. Why, wondered Marina sometimes, when a moth had its choice of bulbs, would it pick downtown Fenworth to burn its wings? It didn't make sense.

And nor did tonight.

From her room, Marina listened to Emily parading to and fro from her bedroom to the bathroom. She was the only woman Marina knew who took as long to get unready as it took her to get ready. Once, in an effort to save on time she had asked Marina to strap her into her bed while she slept. She had hoped that by being tied up, her body would remain still during the night and therefore come morning her make-up would remain perfectly applied. It was an amazing success. Emily had awoken with flawless foundation and mascara. Unfortunately the rope burns on both her feet and ankles had meant she couldn't leave the flat for a week. Marina wondered why looking good was so important. So important to both of them. Why did men have to be so shallow that only looks counted, she thought, drooling over her poster of Robert De Niro in *Raging Bull*. Why did men have to care so much about beauty, she thought, getting hot thinking about Thomas's smile. Surely he had been smiling at her. He had to have been smiling at her.

She stared at her small statue of Shiva. Her private Hindu God. The God who chose her to choose him. The bronze figure made in the hottest flames now as cold as the ice on top of the Himalayas. When she was smaller, the multi-armed creature had seemed like a monster, the circle of fire encasing a demon. Her parents had given her the choice. 'If he frightens you, Marina, *beti*, then choose another.' But something enriching about this deity with powers of destruction and recreation entwined her mind like no other. No, Shiva would be her God. Marina asked him questions from time to time. There was something safe in his darkness. Something magical in his simplicity.

'Aum.' Marina uttered the sacred syllable. 'Aum.' The sound of God. 'Aum,' she continued. A whole bunch of meaning was wrapped up in that noise. It supposedly contained the sound of the universe's creation. Some Hindus begin and end a prayer with the sound of Aum. Marina felt comfortable around the sound. Although when half drunk. Aum sounded more like Aum-hic. Her Aum was interrupted by Emily waltzing in and asking her if she would be going to bed thinking of Thomas Harding.

'Don't be so wet,' Marina said, unfolding her legs from the lotus position. 'Of course I won't be thinking about him.' She unclipped her medium-length hair, gave it a shake, then stared at Emily's talc-white face. 'What's that on your skin? Does Jack Straw know you're borrowing his make-up? You look like a walking corpse.'

Emily pulled back Marina's duvet and tucked herself in. 'I was thinking about having a slice of cheese before bed and then seeing if Mr Harding would come and rescue me in my nightmare.' They sniggered as Emily tried hard not to let her mucky face touch the sheets. 'And no, it's not make-up, it's the Regency Anti-Ageing cream – it makes you look years younger – which fell into my bag *accidentally*.' She rummaged in her dressing gown under the duvet and pulled out the tube. 'It says, "Not to apply to children". Or they begin to look like foetuses, I suppose.' Emily glided into a dream. 'I was thinking, I might get some wedding photos done of me before I get wrinkly. Modern technology would be able to join me up with the lucky man later. Any thoughts?'

Marina nodded her head sagely. 'Better idea. Get married wrinkly and ask them to brush your wrinkles out.' She shook herself out of her dress and hung it lovingly in her wonky MFI wardrobe before stepping into her Betty Boop pyjamas. 'Better still, don't worry about it. Worrying causes worry lines and that's what wrinkles are. That's why Joan Collins looks so good. No worry. No conscience. No wrinkles. And while we're on the subject of taking care of our bodies. I need my sleep.'

'So you don't want to take a peek at this then.' Emily pulled out a glossy magazine from another pocket, opened it to a well-worn page, and passed it to Marina. 'There he is, all six foot one of him. The picture is three years out of date, mind, but still awesome. Thomas Harding. Age twenty-seven. Millionaire. Bachelor number four.'

Marina asked to borrow the magazine in order to have a copy made at Office World. She didn't want to get into that position of having to ask Emily for the picture every time she felt hot. And she didn't want to have to explain why there were lipstick marks on his face and crotch either.

Lying back in her bed, Marina closed her eyes, thinking of how her parents had left her free to make decisions. Free to find herself the man who she thought would make her happy and, when she did so, they would bless her unconditionally. If Marina wanted help finding a man, then they would oblige her also. But being free to make her own decisions meant being free to make the wrong decisions. 'Follow your heart, Marina,' her parents insisted. 'The secret of a happy life is an honest life, and there is no honesty in following the hearts of others.' But Marina had two hearts to follow. Her Western heart and her Eastern heart. Like two drumsticks thumping on a drum. Two different beats to one rhythm of life. Her parents had just left her to it. Removed her Indian stabilizers and told her to freewheel down the English hill. But the hill was steep sometimes, and there were days when her brakes failed. Some days, and today was one, she needed the advice of her mum – but for the last four years her mum had believed that Marina was an independent woman and had simply taken her mortal being by the scruff of the neck, given it a good shake, and declared, 'Life's sweet!' But it wasn't sweet, not by a long shot. God, freedom could be so constraining.

Marina tossed beneath her duvet. Through the thin walls, the sexy voice of Dr Fritzgerald Guztelburg spoke soothingly. The German self-help tapes had been a bargain at a car boot sale and they helped instil confidence into Frau Emily every night – even though she did not understand a damn word of German except for *frankfurter* and Adolf. These were very worrying times indeed for Hilda downstairs, though, whose late husband had been blown into tiny charred fragments by the Luftwaffe – on perhaps one of Germany's most successful bombing raids over London. She still heard the sirens. Marina plugged her ears with tissue paper, blocking out Dr Fritzgerald Guztelburg's dulcet tones as she returned to deep thought. Wondering if God had equipped her with enough natural instincts to navigate her way through this mad world.

Instinct. God's gift to balance out naivety, a bucket of water on a dreamer's fire. Marina knew in both her hearts that Mr Harding, or rather, Thomas, was out of bounds. Off limits. 'Don't Walk On The Grass.'

'Stay Out.' Another woman's man. He was the big UN. The no-holds-barred UN. UN for UNattainable. And this fact begged Marina to say, 'Let's say.'

Let's say, she thought, that Shiva, her Indian Hindu God, had set this all up. Let's say that from the moment Emily and herself had arranged the visit to the Regency, Shiva had been fiddling around with the future trying to arrange Thomas's schedule. No time to prattle around with $E=mc^2$ and arrange travel back in time, Shiva had to act on impulse in the present and arrange Thomas's path to cross with Marina's right now. Let's say that Shiva picked the place and Shiva picked the time and Shiva, in all his wisdom, in all his goodness, was now picking her man. Marina smiled at the thought. Shiva had taste.

Marina wondered if it would be awfully rude of her to ask whether Shiva could now arrange for Thomas and Nicole to split. It was obvious that Shiva had wanted her to see, first-hand, how rocky Thomas and Nicole's relationship was. Surely Shiva would only have shown such a sight with one thing in mind: Shiva wanted Thomas to be Marina's man. It was her destiny. Shiva had given the green light. And who was she to disobey Shiva?

Marina uttered only one word before falling off into a deep and pleasing sleep.

'Aum.'

Chapter Eight

Thomas stared at the thirty brides and grooms. In some ways he was extremely happy for them, the start of a brand new life together. And in other ways he was downright bitter. He folded up his local newspaper and chucked it in the bin beside the park bench. Out of the thirty couples, only three, ONLY THREE had chosen his hotel for their wedding reception. Bastards.

It was Friday, midday, nearly a week since the Cockneys' wedding. Already a postcard from Phil and Tracy Jenkins was pinned up in Reception:

> *Thanking all the Regency staff for a memorable wedding day. If we both re-marry, I'm sure we'll both use the Regency to have our reception.*

Thomas, in just jeans and T-shirt, sat alone in the

blazing heat of an August roaster. For the last half-hour he'd watched a man throw sticks for his Labrador to fetch in the River Isis. Amongst the turds and current, the poor thing battled to keep his master happy. It was a dog's life. Thomas continued to watch one man and his dog while his mind went for a walk. Or rather, a run.

Since the Cockneys' wedding, Nicole had forgotten how to be polite to him. Words like 'arsehole' and 'urchin' kept creeping into the conversation. Words she only used to use when she was hitting PMT. And now she walked about with a force field around her body. If Thomas strayed within a foot of the force field, she threatened to pick up the red phone and ring Mummy. Sex was a no-no. In fact, in the current climate sex was rape.

Pinned on the wall in Thomas's apartment was a large piece of graph paper showing the declining love Nicole held for Thomas. Nicole had plotted the graph paper with pink nail polish. Since Saturday her love for him had gone from a strong 100 per cent and dwindled down to a measly 15 per cent; 10 per cent because he still knew how to make a good coffee and 5 per cent for sexiness. The last two days she'd refused to acknowledge him at all. H.G. Wells had written about this character before. Thomas was now the invisible man. And this was war of the worlds. It was time to fly the white flag. Time to surrender.

From his pocket Thomas pulled out the box and popped open the lid. An expensive engagement ring with so many noughts in its price tag one could make a necklace by linking them together. The diamonds glared, waiting for the applause. Thomas glared back:

I could have had an extension built on my hotel for the price of you.

He thought back to this morning when once more he had read through the letter he had written to himself as a fourteen-year-old boy. It was like looking back on an old diary entry. He'd paid particular attention to page nine. Written amongst a list of fantasies that he should have achieved by now, including sex with an air hostess from Air Canada, was a promise.

I, Thomas, promise myself that I will never be forced into marriage even if I get a woman pregnant.
I, Thomas, promise myself that I will never marry a woman for her looks and packaging.
Dump the leggy blonde, Thomas. Listen to me.
Dump her!!! I know you're with her. I can feel it.
I bet she's out of this world beautiful.
But dump her.
YOU CANNOT, WILL NOT, MUST NOT MARRY A WOMAN JUST FOR HER <u>LOOKS</u>!

He needed H.G. Wells again for the Time Machine. He'd go back and strangle that fourteen-year-old know-it-all, explaining that he was wrong and Nicole was so right. Everything about everything was right about her. Setting aside that she went a bit mental every time it rained. There was something written in the way she was made that other women aspired to. And men from all walks perspired to. Even Sheikh Abe Assop Mohammed Junior, who occasionally stayed at the Regency, took a liking to her, saying he would have one of his wives (the incontinent one) back in Dubai executed immediately so that he could marry Nicole. And if Nicole said 'no', he would fall on his own sword by morning.

Face it, Thomas had told himself after splashing out a fortune on an engagement ring, you love her and even if you lost everything tomorrow and had only Nicole left, you'd still be happy. And no woman was supposed to do that to a man. If she did, you married her. The diamonds still glared. And in some amazing way, the more he thought about marrying Nicole, the better it sounded – and he knew the perfect venue for the reception.

Falling in love with Nicole had been easy. You met her, you fell in love. Very easy. Paul Simon wrote 'Fifty Ways to Leave Your Lover'. But there must be a million ways to meet her in the first place, Thomas thought. Including the grass verge of a dual carriage-way – where Thomas had seen Nicole standing in the lashing rain angrily kicking the wheel hubs of her Mercedes with the pointy tips of her stilettos. Thomas sometimes wondered whether he would have stopped to help Nicole that frightening, lightning night if she hadn't had blonde hair, or if her nipples hadn't been showing through her drenched red cocktail dress, or for the simple fact that she looked so helpless.

Her first words to him could have emptied a man's heart of hope. 'Go away, Mr Harding,' she had said, throwing her Prada handbag at his face. 'Lester has forbidden me to talk to you. And, believe me, I know all about you. So if it's not too much trouble could you please go away. Bog off.'

Thomas could only vaguely recollect seeing Nicole

on the rare occasion that their social worlds crossed orbits. He knew of her. And she would have known of him. She would have made up the numbers in his list of casual acquaintances and, likewise, he would have made up the numbers in hers.

Passing traffic had slowed to look at the scene then sped off towards Oxford. Thomas couldn't help but notice the registration of the new Merc: N1 COLE. It was to be expected. Her family, the Newton-Harringtons, were known importers of wine and stunk of money. Lester, however, just stunk. Lester Leonard Carradine III, Nicole's ex, had studied at Oxford University with Thomas. Undergraduates together. Even on Lester's first day of term, he had arrived in a top hat, tossing out silk handkerchiefs from inside his waistcoat with the words 'I'm a Winner' embroidered in gold. 'You're a wanker,' was the common response. But Lester bought friends quickly and was soon a popular guy earmarked for great things. Thomas was never included in Lester's group of friends – not that he lost sleep over it – it was an impossibility. Their fathers did not belong to the same golf clubs, cigar clubs, polo clubs, squash clubs and, more importantly (there were quite a few zeros' difference between Lester's father's Swiss bank account and Thomas's father's), money clubs. Money didn't just talk in Lester's world, it shouted.

But Lester's hatred for Thomas, and it really was hatred, had nothing to do with Thomas's meagre prosperity, or how unconnected Thomas's family was. It had more to do with sex appeal. Thomas ruled the roost when it came to women. Lester couldn't bear the fact that Thomas's name came up in conversations more than his. Sophisticated, intelligent, beautiful women became giggling schoolgirls the moment they laid eyes on Thomas. On many occasions Lester had been astonished at the crude language these upper-class women would sink to just to describe how horny Thomas made them feel. Not that Lester was unattractive, he was amazing by most standards, but not in Thomas's league. That's why Nicole was so handy. Thomas could never have her. Nicole and Lester had been marked for marriage since the day their families became entwined in a business venture many years ago. Nicole was the jewel in Lester's crown and he forbade her to go anywhere near Thomas. But soon Lester's orders to Nicole were to end.

It was like a monsoon that day he'd stopped for Nicole. Thomas had dumped her Prada bag on the Mercedes' bonnet. 'Look, sit in my car, I'll phone the AA. It's probably just damp. They cut out sometimes.'

Her eyes had clamped on Thomas's. She'd opened her mouth to speak, paused, then did speak. 'I'm a killer. I've killed someone. Their life "cut out". Anyway, I don't think Alcoholics Anonymous can help me tonight.' Nicole's figure had been draped in sadness, shivering violently as she recoiled from the cold. With laboured steps, she'd walked towards Thomas's midnight-blue Porsche, opened the door and nearly fallen inside. 'I can't believe I've killed someone.' Her sobs had dissolved as she closed the door behind her.

Thomas, soaked, had searched up and down the road for signs of an accident. He had felt his heart pestering to jump out of his rib cage. She had said *someone*, not some people, so it was just the one body he was looking for – hopefully still in one piece. Quickly he had sunk to his knees and checked for body parts under the chassis. Nothing. No blood. No guts. Not even bone fragments. He'd jumped back up, maybe the rain had washed it away.

He'd shouted at the windscreen, 'Do you remember which way the body was sent? Did it bounce off the bumper? The windscreen? Or maybe it ricocheted off the bonnet.' Nicole's eyes had registered nothing. 'What was the trajectory when it flew through the air?' He'd pulled open the passenger door. 'Where the hell did it land, Nicole? The body?'

She'd sobbed harder. 'I need a drink. It wasn't even on this road. The accident was about five miles from here.'

Thomas had sighed. 'Hit and run. Of all the stupid, senseless things.' He'd paused. 'Nicole, this is probably going to sound slightly melodramatic, but considering that you've just killed someone, taken their life and ended their existence, I will say it anyway. You are going to need a good lawyer. And I mean the best that Daddy can afford. But first things first, though, we're going to have to drive back to the scene of the hit and run and then call the police. I will help you as much as I can.'

Nicole had mumbled something as she blew her nose into a silk hanky. The words 'I'm a Winner' slightly out of place here. 'I killed Lester,' she'd sniffed. 'He died instantly.'

A frown had formed. 'But he died two years ago. And you didn't kill him. He killed himself.' Relief had moistened Thomas's mouth as he realized that, thank the Lord, no one had died today. He'd spoken firmly: 'Everyone said Lester was the culprit of his own demise, Nicole.'

'That's what most people think. But the truth is, I killed him. If it wasn't for me he would still be alive.' And she'd broken down again. 'I shouldn't be discussing this with you. Lester despised you. He said you would never belong because you're too busy trying *not* to fit in. He loved calling you a cad. Summed you up to a T, he said.' She'd sniffed again. 'I don't think you are, though. A cad. He talked about you more than he talked about me. My opinion? I think he was secretly jealous of you. But,' she'd pulled out another silk hanky, 'we'll never know, will we? Because I murdered him.'

Thomas had begun a cuddle that would last until next morning.

And so it came to pass, Nicole and Thomas fell in love. A meeting of two worlds, a collision of two social breeds. Thomas always climbing the ladder that Nicole's father thought he owned. Each rung a step nearer acceptance but never quite enough. For still, standing at the top of the ladder, and even though now dead for five years, was the memory of Lester, the son-in-law they'd always wanted but the son-in-law taken from this universe. Thomas would never fill those boots in Nicole's family's eyes.

And Thomas would never bother trying.

Here, today, as Thomas sat on the bench watching the River Isis idle past, a thought that would win Thomas no haloes in heaven occurred. He wished that Lester could be here to see how this socially impotent cad, Thomas, had taken his premier-league woman. He stared at the blue sky overhead. A white trail from a plane divided the sky in two. Thomas gazed at the long white line. Maybe Lester was up there after all. Maybe Lester was looking down right now. Thomas leant back on the bench and smiled up at the sun. Oh, how much he loved Nicole.

'Thomas!' Not many people said Thomas the way Thomas liked it said. Some people dragged the 's' at the end. Others placed more emphasis on the beginning with the 'us' added later. Like Thom-arse. This man was right on the money.

Thomas stood up and shook his hand. 'Frank, I'm amazed you acquired it so speedily. I thought this sort of thing took months.'

The tall, thin man in a grey suit sat down beside Thomas on the bench, his briefcase snug between his knees. 'I struck lucky. I think you're going to be surprised at what I've found.' He tapped the case. 'I don't know if it's good news or bad for you. But obviously, at the cost, I hope it's good news.' He looked at the dog nearly drowning with fatigue in the water. 'We said three.'

Thomas nodded. 'Three,' he agreed and produced an envelope tucked inside the front of his jeans. He handed the three grand over and thanked the man. In return he opened his case and passed Thomas a medium-sized cream envelope. The switch was a cinch. There was nothing remarkable in two men talking on a bench.

And two people who had never met before parted.

But there was something remarkable about a bright-red shiny Porsche being parked next to Astras,

Escorts and Cavaliers. A small crowd of teenagers admired the car with nodding heads and erections and rubbed their chins, working out what type of bird they would pull if they drove it.

Thomas sat inside and reversed the car away from the chorus of adolescent voices – 'Oh, come on, mate, give us a spin in yer motor' – heading towards Nicole's parents' mansion, out in the sticks right on the edge of Oxfordshire. Fifty-five acres of land including a small brook and bridle path. A haven for a variety of birds and tiny mammals. You had never experienced true silence until you'd stayed in Castle Cliff Manor. A refuge of solitude.

Until Nicole's mother opened her gob.

'Hello, Thomas, what a pleasant surprise,' sounded Nicole's mother, Marion, greeting him with an embrace at the Manor entrance. Thomas despised the way his future mother-in-law – oh, what a horrible thought – spoke his name. Sounded more like 'Sthom-ass'.

Three huge Dobermanns skidded through the palace hall and out on to the porch. Oh my, you've grown, noticed Thomas, lying underneath one of the dogs on the gravel.

'Pingo, get orf him.' The dog bolted back indoors, with the other two just a tail length behind.

Marion could make a basketball team feel as small as a tribe of pygmies. She could smell the scent of an inadequate man from forty yards away. And all men were inadequate for her three daughters. Thomas was no exception.

Inside the vast hall, underneath a chandelier that looked as though it could bring down a cathedral,

Thomas followed Marion into one of the drawing rooms. To heat this place would cost a small fortune, which didn't matter because they had a large one. Grapes. French vineyards. Millions of pounds from the red and white squashed grapes populating the southern hills in France. And if that wasn't enough cash to warm their cockles, they always had their inheritance to fall back on. They owned enough prime London real estate, handed down from their ancestors, to play Monopoly for real. The Newton-Harrington family was sturdy, the family was powerful and the family spoke very highly of itself. It might be hard to fit into a family such as this. Hence a certain reluctance on Thomas's behalf to try.

Marion was gone and there was that silence again. This room would be torture for someone who couldn't read. Books dominated all available wall space except for the two cabinets, which stood proud, filled with shooting trophies. Edmond, Nicole's father, had bored Thomas shitless discussing how to shoot clay pigeons. 'Just shoot them with a machine gun, I would.' Thomas's suggestion did not go down too well. But Thomas hated licking the arses of girlfriends' parents – it gave him awful hairballs. And anyway, what was the point in parent-creeping when he would never match up to our Lester, the son-in-law they had set their hearts on?

Keeping Thomas waiting longer than necessary was an old trick. And a cheap trick. He'd tried it himself once when interviewing for a commis chef. By the time Thomas had called through to the prospective interviewee, the room was empty except for a note left on the chair: *Stuff your job! You're not that important*. But this was no interview. Thomas was here to ask the woman he loved to marry him. He opened the jewellery box once again. The diamonds and their worth seemed to shrink before him. However much he spent was peanuts to a family like this. Not even peanuts. One peanut. This family, who thought nothing of buying up property the world over, of owning a moored yacht, *Aurora Borealis*, in Monte Carlo, Monaco, of bidding for priceless paintings at Sotheby's, this family who gained millions when the interest rate rose by just half of one per cent; how would they react to a ring that they would think twice about putting in a Christmas cracker? One of Edmond's favourite comparisons was Africa. 'Do you know,' he would say to Thomas's disdain, 'for the money I just paid for that little filly in the stable I could have fed ten thousand Africans for a year?' How many Africans, wondered Thomas, would Nicole's engagement ring feed?

He pulled out a heavy red-leather chair and sat. All he needed now was a stupid white wig and he could have been sitting in the House of Lords. Just then the door opened slowly and Nicole entered. Her modern designer clothes looked almost out of place amongst the antiques. Like the sound of someone hammering nails into oak, she walked confidently across the wooden floorboards in her kitten heels. Like the feeling of someone hammering nails into his skull, Thomas questioned himself one more time, quickly, before Nicole arrived at his feet: did he want to risk losing the hotel for Nicole?

'Mummy said a scruffy little urchin was here.' She checked his tatty jeans.

'I suspect she means me, if you were wondering.' He stood up to kiss her, but she dodged. He kissed the air passionately instead. 'Where's Edmond? Killing foxes?'

She sat side-saddle on the edge of the desk, her long tanned legs dangling freely. 'Daddy doesn't kill animals. We've been through all this before. And he doesn't injure them and watch them wriggling in agony either. If you must know, he loathes it when he goes clay pigeon shooting and a bird gets in the way. Detests it.'

A few seconds of silence while the pair of them looked at each other.

Nicole spoke. 'I would offer you tea but Lilly's on her lunch break.'

'I would gladly indulge in one of your mother's finest brews instead if she is willing to get off her pert backside and make it.' He smiled. 'Second thoughts, no, I abhor the taste of strychnine. It repeats on me.'

Nicole laughed. 'She doesn't think that badly of you, Tom. But we are from different stables.' She rose and hugged him tight. 'I've been doing a lot of thinking. I'm *so* sorry for the way I've been treating you. And . . .' She pulled back and sheepishly watched his eyes, her expression suddenly afraid. 'Please forgive me for what I have done.'

'Forgive?'

Nicole went on to explain how in a moment of rage she had placed the Regency Hotel in *Daltons Weekly* for the measly price of half a million. Including live-in manager called Thomas Harding. Thomas Harding worked like a Trojan. If that wasn't enough, his red Porsche had also gone on sale via the Internet. Measly price of thirty grand. Including a free tank of petrol and a free car wash each month from the previous owner, Thomas Harding. Also . . .

'What haven't you put up for sale, Nicole?' he asked, realizing that she was *definitely* the woman for him. Any doubts he'd had about her escaped like little Harry Houdinis. 'Please tell me you haven't tried to sell my light sabre. A Jedi Knight needs his light sabre.'

The sabre was safe – for now.

Looking around the room in which they cuddled, Thomas then closed his eyes, enjoying the last few moments of the known. For after he had popped the question, after he had asked Nicole for her hand in marriage, he would be stepping into the world of the unknown. From that moment on, Thomas's focus of commitment would swap from his hotel to her. He gulped internally. It was a huge step. One giant leap for Thomas but one small step for mankind.

'Can I ask you a quick question before I ask you to marry me, Nicole?'

Nicole shoved him off her. Shocked. 'You want to marry me?' she said, jumping up and down, squeaking the words out. Over the moon. The very same moon Thomas was trying to land on. 'Quickly then, ask the question.'

'Erm. I'm only going to ask because it would bother me later if I didn't.' He took her hand. His mouth as dry as a salt mine. 'It really doesn't matter what your answer is, it's just that I'd like to know. So, without further ado, I shall ask: when you were with Lester, if he had asked you to marry him, what would your answer have been?' Thomas felt the strong clench in her hand.

'No.'

'No?'

'I've only ever truly loved you, Tom. Lester was my parents' idea of my perfect man. You dug me out of a hell-hole. I'd most likely be dead by now if you hadn't.' She shook her head slowly. 'There is something about you, I don't think you even know it yourself. And it's not about looks.' She paused. 'I'm going to tell you something that destroys me sometimes.' A tear popped out and set up camp on her eyelash. 'I'm actually glad of my nightmare. If it hadn't happened, then I would never have met you. But it doesn't stop me from blaming myself. I know it was my fault, deep down. I really know it.'

'Maybe. Maybe not.' Thomas thought back to the envelope in the car. 'Anyway, that doesn't matter right now.' He pulled out the box. The woman in the jewellery shop had promised there would be tears after he produced the ring. She had said nothing about tears beforehand. Thomas opened the lid and slid the band of gold and diamonds on to Nicole's elegant finger. The smile that followed was priceless.

He was hers to keep now.

Chapter Nine

Fenworth High Street on a busy Friday afternoon. Bustling with passers-by passing through, and, outside the pubs, clogged with people passed and passing out. Many family disappointments ended up in Fenworth. A haven for school drop-outs – and that was just the teachers. You paid so little for accommodation here, you could liken it to the land of rent exile. And anyone with a job was accused of sleeping their way into the firm.

Introducing Napkins Sandwich Bar, home to the Belching Bacon Buttie, employer to both Marina and Emily for the last four years. Four years of filling sandwiches intended to fill bellies. Four years of questioning by the girls: was this really the best they could do? Emily left feelings of failure to Marina, the more grounded of the two. She looked up to Marina and if Marina was happy, filling Hovis nowt taken out bread with pork luncheon meat and cherry tomatoes, then so was she.

But was Marina happy filling pork luncheon meat sandwiches with cherry tomatoes? In her heart she was ashamed. This job was supposed to be temporary when they moved down from Watford. Marina's parents believed that she was working for an estate agent. Napkins Homes. Only her brother, Zaine, knew the truth and could be trusted to keep this secret. She'd only banked on lying to her parents for a few months. But months became years, and last week on the phone her mum was nearly in tears with joy when Marina explained how she had just sold the last of three mansions to a Welsh farmer by the name of Aberwysthworth Lambing-Shepherd. Her savings from her wages were being stashed in a high interest account that did not let her withdraw any money for thirty years. Her father was ecstatic: 'At last you understand how important your future is. Thirty years! The interest must be incredibly high.' And it was. Any interest on an account that didn't exist would be. But telling him the truth would have hurt him too much. Four pounds fifty an hour – before tax and NI – for filling poxy pork luncheon meat and sodding cherry tomato sandwiches. God, Marina thought, I have five GCSEs. I only flunked my A levels by the skin of my teeth. I hate this place.

'I hate this place,' Marina murmured sideways to Emily as she gave one of her regulars his change. 'Ox tongue and granary mustard. With anchovies.' She retched. Marina waited for the customer to leave and then went to join Emily by the coleslaw. 'Tonight, after work, I think we should begin writing our letters of apology. "Instant Karma" was a song by John

Lennon, I believe. And I want it now. I feel like every time I slice another sandwich, I slice away my life. If I carry on at this rate, the poor bloke who ends up with me will get only the crusts.' She spooned creamy coleslaw in her mouth. 'More salt!'

Outside the sandwich bar, the illuminated hulk-green sign of Napkins aimed to attract the cars on their way to Oxford. The shop's reputation for fine quality fillings was on a par with its reputation for fine quality flirting from the two saucy women who worked there. Both Emily and Marina, the only two employees, had noticed a monumental rise in tips when they played with sexual innuendoes. Words such as 'big', 'wet' and 'juicy' were often falling into the chat – or what the girls called 'customer care' – and it helped the day speed by.

Today, with the girls forced to reach into their pasts to grab the names of the people who they'd treated 'unfairly', was a day of apprehension. Nobody likes to apologize. Nobody likes to admit they were wrong. And nobody likes to be treated like a nobody. And that's why Emily's and Marina's Hit List now took up two sheets of A4. Most of the people who they would be apologizing to had, at one time or another, been treated like a nobody by the girls – but only for reasons that had seemed valid at the time. But what constituted valid to a sixteen-year-old girl back then might be considered invalid now. Proving that sometimes, along with spots, pubic hairs and rebelling, obstinacy and stupidity go hand in hand with youth.

'I think we should do a standard letter,' Marina suggested, tucking the list of names back into her blue apron. 'With a self-addressed envelope for their acceptance. You see, it's such a long time since we've seen any of them, just to hear from us will fill them with untold joy.' She pulled out a stool and sat down. 'Karma is breakable but it's also fixable. The clear aim here, Emily, is to be as nice as possible in this life to enable the good to come to us in our next. It's like planting seeds in this dimension only to pick the fruit in the following one.' She paused at the idea. 'Also, it stands to reason that by being nicer in this life our chances of bagging a nicer man are increased many manyfold.'

Listening to Marina loosely, Emily scribbled a few lines in Napkins Customer Suggestions book.

> *If only my wife could make sandwiches this good. And if only she could look this good too. The two girls brighten up my mornings. Mr Saunders, Oxford*

> *Is it a crime to buy sandwiches that taste so good, but which I cannot eat, because I am in love with the delicious lady called Emily? My stomach is churning. Her blond eyes and blue hair are amazing. Look, I must be going mad because of my love. I meant blond hair and blue eyes. Doh! Mr Thomas Gorgeous Harding, St Meridians Oxfordshire*

Emily sucked on the pen end trying to inspire herself for her next entry in the book. Life would be very dull without a flourishing imagination. An imagination capable of scenes that Hollywood would envy.

Thomas, her latest fantasy, had just finished satisfying her completely and . . .

'Emily!' Marina scolded, disrupting the daydream, pointing to the new sign on the wall. 'On second thoughts, I don't think Perv Bazzer *will* find that amusing. I'm taking it down.'

Shaking her head, Emily scowled at her friend. Their reputations were at stake here and all Marina could think about was their pervy boss, Perv Bazzer. He'd most likely get a thrill out of the sign anyway.

Holding the small wooden stepladder steady while Marina climbed, Emily watched the door in case a 'charger' came in and knocked Marina down. The notice was removed and the girls giggled at it one more time before they ripped it up:

The fish smell in here is the fish and only the fish.
Not US!

After being read the rule book of etiquette one must adhere to when one marries a Newton-Harrington, Thomas drove back to the Regency eager to deposit the envelope filled with information into his safe. Nicole was left floating on a cloud of euphoria, her dreams of engagement to the finest man in the land had finally been realized. She chose to show her happiness by uncontrollable squealing. Pingo, Excalibur and Moochy Moo, the three Dobermanns, howled for forgiveness – even dog whistles didn't hit the pitch of an excited Nicole. Within just one hour of Nicole being engaged, half of Oxfordshire's hoity-toity citizens knew all about it. Like a disease, news spread. Some were happy, some dubious, and some depressed. A minimum of nine bachelors would be crossing Nicole off their 'future wife' list. And including one judge, one MP and one vicar, at least twenty-five married men would be crossing Nicole off their 'future mistress' list. The Samaritans, however, would not be crossing Nicole off their 'future suicide' list. One never knew. In any case the most important list at the moment was the invite list for the huge engagement party that was due to be announced in their circles. No one held parties like the Newton-Harringtons.

Thomas closed and locked the door to the downstairs office in the Regency. Sometimes this place, with the number of important calls he had to take here, seemed like it was swimming with sharks. Snapping and biting. But today, his office felt like a tranquil lagoon. A framed picture of the film *The Big Blue* filled a portion of one wall. Below the poster, the words *Find Me The Frenchman*. Just another man lost like me, thought Thomas.

After hiding the envelope away in his safe, he sank into the swivel chair, closed his eyes, and checked out for a few minutes. Enough time to build up the courage to phone his mother who was on holiday in Italy. He hoped that she, or his father, didn't pull any stunts like they had the last time he'd phoned, when they thought it was highly amusing to pretend that Mom was going through her menopause and was finding her own son, Thomas, extremely attractive – in the wrong kind of way. Parents like these were hard to come by. Thomas dimmed the lights with the remote so that just the silhouettes of the computer, printer and coffee machine peeped out, then picked up the phone to dial.

'Mom, guess what? I finally did it.'

'Thank God for that,' she replied in a voice that the Queen would approve of. 'Does it help you swim faster?'

Swim? 'What are you talking about, Mom? I got engaged.'

'Oh. Sorry, darling, that's brilliant news. Excellent. Nicole, is it? Your blonde thingamajig?'

Thomas clenched his fists. 'Yes, Nicole. The blonde thingamajig.'

'Ah. Wonderful. Nicole, well I never. So pretty as well. How long do you think it will last?'

'For ever.'

Laughter. 'Oh come on, Thomas, my darling, let's be realistic. If you last one more year together you'll be doing well. So, when do I get to meet her?' She shouted back to her husband, 'It's Thomas, our idiot son, he's got engaged to thingamajig. The blonde one. You know, the Newton-Harrington child?'

Thomas waited for Mom to rejoin his conversation. 'Okay. I see what you're doing. The senile mother trick. Just out of interest, what exactly was going to help me swim faster?'

A pause. 'Oh that. It doesn't matter now. I'm sure you'll tell me when you're good and ready.'

'Tell you what?'

'Well, I thought you were ringing to tell me that you'd shaved your chest. To help in the swimming pool. You know? To take a few tenths off your times.'

'For fuck's sake, Mom, to shave my *fucking* chest?'

'Thomas! How dare you use such filth when you're

talking to me. I didn't get your father to spend thousands of pounds on a private education for you to use such profanities . . . You sound so common, Thomas, really. Now say sorry.'

'Sorry.' He felt as though he were four years old again.

The conversation turned down a few dark alleys, but essentially, after Thomas had apologized for swearing thrice more, his mother finally admitted to having met Nicole before, on quite a few occasions, and his parents issued a stark warning: beware of Nicole's mother and father. The Newton-Harringtons were to be taken very seriously. Their money and clout could shake the strongest foundations. And if Thomas were to go ahead and marry Nicole and then let her down in some way, bad tidings would surely come Thomas's way. It was as certain as the pop from a Newton-Harrington wine cork.

Replacing the receiver, Thomas held on to an edgy smile. He knew there was no way on earth that he was going to let Nicole down, so he had nothing to worry about.

The smile began to fade. Or did he?

Chapter Ten

Days passed too quickly sometimes and already it was one week since Thomas had proposed to Nicole. Both families were joyous. Party preparations for their engagement were already in full swing. The announcement had appeared in a double-page spread, organized by Nicole's mother, in *Horse & Hound* and *Shooting Weekly*, and a quarter-page advert in *The Times*. The festivities were to be taken to the extreme, no expense spared, no excuses for not attending.

The talk of 'the wedding of the century' was already driving the Regency staff nuts. Stuart, the commis chef, threw another cardboard box of tomatoes across the kitchen floor, where it skidded over the tiles and wedged itself under the stainless-steel food server. He was, apparently, tenderizing the toms.

'You'll fucking bruise those, Stu-pot,' shouted Harry, the head chef, whose humour apparently needed seasoning. He reached down and pulled out the remnants of a tomato, its oozing flesh weeping in his huge, coarse hands. 'Ketchup,' he said with disgust. 'I give up.' He paused, tossing a knob of butter into the pan. 'I don't give up easily. But with you, I give up.'

'Does that mean I can go, then?' Stuart asked, checking the time – 8.45 a.m. – and replacing the tray of eggs he was about to throw at Harry's head. 'You're the twat who told me you'd never have the heart to recommend sacking someone. I'm not being horrible, *Harriet*, but you're too soft.' He pulled off his apron, stained from this morning's breakfasts, and hung it on a peg. 'Toughen up. And remember, the wolf climbing the hill is always hungrier than the wolf on top of the hill. Your job will soon be mine.' Stuart clapped his hands together once and walked out of the steamy, stressed kitchen and into the cool, relaxed restaurant. Now where was the lucky lady? Where was the woman who struck gold this morning? And who *did* make up that wonderful saying, 'When the cat's away the mice will fuck?'

Half an hour later, breakfasts done and dusted, in a vacant room on the second floor, two little mice were at it like rabbits. Stuart and the young, up-for-it, Barbie doll waitress, Penny, squeaked and squealed like it was spring. Thrusting and clawing at each other's bodies before it was time for hibernation – or, in the real world, before lunch time in the restaurant had arrived. Unbeknown to Thomas, his staff had been 'at it' for years. It was one of the perks of the job, or, as Stuart put it, 'porks of the job'. Thomas hated vacant rooms. And this was Stuart's way of filling them.

And filling something else.

Penny moaned underneath Stuart's well-honed body. He was definitely the best commis chef lover she'd ever sampled. All that chopping, dicing, kneading and peeling toned up the bod perfectly. And because the kitchen was where he let his feminine side show itself, the bedroom was where his manliness came to life. Alpha Male Stuart. Hung like a horse, but he'd never cook one.

All their energy spent, Stuart and Penny lay side by side on the king-sized luxury bed. A light breeze wafted through from the air-conditioning. Nothing beat the aftermath of a good bonk – except for the bonk itself. The gentle lowering of heartbeats, the sleepy rolling of the eyes, the carefree roaming of the mind. It was times like this that men exposed themselves. It was times like this that men told the truth.

'I'm going to let you in on a little Stuart secret, Pen.' He lit up a fag and breathed in. 'I've got an agenda.'

She smiled. 'What's that? Some sort of genital disease?'

'Better than that. Way way way better. It's called "Thomas's Landslide". It's better than anything even Mini Me could have thought up. It's slick and sassy. And I give you my code word, "Live". And guess what live is backwards? EVIL!' He imitated a Dr Death laugh.

Penny battered his head with a pillow, then let Stuart continue to explain his crazy plan. The idea was based on jealousy. Thomas seemed to be a man blessed with everything. From a healthy, prosperous start in life, to a good private education, to a first-rate hotel and now an exceptionally beautiful woman who had agreed to marry him. Then there was the Porsche, the money, the connections, the respect, the designer suits, the admiring eyes of hordes of women, the . . . Oh, dear Lord, the list went on and on. Pure, unadulterated jealousy. If Stuart had a middle name it would be 'Thorn'. And he would be. The thorn in Thomas's side.

The room was now filled with smoke. A hue of grey that infected the clean feel to the five-star room in this four-star hotel. If the walls had ears they would have crumbled by now.

'You want to do what?' Penny sat up, giggling.

'I want to sleep with Nicole. I want to wreck something very dear to Thomas. Do you know that he's not had *one* affair since I've been working here? Not one. That's not a man, that's a wuss. I mean, forgive me here, but it's not like spunk costs, is it?'

She shook her head. 'I say forget it. One, Nicole has standards, she'll never sleep with you. And before you give me a cheap shot, no, I do not have standards. And two, I think you should keep away from her. Especially after what happened last year.' She paused. 'You do know what happened?'

His Dr Death laugh returned. 'Enlighten me, Penny, the wise, enlighten me.'

She hummed the theme tune to *M*A*S*H*. No response from Stuart. She jumped out of bed still naked and found the letter opener in the oak drawer by the window. She proceeded to draw the shiny blade across her right wrist. Still no response from Stuart. His eyes squinting in concentration, confused.

She returned to bed. 'Look, Nicole tried to kill herself last year. Blood was everywhere. She slit her wrist, nearly sliced through a tendon. She was hoping to die that night but Thomas found her in time.' Penny watched Stuart's face remain confused. He knew everything that went on in this hotel. Surely a suicide attempt wouldn't have escaped his notice. 'Two pints of blood squirted up the hall just outside this room. She was in a right state. And it made me wonder about things, it really did. I thought she had it all. I thought that Nicole was chosen to annoy us women, to irritate us. And next thing I know, she's worse off than I ever was. Stay away . . . Really, Stuart, I mean it. Don't mess with Nicole and her mind.' She cuddled up to her commis chef. 'See that lovely bracelet she wears? It covers the scar. You'll *never* see Nicole without it.'

The diamond-studded bracelet looked like something stolen from Tutankhamun's burial chamber. Wonder Woman would have been proud of a bracelet as big as that to battle her enemies. But Nicole, as far as Stuart could now make out, had enemies of her own. Herself being one of them. Maybe he'd have to rethink his plan. Maybe now, instead of getting Nicole into bed, he would approach Nicole and be her listening ear. Someone who she could call up and talk to at any time because Thomas was too busy and selfish with his hotel. He would take her to one side and show her that killing herself was not the only way. Suicide has a very high mortality rate and rarely, if ever – as the *M*A*S*H* song goes – is suicide *painless*. Yes, Nicole needed someone to talk to. And if things really went well after that, then who knows, maybe the next stop would be the bedroom.

That would serve that Thomas – the man who had it all – right.

Nicole loved the word 'couple'. But she loved the words 'married couple' even more. They ranked alongside 'Yes, madam, we have got those John Rocha shoes in stock.' To be married meant being in the ultimate gang. It meant sharing and spoiling each other and secret handshakes under the bed sheets. It meant falling in love over and over. And even the worst days together are better than the best days apart. Nicole, with two jewel-like eyes staring at her engagement ring, was smitten, and bitten and floating in a mist of love for Thomas. This wedding of theirs would be the beginning of a new universe, a happy slice of heaven. And her old universe, the one with the pain, could remain in the hell of her past.

And talking of hell, Thomas's apartment now looked like it had been on fire. Nicole frantically tried to vacuum up the last of the smoke with the Dyson on full pelt before Thomas exited from his shower. The breakfast sausages, chiselled off the frying pan with a knife, were so charred you could write with them. But that was okay, because with the burned sausage Nicole could scrawl a stern letter to the manufacturers of that expensive toaster now smouldering on the side, asking for an explanation as to why, after accidentally spilling the juice of *just* two fresh oranges inside the filament, it refused to work. Technology and Nicole didn't gel. She'd rather buy a new mobile than work out how to recharge her current one.

Some people don't look that nice in the morning. Nicole, however, was perfect. She was one of the beautiful people. In her deep-plum silk chemise and stiletto mules, she prowled the apartment kitchen hunting for inspiration. 'You go and have yourself a nice long shower, Tom, and when you come out a delicious breakfast will be waiting,' she had promised. Then disaster struck. Everything she touched caught fire. It was too much for Daddy's little rich socialite. Nicole tried to quell the instinct to reach out for the bell she used to ring to summon her maids. But there was no bell and there was no maid and this was not Castle Cliff Manor. It was the Regency. A hotel. A hotel with rooms. A hotel with rooms and a restaurant. A hotel with rooms, restaurant and . . . Hang on a minute, a hotel with rooms, restaurant *and* room service.

Nicole grabbed for the phone and then saw the deceit in her actions. If a man couldn't fix a car it did not make him any less of a man. Well, here was a woman who couldn't fix a breakfast. She screwed her face up. Or lunch. Or tea. Or elevenses. In fact, here was a woman who couldn't cook at all. Not a sardine. Two Delia Smith cookbooks stood uselessly on the side. Boiling an egg used to be so easy until Delia got involved.

Five minutes later, one huge apologetic look and Nicole held the jug over Thomas's cornflakes. 'Milk?'

With cornflakes? Are you mad? 'Yes please, quite soggy.' Thomas smiled, ignoring the fuming toaster, broken juicer and cracked espresso coffee machine. He was so glad that he'd just washed his hair, as the circling smoke took to it so well. 'Would you be miffed if I ate a banana as well as this?' He began to tuck in to the cereal. 'I'm not saying that this bowl of cornflakes won't fill me. I'm sure it will. I'm thinking, just in case.'

'Would you like me to cut the banana into dainty slices?' She rummaged in a drawer. 'I saw an electric knife in here somewhere.'

'No!'

Domestic bliss. A contradiction in terms as far as Thomas was concerned. How could anything even remotely related to domesticity be bliss? Nicole breaking out of the shell of old with her new-found household beak was making the electric appliances jittery. Who was next? But Thomas could see the good intentions hidden behind the short-circuiting. Beneath the floods, spillage and damage was a woman who was trying her hardest to do things that she'd never done before, like housework, for instance. Now that she was engaged to be married, she would hate Thomas to think he was marrying someone useless.

But there was useless and there was dangerous. Thomas gently eased the electric knife from her hand, already she'd nearly severed the heads from a vase of purple orchids. He kissed her on the lips. He was in love, nothing was going to change that. And the woman who he was going to marry in nine months' time was a home-wrecker. Literally.

The microwave made a beeping noise and Thomas instinctively threw Nicole to the kitchen floor and dived on top, covering her demure body, protecting her from the impending blast. He closed his eyes tight while the countdown continued. Beep . . . beep! . . . beeeeeeep!!

'That will be my leg wax, Tom. Could you let me up, please?' she said, giggling.

'Sorry. I thought . . . Never mind.' He helped her to her feet and brushed down his Armani suit. 'That was a jujitsu move, by the way. Obviously in a real bout I would have given serious consideration to letting you up for *just* leg wax, though.'

'And I suppose in a real bout you wouldn't have had an erection either, Tom,' she said, staring at his nether regions. 'It's times such as this that I wish your willy was detachable. Then you could scoot off into your hotel, like I know you're going to any minute. Regardless of your urges. Sometimes I feel like booking myself into this place so I can finally get your full attention. Look,' she dropped her silk chemise to the floor and, except for her stilettos and diamonds, stood naked against the kitchen cupboard. 'Go on, off you go. I'm sure a guest needs a towel or something.'

Inside Thomas's head he dialled 999. 'Yes, fire brigade, please. There appears to be a raging fire in my pants. No, a Green Goddess will not do. I need professionals.' Nicole's tanned body, under the tinted kitchen lights, looked irresistible. And he drooled a hot sweat. It had nothing to do with missing out on breakfast, or that he was standing in the kitchen, or anything else, but right now Thomas wanted to eat her. His hunger pangs reached from the top of his head down to the head of his knob. Business would have to wait for pleasure today.

Frenziedly he removed his suit, tie and shirt while checking the flashing timer on the microwave. And then, 'We've got twenty minutes to produce something wonderful. Ready . . . steady . . . cock!'

'Wait!' Nicole announced.

'Condom?'

'With or without?'

'You wouldn't want to be pregnant in a wedding dress. And remember, it will be *you* showing the photo album off not me. I say *with* a condom, Nicole.'

She huffed, life was so unfair. 'Scissors, paper, stone?'

'No, I'll fetch a Durex. Don't move.'

He returned with the condom in place and asked Hal to switch on the stereo to add to the mood. U2 – *Sunday Bloody Sunday*. Listening to Bono rock, while giving Nicole a boner of her own, brought the volume in the kitchen up. The rattling pots and pans, the steam, the energy, the fever. The screams of delight. The unashamed ecstasy of enjoying each other to the full. The dirty mouth, the filthy mind, the letting-go of all inhibitions. Thomas glanced to the microwave timer. Only five minutes left. Time to up the ante. He pushed her down on the kitchen table and lodged himself inside her. The table creaked, their minds in a frenzy, their pleasure incalculable, their love . . .

'Oh, yes, right there. Harder, Thomas, harder. There, there, yes, yes, *yes there*!'

The sound of footsteps on the tiled floor. 'Mr Harding. Sorry to disturb you, but I didn't think you'd be here. I did knock but there was no answer. I thought that you'd just forgotten to switch the music off. Sorry, I'll come back later. I'm really sorry.'

Two shocked lovers stopped loving. Quite a lot of naked flesh was on view. Josephine, the chambermaid, stood holding a bucket and mop as she rocked from one foot to the other, not knowing where to look. Her cheeks were rosy with embarrassment.

Nicole giggled uncontrollably – she was, after all, covered by Thomas.

Feeling she needed to justify herself some more, Josephine stepped a little closer. 'I knocked at least three times, Mr Harding. There was no answer. And you didn't leave the "Do Not Disturb" sign on your knob again. I am really, really quite—' She began to sob. 'I'm so sorry. I only came to clean your apartment . . . and . . . Mr Harding, if—'

Thomas, still on top of Nicole, interrupted Josephine. His voice was calm. 'Would you mind turning your head while we separate, Josephine? Or perhaps it might be better if you waited out in the living area?'

'But, I really am—'

'NOW! Please.'

Even though Josephine wasn't remotely religious, she sat on the sofa in the apartment making the sign of the holy cross on her chest. It seemed to help. Her mind was trying to block out what she had just witnessed. It was worse than a porn movie. How could she ever look her boss in the eye again? She couldn't even call him by her pet name of 'Peeping Tom' any more because it was she who was the peeping tom now.

Thomas entered, dressed in his suit, and sat opposite Josephine. 'I wouldn't worry about this too much if I were you, Josie, no one needs to know. Have you ever seen that Ray Mears on TV wrestling with an alligator? Well, just look at it like the naked version of that. Of course, Nicole would have been the alligator.' He paused, wondering if Dulux did a red in the colour of her face. 'And as regards the cleaning, as you might have seen, the kitchen is a complete state. It has nothing to do with the sex you just witnessed, either. Nicole, the alligator, has taken up cooking.' He smiled, and stood up. 'Feel better now?'

Josephine breathed easier and stopped making the sign of the cross. 'I've never walked in on anyone doing anything quite like that before, Mr Harding. It was a total shock.'

He bent down to pick up a few of the sealed condoms that had been ejaculated out of the box on to the coffee table. Obviously he would have been less zealous in unwrapping the Durex if he'd known that his 'sensitive' cleaner was coming. For a joke he was about to offer a strawberry-flavoured one to Josephine, then thought better of it. A brandy was what she needed. A minute later she was sipping on the tipple, easing up on the accelerator to her heart-beat. He felt like he was nurturing someone back from a bereavement.

'Maybe now's the time to—' How could he say this without hurting her feelings? 'Maybe, Josephine, I'm to blame in all this. Expecting you to clean my apartment at all hours. I'll make a deal with you. You give me back my key and I'll only ask you to clean the apartment when it really needs it. When it's a total pigsty. How's that?' She nodded her understanding. 'Plus, Nicole is dying to learn the idiosyncrasies of being a housewife. It's a huge challenge for someone who can't iron, clean, sew, knit, weave, wash up, dry up, make bric-à-brac from straw or even cook.' He laughed. 'I should be marrying *you*.'

After handing Thomas back his key, Josephine brought another potential dilemma to his attention.

'There's a problem in Room 28. The gentleman who checked out this morning must have taken the key and we can't find the spare anywhere. It needs to be cleaned before twelve. Before the new arrivals check in.'

Ten minutes later, Thomas and Josephine were heading towards Room 28.

Inside Room 28, Stuart and Penny were still bonking. He'd proposed to her twice already, just before orgasm. Then just after, with a quick shake of his head, he'd withdrawn his proposal, just before withdrawing his willy. She minded not. Stuart was a darling in bed, but a terrible womanizer. Nothing he said was ever taken without a handful of salt.

The jangling of keys outside the door left Stuart and Penny looking into each other's eyes as they held their breath.

'Don't worry, Pen,' he whispered, 'double-O Stu has taken both sets of keys. Only Thomas has the master key. And . . .' more jangling outside. Their pupils dilated. 'And . . .'

'And what, Stu?'

'And no one disturbs the naked chef!' They laughed until the door swung open. Oops!

Thomas and Josephine stood at the entrance staring shocked at two bare-arsed bodies. Without a second thought, Thomas covered Josephine's eyes with his hand and manoeuvred her back into the hall, while she made the sign of the cross on her chest once again.

Back in the room, Stuart, a seasoned pro of excuses, could think of none that might explain why he was stuffing Penny in Room 28. Or why the floor was littered with porno magazines, or why two condoms were stuck to a framed painting of Oxford University. To top it all off, he had a huge fart he wanted to download under the sheets, and now, if ever there was a time, was not the time. Thomas re-entered, slamming the door behind him. He seemed stressed.

'I want to see both of you – dressed – in my office in ten minutes.' Thomas turned to leave.

Stuart mumbled something. Thomas halted in his tracks. Surely he hadn't heard what he just thought he had. He arrived at Stuart's side of the bed and – with a cold look Stuart had never seen before – asked him to repeat the remark.

Tentatively Stuart spoke. 'I said, Mr Harding, erm, "It must be hell living with you. I would slit my wrists too."' He closed his eyes, slightly ashamed of what had just come out of his mouth. Penny elbowed him hard beneath the sheet. 'I nearly slit my wrists once, in your kitchen, slicing the ends off asparagus, slippery little buggers. Erm.' Clutching at straws. 'I bet you and Nicole will have beautiful children.' He faced Penny. 'What d'you think, Pen, beautiful, hey?'

Penny agreed, still blushing. 'Beautiful.'

Thomas kicked the porn magazines away and a *Kays* catalogue (opened to the bra section). He knelt down. 'Nicole nearly died that night. And I know that the only time you ever shed tears is when Arsenal loses, but some people have higher morals than you, Stuart, some—' Thomas's eyes were drawn to the boxer shorts hanging from the curtain rail. A dirty great skid marked the inside of Stuart's Union Jack boxers. It was pointless trying to converse with a man who would think nothing of getting *back* into a pair of pants that dirty. Thomas stood up. 'You *ever* fucking mention anything about Nicole again and I'll see to it that you suffer. It's a threat and a promise. And I want the pair of you in my office in ten minutes.'

Stuart watched him leave, then began to hum the tune to *M*A*S*H* as Penny sat in silence, shaking her head in disgust.

Finally Penny spoke through clenched teeth. 'You just couldn't wait to let Thomas know you knew about Nicole's wrist, could you?'

Stuart glared. 'Oh shut up.'

Chapter Eleven

Brown-skinned people and white-skinned people mix. It's as simple as that, thought Marina. If God, or nature, intended no mixing, then God, or nature, would somehow prevent it.

She pored over another page in her scrapbook while she lay, stomach down, on her bed, processing a bundle of thoughts that were as muddled as the brain that was trying to decipher them. The scrapbook's title sounded like something she would have written for a school project: *India. What India means to me.* And amongst the many pages of poems, cut-outs from newspapers and odds and sods was a scattering of photos of her relatives. Relatives who had never left the homeland. What would they make of this world that she found herself in? Her gran, who she remembered with a fondness that strengthened as time passed, would most probably have fainted on the spot had Marina mentioned that she was seriously thinking 'bad' thoughts about a man of colour. The white colour. Gran would most likely come up with her famous *haiti* (elephant) story about the young Punjabi boy who fell in love with his elephant and wanted the village's approval of marriage. 'And what would the offspring look like? Would it have a huge nose? And what would you call your child, a *haitiman* (elephantman)? No, young boy, you cannot marry the elephant no matter how much you love it. Some things don't mix.' And Marina's whole family tree in India would duplicate that message: 'Some things don't mix.' Especially white and brown.

Marina ached for the advice of her mother. Shiva could only help so much. Sitting innocently on the chest of drawers by the open window was a pile of envelopes with a guilty conscience inside. Emily and Marina had been carefully signing their letters of apology most of yesterday evening and now all they had to do, to improve their karma, was to send the letters out. Marina huffed at the pile. Money was tight. These were first-class grovelling letters being sent with second-class stamps. Location location location. Finding the location of some of their old school 'acquaintances' in Watford had been a nightmare. Telephone directories were only so much help. Then Emily remembered she'd slept with someone from the Inland Revenue a few years back, who could trace anyone she wanted. His chat-up line, 'I will fuck you into the higher-rate tax bracket,' had bowled Emily over. Her assets became his.

Hilda could be heard vacuuming downstairs. She hated it when either of the girls were off work, making great efforts to wreck their lie-ins. 'Girls didn't get sick in my day,' she would say. 'Women were *real* women back then. We grafted until we fell asleep on our feet.' But today, the noise came to Marina's rescue, blocking out the thoughts that had kept her awake last night. Today was going to be a benchmark in Marina's life, and there was no one in the world whom she was willing to discuss this with. Not even Emily. She was at work, unknowing, buttering bread, under the impression Marina was sick. And in a way Marina was sick – in her stomach.

What to wear? The beginning of September and as hot as a volcano outside. It must be the ozone, thought Marina, remembering the Septembers of her childhood being wet and chilly. She was sure Emily's economy hair spray was the cause. Two cans a month! Now, how to make the best impression? She fondled through her wardrobe searching for items that might cause blood pressures to rise. How to make the man fall in love with you? High Street wear was out. No, actually, High Street wear was in, it was all the rage. It had to be. It was all Marina had. She settled on casual and sexy. Sophisticated but daring. Passionate and womanly. Jeans and a crop-top T-shirt. It's not the T-shirt and jeans, it's what's *in* the T-shirt and jeans, she told herself, over and over, admiring the beads and sequins that she'd sewn into the denim. They sparkled in the sunlight, giving them the feel of India; spicing them up. Like adding cumin to a bag of soggy chips.

She checked out her complexion. God, she *felt* like a bag of soggy chips right now. How could she compete with beautiful Nicole? Whose skin was polished and pure, whose body was designed as a man's wet dream, whose aura transcended anything Marina had seen before. Stick a crown on Nicole's head and call her Ma'am. Simple as that. She was groomed to be a queen.

Off with her head!

Would Thomas ever go for a brown woman? It was a big question and it came with one of two little answers: yes or no. She couldn't even hope to guess. As she combed her hair, a voice with an American accent sprouted in her mind. It sounded like someone from a *Montel* show. 'Helloooo,' it began, 'what planet are you on, Marina?' Go away, American loudmouth, she thought. The voice continued, louder, even more whiny and Yankee. 'Helloooo. Wake up and smell the roses. As if *you* have a *hope* in *hell* of getting it on with Thomas.'

She finished combing her hair in a sulk. It was the first time she could remember sulking at herself. Since seeing Thomas at the Cockneys' wedding, Marina had being waiting for Shiva to show her the sign. To give her the go-ahead with Thomas. Day and night she waited for the moment. Anxious and nauseous with hope it would come soon. Maybe his name would be written in the stars. Nope. Or maybe when she switched on the TV, an advert for the Regency Hotel would appear. Nope. Even the letters 'T' and 'H' inside the middle of her apples would have done. Three bags of bruised market apples later – still nope. How would Shiva show the sign? A customer had come into Napkins last week and asked for a sandwich: 'A cheese and *Tom*, sandwich. And could you make sure the tomatoes are *Hard*, not soft, wet and juicy like last time.' Tom and Hard. Thomas and

Harding. Was that a sign?

Nope. (Well it was until the customer brought the sandwich back – Emily's plaster had fallen into the margarine.)

And then, like a new day, it dawned on Marina: signs were not always visible. Scientists know that black holes exist even though they've never seen one. The behaviour of surrounding stars shows them it's true. Maybe, like a black hole, Marina's sign was also invisible; Shiva would never be so blatant as to show fireworks. And the fact that she'd been thinking about Thomas, constantly, for the last two weeks *must* be *the* sign. No man had ever done that to her before. And like a black hole, the thoughts of lying in bed with Thomas were sucking her in. Mentally, she apologized to her dead gran for such a wickedly sexual vision.

It was a shame the young Punjabi boy didn't get to marry the elephant, she thought, slipping on her suede boots – still damp from the kettle steam – then tumbling to the mirror in her heels. The finished result staring back was not bad. But would it win a man's heart? In her own heart she knew something was amiss in her thinking. How dare she even assume that she could waltz into someone else's relationship and steal the man. Thomas, like Nicole, like the elephant, was a different breed. Upper class. Her mum and dad would metaphorically clout her round the mouth for having such ideas. Her whole childhood had been infused with one notion: no one is born better than anyone else.

It was with this thought that she removed the large copper bottle filled with Ganges water from the shrine. Today was *the day*. She made a small prayer in front of the statue of her God. 'Shiva, if we are meant to be, please let this water work.'

An hour's bus ride later, after another prayer to Shiva – 'Please let my deodorant last' – she stood by the open gates that led into the Regency Hotel car park. Sharp nerves scratched at her insides like a gang of frisky kittens. Stupidity and naivety were traits of a woman in love. She just hoped it didn't all end in calamity.

Two shirtless window cleaners perched on sturdy ladders cracked jokes thirty feet up. One appeared to be demonstrating to the other what he could see through his window. His hips rocked to and fro, his face like a chimp's, wobbling the ladder like a jelly. Marina giggled then headed in, her inner voice singing a tune, 'Who's afraid of the big bad wolf? . . . I am.'

Background music played quietly in the lobby. Marina was sure she'd heard it before, it sounded like the theme to *Silence of the Lambs*. A few men in expensive suits lounged around small circular tables with newspapers, phones and coffees, and the receptionist in her blue suit made a point of noticing Marina immediately, standing rigidly to attention, obviously well trained. Marina glanced quickly at the grandfather clock noisily ticking in the corner: 11.45 a.m. Two possible plans here. One, ask the receptionist for a room near the window cleaner's ladder and push him away from the wall for being so crude. Or, two, walk right on up, confidently smile and then ask to speak to Mr Harding. She shook her hair, raised her chin up and presented herself at the counter.

'Would it be possible to speak to Mr Harding,

please?' Marina said. 'He's the owner.'

The receptionist, her name tag said Cheryl, fluttered her heavily mascara-ed eyelashes. 'I know who he is. Have you an appointment?' She looked down a book of entries, and in a casual, I-think-you're-wasting-your-time manner, stared up again at Marina. 'No one is listed for this morning. And why did you say you were here?'

Yikes! Marina hadn't thought that far ahead in her plan. 'I've come for the receptionist job,' she blurted out, without thinking.

Last week, just after Stuart had bonked Cheryl in Room 29, or, as Stuart put it, 'fed her fire of passion,' he had mentioned that Mr Harding was going to be making some major changes. Stuart had remarked that the Regency didn't tolerate bad smells, so it would be getting rid of the bad eggs. Stuart's job was safe though, he'd reassured Cheryl smugly, because he was – as a certain butler once said – Mr Harding's 'Rock'.

Composing herself, Cheryl picked up the phone angrily and dialled through to Thomas's mobile. Only to be used in emergencies. He answered immediately. 'It's Cheryl here. My replacement has arrived. She's waiting at Reception. Thanks for absolutely nothing, Mr Harding. I used to think you were a cool boss. Fake!' She hung up.

'I'll be over here, then.' Marina tiptoed to the corner and parked her contrite bottom on a comfy leather armchair. Her *Charlie's Angels* bag was too small to hide in, but she felt like giving it a go. A bag in a bag.

The great thing about a wide, echoing Reception

area was that you were always within earshot. Marina sat listening in to five or six conversations: how money was the root of all evil, how oil was the new religion, how world leaders corrupted the planet. She eavesdropped on one bloke talking to another about how he had been wide-hipped and fat all his life and how his middle-age spread had come early – in his teens. Then her wandering ears picked up a posh man apologizing to a woman about her job. Her heart hammered. It was Mr Harding. Even from behind, his looks were amazing. She would love to lick the soap suds that had washed his fabulous body this morning. If only.

'Look, I can assure you, Cheryl, I have no intention of replacing you. And, no, I don't know who that lady over there is.'

'Stuart told me that some of us would be getting the chop. Is that true?'

'Not this again. He's always spreading rumours. Last year, this was just before you started here, I had to hold a meeting with all the staff and explain that their jobs were all safe. Two of the chambermaids were in tears. They only went to bed with him because he offered a consoling arm.' His voice had become a whisper, Marina strained her ear to hear. 'And it was Stuart who bloody started the rumour in the first place. Honestly, why some of you women fall for his claptrap, I'll never know. He makes you vulnerable and then he takes you to bed. Don't go falling for it, Cheryl. Don't . . .'

Cheryl was now in tears.

Marina watched Thomas hand Cheryl a tissue. If only she could have a boss so sensitive. All she had was

Perv Bazzer. The only tissues he would hand her . . . It didn't bear thinking about. She hoped Emily was coping all right with him today. They had a system in place if he ever tried touching either of them. They would kill him. Zero tolerance. Innuendoes were one thing, but fingers and tongues were something else.

Thomas made his way towards Marina. The clock struck twelve. He looked like a man with many things on his mind. Marina was about to add another. But first, she had to ogle. He was spectacular. Above the confidence in his walk, above the expensive sheen to his suit, above the designer messy hair, above his tantalizing dark-blue eyes. Above it all. Even her wildest fantasies could not have invented a man this darn good. All other men from now on would be ugly in comparison. He moved his lips with such elegance, his voice was so sexy, even the way he used his arms to explain himself. Riveting stuff. But it would be so much better if she had actually heard any of it – rather than dribble, drool and desire him.

Thomas stopped speaking, puzzled. He loosened his tie a little. 'You do speak English, don't you?'

She nodded.

He continued. 'As I was saying, all the posts are filled at present. But do feel free to leave your CV with the lady at Reception. We are always on the look-out for hard-working—'

'Slaves!' Marina interrupted a shocked Thomas. 'Sorry.'

Like red salmon swimming back upstream, memories flooded back to Thomas: saunas and cocktails. He tilted his head as recognition set in. Yes, it was the Fenworth girl. His head snapped around quickly, where was the other one?

'No, not slaves. This isn't a Roman galley ship,' he answered, his voice low. 'Anyway, I'm a bit tied up at the moment.' He turned to leave, taking one last glance back to look her in the eyes. 'Nice to see you once again. It's been a pleasure.'

Has it, thought Marina. Has it really been a pleasure? Or will you just forget about me the minute you walk away? A grinding determination swept over her. She was going to see this through. On the bus journey up here, she'd imagined that a weakness in her character would prevent her from completing her task. She would become a mouse. An Indian mouse destined to be left on the Indian shelf, where she would join turmeric and curry powder. No! She would definitely see this through.

A quick twist of the copper bottle, loosening the eighteen-year grip on the cap, and finally the sacred Ganges water could taste the living air again. English air this time, not Indian. With a steady hand, Marina held the ancient container and picked a target area on Thomas's head. His hair. Then, with a sudden jerk of the wrist, the contents of the bottle, about one snotty-brown pint's worth, shot through the room and landed on Thomas's head, neck and Armani suit. Marina's favourite part of the day, she would most likely tell the police later, was when Thomas spun back round. His face . . . what a monster.

'What the fucking hell have you just thrown on my fucking head?' he shouted. 'Look at the fucking state of me. This stuff STINKS.' The brown liquid dripped on to the floor. 'What is it?'

'I'm hoping that one day you will thank me for

this,' she said, with a tandoori-red face.

'Are you seriously ill or something?' He swiped a few tissues from Cheryl's outstretched hand. 'Thanks, Cheryl. Could you do me a favour and get someone to mop this shit up?' He turned to the enthralled guests with an apologetic look.

'It's not shit, thank you very much, Mr Harding, it's sacred water from the Indian river of the Ganges. It's travelled ten thousand miles and eighteen years for what I just did. So, please, give it some respect.' Marina grabbed a pen and scribbled her name and address on the back of a Regency tariff brochure and handed it to Thomas. 'Here. Bill me for the suit and any damage. I'll wait to hear from you.' And then under her breath she whispered to herself, 'My love,' as she left.

Chapter Twelve

DO
NOT
DISTURB

There were rare occasions when Thomas wanted to erect a forty-foot 'Do Not Disturb' sign outside the hotel. Today was one of those occasions. After being caught bonking, catching someone bonking and then being doused with Ganges water, what more could go wrong?

At 12.30 p.m. there was still a lot of day left to be ruined.

Thomas turned the shower on full. The only thing he could be glad about was that Delia Smith hadn't devised some way that a power-shower could be incorporated into cookery, or else Nicole would have broken that too. 'Sorry, Tom, darling, but I was cleaning the King Edward potatoes when the shower exploded. The broccoli is being spin dried in the washing machine as we speak.' Thomas's mind scanned through diseases he might have picked up by virtue of the smelly brown Ganges water he was trying desperately to scrub away. There was typhoid, rabies, Japanese B encephalitis and TB, and good ol' malaria, you had your usual diarrhoea, stomach bugs and vomiting viruses. Skin lesions, welts, throat, mouth and nose eruptions and the most severe of them all – death. He doubted his Eternity body wash would combat the army of germs, it would be like the Northern Alliance fighting the USA, but it was all he had on hand. His private doctor, Dr Belveder, had calmed him down a little on the phone by explaining that the 'Ganges' water was most likely fake. 'Just tap water,' Dr Belveder had said, 'sold off to naive student tourists on their way back from Uttar Pradesh. I've got some myself. But, just in case, I will call the intensive care ward for you. Are your eyes bleeding yet?'

Why were women such strange creatures? They were filled with a different energy from men. It confounded Thomas immensely. Why were they so unreadable? He knew from experience that it was a pointless waste of time trying to read anything into why the mad Indian woman might have thrown Ganges water over his head. Totally pointless.

Something sludgy fell out of his hair and on to the shower tray. It landed with a thud. Thomas waited to see if it moved. A leech? Trying hard not to gag, he did his best to keep his feet well away. There was no chance that Nicole would suck his toes if she knew they'd been near a leech. He had a hard enough time getting her to suck 'em when they'd been in his trainers. The shower continued to rain down, invigorating and hot, one of the few true pleasures of life.

The Armani suit lay crumpled in the pedal bin. Stuffed down with an angry shove. Sketchley may know the meaning of cleaning but they didn't know the meaning of stinking until they'd sniffed that water. Phew! And a bill of £2500 would soon be on its way to the Indian girl with the smart mouth. Plus the cost of his rabies shot. Yes, this really was a 'Do Not Disturb' kind of day.

With a towel tucked round his waist and a hairstyle that could only be described as wet, Thomas ironed a new shirt with the new iron. Like a fresh page to a book, he would begin the day from now. Chapter One, page one, word one . . .

'Tom!' It was Nicole. Back from shopping. 'Are you here?'

'Bedroom,' he replied, readying himself for the bags.

Thomas tried to gauge how many items she'd dropped on the wood of the living-room floor. Five paper, two plastic, one small box and one metal container. Sounded like ten grand's worth. Shops loved Nicole and Nicole loved shops. It was a loving relationship that Thomas could only aspire to. Nicole always seemed to come back coated in store manager's saliva. They drooled as soon as she was spotted on the CCTV cameras coming in. Nicole meant money. Platinum and gold credit cards. Funded by a conglomerate of both Daddy and Thomas.

'How big is your head, Tom?' Nicole shouted through.

He was about to answer with a witty penis joke, then changed his mind. Head size? Now why would she need to know that? 'You haven't bought me a hat, have you? I only said I liked Badly Drawn Boy's headgear as a joke.'

The squeal of a happy bunny. Nicole shot through, excitable in her peach-coloured designer summer dress, her arms outstretched with a tape measure. 'Mummy needs to know the approximate diameter of your head for the top hat.'

'You mean the circumference.'

'From ear to ear.' Nicole paused. 'Daddy said something about measuring your ear to your nose then multiplying it by pi squared?'

'I think he means taking the radius of my head, then multiplying it by two pi.'

'Anyway, Mummy mentioned it was best to measure your skull in the morning rather than later as the blood works its way down to the feet. But not to worry too much, there'll be a proper fitting at the hat shop.' She smiled at Thomas in just his towel. What an immaculate specimen of a man he was *and* he was all hers. The day was turning out wonderfully. Sex, then shopping, and now it looked like more sex. Wonderful. She squealed again, causing Thomas to scald his arm with the jet of iron steam.

'What?' he questioned, rubbing his forearm.

Nicole stood close and stared right in his eyes. 'Guess?' She giggled.

Thomas recalled the conversation he'd been having to himself just before the leech popped out of his head. Women were completely nuts. 'What???'

And then Nicole's smile faded. 'You haven't even

noticed, have you?' She stamped her foot on the floor. 'What colour eyes do you think I've got, Tom?'

He shook his head, resignedly. The old contact lens trick. Make a man feel like shit by turning up slightly different and then crying when he doesn't notice. Women, fucking mental, the lot of them. 'Sorry. You have the most beautiful blue eyes, Nicole. And yes, yellow lenses with green flecks *do* suit you. Science fiction, almost.' He switched the iron off. 'Were you running out of things to buy today?'

Apparently not. The bags were a sea on the living-room floor, lapping at Thomas's ankles as he struggled through to fetch them and bring them back to the king-sized bed. And Nicole's mood was beginning to change like the tide. Thomas checked through the huge balcony window for approaching storm clouds. Not even a tuft in sight.

'Who is she?' Nicole said, her voice trembling.

'Who?'

Nicole picked up the various body gels, sprays, aftershaves and hair mousse scattered on the duvet. Ignoring the Dettol, TCP and sterile wipes balanced on the pillow, she launched an offensive strike. 'What woman needs you THIS clean, Thomas? Well?'

Your sodding mother for one. 'Erm.'

He stood there in a towel while Nicole played her eyes up and down his body. Men used showers for two reasons: cleanliness and guiltiness. Either Thomas had just had sex with a woman and was wiping her scent away. Or he was about to have sex with a woman and was wiping Nicole's scent away. Either way deserved a small punch in the stomach. She tightened her left fist and jabbed him hard in the solar plexus. 'Who is she, Thomas? Why are you taking your second shower of the day? You weren't expecting me back this soon, were you? I've caught you out, haven't I? You've been had.' She tried to jab him again but he caught her wrist.

'I suggest you go and sniff one of my shirt armpits, Nicole, and see how hot it can get in the hotel this time of year. It's like being inside a sumo's loincloth. You try explaining to the guests, "No, sorry, sir, we have not got a sewage blockage in the hotel, the smell putting you off your cheesecake is, in fact, *me*. It's just that I'm not allowed to wash any more because my fiancée thinks I'm fucking another woman when I take more than one shower a day. Anyway must dash, toodley poops."' He let go of her wrist, grabbed the white shirt from the ironing board, and began to dress.

'Don't be so flippant.' A huge open book on the writing table caught her eye and she quickly wandered over. The facing page was titled *Diseases*. Horrified she shouted, 'What type of woman have you been sleeping with to pick up a sexually transmitted disease? Some sort of ho?' She thought back to the Hobbs key that she'd found in his jacket pocket on the night of the Cockneys' wedding. Maybe the key opened a secret metal box. Maybe inside that box was Thomas's stash of pills, injections and concoctions for his list of sexual diseases. No doubt including AIDS. No wonder he always wanted to wear a condom. No wonder he gave so much money to charity. It would only be a matter of time before he was a charity case himself.

She sat on the edge of the bed with her hands

covering her eyes. Her long blonde hair flopped limply down as her head slumped. 'Are you dying, Tom?'

'Of course I'm not dying.'

Thomas overheard his conscience talking: *Tell the truth. A woman came into your hotel and threw Ganges water over you. Simple!* But it wasn't. Nothing was simple when *another* woman was involved. Why couldn't it have been a man who threw Ganges water over him? At least then if he told the truth he wouldn't be subjected to a barrage of questions – You must know her! Is she an ex? Is she pregnant with your child? Is she prettier than me? Did you treat her badly, is that why she threw the Ganges water over you? And so it would go on.

Pity took precedence at that moment and Thomas hugged Nicole tight. He said softly, 'You know I could never betray you. You're the most beautiful woman I have ever seen, why would I look at anyone else? I'm so lucky to have you.' He kissed her on the neck. 'Come on, we're getting married in nine months' time. Nothing means more to me than to see you happy on that day.'

Through watery eyes Nicole looked up. 'I just think that you're going to leave me. I know you think I'm crackers. I'm sorry.' She paused. 'What about the diseases?'

A lie worthy of a lawyer was needed. Fortunately, apart from the shitty day he was having so far, in one respect circumstances were on his side this morning, and after a quick private telephone call to Reception he bounded out of the apartment, in his jeans and T-shirt, with Nicole, and down into the foyer of the hotel. She wanted to know why a man might need to have a second shower. Well, she would soon find out. And shortly he would be taking his third shower of the day. Maybe he really was diseased. With genius.

'Stand here and watch,' Thomas said to Nicole as she waited by the Reception counter, then he dialled a number on his mobile. 'Is it all clear? . . . Sure? . . . Right, I'm coming through right now.'

He marched towards the main door, a beaming smile of confidence attached to his face. It was just like being a kid all over again. Five seconds later Thomas stood just outside the entrance, while a bucket of dirty, soapy water dropped from the window cleaner's ladder above. Six seconds, Thomas was drenched. Ten seconds, Nicole was at his side, squealing with delight and uttering her apologies ten to the dozen. Oh how she hated doubting her fiancé. With the security of being engaged also comes suspicion. And already suspicion had reared its ugly head. They headed inside.

Thomas winked at the receptionist, Cheryl. 'That's exactly what happened, wasn't it, Cheryl?'

Cheryl smirked. 'Why, yes, Mr Harding. Just like that.' She paused, thought about a pay rise, then added, 'Except earlier you were wearing an expensive suit.'

Nicole smiled, Thomas smiled. Bingo!

'I can't believe there are seven chickens in there,' Marina said, lifting the lid off the huge Tupperware container that Emily had swiped from Napkins.

'There's a dozen pork bangers at the bottom as well, just beneath the blanket of coleslaw.' Emily flopped on a kitchen chair next to Marina. 'We deserve it for working with Britain's Most Disgusting Boss.'

They laughed but it was true. Perv Bazzer was a customer repellent. Upon seeing him behind the counter, with his dirty knotted ginger beard and wing-mirror sideburns, customers often walked out quicker than they walked in – never to set foot in Napkins again. Bazzer said that his fortunes had taken an upturn and a U-turn when Tesco had gone twenty-four hour. He would shop in the wee hours buying up all the knock-down-priced food and palm it off to his clientele as 'fresh' the next day. On pay day he would remind the girls of a few sayings he lived by: rope for old string. If you save the pennies, the pounds will take care of themselves. Who spends before he thrives, will beg before he thinks. Marina and Emily had a saying of their own: 'Tight, stingy bastard.' And he was.

Emily spoke. 'Most of your customers asked me to wish you to "Get well soon". Bazzer only put a bleeding sign on the window saying you had an "alleged" stomach upset, didn't he? He said it would stop us taking unnecessary sick leave if he made an effort to shame us.'

'Bastard.' Marina felt her skin redden with guilt for lying to her friend and jumped up to fill some snappy bags with chicken for the freezer. Being poor had its advantages. When you did get nice food, you damn well appreciated it. Even her relatives in India would eat finer food than she and Emily were used to. One brand dominated Marina's and Emily's kitchen cupboards: economy brand. Economy this and economy that. The blue-labelled sign that really should read 'poor'. Tins of tomatoes 9p. Beans 3p. Bread 22p. Tampons – their most expensive item to date, and they couldn't even eat them – £1.06. Although once, when Emily was drunk, she did try to spread economy strawberry jam with an economy tampon when she couldn't locate the plastic knife. Hilda found the tampon in the bathroom bin on one of her Inspector Clouseau snoops, surgical mask in place, Marigolds at the ready and, once again, she thought the worst of her lodgers: 'Dirty girls. Used tampons are to be flushed.'

'I lied to you today, Emily,' Marina said, handing her flatmate a mug of economy coffee. 'Sorry. But I wasn't really ill.'

Emily slurped, her eyes just above the rim of her Daffy Duck mug. 'Continue with this explanation.'

A dragonfly flew awkwardly across the windowpane as Marina watched. 'I went to see Mr Harding today. Thomas.' She sat down. 'Oh, Emily, he was gorgeous. Lock, stock and barrel.' Oh what a barrel he must have, she thought, grabbing Emily's arm. 'I know I shouldn't have lied but it was my destiny calling.'

'Destiny?'

The explanation that followed did not fulfil the Emily water test. Leaks were everywhere. How could what happened in India eighteen years ago affect what was happening today in Fenworth? Marina explained about the butterfly's wings flapping in China, causing a hurricane in America. Cause and effect. Yin and yang. Emily was more confused than ever. How on earth could Ganges water from India trap a man from England into loving you? It didn't make sense.

But nor did love.

Marina went on to explain in more depth how eighteen years ago on a visit to see her dying gran in India, Marina's ten-year-old life was enlightened by the power of her gran's wisdom. If Gran had told her back then that a stick on the ground was a snake, then a snake the stick would be. As a young girl she'd had total trust in whatever her gran told her. A trust that still lived with Marina today.

Gran was sick. The nurses at her bedside were shooed away as Marina stood at the hospital door with her brother, Zaine, clutching her parents' hands. And even though Marina was very young, she knew her gran was not long for this world – even though her eyes still shone with the zest of her eternally youthful mind. But her body, as thin as a twig, ravaged by unknown forces, was soon to be stolen by death.

'You don't look so well, Nanna,' Marina had said, crying.

And sitting on the bed, Marina had listened to her gran explain reincarnation. She remembered her gran's smile lighting up her grey face as she described the Hindu way of eternal life. Gran had pointed to a cockroach scuttling in the corner. Apparently a few of the bad men in Gran's village were destined to turn into them once they were reincarnated. There are rewards for being good in the Hindu life just as there are punishments for being bad. Marina knew her gran was a good woman and she would be rewarded accordingly.

Before her gran's eyes closed that day, for what would be her last short sleep, Gran had explained men. How picking the right man would help in a happier life. She had told Marina to go down to the Ganges after she had been cremated and scattered over the sacred river. 'Take a bottle and fill it. My prayer for your future happiness will be in that water. When you find the man who is right, you will know; pour the water on his head. It will work. It always works. He'll be yours. My village, Jhunjhunu, swears by it.' She had winced in pain. 'There is one catch, Marina: in order for the Ganges water to work you must receive the blessings of your parents.'

Now, in the dimming light of a Fenworth sunset, Marina felt empty. Half her secrets finally shared. Before long, she was sure, she would feel brave enough to tell the other half. The shameful half. The half that left her feeling less than whole. Forgiveness comes in many brands. Marina hoped that once she told her family of her unspeakable sin, they would forgive her, and it would not be forgiveness of the economy brand.

The girls dried the dinner dishes in silence until Marina was prompted to continue her explanation. 'And that's it, that's why I poured the water over Thomas.' Marina paused. 'Now do you see why I never wanted you to open that bottle? You always thought it was booze. I think Thomas is The One, Emily, I really do. As hard as I try, I can't ignore that look he gave me when he picked me up off the beauty salon's floor. We connected. We shared a moment together. It's so hard to explain, there's just something about him.'

Emily agreed. There was just something about him.

Night time crawled in. Emily found herself tucked up in Marina's bed as usual. Many a time they'd lain in that very spot slagging off men. From news readers, to Hollywood stars, down to ex-boyfriends. It was a never-ending job. But not tonight. Tonight, men were the biz. Well, one man was. Thomas was being planted on a pedestal. A throne, almost. He had been elevated to King Tom.

Emily, although jealous of Marina's private liaison, could not take it too seriously. Throwing stagnant water over the man of your dreams was a fairly intense way to start a relationship. More like a one-way ticket to the retard home. Anyway, there were other reasons as to why Emily lay back with a smugness so thick it was clotting the air. One, Thomas obviously went for blondes. Nicole was proof. Two, Thomas was a snob, snobs don't go for Indians. And three, Marina had smaller breasts than Emily.

'And four,' she said out loud, without thinking, 'I've got bigger tits than Nicole.'

Marina jumped up. 'Sorry, what did you just say?'

Emily fumbled, 'I said . . . er . . . has he finished with this criminally beautiful Nicole?' She bit her bottom lip in the dark, was about to say something horrid, thought better of it, then changed her mind. 'What colour hair has Nicole got? It's blonde like mine, isn't it? Long and blonde.' She brushed her fingers through her hair. 'Makes you wonder, doesn't it? If he goes for blondes.'

'Only a feeble man would set his heart on a sexy blonde. He doesn't look the sort to go for just looks. He seems the type of man who would rather have a good chat with an intelligent woman.' Marina's mind's eye glimpsed Nicole standing on the podium at the Cockneys' wedding a couple of weeks back.

Nicole's well-spoken voice over the microphone, her designer red dress and fabulous figure. It was time Marina's imagination gave perfect Nicole a Medusa makeover. She began with a few spots, a harelip, bushy eyebrows, a bloated neck, and finally a crew cut. She imagined Ann Widdecombe.

Pushing a sleepy Emily out of her bed, Marina added a few comments to tie up the evening. 'Thomas looked like a man who hasn't had sex for weeks. Since that wedding. I think he's finished with Nicole.' She opened the bedroom door, pointing to the hall. 'And you just had to be there to hear it, Emily. In his sexy voice he said to me, "Nice to see you once again. It's been a pleasure." Honestly, Emily, I could have melted with the look he gave me. Right in my eye. I felt it in the root of my pelvis. Now off you go. To bed with you. And don't forget to hang up your dream-catcher. You were screaming last night in your sleep.' She closed the door, smiling, as Emily ambled to her bedroom.

In her own room, amidst the subtle glow of a pink light bulb, Emily removed her T-shirt and denim skirt and stood naked in front of her full-length mirror. The girls had often worked as a team to bed men, using bully-girl tactics to achieve their goals. Marina likened it to battle. Attacking from more than one front. Emily smiled at her breasts in the mirror. Now *there* was a front.

And now the team had split. The army all but disbanded. Marina had broken protocol by going behind Emily's back – sneakily crossing over no-man's land (or rather no woman's land) and trying to wage her own private conflict with Thomas. It wouldn't do. Not by a long shot. Especially when Emily already had her heart set on him. It was time for Emily to retaliate. Her body was her weapon, her breasts her missiles. Thomas was the main target on her *Axis of Sexual.*

As the war bugles sounded in Emily's ears, she dived into bed, and switched on her German self-help tape. Dr Fritzgerald Guztelburg continued from last night's lecture in his sexed-up voice until Emily dropped off to sleep.

'*Gute Nacht.*'

Chapter Thirteen

Saffron, gram for gram, is more expensive than gold. A luxury item in the kitchen. The aristocracy of all spices.

Alone in the Regency Hotel's kitchen, 11.00 a.m., after breakfasts had been served on a Saturday morning, Stuart sipped his home-made chicken, almond and mushroom soup. His mind was deep in jealous thought. It had been a week since Thomas had caught him in bed pleasing Penny. A week since his first warning. Stuart stirred another £40 worth of saffron into his mug, dissolving Thomas's profit margin with each delicious mouthful. How dare Thomas reprimand him in front of one of his lovers. And that joke about bringing in someone wearing a germ-warfare suit and asbestos gloves to handle his underpants was not even close to being funny. Penny had only laughed out of nerves. The microwave beeped and Stuart crossed the floor and reset the dial for a further fifteen minutes. Time for a fag.

The huge lawn of the Regency garden was a sight to behold. Stuart opened the kitchen back door and walked down the three steps. He was at once standing in one of Oxfordshire's finest horticultural masterpieces. Flowers and plants clambered for attention amongst the spacious rockeries that blossomed on the vast lawn. A hundred different trees spread out towards the open country that tightened around the garden. Just one breath of this air was worth ten from a city.

Stuart breathed in his high-tar Marlboro and sat back on one of the many wooden benches. His whole life was high-tar. 'Dangerous,' he'd told his career officer, 'I want a job that's dangerous, nothing goofy or poofy like a career officer's. Something with bite.' And in a way his commis chef job did have bite, in the literal sense. But it left him feeling like a loser amongst men like Thomas.

Stuart eyed a couple of squabbling pigeons. Crusts and whatnots thrown from this morning's breakfasts were all but gone. He liked pigeons. They made excellent pies. He threw his fag on the grass and breathed another healthy mouthful of sweet September air. The summer heat was fading away and winter would soon be here. And what did winter bring? Rain. Lots of rain. He thought about Nicole. Nicole was just 'mad' about rain. It was like some spirit was being exorcized from her body the minute rain began to fall. When the heavens opened above, so, too, did the hell beneath her feet.

But how did a beautiful woman like Nicole ever become so mixed up in the head as to want to kill herself? It's not like dead people wanted to be beautiful so why should beautiful people want to be dead? It was stupid. Didn't she ever wonder what death was going to be like? Most likely worse than this life, that's for sure. She just needed someone with understanding to provide her with the answers. To help her in times of need. To listen, perhaps, when others did not. To wipe away those painful tears.

Sitting on the work surface next to the carrots in the kitchen were two books he'd picked up in the library: *The Failings of Success*, by Professor S. Bridge and *Bipolar Affective Disorder*, by Dr S. Mile. Stuart had asked if there was *An Idiot's Guide to Suicide* and was pointed in the direction of Health and Beauty. 'Don't worry,' he'd told the librarian, 'I'm not thinking about topping myself at Beachy Head. I just want to make a murder look like suicide.' The joke was lost on the librarian, who had continued to stamp things with an inky thing.

But the books made excellent reading. God, he'd never realized *quite* how mental people got. Some people would resort to just about anything to make their lives better. And in a few weeks, after studying the books, after a few pep talks and serious conversations with Nicole, he was sure that a huge 'thank you' would be his for the asking. Nicole would have been cured of her depression by the one and only . . . Lothario Libido . . . Stuart. Maybe, if things went smoothly after he'd sorted out Nicole's mental illness, then she would grant him access to her body. Just the idea of removing her designer straitjacket straps and buckles was giving him a hard-on.

Inside the kitchen, a delicious cream and

mushroom sauce simmered in the copper pan. Stuart gave the pan a vigorous shake. Professional chefs did that sort of thing. In emotional terms, this week had been the worst of his life since his parents had split ten years ago. The announcement of their divorce had come during an Arsenal and Liverpool match on the box. Stuart had cried that day. And it wasn't just because Arsenal had lost. Stuart had also lost. His family.

With a finger, he scooped up some sauce and tasted the flavour from his digit, sucking on the blue plaster. Professional chefs did that sort of thing. Mmm. And why was he so emotional this week? Why did he suddenly hate Thomas more than he'd hated the man who'd run off with his own sweet mother? The answer was simple: sex. Stuart added a few strands of saffron to the bubbling mixture of mushrooms. Gram for gram saffron might be the most expensive item known to man. But when it came to the most exciting, nothing beat sex (except, maybe, sex while watching Arsenal win). Stuart didn't need to be a mathematician to work that one out.

But there was no point in doing sums. Stuart had bonked many women in this hotel. Staff, guests, even people simply passing through. Professional chefs did that sort of thing. He was, as he was known to be, the Lothario Libido. Women always came back for desserts after a very satisfying main course. His boyish good looks, his animal lust, his actions-speak-louder-than-words thrustings. His mind. He might only be a commis chef in the kitchen, but in the bedroom he was Mr Cordon Bleu. Three Michelin stars.

Or so he had thought.

Stuart smirked at the fire blanket on the tiled wall. Could have done with one of those last night. Which was why he was confused right now. Women were such riddles. How could a whole group of women possibly believe that Thomas could be better in bed than him? He was sick of catching the waitresses talking about Thomas with their starry eyes and bleeding hearts. 'Oh, imagine Mr Harding undoing your buttons,' blah blah blah. 'Oh, imagine Mr Harding lying on top of you,' blah blah blah. Imagine this, thought Stuart, picking up a meat cleaver and swinging it down on a Savoy cabbage, blah blah blood. They haven't even slept with Mr Fucking Harding yet, and already he's a stud capable of providing multiple orgasms on a cosmic level. Just yesterday, Sarah, a full-time waitress, had compared Thomas to a modern-day Mr Darcy. 'Well, Sarah,' Stuart had taunted, passing her the plate, 'I hate to destroy your little vision of life in the olden days, but they didn't have washing machines back then. Mr Darcy had skids just like me. Now, would you please take this fucking duck to table three, before you dribble over it. Quack quack.'

The kitchen clock ticked past twelve o'clock. To be able to hear a clock tick in a restaurant kitchen means either everyone has been poisoned or everyone has gone home. The kitchen is the restaurant's motor, it's where all the noise happens. All the action. As Stuart stood in a silent kitchen dressing the meal he had just prepared, he noted the time, grateful for these extremely rare days when no one wanted to eat his food. Not that his food was bad, far from it. If anyone ever wanted proof that Stuart was a brilliant chef, then here it was. A plate that seemed to explode with colour and flavour. Only the most well-tuned palate could appreciate the subtle tastes that Stuart had added to bring this dish to its magnificent conclusion. Only a blind person wouldn't see that this meal had an alternative motive than just to fill a stomach.

A few minutes later Stuart knocked on Thomas's apartment door, then grinned down at the tray he was holding. A silver lid covered the surprise lunch and mirrored back Stuart's devious smile. There is no finer treachery than abject servility.

'I've got a joke for you, Mr Harding,' Stuart said, as a shocked Thomas took the tray from him. 'Do you know why Bruce Springsteen could never get a job? Because . . . he was already the BOSS. Get it?' Stuart stepped in and glanced around at Thomas's open-plan apartment. His nipples hardened at all the gadgets and boy's toys. Spoilt rich kid, he thought, drooling at Thomas's light sabre leaning against the 5000-watt tower speaker. 'This meal is to show my appreciation that you didn't sack me for my unspeakable behaviour last week. Where's Nicole? I would like to apologize to her, too. Explain I didn't mean anything by it. The last thing she needs is idiots like me mentioning her slitting her wrists.'

Thomas placed the tray down on the dining table and sighed. 'She doesn't know anything about it. Do you honestly think that I . . . Never mind.' He lifted up the lid, nodding his approval. 'Steak! Smells great. Thanks!'

'Medium-burned fillet, just as you like it.' Stuart beamed at his creation. 'Cook it too long and the steak is all wrong. Cook it just right, it's flavour dynamite.' He pulled out a chair and parked himself opposite Thomas. 'I cook a mean steak. I can turn a carcass that even the flies won't go near into something spectacular.' Stuart couldn't help noticing how ragged Thomas was looking. 'Rough night?'

Three bottles of champagne. One tray of bacon and cream cheese vol-au-vents. Two slices of strawberry and cream sponge. Quarter bottle of Jack Daniels washed down with dry martini. And three mates, including his best mate Nathan, toasting his future happiness with Nicole. A night to forget. A night he couldn't really remember. Rough night? Thomas stared at the creamy mushroom sauce topping the steak, recollecting a bathroom episode in the wee hours. He also vaguely recalled trying to remove the vampire-red contact lenses this morning before realizing that they were his real bloodshot eyes.

Thomas tucked into the steak. 'It's good,' he said appreciatively. 'And before you go, I'm going to leave you a tip.' He noted Stuart's sheepish smile. 'It's not a cash tip, it's a verbal tip.'

Stuart jumped in. 'Well, if your money tips are anything to go by – I saw how generous you were to last year's carol singers – then your verbal tip will be an hour-long lecture.' He couldn't hold out any longer, shot off the chair and grabbed the light sabre. 'Do you mind?' *Star Wars* sound effects came from the sabre as Stuart waved the glowing-green weapon around. 'Chef's apprentice, I am. Yes, Yoda approves, he does? Be mindful of the sauce, Obi-Tom Kenobi. Mindful of the sauce.'

Thomas tried to conceal his smile as Stuart, in his chequered black and white commis chef outfit, wooshed the sabre over his head like a swashbuckling pirate. The pantomime was allowed to continue until Stuart stuck the sabre between his legs and said something about the girls feeling the master's force.

'Enough, Yoda. Keeping the food down is hard enough without your pornographic light sabre show. Sit down. No more pole-dancing.' Thomas waited for Stuart to sit before continuing. 'Did you ever understand maths at school?'

'Bits.'

'I don't suppose you remember a branch of mathematics called statistics, do you? No? Never mind. What I'm coming to is this. Every time I enter the hotel kitchen you seem to be in the middle of a charade. In this charade you happen to be pretending to slash your wrists with a knife. Not once, but the last six times I've come in, you're there, facing the door, knife in hand, rubbing it across the main artery on your wrist, twisting your face in fake agony.' Thomas pushed the empty plate away. 'Statistically, six times out of six means that this behaviour is not a coincidence. Which leads me to believe only one thing . . .'

'Which is what?'

'You're doing it deliberately.' Thomas stood up. 'My tip to you is this: stop it.' He handed the tray to an embarrassed Stuart. 'Ask yourself this, Stuart. Who has got more to lose here? You or me? Take it from me, you are a good chef, and one day you will be head chef, but get in my way just one more time and you're out. This is your second warning.' He opened the door and ushered Stuart to the hall. 'Thank you for the steak. I think my hangover is nearly cured already.'

Inside, Thomas lay back on the sofa. If only Nicole was here to dab my forehead with an icy flannel, then I would be totally cured of my hangover, he thought selfishly. But Nicole and her two sisters were at Castle Cliff Manor helping Mummy with some fund-raising paperwork for the Parish Council and organizing God knows what for the looming engagement party. Thomas had seen little of Nicole in the last few days and he missed her. But stints away from Nicole were not uncommon and they normally involved 'Mummy'. Party preparations. Gymkhanas. Summer fêtes. There was even the time that Mummy needed Nicole when she was recovering from a nose job. Mummy wanted her nose to be more like her sweet daughter Nicole's. It was a never-ending circle. Nicole's sisters wanted their noses to look like sweet Mummy's. And so it went on. Thomas thought of the irony if Nicole wanted her nose to look like his. Mummy would follow suit, then the sisters, and before you could say, 'Pinocchio', he would be faced with a wife, mother-in-law and two sisters-in-law with matching noses. What a hoot. Or rather, what hooters.

Thomas pushed open the door to his apartment office. A huge painting by Blaise de Vigenère, titled *Who Beat Goliath?*, greeted him. The giant is being hacked to pieces by the warrior's sword, upon which are engraved the words *Mef Ubk Obso*. Thomas had an idea what the hidden message meant. He smiled at the oil painting – he liked the symbolism. It reminded him of small businesses taking on the giants of the Inland Revenue. As he pressed a switch on his DeLonghi coffee maker, his eyes caught a light blinking. The laptop on the oak desk flashed 'Mail'. For all the room's pleasantness, the decor bright and airy, the tidy books and staff files, even the heavy safe surrounded by potted plants, for all that, Thomas always felt slightly uncomfortable doing business here, having promised Nicole he wouldn't – Nicole demanded that a home should be a home, never a home-cum-office – but for what he was about to do next he needed complete privacy, and the office downstairs didn't always provide that.

From a CD case, *Relics* by Pink Floyd, he produced a neatly written telephone number. No name. Thomas dialled and hung up. He dialled again and hung up. The man had told him to dial twice, hang up twice, and then on the third attempt he'd get through. It was true; Thomas said, 'Is this Terence? It's Thomas.'

'The very same.' His Eton-school accent was overpowering. 'And would this be a certain Thomas who neglected to attend my thirtieth-birthday bash last year?'

Thomas said, 'The very same.'

'A call out of the blue from an old university chum. One wonders at the motive, doesn't one, Thomas? How's the lovely Nicole?'

'She's better.'

'Terrible business, what happened. Completely took us all by surprise. Really. Although, please don't take this the wrong way, it was always on the cards. Lester's lifestyle gravitated that way. He said to me once, "Life's just death but speeded up." Didn't have an inkling what he meant. Still don't. Any ideas?'

'Lester and I weren't exactly . . . chummy,' said Thomas.

'Figures.'

'How's that?'

'Wellllll, he always looked down on you. Let's face it, I think he black-balled you from day one. Silly really, looking back. Anyway, we were all young and stupid with too much money in those days. Too many women. Too many drugs. Too many—'

'Mistakes!'

The echo sounded sad. 'Yes, too many of those, too.' Terence cleared his throat. 'So, what can I do for you? I take it that's why you called.'

It was and Thomas felt odd for asking. 'I need some cocaine.'

A pause. 'Well, well, well. And here was I claiming you as the last survivor of the white-powder holocaust. My faith in humanity is dented for ever.' A sudden burst of Eton-boy giggles. 'I take it this is for you and not for angelic Nicole? Please say it's so. I could not imagine Nicole on Charlie. Please.'

Nicole didn't need cocaine, just cold rain to look like she was on drugs. 'No, it's for me. I don't like discussing this on the phone. Can we meet?'

A place and time were arranged. Terence's last comment, 'It's amazing. No one is quite who you think they are,' hit home to Thomas.

And it was true, thought Thomas, no one is *quite* who you think they are.

Especially him.

Chapter Fourteen

Apart from insect pie, the hardest pie to eat is 'humble pie'. Flavourless, unnourishing and nauseating. Parents, in all their wisdom, sometimes wait for the day that humble pie is force-fed down their children's throats. Open wide and take your humble pie. 'Now, do you understand why we wanted you to study? Now, do you understand why you were not allowed to sleep over? Now, do you understand why sex before history homework ruins your concentration? Now, do you understand?' But kids don't. Who wants to understand parents? What sort of geeky kid stands up on the school playing field and says, 'I want to grow up like my parents'? Who would understand that???

Kept safe in the warm oven of Marina's mind was a fresh slice of humble pie. Baked especially for today's visit to her parents in Watford, where she would have to go back to the family home and explain that she could not find a man of her own. Marina's whole life so far had been open, free and crazy. And not once, in all her years, could she remember a lecture from either Mum or Dad that began with the words, 'I told you so.'

After a National Express coach ride to Watford, Marina hailed a cab.

The familiar roads, the various pubs, parks and schools; to Marina, coming back to her home town was like a trip to the funfair. A place of laughter, happiness, noise and innocence. So why had she left? It wasn't as if Fenworth streets were paved with gold. In fact, they were hardly paved at all.

Leaving home had knocked the wind out of Marina. The idea of abandoning Watford ASAP had been hatched in the playground of Florence Nightingale School with her best friend Emily and remained incubating until four years ago. Watford was where they had grown up, it was where their friends and family lived, it was where they belonged. But it wasn't where their dreams lay. 'Try or die' was their key phrase back then. And if they didn't try for their dreams somewhere else, then their dreams would die in Watford. Of that, they were sure.

Marina's parents had listened quietly as she explained her plan of moving to Oxford with Emily and becoming successful. 'I want to prove to you both that I can make it without your help. No disrespect. But I would love to come back one day and say, "Mum, Dad, put down your *dhal*, open the champagne, your only daughter has made you proud. I am a huge success."' Mum had cried litres while Dad had explained the meaning of life: high interest accounts.

Leaving them both standing at the door had been the hardest chapter in her life so far.

At this precise moment, in the back of a Vectra taxi, Marina was just about clinging on to her life, what with the ferocious road-kill speed of the cab driver, the *Nightrider* theme tune, the G-force when taking roundabouts at 70 m.p.h. Every new job that came up on the CB, the driver accepted, mentioning something about having to feed four kids. With the cost of cigarettes nowadays, he shouted above the roar of the engine, he was nearly on the breadline.

Finally, two flatlines later, after leaving a 50 pence tip for the thrill, Marina stood outside the iron gate to her old home. Seeing her parents always tore at her nerves but it was important that her mum and dad only ever got to see the happy Marina, the young Indian girl they let fly free from their nest. It was important that her mum and dad did not become overly concerned with Marina's direction in life. Her parents' house was not a car boot sale where she sold off her worries cheap. And it was important that she left Watford knowing that her parents were proud of her.

Walking up the garden path, Marina smiled. The front garden was huge and she remembered how Dad had taught her and her brother Zaine the geography of Asia on the lawn. The main road was the Indian Ocean – dangerous and busy. Sri Lanka was the front gate. Next up, at the beginning of the path, was southern India, which included Madras. Calcutta was the apple tree on the right, and on the left, in the rose bushes, was Bombay. Through the front door was Delhi, where Dad was born. Next door was the

Bay of Bengal. And in the back garden, with the wild flowers, where the smelly wheely bin was parked, that was Kashmir. That's where everyone dumped their problems.

'*Namaste*,' Mum greeted Marina from the doorstep with a hug. 'Your father's on the toilet.'

'*Namaste*,' Marina replied, then shouted up the stairs, '*Namaste*, Dad.' A weak response was followed by the pull of the chain. It must be 2.00 p.m. thought Marina. Dad always went at 2.00. As regular as an atomic clock. As explosive as an atomic bomb!

Mum's smile lit up the narrow hallway and after taking Marina's bag and jacket she herded her into the huge living and dining room to join her brother, Zaine, and his wife, Shabana. Joyful laughter filled the room while Mum organized tea and sweetmeats in the kitchen. Yesterday may have been about bills. And tomorrow may be about worry. But today was about brothers and sisters.

And the moon.

Most Indian men are linked by the moon. That unstoppable circling timepiece in the sky. On the last full moon in August each year the sisters of all brothers must drop what they are doing and come running to meet their respective siblings. No matter what. Even if the girl detests the brother, or he detests her, attendance at the ancient ceremony called *Raksha Bandhan* is expected. '*Raksha*' means 'protection' and '*Bandhan*' means 'to tie'.

And '*Let auni!*' means 'Late!'.

Marina was three weeks late for *Raksha Bandhan*, better known as *rakhi*. The full moon was now empty; just a smudge of white light in the September night. In most Indian families turning up three weeks late for *rakhi* would be considered downright disrespectful. But Marina's family was not like most Indian families. Its rules were like bananas. Very bendy and, sometimes, quite slippery. Being late for *rakhi* in this family was definitely not a sulkable offence. Especially when, for the last month, Marina's brother and his wife had been sightseeing in Egypt. Flying out to Cairo was not an option a Fenworth sandwich filler could consider. Just affording the coach up to Watford today had meant sacrificing next month's mascara. She only hoped her brother had received her text in time.

Bring me back some duty-free Pharaoh eye mascara and some Valley of the Kings lip gloss. Please.

Zaine and Shabana sat close on one of the sofas, their hands entwined, love obvious in their eyes. Their marriage had been a love marriage and they wasted no opportunity in proving to their relatives that it was working. At first, their chosen path had been looked upon with scorn at the various Indian dos that they attended. 'You think you know better than your own elders, do you?' was the commonly asked question, and amongst the angry sounds of *bhangra* drums at Indian weddings came the angrier sounds of uncles and aunts. 'You've married against the wishes of us all.' And over and over again they repeated a Frank Skinner phrase, 'It will never work. It will never work. It will never never work.' But it worked.

Marina sipped tea while dreamily contemplating her brother's oh-so-sweet life. This was what she wanted. Love. To live in a world of contentment with the blessings of her family; a fantasy that seemed only too far away right now. She recalled the dreaded burn in her stomach when the letter from The Regency Hotel had arrived a few days back. Surely with the confidence Thomas Harding portrayed he would not be proposing marriage by mail? Maybe that Ganges water was stronger than she'd originally thought? She'd ripped open the letter and her smile evaporated quicker than camel sweat. Oh, yeah, that Ganges water *was* stronger than she'd thought all right. Two thousand five hundred pounds' worth stronger. The bill for his Armani suit.

The romantic compliments slip that accompanied the bill had nearly brought tears to already wet eyes.

Ms Marina Dewan,

I might have understood you throwing water from the sacred river of the Ganges over me if it was for Children in Need. I am a charitable guy. It would have been a worthwhile cause. Rather ominously I fear that your action was more akin to a Child in Need. And the child in this case is YOU! Perhaps, if I may be so bold, I could suggest a course in Social Behaviour Skills. You may find lesson one deals with not throwing excrement over strangers. No matter how sacred the excrement may be.

Unfortunately, my NEW Armani suit went the way of the incinerator. Nuked! I therefore bill you for the complete suit and not just the cleaning of the suit. £2500 made payable to the Regency Hotel. Non-negotiable.

I will end this note with a piece of advice: don't refill the bottle.

Yours disgusted at your actions,

Thomas Harding

Thomas Harding

After reading the letter, Marina had nearly broken the laws of science by folding it up eight times (apparently no sized paper can be folded more than eight – although legend has it that Fatima Whitbread could fold a Chinese menu into nine), until it was just a nugget of dense anti-matter. And she'd thrown it across the room like it didn't matter. But it did. It mattered a lot: the Ganges water wasn't working.

An hour later she was filling her iron with tap water. Why am I punishing myself, she'd wondered, steam ironing the creases out of Thomas's letter. What good would this do, she'd thought, spraying the edges with economy starch. A word sprung to mind, 'graphology', the study of handwriting. A man can hide a whole lot of emotion in his face but, allegedly, nothing can be hidden from the pen. The written word can so often be a man's Judas.

Unfortunately, the words were just words. Beautifully written, in a posh fountain pen no doubt, but words all the same. Nothing romantic or warm at all. Her last-ditch hope of finding something to cling to had been dashed when she removed the scorched letter from the oven to find, no, alas, he had not written a secret message of his undying love with lemon juice. Balls!

There was only one thing for it she'd decided, after stuffing the letter in her *Charlie's Angels* bag with her oven glove, the first chance she had upon returning from visiting her family in Watford, she would make another visit. This time to see hunky spunky Thomas in St Meridians. How dare he use words like 'akin' and 'ominously'! It was so 'pretentious'! The moment had come for Thomas to see another side to Marina. And this side would be, like the letter said, *non-negotiable*. Where the hell was she going to find £2500?

Marina sat amongst the harmony of her family; all in their favourite seats, a woven unit of solidarity. Moments like this were precious and they never lasted long. Then again, precious moments never do.

'I'm thinking of forgiving uncle-ji in Ghaziabad. He's not getting any younger,' Dad said, slurping his lager from a pint glass. He was referring to a bitter dispute that had raged through the family for twenty years. 'If he says he accidentally ploughed up my mango tree, then I suppose I will have to take him at his word. I planted that tree when I was only ten. The day was so hot my skin refused to sweat—'

'Good,' Marina said, all smiles. 'It's bad karma to hold a grudge. When are you going to tell him?'

Dad crossed his feet, kicking off one of his tartan slippers. 'It's up to him to come to me if he wants my apology. I'm not begging him.'

A Mexican wave of nodding heads. The family dispute would live on.

'Do you want to get this *rakhi* out the way, sis?' Zaine said. He always looked smart and dashing (for a brother); even today, in just T-shirt and jeans, he appeared fresh and sparkly, with his bare arms bearing evidence of a month in the sun. 'I suppose you've brought an empty purse for me to fill?'

I've brought an empty Charlie's Angels *bag and even that won't be enough for Thomas's posh suit bill.* Marina smiled. 'I'm not here for the money. I come out of kindness and duty.'

'You must always take the money, Marina,' Mum said, walking out to the kitchen; her expensive silk sari, the colour of Paul Newman's blue front door, fit her neat body and made her look like an Indian princess. She disappeared, only to return with a stainless-steel tray ornamented with a marigold flower, a couple of clay pots, and a china bowl of Indian sweets, which she placed in Marina's out-stretched hands. 'We give so much to these men and take so little in return.' She eyed her son. 'You give generously, Zaine. There is no prosperity in selfishness.'

Dad swapped a beleaguered look with Zaine, while Shabana and Marina giggled. Today, the women out-numbered the men. So, today, the women would out-talk the men. Fair's fair. But only after *rakhi.*

Performing rituals in front of relatives was part of the Indian way of life. It was no use turning around and saying, 'I'm shy,' you just got on with it, no matter what it entailed. This Saturday afternoon, Marina needed to get her hands dirty. The mushy red paste, called *kum kum*, was scooped up from one of the clay pots and deposited on Zaine's forehead. The first time Marina had performed the *rakhi* ritual she had accidentally poked Zaine in the eye. Unfortu-nately for Zaine five-year-old Marina was in a naughty mood that day and had decided to add Birds Eye chilli paste to the *kum kum* mix – payback for breaking brown Barbie doll's neck. Brown because at five years of age Marina felt she couldn't identify with a white Barbie doll and had rebelliously dyed her doll's face and hair with henna. So Barbie the Blonde Beautiful became Barbijit the Brown Paraplegic. And Zaine had cried buckets as the chilli paste sizzled his eyeballs.

During the anointing of the *kum kum* a brother and sister may steal a glance at each other. It's probably the closest the two will have been all year. All grievances are to be thrown away right then! Marina enjoyed these Indian traditions and festivals. Even when she was at school her calendar of celebrations didn't always match the other girls'. For sure she would take advantage of the good ones they had, like Christmas, Valentine's, Secretary Day, even Easter, but it was nice to hold another set of dates in her heart that were special only to the Hindus. *Diwali*, the festival of lights. *Dassehra*, meaning nine nights. *Mahashivratri*, the great night of Shiva. And even *Krishnajanmashtami*, which remembers the birth of Krishna. All celebrated in their own way depending on which part of India your relatives originated. All celebrated with various degrees of enthusiasm depending upon how strict your upbringing. And all with one thing in common: each festival is impossible to pronounce correctly when drunk.

'Have you brought the *rakhikiki*?' Dad mispronounced, now slightly drunk.

Marina giggled; yes, she had brought the *rakhikiki*. '*Rakhi*, Dad. Yes.' From her bag she produced a delicate glittering silk thread which had a shining colourful disc attached. Much like a Christmas bauble. She tied it to Zaine's right wrist. 'May your ambitions be fulfilled,' she uttered, then placed a blessing of a milk sweet, *burfi*, in his mouth.

Now for the money!

In return for Marina's sweet gesture, Zaine reached into his back pocket and pulled out his wallet. With an air of showmanship, he unfolded a crisp £50 note (Marina was glad to see that the note was not folded more than eight times) and handed it to her, making a promise to protect her throughout her life.

'And this,' Shabana held out a small silver trinket, 'is water from the River Nile. Zaine assured me that you would be extremely grateful, as you collect sacred water. He's not winding me up, is he?'

Zaine and Shabana laughed while Marina opened the engraved box and stared at the glass vial of murky water lying on a bed of purple velvet. It was at moments like this she wished she was an only child. And it was at times like this that Marina was grateful that Zaine didn't know all her secrets. Especially the shameful family-wrecking one.

'Thanks for telling her, Zaine,' Marina said, slightly embarrassed.

'If it makes you feel any better, sis, the vial contains King Rameses the third's urine. Guaranteed by a camel herder we met in the desert. By the sediment at the bottom I would hazard a guess that poor old Rameses had kidney stones.'

'Probably the heat,' said Dad. 'You've got to drink more water in those deserts. Uncle Dilip suffered from one the size of an orange. How he passed it through his penis, I will never know. You could hear his agony from two villages away.'

Marina shook her head at Dad, he was getting drunker. 'Mum, come on, I'll help you with dinner.'

Chapter Fifteen

On a wooden bench in the hotel garden Thomas chilled out, the mild sun massaging his skin. The morning had been eventful. First that dealing with Terence regarding the cocaine – their scheduled meeting was a few days from now and seemed like a lifetime to wait. Then watching with horror as a pilot landed a helicopter on the huge back lawn, asked if there were any vacancies at the inn, then flew away, yawning, leaving a hundred pounds for the flowers that he had decapitated upon landing. If that wasn't enough, five of his waitresses had signed a petition asking him to withdraw the second warning he'd given to Stuart earlier or they would resign. Apparently, they couldn't function at functions without him. A humdinger of a day already.

His eyes caught sight of the weeping willow tree near the back fence. The branches shook, and Thomas smiled as two love-struck pigeons landed together.

Ahh, the joy of romance, he thought, then watched with distress as one of the pigeons squawked and fell dead to the ground below. What the blinding hell had just happened? And then the second pigeon squawked and dropped out of the tree. Thomas stood up. As far as he knew, scientists had not added the lemming gene to pigeons. Something was amiss. And when something was amiss, it normally involved Stuart.

From behind a bush, sculpted of all things in the shape of a bird, Stuart, dressed in camouflage gear, appeared with an air rifle slung over his shoulder. His smile proved one thing: he didn't think he was doing anything wrong. He'd given the same smile to the police officer two years back who had stopped him in his car doing 90 m.p.h. while reading his *Playstation* 2 magazine over the steering wheel.

'Hi, Mr Harding. Guess what's on the menu tonight? Don't worry, I'll make sure head chef removes the pellets. Nothing like hunting your own dinner. Two shots, two deaths. What a buzz,' Stuart said, yawning like a guppy fish.

'I want you to bury those birds by the tool shed – a full service with prayers. And make sure you bury them far away from my gravestone. Make a couple of wreaths from that pile of geraniums on the lawn.' Thomas motioned to the decapitated flowers. He wanted to make a point here: you can't just shoot anything that moves. 'I cannot believe that you have turned two beautiful animals into pie filling for a thrill; we don't even serve pigeon, for God's sake.' He shook his head. 'We buy all our meat from the butchers, Stuart, you know that. What might our guests think if they saw you shooting their dinner? If I catch you doing this sort of thing again, you'll be next on the menu. Now go and get a shovel, you murderer.'

Stuart smarted inside. Oh, how he was going to punish Thomas now. Nicole would soon see the *real* Thomas. The one no one else seemed to see but him.

If outside the hotel wasn't free of problems, then maybe inside would be. Thomas aimlessly drifted through the premises, his hangover only partially cured by Stuart's breakfast steak. He just prayed that sometime during the day Farmer Paintly from up the road didn't drop by to say that one of his cattle was missing – possibly shot by a smiling man in a bloodied chef's uniform, toque on his head, holding an air rifle.

Hogging the main bar, sisters Daisy and Maisy sat before a huge tray of dips and snacks waiting to join the other twenty-thousand calories already consumed in their vast bellies that morning. Food never had to wait long around these two. Since they'd taken up residence within the Regency about a year ago, they had become part of the furniture – and it would take one hell of a removal van to take them away.

'Good afternoon, Mr Harding,' Daisy said, a fistful of French fries at the ready to jam in her mouth. 'Is it casual attire today?' She eyed his black jeans and T-shirt, which read: *Don't Yawn*. 'Did Paul McCartney arrive earlier? The helicopter?'

Maisy giggled sheepishly. 'We thought it was royalty at first. A secret rendezvous for Camilla and Charles. Oh, my . . .' She opened her mouth wide and yawned. 'Come and join us for a drink, Mr Harding, you look all worn out.'

Daisy patted a stool next to her with one hand, while with the other she scooped up another handful of fries. 'We don't bite.' Which wasn't what the food thought.

Thomas smiled. The last time he'd become 'chatty' with these two he'd lost the desire to live. As today stood, one five-minute chat with the dynamic duo and he'd probably be asking Stuart to aim the rifle at his body.

'Can I take a rain check? You see, I've got so much to do.' His eyes focused on a blonde woman hovering by the entrance, wearing a mini-dress and knee-length boots. 'See the lady standing by the door, she's here for a job interview.' Thomas waved to the blonde, then said fairly loudly, 'I'll be with you in a minute, just let me finish talking to my two favourite guests.'

'Oh, Mr Harding,' they said in unison, yawned, then stuffed their gobs with fries as Thomas nearly tripped over himself to get away.

With an eagerness normally saved for major room bookings Thomas whipped out his hand like a snake's tongue and shook the blonde lady's hand heartily. 'Mr Harding, how can I help you?'

'It's you I've come to see.' Her smiling face became downcast. 'You don't remember me, do you?'

Thomas recognized the lyrics – a Hot Chocolate song – but he didn't recognize the woman. 'No. Should I?' In the old days, he would have lied. In the days before Nicole, not only would he have said he remembered her, but he would have convinced this pretty blonde woman that he had been thinking about her every second since they last met. But now, he was a kept man. Things were different. 'There *is* something about you. Were you ever employed to clean rooms here?'

Bloody cheek! 'Do I look like a scrubber? Is that what you're trying to tell me?' Emily said, her face changing from downcast to down-right-annoyed. 'Where's your suit? You haven't exactly made an effort yourself, have you? Or are suits a sore subject?' She yawned. 'Did it really cost £2500, or are you out for a quick buck? Emily's the name, by the way.' She dropped her heavy bag; the sounds of metal on metal jangled within. 'Call me M for short if you like.'

The common London accent rang a bell – not quite a Bow Bell – and recognition ripened quickly in Thomas's mind. It was the Fenworth girl. But was she alone? With a speedy sweep of the bar, he checked for the mad Indian woman. Two smartly dressed barmen, one waitress, half a dozen or so guests, and the dynamic duo food-processing factories – Maisy and Daisy. But, thank God, no mad Indian woman waiting to throw putrid water over him. His anxious sweat retreated back into his pores as he ushered Emily over to an empty table overlooking the back garden. If she wanted to cause a scene then the Fire Exit was only a foot and a shove away.

They both sank into the burgundy-leather armchairs. The two barmen and waitress forgot what they were doing and scrambled over to take Thomas's order. The boss rarely ate here and it was the perfect opportunity to suck up to him. Two glasses of white wine were ordered and swiftly brought over to the table just as the background music changed to Thomas's favourite classical piece – *Cosi Celeste* by Luciano Pavarotti with Zucchero. The creeping in this place never ceased to amaze Thomas.

He eyed Emily suspiciously. 'Subterfuge is an erroneous way to go about getting what you want,' he began. 'We are not all as foolish as the Trojans, Emily. And it's inconceivable to think that—'

'Was it Oxford Uni you studied at?' Emily interrupted.

Baffled, he replied, 'Yes, why?'

'Well, don't make it *so* obvious. Have you heard the way you talk? Do you think that the average person can actually understand all this malarkey that comes from your gob?' She sipped her wine, enjoying the obvious embarrassment she was causing. 'I can handle the posh accent, it's quite sexy in fact, but there's no way I can have a conversation with you when you use all that posh Oxford muck.'

Stunned, he answered, 'Sorry, but I don't mean to sound patronizing or condescending or even—'

'There you go again. A clever person would be able to talk on *all* levels. You're a businessman, you should be able to adjust to your client's IQ. You probably cream your pants when *Newsnight Review* is on, am I right? All those long words.'

Honesty shone from Emily's personality and to Thomas it was as refreshing as the wine. But why was she here? What was he doing talking to her? Why did his Oxford degree in English suddenly seem so crass? And, more importantly, why was he staring down her top?

He changed views and looked into her blue eyes instead. 'What I'm trying to say is this: it seems to me that you and Marina are having a laugh at my expense. Is it a bet? Or a dare? And if the object is to out-do one another, I can assure you that Marina has won. Nothing beats throwing shit over someone. Plain enough for you?'

'It's not a bet or a dare. This is about you and me.' She took a gulp of wine for courage. 'I've come to ask you out on a date. I see great things for us two.'

'The answer is no,' he said. 'Thank you anyway.' He stood up to leave.

'You at least owe me an explanation. I took the bus to get here, you know. At least show me that an Oxford boy can be truthful.' She squeezed her eyes shut. 'Tell me, is it because I'm not pretty enough for you?'

Thomas stared at the ridiculous woman and sat back down. 'It's not that.'

One eye of hers opened. 'Well, what then?'

And Thomas went on to explain about the social gap between the two of them. How he wouldn't be able to explain how much he loved her without a dictionary nearby. A picture dictionary. How he believed classes should remain divided and never meet in the middle. How they were from different backgrounds.

And infinitely more important: how he was already engaged to Nicole, the woman he loved completely.

Emily raised her perfect eyebrows. 'So, basically, you're too good for me? That's what you're saying. You wouldn't be seen dead with me in public? Is that what being a snob is?' Emily cast an eye to a wall speaker above her head and sighed miserably. She hated opera music. 'What about Marina? Is she classy enough for you? Does she fit the mould of a snob?'

Thomas fidgeted in his seat. 'I hate the word "snob", but I don't know. Maybe in India she is a "snob". But to me, she's a different culture entirely and I could never even entertain the idea of . . .' He stalled. Why was he still having this conversation? 'Look, Marina is a different skin colour and class to me. I just don't think cultures should mix, that's all.' He handed the waitress the empty wine glasses and waited for her to leave. Thomas felt shallow; not as shallow as the day he and Nathan were caught at university trying to graffiti a wall with plaster of Paris in Braille for the blind, but close enough. Why did he feel this way towards cultures mixing? He couldn't blame his parents for this one. Maybe life has proved that people of different races rarely get on like a house on fire – they are more likely to set each other's houses on fire. Wars, battles, death – all in the name of religion, culture, and the upkeep of what one party believes is 'the right way' but the other believes is 'the wrong way'. Trying to have a relationship with a woman of a different culture would be asking for trouble – there would be just too many obstacles – especially when Thomas was having enough trouble understanding women of his own culture.

Thomas looked at Emily. 'I'm not racist, but if Marina was the last woman on earth, something inside tells me it would be wrong.'

Emily kept a smile at bay. 'So, ignoring that you're engaged for one moment, Marina is *definitely* out of the question – even if she was the last woman on earth?'

'Absolutely.'

She giggled. 'God, I'd hate a bloke to say that about me.' A worried expression took hold of her face. 'If *I* was the last woman on earth, would you screw me?'

Thomas stood up. 'Well, seeing as you put it so nicely, yes, I'd give you a good fuck.' He walked off leaving Emily basking in smiles.

Outside the window, on the deep carpet of lawn, a group of waitresses, dressed in their working uniforms, stood huddled around a chef in his chequered overalls. Emily watched, intrigued by the strange-looking funeral being conducted in the garden.

Stuart stared gloomily at the two mounds of earth next to the tool shed. His face was like stone. He told Jenny to stop digging now, the holes were deep enough. The five waitresses were encouraged to hold hands as Stuart made a small speech. No one liked losing a pet, especially Stuart, but to lose two in one day, it was heart-breaking. He laid the two bundles, wrapped in baking foil, into the ground.

Opening his mouth to speak, Stuart's voice quivered with emotion. 'Ashes to ashes, feathers to feathers, beaks to beaks.' He wiped the corner of an eye. 'I would like to say a few words before I bury my garden pigeons. Two lives snuffed out by an act of pure evil.' He paused to whisper into Jenny's ear, 'I'm going to miss those two little terrors . . . so much . . . I think I may need some company tonight.'

Jenny cradled his head, nodding she would be there for him if he needed her. 'Poor Stu-pot, you are such a soppy darling underneath.'

Stuart continued. 'They didn't stand a chance, caught up in the centrifugal force of the helicopter's propeller blade and then hurled against that tree over there.' He pointed to the weeping willow. 'I called out to the pilot, "Don't land there, please don't land there, my pigeons, my pigeons." But he didn't hear me. And then . . .' Stuart bit his bottom lip. 'And then, they were gone. This is all Thomas Harding's fault, allowing his yuppie friends to show off their rich toys on the hotel lawn. But my pets died today, not his. Thomas said to me, "They are just meat with wings, Stuart, that's all. Just meat with wings."' The waitresses gasped at the comment and then watched as Stuart stooped down and lowered the two geranium wreaths on to the mounds. He choked out, 'Rest easy, my little ones, I'll be joining you one day.'

All five waitresses cuddled him. Stu-pot was *such* a darling. He would be needing a lot of support over the coming weeks. Whatever that entailed. Stuart's erection went unnoticed during the group hug.

On a piece of cardboard cut from an empty box of courgettes Stuart had fashioned a makeshift headstone. It read:

R.I.P.
Delightful Delia
Randy Rhodes
Two small birds
Killed by
One big bird.
Sponsored by OXO Gravy Granules

Chapter Sixteen

Six female Indian hands prepared a meal fit for the God Shiva himself in a vast kitchen worthy of a temple. The order of spices, the slicing and cutting, even the display of food on the plate, all had to be done a 'certain' way. And the certain way with regards to food in any Indian household belongs to the mother. With a wooden spoon for her baton, she commands the gourmet Hindu symphony orchestra, yelling advice in Punjabi, dishing out orders in Hindi and offering up compliments in English. Amongst the noise and tittle-tattle, the subject of all subjects emerged. The subject Marina detested discussing with her mother. It began with an 'M', it ended in an 'N' and somewhere in the middle there was an 'E'.

'Men!' Mum began, her voice echoing. 'Have you found one yet?'

'No. Still looking,' Marina replied cautiously, careful not to tread on a word-mine hidden in Mum's question. 'Every day I'm on the look-out for potentials. Twenty-four seven. I know he's out there, I can feel it, it's just a matter of our paths crossing.'

'So we all just wait, do we? Until your paths cross. Your father and I are the only relatives out here with a daughter nearly thirty and without a wedding ring.' Pop pop pop. The coriander seeds exploded like midget's popcorn on the frying pan and Mum gave a quick stir. 'You've got a wonderful job, you're so very pretty. But you can't outwit time, Marina, it will take your looks before you know it. Remember your cousin Pepi in Wolverhampton? Remember how one day she was like Twiggy and the next day she was breaking the bathroom scales? And then, in a panic, her family put Pepi on Slim-Fast and made her wrap her bulging stomach with cling film beneath her *shalwar kameez*.' Mum stared sternly at Marina's and Shabana's giggling faces. 'It's not funny, no man wanted to marry her afterwards. Her parents had to settle for that peasant from Partapgarh. No teeth. Spitting everywhere. Horrible man.'

Mum had forgotten to mention the peasant's missing ear. Blown off in that most traditional of all traditional Indian peasant farmer's games: 'Can you shoot me?' But Mum had made her point. And Marina heard it loud and clear. With both ears.

Marina's family were ripping up the rules of marriage generation by generation. Her own parents had married against their parents' wishes. Mum was a lower caste than Dad. Less pure. Less worthy. But Dad didn't care, he'd loved her from the moment he'd seen her cross the stream outside his small white-washed house in Delhi and had watched how gracefully she trod the stepping stones in her bare feet, carefully pulling up her robust-red *chunni* to cover her face as she stepped to the far side. One look back at Dad was all he had needed to pursue her down that path called destiny. His eighteen-year-old heart had pounded as her figure blended into the sinking sunset. That was the woman he would marry. Regardless of whether their families disapproved, regardless of whether their friends disapproved, regardless even if India disapproved. Regardless!

They had leapt the chasm of the caste system, shrugging off the sulks, stares and whispers of relatives, their naive teenage heads filled with a thousand questions. Why should a baby be labelled at birth *Hari-jan*, 'untouchable'? Who defined the score chart of the Indian caste system? Why is one shade of skin more acceptable than another? Questions they couldn't just stick in the deep freeze and thaw out when they were seventy. When it was too late. They had wanted the answers now! But all that had been forthcoming was one word: tradition. Surely tradition wasn't big enough to lose out on true love once you had found it. For Marina's parents *had* found true love together. And at the time they'd asked for only one thing in return: the blessings of their elders.

It took the birth of their first child, Zaine, before the blessings arrived. And even though Zaine had been formed from the mixing of castes, he was born with two arms and two legs just like most babies. Not a third eye in sight. By the time Zaine was twelve and asking twelve-year-old questions about fully grown women undressing in the shower, England had become home for Marina's parents, and India had become abroad. Parental guidance to a hormone-busting, mixed-caste, Hindu-Watford boy was about to become interesting. Both parents agreed that Zaine should be left to think freely, but deep down, in the marrow of their bones, they'd hoped he would come home one day smitten with desire for a good Hindu girl. 'Are we wrong to want this?' they had asked themselves. 'Is this the request of a hypocrite?' they'd hypothesized. 'Should we not be pleased whoever he brings through that front door – as long as he is happy? Regardless?' It was a good question. One that never saw its own answer; for one fine day in summer, not too long after Zaine had completed his chemistry degree, he'd arrived at his parents' house with a pretty-faced Hindu girl on his arm and a cheeky glint in his eye. Shabana, sculpted from pure love stone, would be Zaine's princess. Clearly, his parents were happy. Without pressure, without threats, and without capital punishment, their own son had chosen for himself an Indian girl to marry. But it would take diplomacy of the highest order to persuade the rest of the relatives why – yet again – the family was in breach of the Hindu customs, where the arranged marriage takes prime spot. Yet again, the family was ripping up the rules of marriage. And by now one might think that the elders would submit to change, but like a tree grows rings, an Indian grows more stubborn. The oldest relatives, the hardy oak trees of India, being the hardest to please. Out with the chainsaw. Down with the trunks.

And now Marina stood poised. Her finger outstretched waiting for a wedding ring. But who would be placing the band upon her finger? And how old and wrinkly would that finger be when it finally happened? Dad was beginning to despise the word 'freedom'. They'd hoped that Marina would have used her freedom wisely and found a husband who was Hindu. Time, like the future, was running out.

There was only one way to describe the smells wafting from the kitchen: 'Mmmm.' Dinner was nearly ready. Shabana, Marina and Mum sat on kitchen stools, sipping red wine, enjoying each other's company. A CD from *Bombay Dreams* played on the stereo.

Mum frowned. 'I think you're missing out on much happiness, Marina. Your father and I can't understand why you can't find a husband. You haven't even brought a single man back for us to—'

'Rate? To score? Belittle?' Marina interrupted. 'Look, Mum, the only man I'll ever bring home for you and Dad to see will be the one I marry. Until then, the only thing on my arm will be my *Charlie's Angels* bag. Quite a stud I can tell you.'

'It's old and battered. Is that how you want to look when you get married? Already you are being talked about as a spinster.' Mum touched Shabana's hand. 'Tell her how lovely Hindu men are. *Fantastic*. Tell her how lucky you were to find my son.' Mum didn't wait for an answer. 'If it's a confidence problem, Marina, then your father and I can help. Just give us the go-ahead and we could have twenty meetings arranged within a month, thirty even. *And*, this is the best part of the plan, you could go out for romantic meals with your Hindu man and even the cinema and then you wouldn't even have to call it an arranged marriage. It would have been all your own choice.

Fantastic. Imagine it, you would have a Hindu man all to yourself.'

'Plan?' Marina hated the sound of this. Mum and Dad had never gone so far as planning anything before. The odd hint here and there but never anything so devious as a plan. 'Look, at the moment the house prices are so unstable. My work needs me to be as sharp as a tooth. I can't even begin to think about Hindu men until the housing crisis has been sorted out. It could be a month, or a year, but Napkins Homes needs me. Without my input they would crumble.' She stared shamefully at the bubbling saucepan. God, she hated lying to her parents about her job. 'Times are dire.'

Indeed they were. Mum spooned pilau rice on to the dinner plates. Her mind was in flight, heading towards India. It was a sad day when you had to go behind your own children's back. From what Marina had just said, from what she had always said since moving down to Fenworth, she would continually place her job before her love life. Her ambition, although commendable, was also something of a stick in the mud. It was preventing Marina from settling down and having children. Maybe it was time for some assistance. Maybe it was time to phone Uncle Palekji again, see what good Hindu boys were on offer over here. And if not in England, then in India.

India was chock-a-block full of good Hindu boys. Mum smiled at Marina. Her daughter would soon know the happiness of a blissful married life. Oh how thankful Marina was going to be for her mother's interference.

Fantastic.

Chapter Seventeen

Because of the extreme isolation of the Regency Hotel, its central spot in the countryside meant it was always caught in the Sunday crossfire of church bells, each church desperate to out-ring the other. Rumour had it that the women bell-ringers of Holy Trinity Church on the north hill had twenty-three-inch diameter biceps; in an effort to ring louder and for longer than the women of the Church of Jesus Christ on the other side of the hill, they had taken to injecting themselves with anabolic steroids. Bell Rage was not uncommon in these parts, and most people who joined rambling clubs in the area were deaf within the year. A note of trivia that was not pointed out in the new Regency Hotel colour brochure.

Sitting at a small round table in the hotel Reception, Thomas pushed the box of brochures to one side as a waitress poured a refreshing cup of black coffee into a large Regency mug. Sunday roast was in full swing in the restaurant, an ocean of activity, while out here, with just one waitress on hand, one receptionist, and a grandfather clock ticking, he was in a desert of solitude. He eyed an excitable kid in a tuxedo chasing another across the marble floor, with a snotty tissue. Well, maybe not quite a desert, more like a beach. The lads both stood up, burped out their own musical score, bowed to the watching receptionist, Cheryl, then sprinted up the stairs like gazelles. It wouldn't be too long, Thomas worried, before children like this would be running the country. If only he'd *not* listened to Health and Safety when they advised him to round off any sharp edges in Reception.

The Sunday Times waited to be read. It waited to depress. But being uninformed in the world of business was tantamount to commercial suicide. Anything even slightly related to hotels was greedily absorbed by Thomas. Even the price of butter stocks could in some way affect his profit margin. When the petrol strike was in motion, then so, too, were Thomas's bowels. He'd lost thousands in bookings through cancelled events. If he'd taken the precautionary step of enforcing higher deposits back then, and a couple of Imodium tablets per day, his suffering would have been minimized. Nowadays the required deposit was nearly the full balance. And thus, rarely were there cancellations.

Apart from today.

The Steadfast family had cancelled this morning. A booking of four luxury rooms. The rooms were paid in advance in full, so no money was lost, but if the truth were to be known, Thomas was hurt. How dare someone cancel at the last minute using the sex excuse. Just because the Regency did not show hard-core pornography on its satellite channels, only soft porn, they would find a hotel which did. Pervs. They'd even left a few words of advice: 'Modernize or Die.'

Thomas sipped his coffee, coordinating his thoughts. It would take more than a lost booking to bring him to his knees. He would just ignore it. Just like he'd ignored the black armbands that the waitresses and Stuart had worn this morning at breakfast – in respect for the pigeons. Just like he'd ignored the second mattress of the week stacked up in the bin area round the back dripping with Mr Whittleworth's liquor urine. And just like he was going to ignore the blonde, tanned woman who had just swum into Reception on a sea of perfume.

But ignoring *her* of all people was going to be near impossible. He hadn't seen her since she'd jetted off to Italy. And now, with most of the Mediterranean marinating her skin, she had returned. Her question to the receptionist was never in any doubt and Thomas waited for a count of three. Or rather, *uno, due, tre*.

'Where's my son, Cheryl?' the blonde lady said, her face as pretty as any fifty-five-year-old was allowed to be – without copious amounts of plastic surgery. 'He's not *still* in bed, is he?' Her words were as well-spoken and manicured as could be.

Cheryl stared, impressed as ever at how young and sexy Mrs Harding, Thomas's mother, looked in her pristine white Chanel dress and matching kitten-heeled mules. Her curves and breasts had openly disobeyed time. And maybe, if Newton was around today, he would have been as confused as anyone about the laws of gravity.

Thomas skirted across the floor and planted a kiss on her cheek. He was used to his mother turning up unannounced by now. 'You look like a prostitute, Mom. You look great.'

'Thank you.' Victoria Harding smothered her son with lipstick kisses. 'Now, darling, don't get yourself all upset. It's only material after all, and you've got plenty of money to buy a new one, but—' She paused and took his hand in hers. 'Your father is outside. Now, I don't want you to worry about this, he is all right. He's not hurt at all. Just mild whiplash and a sore thumb.' She squeezed his hand and closed her eyes. 'I accidentally smashed my Mercedes into your Porsche. Head on. I'm so sorry. Really sorry. The right wing has caved in and I think, judging by the amount of debris in the car park, you will need a whole new bonnet. The windscreen is not looking too healthy either.' Thomas was quiet and looking paler by the second. 'I made a quick count before I rushed in here, so I can't be one hundred per cent sure, but out of the three original doors you had when the car was new, I think only one survived the collision. I'm just surprised you didn't hear it. Do you want to sit down?' She nodded to Cheryl who was listening open-mouthed. 'Go and fetch him a large brandy. My son has had a shock.'

'And you're both okay?' he asked, really meaning, my poor car is dead?

'Oh, don't you worry about us. We're fine. I think your father may have slightly pulled a muscle in his thumb, though, when he grabbed the handbrake for the handbrake turn.' She paused. 'Damn shame, we were so close to a three-sixty spin as well.'

Thomas leant backwards. 'You mean you were both doing a handbrake turn in my car park? A stunt? A three-sixty spin?'

She aimed her head away nonchalantly. 'I saw the gap, I took my chance and I went for it. A slight misjudgement on your father's part. He said that there was room for a bus.'

'Mom, you're not twenty any more. You don't do handbrake turns in hotel car parks. What next? Demolition Derby?'

The first time he'd bought an expensive car, Thomas had told himself that if he were to enjoy the motor, then he was not to get too upset if the paint got scratched or the window got broken or even if the stereo got stolen. What was the point in having an expensive car if you worried about it all day? So, it came as some grave concern to him to find that tears were now welling in his eyes. Oh God, he loved that car – his third Porsche to date, and his favourite by far.

Led by the hand of his mother, Thomas could feel the diamonds of her rings cutting into his fingers. She was obviously as worried about this as he was. He would make a huge effort not to lay blame. The last thing she wanted on returning from her holiday was an ear-bashing.

Pops stood grinning nervously by the red Porsche, puffing on a cigar. Thomas circled his car, assessing the damage, calculating which one of his parents he would murder first. They were both culpable. Both adults. Both in big big trouble. How much more could a son put up with? What sort of family was this? Nearly in the words of an *X Files* episode, 'This was not happening.'

'I would like you both to leave, please,' Thomas said, his anger neatly displayed in two clenched fists. 'We were thinking of holding Murder Mysteries here. You two might be the first if you hang around.'

The parents laughed hysterically. Falling into each other's arms displaying actions similar to children in a school playground. The Porsche had not been involved in any catastrophe, any accident, any collision! It was exactly as Thomas had left it last night. Polished, clean and perfect. Once again, his parents had taken great pleasure in winding up their only son. A plan that had been hatched on the flight out to Italy. If giving their son a stomach ulcer kept them looking young, then so be it.

Pops held out his hand. 'It does no harm to lose things from time to time, son, even if it is only for a few minutes. I expect that your Porsche means even more to you now. Am I right?'

'Yes. And my parents mean even less.' All three laughed this time.

It was hard to think that Pops used to be one of London's high-flyers. A stockbroker with an uncanny ability to buy up shares just before they shot up in value. But a near-fatal heart attack had shown Pops that the value of stocks paled into nothingness when compared to the value of life. Get out, take the millions he'd made, and enjoy the rest of his days with his wife, was what the doctor had ordered.

And ever since then, life had been crazy for Thomas's parents. Collecting enough air miles to wallpaper their luxury home in Oxfordshire. Grabbing each moment and stretching it until it snapped. And proving that old age was not a station that life's train needed to rush to. If any proof was needed that all middle-aged people are not miserable bastards, then *they* were it.

After showing Thomas her tan and offering to prove it was all over, Mom reached into her suede handbag for the tissue she knew she would soon need. She'd been saving the tears since Italy, since Thomas informed her of his engagement to Nicole.

'You and the Newton-Harrington child must come round for lunch,' Mom said, after a little cry of happiness. 'We'll hire a butler for the day. Make Blonde Thingamajig feel at home.' She smiled over to her husband. 'You've been practising sitting on the kitchen stool side-saddle, haven't you, darling?'

Pops nodded. 'Plays havoc with the shins, but I'll do anything to make a good impression on Thingamajig. It's either that or I phone the local zoo and order in some foxes for me to shoot. That should please her.' The parents laughed.

'Her name's Nicole. She doesn't shoot foxes. She is one.' Thomas turned to his mother and spoke in Italian so Pops couldn't understand. '*Vedo che papa continua a comportarsi come un bambino.*'

'*Tuo padre non ha mai smesso di comportarsi come un bambino,*' she replied laughing, then faced her husband. 'Your son, whom I love from all four chambers of my heart, just asked me if you were still behaving like a child, a *bambino*, and of course I told him you were. Why lie?'

Pops scoffed, 'Lie? I'm not the *bambino* whose

latest hobby is phoning *Crimewatch* and telling them I know who did it.'

And with that comment, after a quick cuddle each, Thomas waved them goodbye from the car park. The personalized registration of the Merc made him smile: BMW N0T. Then his thoughts turned to the observation that might sum his parents up: NORMAL N0T.

Inside the hotel, traffic in the lobby had increased dramatically: people sitting around digesting their roast dinners, keys being collected from Reception, staff, still wearing their black armbands, marching through. A team of ramblers sat shouting at each other in the corner, arguing over a map. Two kids pulled on a chicken wishbone given to them by head chef, Harry. And Thomas smiled internally, oh how he loved a busy hotel. Busy rhymed with money in Thomas's world.

And money rhymed with fantasy in Marina's world.

'Hello, Mr Harding.' It was Marina. Black combat bottoms, a tight, white vest top showing off her slim tummy – her navel pierced with a blue stone – and black trainers. Casual but sexy. Her slender figure displayed the clothes just how the market-stall clothes designer had envisaged. Marina waited for Thomas to look up from his *Sunday Times*. 'I'm a little bit disappointed in you.'

Thomas folded the paper into four, fearing that if Emily had relayed yesterday's conversation in its entirety to Marina, then it would be *him* heading tomorrow's newspaper: *Oxfordshire Hotelier Accused of Racism. Boycott the Regency Hotel.* Thomas had found over the years that delicate topics like this needed the soundproof touch. It was not so long ago that he had been accused of Farmerism, when he refused to let a group from the Young Farmers Association use his conference room for a talk on sheep culling, because of the amount of horse manure dwelling on their wellingtons.

He stood up. 'Would you like to come into my office and we can talk about this in private, Ms Dewan?' Not waiting for a reply, he walked off.

Inside the office Marina was offered a seat across from Thomas's desk and without a word being said he poured out two cups of coffee. It was important to seem important in circumstances like this. Keep them waiting. Make sure their chair is lower than your chair. Make them repeat things, keep them on edge. Above all, use eye contact as a weapon – hold their gaze until they look away embarrassed.

Thomas swivelled the VDU screen his way and quickly tapped in 'India' on the Internet search. 'I've got nothing against you or India. I want to make that crystal clear right from the off. And, I'm not being patronizing or condescending here, but if I say a word that is too clever for you I want you to tell me straight away. Don't leave it until you've got a huge list.' He held her gaze. 'So, enlighten me, Ms Dewan, what blatherskite have you been paying heed to?'

She held his gaze – oh what lovely blue eyes, she could look at them for hours. 'No one. I don't pay "heed" to gossipmongers anyway. I'm here, one, because I don't think what you say is fair, and two, it's my own ethics at stake here.' And three, she thought to herself, I was hoping you might let me off the money for the suit.

He continued holding her gaze – it had been nearly a minute. 'Well, I'll ignore the fact that you just contradicted yourself, Ms Dewan, as you're obviously here because of the gossip, but, with regard to your skin colour, I have nothing against it. Just, I hope, as you have nothing against my skin colour.'

Marina held his gaze while taking stock of the situation. The man was obviously mad. Gorgeous still, but mad. 'Okay, I'll cut to the chase.' She plucked from her combat bottoms the £50 note that her brother had given her yesterday for *rahki*. 'My first instalment.' And still holding his gaze, she slid it across the polished wooden top, wishing he would just forget about the money, wishing that her debt to him could be paid off in cuddles and kisses instead. 'I'm going to be honest with you, I can't really afford £2500. If I had that sort of money I would have had a nose job by now.' She turned her head to the side, not losing eye contact, and pointed to a slight dent in the bridge of her nose. 'I fell off the carnival float when I was eight. Nearly wrecked my life.'

He smiled. 'And what were you dressed as?'

'A samosa.'

'Vegetable?' he asked, still holding her gaze.

'Meat. Minced meat and potato. And my brother was an onion bhaji. We were dancing on the Hindu float. Anyway, back to this debt, the most I can offer, and this is cutting it fine, believe me, is £2 per week.' She paused, still holding his gaze. 'And before you ask how I can manage to pay twenty-five weeks in one go, don't! It was a gift from my brother to me and he would die if he knew. So, please don't ask. It's personal.'

His vision was now blurred; Thomas's eyes were weeping from the strain of eye combat, and for the first time in his entire life he had to break the gaze. She was a pro. While Thomas had been staring, his hand had been fidgeting with the mouse. The VDU screen was flashing. Somehow he had reserved five tickets for *Bombay Dreams* and was just about to order a set of *Monsoon Wedding* bathrobes. How the hell did that happen? This woman was turning into a jinx. What's more, she obviously didn't have a clue about what he had said to Emily yesterday: how if Marina was the last woman on earth he wouldn't sleep with her because of her skin colour.

Suddenly the noise of an Indian sitar came from the computer speakers. Thomas smiled and swung the VDU screen round to Marina. 'See, I have nothing against India. Look at my screen saver.'

Marina watched the moving picture of the Taj Mahal on the screen. It would have been a nice scene if it wasn't for the eunuchs dancing seductively in their saris in front of the sacred monument. 'Lovely. So, about the money, £2 a week okay?'

He stood up. 'No, it's not okay, Ms Dewan. It's obvious to me that you can't afford it, so we'll call it quits.' He dropped the £50 note into her lap. 'And before you say "I don't accept charity" or—'

'Oh, *I do* accept charity, Mr Harding,' she interrupted. 'You're a very generous man.' Marina jumped up and scored a couple of lipstick kisses on his cheeks – inhaling his fantastic smell. 'I'm really sorry I wrecked your suit. And please don't ask me why I did it, it's embarrassing enough as it is.'

He agreed not to and escorted her out to Reception. Proud to be seen with an Indian woman now he was confident she wouldn't yell 'Racist pig!' across the room. It was good for public relations. This day was becoming more memorable by the minute.

'I guess this is goodbye?' Marina said, praying it wasn't. 'I suppose I won't be hearing from you again. No more dry-cleaning bills?' He shook his head. 'So, I'll see you next year on my Regency Special, then?'

'It will be worth the wait. I'm sure you'll be pleased to hear, I'm thinking of adding a new range of quick-fry sunbeds to the special.' He paused. 'Erm. Not that you'd need a sunbed. You're quite brown enough as it is.' Thomas flushed with pure embarrassment. 'Well, goodbye then.'

Marina giggled. How cute could a man get? He was adorable. 'Do you know what time the next bus is to' – and she whispered – 'Fenworth?'

He checked the grandfather clock, 4.00 p.m. 'It's rather a long wait for your bus. I understand the next one doesn't leave until six.' Something cracked in Thomas's armour. This woman, obviously demented in some way, had travelled all the way up here on a bus to arrange a payment plan for ruining a suit. He hadn't felt this touched by a stranger since the time he saw a tramp give another tramp his last cigarette butt. Thomas had stepped in that day and given each of them a £50 note. Maybe he should step in and give Marina a lift, Fenworth was only fifteen miles away – it would also be a good excuse to take his baby out for a ride after Mom's cruel attempt at a joke this morning. Poor baby Porsche.

The Porsche experience was a new one for Marina. The low seats, the maximum overdrive, the instant roadside audience, the sexy feel of cooling leather. Watching Thomas as he smoothly left traffic for dust, screeching round the country roads like a heat-seeking missile, bloated her pupils and dilated her heart. She giggled nervously and every now and then checked the windscreen for Thomas's score. Oh, no, this was real life, not a computer game after all. She could actually die here. Not just lose her bonus points.

But at least she would die with him. *Their love was short and sweet on this earth, but in heaven it will be eternal.*

The graffiti-covered sign to Fenworth jumped up in view. If only the graffiti artist could have spelt 'cocks' properly, then all Fenworth men wouldn't be known for having huge 'cooks'. Marina glanced at Thomas who was smiling at the sign. The knowing smile of someone who knew Fenworth for what it was: a dump filled with losers. And Marina smiled back. The knowing smile of someone who knew the Ganges water was finally working. Thomas would soon be hers. She was more certain than ever now. Her reasoning was simple: Thomas had gone out of his way to impress her with talk of India. He had got himself in a pickle over trying to explain that colour didn't matter to him; in other words, he wanted to let her know that he was open to a relationship with someone of a different culture. So cute. And then, if that wasn't proof enough, what else does he do? He only lets her off the money that she owed on the suit;

£2500 was a lot of love. And now this lift. What man, apart from a man deeply in love, would risk taking his beautiful red Porsche to Fenworth? The Ganges water *had* to be working. Mum and Dad would soon have an engagement on their hands, she could feel it.

Thank you very much, Gran. And thank you very much, Shiva, Marina chanted within.

Outside Marina's abode, he parked behind a burned-out Cortina and finally turned off the deafening thrash-metal music – a cheap trick to avoid conversation – and faced her. He wanted to ask why most of the windows in the area were boarded up, but, deep down, he knew why already.

He spoke. 'Well, it's been nice.'

'Thanks.'

'Just before you rush off, may I ask you a quick question?'

She nodded smiling. It *really* was going to happen, Thomas was about to ask her out. She doubted he would appreciate her wetting his leather seat, but she nearly did with excitement. Where would he take her? Which posh place would he impress her with? Why was she staring at him with her tongue out?

He continued. 'It's about India. I'm getting married in a few months and I haven't decided where to surprise Nicole with the honeymoon. I was certainly thinking about India. Any recommendations? It's such a big country.' This minor fib should convince Marina he wasn't racist, he presumed. As *if* Nicole would set one Prada-clad footstep into India. Too crowded, too disorganized, too backwards. He finished, 'Who better to ask about India than an Indian?'

Her face dropped. 'Oh yes, I can think of a great place in India.' Her voice was cutting. 'It's called, "Stick my boot up your pompous backside". Heard of it?' She opened the car door, jumped out and violently slammed it shut behind her.

Inside, she thundered up the stairs, threw open her bedroom door and stared hatefully at Shiva. Is this what Gods do? Give us men, then take them away? Are we just pieces on a game board? Some to be sacrificed, others to be crowned, and the rest to be shunted around the squares. Is this why the arranged-marriage system came about? To save the misery and hurt?

Marina lit a sandalwood joss stick and swung it about the room. The grey ribbons of smoke dangled in the air as her eyes found the spot on the wall. Office World had done her proud. A poster-sized enlargement, taken from Emily's magazine, of Thomas, smiling. Normally she smiled back. Not today. Today she hated freedom. She hated finding her own man. She hated being hurt and shunted around the board. Maybe her relatives were right when they said, 'Arranged marriages are our way, the only way, the best way.'

Maybe to Indians, there is no other way than the Indian way.

She'd lost Thomas before she'd even had him and she stood boiling with frustration.

'Sorry for hating you, Shiva,' Marina said, as she knelt in front of her statue. 'Truly sorry. It's just so hard not knowing what to do with my life. I've got a feeling that I'm letting my whole family down. All I want is a decent man to settle down with. Why couldn't it have been Thomas?'

She lay back sulkily on her bed. Emily had mocked her picture of Thomas: 'You can't cuddle up to a poster on a cold night, Marina. You can't give a poster sexual pleasure. Take it down, it's ridiculous.' But it was staying up. After splashing Thomas with the Ganges water, it was important that all her spiritual energy was focused on him. And what finer way to focus was there than having a seven-foot poster in your face at all hours? Plus the minor fact that every time she saw his gorgeous face she could feel her womb getting excited.

Chapter Eighteen

The spirits never die down Lamppost Lane. A four-mile stretch of narrow curves, sudden corners and even more sudden death. Spread erratically along the treacherous expanse of road, lampposts adorned with bunches of old and new flowers marked the spot where loved ones had died. Petitions achieved little to widen the route as farmers complained it would encroach on their land. Over time, as the accidents piled up – literally – most drivers began to slow.

But some drivers began to speed.

Nicole, who never felt quite in charge of her beast of a Mercedes sports car at the best of times, who sometimes mixed up her tachometer with her speedometer, would travel Lamppost Lane like a Formula One driver on heat, her high heels slipping every now and then on the accelerator. Her wing mirrors didn't even need to be aligned properly as she never used them. But the rear-view mirror – the one that had reflected many two-finger gestures from the vehicles following behind – was aligned to perfection. For one purpose only, mind you: make-up duty.

Nicole slammed the gear stick into fourth as she passed the spot where her ex-boyfriend, Lester, had died. A pile of bouquets gave the lamppost its own rainbow hue. And as always, Nicole's foot hit the accelerator while her eyes closed tight, as the road that had been an accomplice to Lester's death shot beneath the wheels at speeds that speed guns were designed for. Nicole had nearly died that night. Scared out of her wits that he was driving too fast in the thrashing rain, she had made the mistake of asking him to slow down. No one told Lester, the son of a multimillionaire shipping tycoon, what to do. No one ordered Lester, an ace graduate of Oxford University, to slow down. No one had the right to . . . and then the car had spun off the road, no fuss, no screams, just a sudden smack into the lamppost, and Lester was dead.

No one told Lester, the man with his head poking through the smashed windscreen, how to die – Lester was no longer a winner.

Nicole pulled into the Regency car park, grateful as ever that the journey from Castle Cliff Manor to Thomas's hotel, using the only route that didn't involve opening a farmer's gate and dodging rutting bulls, was over. Taking Thomas's reserved parking space, she wondered where he could have gone. Thomas wasn't the sort to just 'pop out' on a Sunday. He'd declined Mummy's offer of lunch at Castle Cliff Manor owing to masses of paperwork. So where was he? He was wrecking her surprise visit already.

Reception was chock-a-block. Some days people just didn't want to be in their rooms. Lingering, waiting, expecting something to happen. Nicole excused herself as she pushed through a group of businessmen, ignoring the quick-fire sexual innuendoes that the wine had encouraged them to utter, and landed at the Reception counter.

'Cheryl, where's Tom?' Nicole asked, trying to sound jolly.

'Erm. He's gone out, I'm not too sure where. Do you want me to tell him you're upstairs when he comes back?'

Nicole wrinkled her forehead, thoughtful. 'I think I'll wait down here.' She gave a quick look around and spotted a spare table by the piano. 'I'll be over there, Cheryl. Is it possible for someone to bring me over a coffee?'

A loud thud on the floor made Nicole jump. A huge sack of Maris Piper potatoes now sat just an inch away from her Manolo Blahnik diamond-studded lavender sandals. Ironically, just an inch away from *mashing* her lavender-painted pedicured toes. It had to be the act of someone vulgar.

'All right, Nicky?' Stuart said, his chef's outfit deliberately brushed with tomato ketchup to upset the guests. 'Sorry about the bloody uniform. It's only pig's blood, occupational hazard, I haven't tried to kill myself or anything like that, no suicides in this hotel, *Nicky*.'

'Nicole, to you, Stuart.' She felt his dirty eyes crawling underneath her dress. 'Would you happen to know where Thomas has nipped off to?'

A silent slanging match between Cheryl and Stuart

took place. Cheryl's sign language appeared to indicate that Stuart should not tell Nicole the whereabouts of Thomas. They were his staff and loyalty was paramount. Stuart, on the other hand, just stuck his middle finger up – sod loyalty, he was telling the truth, it was time for Thomas's landslide to begin. And if Cheryl didn't like it, then she should have thought a little bit more about that before she'd confided in Stuart about her bedroom fetishes. Blackmail was invented for information like that.

'I think it's best if you're sitting down when I tell you the news, Nicole,' Stuart said, still ignoring Cheryl. 'You must promise to keep this between us; my job's at stake here.'

The promise was promised and they took a seat at the spare table. The grandfather clock struck five. Nicole's hands trembled, tinkling the diamond bracelet, moving it slightly up her arm. This was noted by Stuart. There had to be a way of making her *so* nervous that her shaking would cause the bracelet to rise even higher up and reveal the alleged suicide scar that he was so desperate to see. This was all the fault of Thomas. A woman should not have to suffer with nerves like this. A woman like Nicole needed a sensitive man. He rubbed his black armband. Someone who cared about animals.

'Are you and Thomas close?' he asked, pouring milk into her coffee, stirring in the creamy whirlpool.

'What do you think? We're getting married. What *is* all this about, Stuart?'

'You're *not* the only woman he's got.' Stuart flashed her his look. The one he'd seen Paul McKenna do on TV. The 'empty your heart to me' look. 'Some men need more than one woman. In Thomas's case, he needs two. You for functions, ballroom dances, to look good on his arm and, let's call her Ms X. Ms X for sexual entertainment.'

'Don't be so ridiculous. Thomas is a perfect gentleman. He's the one person I could lay all of Daddy's money on that he wouldn't have an affair. You're making this all up.'

Stuart nodded. 'For sure. For sure. You would think that. You don't see the Thomas that I see. The one who walked out today with a woman. Ms X? I mentioned her earlier? The one who sat in his Porsche and drove out of the grounds with your Thomas beside her.' He sighed. 'Not such a perfect gentleman after all, hey?'

Words have a way of meaning different things depending on who says them. And more importantly *why* they say them. Stuart was here for one reason only – jealousy. He'd read about the importance of gaining trust with prospective suicidals from one of his library books called *The Edge (Don't Push Them Over It)*. And what better way of gaining trust than by telling Nicole the truth? The truth about her lying, deceiving, philandering fiancé. And in Stuart's experience, it was never too long after you'd gained a woman's trust that you gained permission to screw her. Maybe after Nicole had experienced a real man, she wouldn't be able to resist boasting to the other waitresses how godly Stuart was in bed. Shut them up finally. Stop their drooling and fantasizing over rich-boy Thomas.

Words have a way of meaning different things depending on who says them. Except for one word . . .

'*Adulterer*,' Stuart stated clearly. 'Your Thomas is an adulterer. A sneaky one mind, but aren't they all?' He had expected silence in return and knew that now was the time to grab her hand and stroke it like a cat. 'I can tell you're in shock. Don't worry, Stu-pot's here.' He felt the delicate texture of her skin – skin that hadn't done an ounce of work in its life. 'Were you looking forward to marrying him?'

She pulled her hand away and picked a mobile phone from her handbag. 'I'll just ask him. Maybe you misread the situation.'

'No! You need to hear the whole story.' He shook his head in disgust and tutted. 'And, Nicole, I'm surprised at you. You *never*, *ever* let a man know you know. You don't do that, Jesus Christ, you catch him out and collect the evidence. Or he'll wriggle his way off the hook like the maggot he is. Like he did to you just the other day in fact. The eye of the tiger, Nicole, eye of the tiger. Let Stu-boy explain.'

Amongst the chattering guests, stressed staff and ringing phones, a subtle tune weaved its way round the room like smoke. Background music requested by a certain commis chef named Stuart. The theme tune to *M*A*S*H* – 'Suicide is Painless' – eased its way out of the ceiling speakers on repeat. Nicole, unaware of the significance, listened with an ever-cooling heart as Stuart told his tale, while tapping away to the music with a teaspoon.

The details were quite incriminating for Thomas. Stuart explained how the real reason why Thomas had been covered in water that day Nicole confronted him had nothing to do with a window cleaner's bucket, but had everything to do with a flask of

Ganges water being chucked over him by a very pretty Indian woman. Ms X. The very same woman who Thomas had invited into his office earlier today. The very same woman who had jumped into Thomas's Porsche this afternoon. And what's more, the pair of them hadn't been seen since.

Ms X had a lot to answer for. But not nearly as much as Thomas. Who, if things turned out the way Stuart was describing, might well find he was Mr Ex himself. Mr Ex Fiancé to Nicole.

'As you can see, Nicole, I have just relayed information that could see me fired. I'm only telling you this because I know what a hard time you had last year.' He stared openly at her wrist. 'And the last thing you need is a false marriage.' He rubbed his black armband. 'I too know pain, Nicole, it gets us all in the end.'

'Well, thank you for telling me, Stuart. You have my word that your name will stay out of this. I know how much your job means to you. And I would appreciate it, if you hear anything else, to discreetly let me know.' She patted his hand. 'Would you by any chance have any idea where this Ms X lives? No, I don't suppose you know that, do you?'

Stuart grinned. One, because she was touching his hand. And two, because he knew exactly where this Ms X lived. Cheryl had jotted it down in the Reception diary for Thomas's suit invoice. 'Give me five minutes, I'll get shot of those spuds, and then I'll go and fetch her address for you. Her name's Marina, by the way.' Stuart headed to the counter, wondering which boxer shorts he would wear on their first night of passion – if she was fortunate, they would be clean.

Nicole felt her heart race. Fight or flight? The adrenalin was pumping through her like a Spartan fighter's.

Why would God take Thomas away from her after already taking Lester? She felt the itchy scar beneath her bracelet with her fingers. The four-inch gash that made her feel ugly. A deformity of her own making. If God had wanted Nicole to die that day, then why had Thomas come in the nick of time to save her in the hall upstairs?

No, God didn't want her to die, he just wanted her to suffer.

Chapter Nineteen

When mayonnaise was first spotted in a Fenworth supermarket, no one knew what to do with it. Was it a cheese? Or some sort of ice cream to be eaten warm, or maybe it was an expensive sauce to be added sparingly to chips. The day Spit the Dog was seen advertising it on TV – 'Don't save it for the salads' – the news spread quickly. Mayo was the new salad cream. Before long the use of mayo had reached epidemic proportions. Mayonnaise had been given the title of the Fenworth Caviar. Consequently, whenever a customer asked Marina, Emily or Perv Bazzer, 'What in jumping gypsies is a mayonnaise special?' it was immediately obvious that the customer was an out-of-towner. Everyone in Fenworth knew what a mayonnaise special was. Two slices of bread filled with mayonnaise.

So, when Emily was seen walking up Fairground Road, known locally as Baghdad Britain, heading home with a huge tin of Hellman's Mayonnaise under each arm, mouths salivated with jealousy. From behind the cracks of boarded-up houses, envious eyes registered gold in the neighbourhood. The white creamy gold.

Emily staggered under the weight of five-hundred sandwich fillings. If Perv Bazzer wasn't going to put his greasy hand in the till to hand over today's wage, then she'd pay herself. Life was a cruel business sometimes. But working on a Sunday for nothing was a mug's game. And Emily might be a lot of things, she thought, taking a quick breather outside a house with a rubber lawn, where used car tyres covered the whole garden, but she was no mug.

'And talking of mugs,' she said out loud to herself. 'Here's one now.'

A brand new red Porsche flew past, its windscreen wipers set on maximum in preparation for the drive through Fenworth High Street, where gobbing on expensive cars had become the latest craze. Emily shook her head; the driver was obviously lost, and it was a good job that whoever it was hadn't driven through last month when the craze had involved hurling white sun-dried doggy poops.

Home at last, and just before Emily climbed the stairs to her flat, she marvelled at Hilda's dedication, or, more accurately, her cunningness at car boot sales. By the front door was a green Safeway's box filled with mostly crap items. A vase (chipped), two porcelain wall ducks (third one missing), various 78″ records (broken), a framed black and white picture of a woman (name unknown), a hot-water bottle (leaking), and a bone-China plate (worth £3000).

Hilda's thrill was watching the car-booters pass her stall by, sneering at the 'worthless' junk on her pasting table, not realizing that they were only fifty-pence away from a fortune. The buzz she got was better than any prescription drug. So near and yet . . . so far.

As she entered the flat, the smell of garlic grabbed Emily's hand and led her to the kitchen. Marina stood over the stove, a ring of fire beneath a bubbling mixture of Indian spices belching out smells that were strong enough to mess up Emily's middle-ear, ruin her balance and send her toppling down to the begging position on the floor – placing the mayonnaise tins beside her like temple posts.

'Please feed me, Marina, it smells gorgeous,' Emily said, her head bowed in mock prayer. 'I'm starving.'

'I don't think you understand the consequences of eating my mum's famous chicken dish.' Marina screwed back the jar lid. The special blend of spices in the saucepan before her glowed a reddy-brown and hinted at fiery, saucy flavours within. Each visit to Watford had Marina returning with a new recipe of Indian magic. Marina eyed Emily. 'You do know that even one mouthful of this will keep the boys away for weeks?'

Emily stood up from her prayer and tapped her back pocket. 'That's what Tic Tacs were invented for: curry breath. Anyway, true love bypasses the senses. Except the eyes, of course. It's no good smelling like a rose bush and singing like an angel when you look like Nosferatu The Vampyre's uglier brother, is it?' She sidled up to Marina and sniffed the saucepan. 'Yum yum fill my tum.'

Marina admired Emily's flat stomach. You couldn't

really describe it as a 'tum'. It wouldn't take more than a spoonful to fill that tiny waist. Unless, Marina raised her eyes to Emily's enormous breasts, unless she stored her food in those two conversation starters. They do say cows have two stomachs. But Marina didn't like to think of Emily as a cow just because she was having such a crap day. It wasn't fair on their friendship. It was hardly Emily's fault that Thomas was engaged.

Cheap wine filled cheap mugs and was drunk by two . . . women. It was early Sunday evening down Fairground Road. Marina and Emily discussed their weekends as they stared out at the unkempt gardens round the back, enjoying each other's gossip while dinner simmered obediently. They worked their way steadily through the four categories of gossip. D = famous people. C = family and friends. B = ex-boyfriends and lovers. And now to class A = oneself. Or, in this case, themselves.

'Shall I go first?' Emily didn't wait for an answer. 'Firstly, and don't throw a wobbly until you know why I did it, but I went to see Thomas yesterday. Thomas Harding.'

'Right, I'm listening.'

'He's gorgeous. Anyway, I'll come back to his looks later. I asked him out on a date, while you were up in Watford.'

'Just a quick check, best friend, but am I allowed to throw a wobbly yet?' Marina asked, playing the game, but feeling the desperate need to slap Emily round the face. 'I'm getting instructions from Shiva to wallop you one.'

'Just wait. If you only hear half the story, then I'll

look like a bitch.' Emily gulped a mouthful of wine. 'You *are* my best friend and I would never betray you, but, Marina, it was you who broke the oath. You said that we were identical twin sisters and all decisions regarding men should be discussed together.'

'So?' Marina could feel energy building in her slapping hand again, but this time to slap her own face. Emily had made a point. Feebly, she spoke, 'I say that to all my identical twin sisters.'

'*You* sneakily threw the Ganges water over him and then declared Thomas as your man. That was low. I would never have picked up a bottle of Thames water and thrown it over him and declared him mine, would I? Not once did you think to ask me whether my lustfulness for him was serious. Not once did you consider whether I wanted him – come on, Marina, you *knew* I wanted him. Anyway, it doesn't matter now, he turned me down. And his reasons were shocking.' Emily paused. 'Sickening even. I don't think Mr Harding is all he makes out he is. Far from it, in fact.'

A brief silence as the two of them stared out of the window. The ginger cat, Pinstripes, wandered the back gardens, looking up at the odd window, deciding when to come back home to Hilda – it wasn't so much Hilda's face that Pinstripes couldn't abide, just her breath. Pinstripes spotted the girls watching him, their glum faces imprisoned behind the glass. He raised his tail, sprayed a dustbin, then staggered off – spent.

More cheap wine was poured. This could turn out to be one of those 'gloves off' evenings, where minds were emptied as quickly as bottles. Men could be sickening in lots of ways. Some should come supplied with buckets. So what made Thomas Harding sickening? It certainly wasn't his looks, money, charm, smile, body, hotel, car, voice, eyes, sexiness, humour, intelligence, ambition, style, class. No, it was none of those things. What made Thomas Harding sickening was . . .

'He's a racist, Marina. An upper-class, toffee-nosed, stuck-up, la-di-da, hoity-toity, still living in the past racist.' Emily picked at the wine bottle label with her fingernail. 'The things he said to me were sick. To look at him you would never think that—'

Marina interrupted. 'Will you just tell me what he said.'

'Sit tight. Don't wet your pants. It's important that you hear this at the correct speed. If I blurt it all out, you're likely to feel hurt.' Emily stared up at the kitchen bulb and dramatically declared, 'And God knows, Marina, you're going to hurt enough as it is. He told me – and this was after turning me down and telling me he was engaged – he said, if we were the last two women on this planet that he wouldn't sleep with us. At first I thought he must be joking or drugged-up but he said it deadpan. No smile, no laughter. He was serious, Marina. The last two on earth and he wouldn't sleep with us. He's sick. Maybe it's because we are identical.'

Marina assessed Emily. Her body seemed to have developed Tourette's syndrome, nervously jerking and fidgeting, eyeballs flicking from left to right. She watched as the bottle label was curled into a sticky ball and flicked against the window. Emily was anxious about something. And Emily became anxious when Emily lied.

'Tell me the truth, best friend, twin sister. What did he *really* say? Including the racist remarks this time.' Marina rose to stir the curry. 'I'm not going to be hurt. Because I'm over him.'

Treading softly over the colour issue had always been like walking over a minefield for Emily. Brown – Bang! Ethnic – Bang! Not Welcome – Bang! Paki – Thermonuclear Explosion BANG!!! Emily loved Marina as a friend and had seen her upset sometimes over snide remarks. Silly little men, mostly, showing off to other silly little men. Napkins Sandwich Bar was a classic example. Certain customers, who had asked Emily on the sly if it was possible NOT to be served by the Indian girl, the brown, ethnic, not-welcome Paki girl, had given Emily a glimpse of the cruel world that white people sometimes don't realize exists. Marina would never find out which customers had asked for those special favours, and most likely those same customers would never find out who had spat in their coleslaw, or who saved up dead creepy-crawlies off the floor, blended the little blighters together, then added them to their favourite Gentlemen's Relish sandwiches. Emily often wondered why racist white people assumed that all white people felt the same way. One thing was for sure, though, Emily thought one day, watching Mr Saunders just outside the shop window munch away on his six-centipedes-and-a-spider sandwich, those racist white people are just like the slitty-eyed bunch – they'll eat anything.

But did Marina need to know what Thomas had said? Was it a mark of true friendship to upset a friend in the name of honesty? What if Marina still had feelings for this Thomas even though she was 'over him'? Was it fair then? Or was it more unfair if she left Marina to still dream about this Thomas when in reality this Thomas was nothing more than a nightmare to someone like Marina. Someone who took her colour very seriously.

Emily decided to tell the truth; how she understood it. 'Okay, he said that he wouldn't bother sleeping with you *even* if you were the last person on earth because you were brown. He said cultures and classes shouldn't mix and he was sorry but—' Emily saw Marina's expression fall. She took her hand. 'Forget him. He's not nice. He talks down to people and thinks his intellectual brain is superior. He thinks that belittling people gives him the edge.' Emily wondered if Marina had been dissuaded yet. 'Above all that, he's a racist.'

Marina attempted a joke. 'Not raciest, then?'

'Racist, Marina. He discriminates.'

But Marina had heard loud and clear. Men can be sickening in many ways. Being racist topped Marina's sick chart. Despising someone for being a different skin tone or race. Changing lanes in the supermarket because they didn't want to stand behind someone of colour. Paying the exact amount of money for their tinned chunks of pineapple to the Asian cashier because they didn't want to accept any change – change that had been touched by non-white skin. Change that had been contaminated.

Marina smiled wryly. Oh how nice it would be if people *could* change. Somewhere along the line something had to have gone wrong for people to have grown up hating each other for being different. Maybe evolution took a wrong turning somewhere –

between *Homo erectus* and *Homo sapiens* it threw in *Homo discriminates*. A get-out clause for humanity. When things are going wrong in your life, find someone to blame. If you've just lost your job, look out of the window, spot the nearest Asian and blame that person. If crime has soared in your neighbourhood, look out of the window – if you still have windows – and blame the nearest gang of non-whites. Perhaps evolution got it wrong somewhere. Maybe it's not only the strongest who survive, but also the nastiest. Let us hope not, prayed Marina.

But Marina used to justify the thinking behind racism, if thinking was what it was; she used to believe that being racist ultimately meant being thick. No-hopers with no brains. People who had not only been swindled in the queue of kindness but also in the queue of IQ. The losers of this world. So how would that explain Thomas?

Thomas was intelligent beyond the norm. An Oxford grad with a future. Someone who was going places. Marina considered the painful facts. Life was weird. She'd heard of hostages falling in love with the hostage takers. Or relatives of murder victims falling in love with murderers. Could it be possible for an Indian woman to fall in love with a racist?

No way, she thought. Something very apparent was happening in her mind and nothing could undo the chemical process. Her love for him was changing to hate. A reversal of nature. Like a sweet butterfly returning to its cocoon and reforming as the nasty maggot. Thomas Harding's life as a hotelier with a clean-cut image, excellent public relations, and a healthy list of supporters, was now irrevocably tarnished.

Dinner was served on platter plates while Evanescence's 'Bring Me To Life' played from a tape. The dish was heaving with chillies. A jug of cool water waited on call-out duty. Marina had often told Emily how her parents used to punish Zaine and herself for swearing by making them eat raw chillies. Pretty ironic, really, as the chillies made them swear even more and with greater vigour. In fact, the C word had never been heard in the house until Zaine was forced to eat a Birds Eye chilli for saying the word 'fuck'. Funny days.

Today was just as funny. Between munching and eye watering, Marina went on to explain to Emily that she, too, had been to see Thomas today. She explained his odd behaviour regarding India and how *now* it was all making sense. The Taj Mahal screen saver, the Indian honeymoon, the references to 'skin colour'. Marina coldly relayed how Thomas had given her a lift home. She explained it all. She even mentioned how upset she had been when Thomas mentioned his wedding plans. Now, it was Emily's turn to explain further.

'I've accepted I'm a bimbo, Marina, but this is the age of the new-age woman. We don't wait for men to ask us out any more. We pick 'em fresh rather than wait for the mouldy ones to ask us out.'

'I can't believe the nerve of you, Emily,' Marina said, amazed still at her friend's forwardness. 'You just asked Thomas out! Weren't you even slightly embarrassed?'

Emily thought back to the cringe-making moment. 'Look at me. This isn't really me, Marina. The real me died of shame back in the hotel. As soon as he said no, my heart stopped beating in this world. This is just my aura. My afterlife.' She swallowed a glassful of water, almost panting with the meal's heat. 'I know it sounds big-headed but I honestly thought I would be having bondage sex with him right now. All-night sex tied up in one of his spare rooms. I'd even packed an overnight bag. You should feel the weight of the chains.'

They both laughed. Thomas had turned out to be a right shocker. There was a lesson to be learned there. Never try to calculate a man with facts and figures – how much he earns, how good-looking he is, how well-spoken he is – because if you try to calculate a man, you'll find in most cases that, ninety-nine per cent of the time, he cooks the books.

It was hard to be lonely when you owned a hotel. Thomas nodded to the many guests in Reception (a home-coming party every day in the Regency) not even remembering the drive back here from ghastly Fenworth. With the car on auto pilot, he had let his mind wander, angry and insulted at Marina's parting comment. Where did she get off treating him like that? It was at times like this that he wished he was a lowlife racist, then he would have no end of insults on hand to console himself. Like, 'Get back on the plane and go back to where you come from, goat breeders.' Or, 'You lot are all the same.' And finally, the crème de la crème, 'Paki!' But he was not a racist, and he was not a lowlife. He was, in Marina's eyes, a pompous man who needed a good butt kicking. How dare she?

Thomas habitually checked all corners of Reception. Ah, a lovely surprise, Nicole was here. But he knew that already as her Merc was sitting in his car parking space. It had been four long days since he'd last seen her. And four days can play havoc with a man's memory. God, he'd forgotten how beautiful she was. He bent down to kiss her, but she withdrew sharply.

He quickly sniffed his breath – passable – then whispered, 'Some wench has just parked in my space out there. If I get my hands on her, I'll—'

'You've got lipstick on your face, Tom, darling.' Her eyes rested on his.

He sat down opposite her. 'That will be my mother, back from Italy. She said to say how sorry they were to have missed you. You look amazing, by the way. *Stupenda.*'

Nicole continued to study his face, her eyebrows raised uncertainly. 'Thank you. Back to the lipstick. Does your mother make a habit of using two colours on her lips? Brown and pink? And, this may sound slightly sarcastic because I mean it to, but does she kiss you with one set of lips, then rush out to the nearest clinic for collagen injections, rush back, then give you a kiss with the bloated lips?' She paused. 'Thomas, you have two colours of lipstick on your face and the lips are two different sizes.'

An echoing silence. Thomas's brain fluid was having a drought. He had found over the years that there were delicate topics that needed the soundproof touch. This was the first one he could remember that involved Nicole.

Nicole continued. 'I take it that the pink is your mother's, so it leaves the question of the brown. Who has been kissing you with brown lipstick, Thomas, darling? And if you joke about this, I will slash you with the knife I have in my bag.' She smiled meekly. 'And *that* was not a joke, by the way.'

And didn't Thomas know it.

Marina *was* a jinx. There was no doubt about it. Right now, however, he didn't need a jinx he needed a genie. Someone or something to wish away this situation. He couldn't even blame this on Stuart. This was all his own doing. Why did he ever lie about the Ganges water? Why didn't he wipe Marina's lipstick marks from his face? (Her sweet thank-you kiss, earlier in his office, could now be his downfall.) And more importantly, why was he about to lie now?

He took her hand in his. 'Nicole, babe, it was Cheryl who kissed me. I gave her a small raise and she just thanked me with a few pecks. That's all. No big deal, let's not blow this all out of proportion. You know how much I love you.' Thomas and Nicole both looked across the floor to see Cheryl working hard, quite happy, humming away to 'Suicide is Painless' in her own little world with, not pink, or even brown, but bright Tango *orange* lipstick on. Oh dear.

Nicole did her best to smile. 'Well, that solves the mystery of who you have been kissing today. My next question is not about *who* so much, but *where*?' Acting dippy wasn't in her nature, but if it helped squeeze out more lies, and ultimately more truths, then an Oscar wouldn't be beyond her. 'Where have you been? You told me that this Sunday would be devoted to paperwork. That was the sole reason you gave as to why you couldn't attend Mummy's Sunday lunch. So what paperwork was so important that it needed you to take a drive, Thomas, darling?'

A strapping ginger-bearded guest, kitted out in kilt

and sporran, arrived at Thomas's and Nicole's table and sat down. The token tartan guest. Every hotel had to have one. A true Scotsman.

He spoke with his Highland drawl. 'Thanks for arranging the bells, Mr Harding, it made the McIntyre family's day. A real canny idea indeed. Gives this place a certain . . .' He massaged his beard as if he might find the word hidden in there amongst the Sunday roast's debris. He found the word. 'Ah yes, a certain, *panache*.' From beneath his green-chequered kilt he pulled out a small wad (of notes) and proceeded to count, licking his counting thumb in between, and then handed the money to Thomas. 'Forty pounds even.'

'For the bells?' Thomas queried, not having the foggiest what the man was referring to. 'Sorry, Mr McIntyre, you've lost me. The bells—' He was interrupted by a sharp needling pain in his ankle delivered by Nicole's shoe. Either Nicole was practising a primitive form of acupuncture, or it was her way of saying, 'We are in the middle of a private conversation, get rid of the ginger bonce, or I will.' Thomas concluded it was the latter. 'Grab yourself a free drink in the bar and just say . . .' The kilted man was gone before Thomas could finish the sentence. The Flying Scotsman.

Nicole pressed on. 'So, where were you?'

He sighed. 'I went for a quick drive to clear my head. It's hardly the same thing as having a five-hour lunch with your family, is it? I needed a bit of silence to sort out those complicated figures. That's all. Nothing more than that.' Thomas stood up, pulling her up with him. 'Come on, we haven't seen each other for days. I've missed you, let's not spoil it with suspicion.'

'You're right.' She wrapped her arms round him and added a third colour of lipstick to his palette – deep plum. 'Why don't we go upstairs and forget about your paperwork today.'

He took her hand as they walked through the Reception, stopping to discreetly ask Cheryl to *never* play the theme tune to *M*A*S*H* again, and chuckled to himself at how smoothly he had talked his way out of the mess.

On the bed, Nicole pushed herself against Thomas. She dreamily looked into his eyes. 'We should get out more ourselves, you know? Take trips, see places together.' Thomas smiled, nuzzling into her neck. 'I just love being with you, Tom. Why don't we go somewhere soon?'

'Anywhere; you name it and we're there, consider it done,' he said, imagining her naked, on top of Mont Blanc, or naked, beneath the gushing, foamy water of Victoria Falls, or naked, in the cockpit of Airforce One while Bush's World War Three was in progress, or naked, on a . . . He smiled to himself. Why leave it to the imagination when – he unhooked the two straps keeping up her dress – right before him was the real thing, almost naked, in just her purple, skimpy, lacy underwear? Nicole topped any list of any fantasy (bar the one with six lesbian dominatrix sex goddesses from the planet Zarg, of course – every spotty schoolboy's bread and butter fantasy). Thomas kissed her stomach then said, 'A museum is good if it's intellectual stimulation you're after, or if it's activity, what about bungee jumping? But if it's sexual,' he ran his tongue underneath her knickers, 'if it's sexual, I suggest a good, respectable, five-star hotel with a sturdy bed and soundproof walls.'

'Not the Regency, then.' She giggled. 'No, I was thinking more outdoors. You know how much I love yachts. Why don't you take me to a *marina* somewhere. It might be fun.' She watched his face. So perfect, so handsome. 'We could go sailing.' So guilty?

'A marina, sounds great.' He pulled off her G-string, barely digesting a word. 'Sailing, can't wait. Just call me Shackleton . . . Shagging Shackleton.'

Having sex with Thomas that evening had been hard even though Thomas had been *extremely* hard. Her orgasms tainted by the fear of betrayal. What if Stuart was right? He had seemed sure enough. And what if this road led to places she didn't want to go? Like a T-junction – like separation.

Nicole lay naked next to Thomas in the failing sunlight, her worried eyes staring up at the ceiling. She wouldn't allow *anyone* to separate them. No matter what.

Especially a money-grabbing trollop from Fenworth.

Chapter Twenty

Once you've experienced home-made Italian ice cream, then Mr Softy just won't do. Once you've experienced a multiple orgasm, then a solitary orgasm just won't do. And once you've seen how the other half live and dreamt of what having a relationship with a snobby man could be like, a Fenworth man just won't do.

It was Tuesday evening, two days since 'The Thomas Losing His Crown Affair' drama. Marina had been busy making Emily an 'office environment' tape in her bedroom. Recording the sounds of landline and mobile phone rings on a cassette, plus various versions of the office 'giggle'. The plan was simple: next time Emily was asked by a man what she did for a living, instead of saying she filled sandwiches, she would reply, 'I am an office group leader.' Upon receiving a call from the potential boyfriend, the tape would be switched on and the office environment would be created. Her chances of jumping off the slag ladder and climbing the respectable shag ladder would surely be increased manyfold.

After finishing Emily's tape, Marina did what she promised herself she wouldn't do: she forced herself to look at the picture of Thomas on the wall. Still up there. Still staring at her while she slept. Still gorgeous in the extreme. What kind of mad Indian woman keeps a picture of a racist up on her wall? Do Jews keep pictures of Hitler? Do vegetarians keep pictures of pig carcasses? Did Saddam Hussein keep pictures of a poodle? Marina felt as if Thomas were a head cold, stifling her mind, clogging her thinking. A raw feeling of betrayal had set in. A man with a privileged upbringing was showing signs of a man brought up on the moral breadline. Marina hated this man, but she hated to hate this man.

Shiva waited patiently, his cool energy at rest, an open book of answers – if only Marina knew what to ask. If only her gran were here now, to tell her what to do. Unfortunately, Gran was gone, floating in the other universe, her life-force strong in a new heaven – she hoped, or waiting in line for reincarnation. Marina could almost feel a sense of betrayal if she were to give up on Thomas so easily. If she gave up, then the Ganges water would have meant nothing. Which in turn would have meant her gran's words meant nothing. And in a life as difficult as this one, good advice is hard to come by. Marina would not give up on Thomas just yet, even if only out of respect for her gran.

The evening light brushed the street outside with a dusky yellow. If one listened hard at this time of night, the cheery sound of babies crying, dogs barking and sirens wailing could be heard. The beauty of Fenworth had to be somewhere. Marina watched a man stagger along the pavement just below their flat, bend over and barf the remains of his lunch into a once-healthy bush. There had to be beauty here somewhere, Marina thought; oh please, get me out of Fenworth. It had turned out to be such a bad choice.

Marina wanted to feel proud of her choices in life. Her job, her house, and especially her man. She would love to have a partner who she could talk freely to. A man who understood the important things in life. Marina could count on two fingers the number of men with whom she felt totally at home. Her brother and her father.

It would be great to add a third, she thought wistfully, nodding her head sadly at Thomas's picture. Oh why, oh why, did you have to turn out to be such an arsehole? Marina slumped back on her bed, closed her eyes and waited for the inevitable knock on the door from Emily, who should be close to finishing her bath by now. To prevent going stir crazy in the flat, to save each other from going bonkers with claustrophobia, the girls would sometimes get ready in each other's rooms. It gave that important feeling of extra space, especially as they didn't have a living room.

There came the bang on the door. Marina kept her eyes closed. 'Come in, Fenworth Tart.'

Hilda shuffled in and stood at the entrance. What a picture! Varicose veins mapped her legs like an *A-Z*, a thousand rollers pierced her thinning hair and a green surgical mask covered her weathered face. If there was life after death, then this was what it must surely look like. As for death after life – then this, definitely, was what it smelled like. A mixture of rose perfume, moth balls and dried skin.

Marina recognized the scent of the deceased and abruptly sat up. 'Oh, sorry, Hilda, I thought you were Emily.' She spotted, amongst other things, the letters held in her landlady's hand. Surely not more bills? 'Garlic's a bit strong today. We cooked Indian the other night. Sorry about that. Are those my letters?'

'Two letters, MaryANNA, one for you and the other for Emily.' Hilda's muffled voice just about made it through the mask. 'You don't have to worry, though, I haven't steamed them open. Both are postmarked from Watford, sent yesterday no less, first class. Must be important, I would imagine, if they are sending them first class. That's the thrill about letters, you don't know what's inside until you've opened them up.' She held out the envelopes. 'Beats me as to why you've both got letters all of a sudden. Not done anything untoward lately, have you?'

Marina walked across the room and accepted the mail from Hilda's outstretched hand. 'Thanks. We can't help being popular. I'll see you out.' She gently shoved Hilda on to the landing and closed the door.

Jumping back on her bed, Marina ripped open the mauve-coloured envelope. Normally she opened her post with a certain amount of fear: another bill, another demand, more debt. But this was obviously a return from their Hit List. She was right. The letter came from an old school acquaintance, a woman by the name of Becky Anderson.

Gluing her eyes to the paper, Marina savoured every written word. She had been exonerated.

Complete forgiveness for a minor incident involving baking powder and a cake competition. Becky's cake-making prowess was legendary. She won prizes yearly. Until year four, that is, when it all went so terribly wrong.

Marina had wanted that cake trophy *so* badly. Sick and tired of being kneaded into second place, she had tipped a full tub of baking powder into Becky's mixture. The cake had risen like the Tower of Babel, changed to the Leaning Tower of Pisa, then flopped, turning lastly into a burning, smoking, cruddy mess that nearly cost the school the price of a cooker – *The Towering Inferno*. The distraught Becky could be seen after last bell cleaning the bottom of the oven with a wire brush while Marina, who now had her heart set on *Junior Master Chef*, could be seen showing off her first-prize trophy just outside the school gates. It had proved to Marina that sometimes you could have your cake and eat it too.

But could you? The whole reason that Marina and Emily had been forced to look for ways to improve their karma was because it seemed that you could not have your cake and eat it after all. What goes around comes around.

Becky's letter cheered Marina up considerably. A positive response to a positive idea. Not only did she feel better about today, but she felt better about her past. The only thing left to sort out was her future.

One more read-through of Becky's letter and Marina allowed herself a small smile. This was a good start to getting her life balance back on target. Keep correcting her karma, keep thinking good and acting better, and surely, with the help of Shiva and her own positive attitude, her man would come to claim her.

Her eyes met those of Thomas staring down from the wall. She sneered, 'Loser.'

The undergraduate studying French at St Hilda's, Oxford, stood on the table and dropped her lacy 36DD bra down by Thomas's wine glass. Her mile-long legs were whipping up a frenzy among many of the onlookers. Graceful moves, sleek and energetically sensual, offered glimpses of heaven. Her two motives were as see-through as her knickers. Firstly, she wanted men to desire her, to fantasize, to want her. And secondly, she wanted them to pay. Amongst the throbbing music and throbbing penises, a meeting of huge significance was taking place. Thomas, by now, was becoming sick of nipple tassels being thrust in his face. But what did he expect from a venue chosen by Eton Boy Terence, who had requested the rendezvous at VooDoo Dolls?

VooDoo Dolls, situated just beside the calming waters of Knight's Armour Canal, was a bit of an enigma to some. The entertainment on offer was pure sleaze, but the members were upper-class rich boys. A crazy club catering for that rebellious feeling posh boys miss out on. From birth to boarding school they hibernate under Mummy and Daddy's protection, never facing the real world, blocking out the underprivileged people like the glare of a raging sun. VooDoo Dolls gave the rich boys the buzz of non-conforming without disobeying Mummy and Daddy. What happened inside VooDoo Dolls was for VooDoo eyes only. *Members Only* had a different meaning here.

Thomas, dressed in his Yohji Yamamoto jeans and burgundy Fendi shirt, sat across from Terence, who was never out of a suit; they'd been discussing their shared history while drinking a bottle of top-notch white wine. Teasing lights flickered off the naked women dancing on the tables. Cleverly structured sentences were just about useless here with the intense beat blaring from the speakers. So talk was kept to the point; pure and cut to the minimum.

A bit like their next topic.

'Take this, go to the Gents'; inside is a small sample.' Terence slid his wallet between the dancer's ankles. 'If it's been a while, my dear friend, I would suggest waiting until you get back home. It will knock you for six.'

Thomas sipped his wine. 'And this stuff is pure? I heard the same thing said about Lester's batch and look what happened to him.'

Terence picked a toothpick from a small dish on the table. He chewed it while he chewed over Thomas's comment. Finally he spoke. 'Lester was a coke head, a druggie. I hate to use a pun in here, Thomas, my man, but he needed a good smack.' The toothpick rolled across his bottom lip. 'Lester didn't like to be told what to do. *His* body, *his* rules. You know he nearly lost the end of his penis once?'

Thomas shook his head. No, he didn't know; and, judging by the temporary stall in tassel spinning, nor did the dancer listening in. Apparently, in an attempt to prove to a group of friends the amount of control he had over his manhood, Lester organized a stunt: coked-up, with an erection, he was tied to the top of a lorry and driven at speed towards a low bridge. He had planned, with mind control alone, to lower his willy just before he reached the bridge. Unfortunately coke left little room for mind control and Lester clipped the bridge at 20 m.p.h. and spent the next three weeks in a top Harley Street clinic hoping he was still a man and praying that his medical insurance covered 'whacking his todger against railway bridges'.

'How Lester managed to win Nicole's heart is beyond me.' Terence began his Eton-boy giggles. 'Then, who am I kidding? We all know Nicole is a headcase. You can't really lay the blame on her, though, my dear friend. I mean, anyone born into the Newton-Harrington family must be short of a few marbles.'

'No one's completely sane, Terence, you should know that better than anyone.' Thomas smiled, thinking back to the poster Terence had erected in St John's Beehives many years ago.

In Pursuit of Science
Watch Scholar Terence Miles Bramble
Perform His Own Colonic Irrigation.
Next Tuesday 7.00 p.m. Inside Baylie Chapel.
Seats £35.00 (includes glass of champagne)

Insane or sick, it didn't really matter, the event was a complete sell-out for the chapel and a complete empty out for Terence. Thomas and his best mate Nathan had cheered the loudest, demanding an encore. But Terence had given it all in this one-off performance.

And talking of performances, that of the girl

dancing on the table could only be described now as lacklustre. Thomas stared up at the topless brunette, more eavesdropping than panty dropping at the moment. 'How much would I have to pay you to leave us alone?'

'Three hundred. As long as you promise to stay away from bridges.' She crouched down to Thomas with her hand out. 'You are temptation itself. We could go private if you want a bit of seclusion.'

Terence interrupted. 'He only goes for blondes. Quite shallow, if you ask me.'

Taking Thomas's money, she stepped off the table, kissed his forehead and sashayed away mumbling, 'Shallow? And what do you call this place?'

How Terence could look so at home in a club like this, was beyond Thomas. And yet, maybe he looked so at home because he felt so at home. He marvelled at how the fat-bellied men's faces would light up with pure energized ego when a naked limb planted itself near their goggle eyes. Didn't they realize that the women here wouldn't give them the time of day if it wasn't for their money?

Terence returned to the conversation. 'Still got a thing about blondes, I see. You have kept to your guns, haven't you? A man of principle, I like that. I don't think I can remember ever seeing you without a blonde on your arm.' He plucked out another toothpick. 'Let's hope that Scandinavia keeps churning them out. I wouldn't want one of my old chums to go short.'

Thomas laughed. 'I've got Nicole, she's more than enough.' He paused to take a gulp of wine. 'We were discussing Lester? The night he died. I know you know what kind of state he was in that evening. Is there some way you could tell me if Lester was *using* that night, without compromising your loyalty to him? I mean—'

'Listen here, my good friend,' Terence interrupted. '*I* supplied Lester that night. See over there.' He pointed to a table near a fountain where two jugs of water were being eternally emptied by two Japanese women figurines. 'Within the space of one hour he had snorted six lines off that very table. That was just the warm-up. He could hardly walk, let alone drive. I tried to hail him a limo but, you guessed it, nobody told Lester how coked-out he was. "As safe as Schumacher." His very words.' Terence shook his head, a gleam in his eye. 'The last words I ever heard from that daft git.' His voice dipped, sad recollections of a good friend. 'As safe as Senna more like.'

The two lost themselves in memories of university life, recalling the brash confidence of living amongst some of the best brains in the country. If the world was going to be made better in some way – then it was this group of men who would lead the country into battle. If all these top-quality boffs couldn't make a difference to the world, then God help it. Thomas listened intently while Terence explained his theory of a new world order. How everything would be changing within a few years and all he needed was proof. A good conspiracy always needed proof.

And so had Thomas needed proof up until today. Proof that would, he hoped, lay Nicole's ghosts to rest. Thomas could feel the puzzle finally being solved as he tucked the small packet of cocaine in his jeans pocket. Terence had confirmed what Thomas had guessed already regarding coke-head Lester. Nicole's fears were unfounded. Her mountain of guilt was nothing but an imaginary Everest.

There was just one item needed before he could rescue Nicole from her nightmare. To rush this too early, without possessing all the evidence required, would risk her disbelieving him and falling further down that path of misery again. He couldn't let that happen. Nicole was just about the happiest he'd seen her in years. It was his job to keep her that way. But he didn't like hiding secrets from her. She didn't have the vaguest idea of where he was off to tonight. And it was a shame he'd had to leave, considering she was wearing only the vaguest of dresses when he left her. A Vivienne Westwood, no less. Far more sexy than anything that he'd seen bobbing around in VooDoo Dolls this evening.

Chapter Twenty-one

Nicole's suspicion was on steroids today. A pumped-up, hormonal frenzy of nail-biting suspicion. Thomas had had cause to vacate the hotel AGAIN, leaving her on her own with her fears. Nicole's mind had patched into a network of neurones in her brain searching for 'Indian Women'. A mini-Nicole Internet search brought up just three. Miss World 1994. Miss World 1997. And Miss World 1999. Thomas was having an affair with an Indian beauty queen, he had to be. And when she had asked him where he was off to this evening, his answer was riddled with holes. He'd said, 'Nicole, babe, I'm just meeting an old friend, you wouldn't know him: his father earns less than ten million a year. Don't wait up.'

Oh, but she would wait up. When he came through the door he would be subjected to a full body sniff. No quick showers, no sneaking on to the trusty couch, no getting away with it. If Thomas had been within erection distance of a woman tonight, then Nicole would know immediately (a woman's scent would surely attach to him at distances of less than ten inches).

Daddy had made it plain. If Thomas cheated on his baby Nicole then, make no mistake, Thomas would suffer. His hotel would disappear quicker than an Enron Director, his car would be impounded, and his life would be in tatters. Never, ever, underestimate a Newton-Harrington.

Nicole continued to remove Thomas's suits and lay them carefully on the bed. So many suits, so many pockets. Nicole had even chosen which dress she would be snooping in today: her Vivienne Westwood number, short, black and clinging. Daring and sexy like a Bond Girl. After all, even though she may not be saving the world today, she may well be saving her sanity. Even a Bond Girl needs to know if 00Bastard is being faithful. The thought of having Thomas's willy inside her just hours after being inside another woman was enough to make Nicole pick up a pair of scissors from the writing table. So deliciously sharp. So sensuously dangerous. They would glide through the designer-suit fabric so beautifully.

A mixture of Armani, Paul Smith, Gucci and D&G suits awaited a fate worse than death.

The stereo played a CD of Strauss. Nicole thought that after tonight she might well re-title the piece 'The Suit Chopping Waltz'. She began to search the pockets, her eyes on standby for tears, her fingers on standby for the scissors, her heart on standby to . . . stop.

Darkness swamped the sky outside and Nicole watched her reflection in the window. Her dress was so black in the glass that her head seemed to float like magic. The optical illusion was lost as soon as she called for Hal, the voice-activated computer, to switch the lights on full. Like her mind was switched on full. And it had to be when dealing with men. As far as Nicole knew, there was a rule of thumb when dealing with the weaker sex: to know what went through a man's mind you sometimes had to know what went through his pockets.

Nicole stamped her stiletto angrily on the wooden floor. Thomas must have an empty mind; his pockets were mostly deserted. An unfamiliar feeling joined her steroid-loaded suspicion. It was hard to put into words, so much easier in actions. Nicole hurled half of Thomas's suits across the room. A cocktail of dejection, anger, sadness and frustration let loose. It was almost as if she wanted to find out he had cheated. Rather that than finding absolutely nothing. Could Thomas be one step ahead of the game? Was he watching his tracks, or, more importantly, covering them?

Suddenly she was reminded of what she loved about Thomas. His fidelity. His total commitment to one woman. He had once even volunteered to go into regression hypnotherapy to convince her of his noble intentions with women. It would be a sad slur on their relationship if it took only a few remarks from a commis chef and a couple of suspicious actions from Thomas to declare him an adulterer. It wouldn't hold up in court. The judge would ask for more evidence.

So more evidence would be gathered.

The hands on Nicole's diamond-encrusted watch said 10.00 p.m. Thomas had been gone for nearly two hours. His suits had been given the all-clear, which was suspicious in itself. Shouldn't a man have at least one item in his pockets that needed a good explanation? When she and Mummy used to snoop when Daddy was on his trips abroad, they would find a treasure trove of items hiding in his pockets. Lists of phone numbers, small hand-drawn local maps, meeting times and even Interflora receipts. Mummy refused to believe an affair was taking place, preferring to think of the evidence as booze-related, secret alcohol drops and private supplies of liquor. She ignored the Interflora flower receipts completely. Unfortunately for Daddy, she couldn't ignore the photograph of a half-dressed woman stashed away in his briefcase. Especially as the woman in question was none other than her contract bridge partner – Daphne Lillytwait-Potter, the Grand Slam Queen. And even more especially as the man in question holding the horse crop against Daphne's bare buttocks was none other than her husband – with his Sherlock Holmes shooting hat on. It didn't take a great detective to establish what they were doing, my dear Watson. Nicole saw her mother swallow great mouthfuls of pride back then, just getting on with her life, ignoring the agonizing truth. She watched her become half the woman she had been. And it was a sad pain. Nicole couldn't afford to be half a woman, she had a hard enough time being a whole one. And anyway, they say women are no good at fractions, well, they're no good at being fractions, either.

But they're masterly at interruptions, dividing up

two people – which, in a way, is sort of a fraction. Nicole wasn't too brilliant at maths, but she wasn't too bad at chemistry. When two liquids cannot mix they are said to be immiscible. When two solids cannot mix, they are said to be immutable. But when two people do not mix they are said to be incompatible. Surely a white-skinned man couldn't mix with a brown-skinned woman. The chemistry, surely, wouldn't be there. There would be no compatibility.

Nicole stood at the window, peering at the countryside out back. Apart from a sprinkling of lights randomly scattered in the hills, it was like blackout in wartime. But there were no bombers flying overhead tonight, just the shrilling siren in Nicole's heart to take cover from the fallout of the J-bomb. The Jealousy Bomb. Her imagination was taking trips to places that her parents would be ashamed of. X-rated scenes in which Thomas was undressing a beautiful Indian woman and then making love to her with more passion, more excitement and more pleasure than he'd ever experienced with her. Nicole wiped away a tear and rested her head against the cold glass. She briefly smiled as a cliché came to her rescue: Indian woman are subdued lovers. No doubt this Indian woman from Fenworth would just lie back while Thomas delivered the goods. Nicole fiddled with her engagement ring as her smile intensified. Thomas loathed the subdued lover. On their first bedroom encounter, while naked in the candlelight, Thomas had explained how he loved a noisy lover. How he hated women who were ladies in bed. How he . . . and then Nicole had jumped on top of him, thrown his head back and said, 'Shut up, bitch, this is my world now. I'm taking you to paradise.'

After drawing a smiling face with her nose on the window-pane's condensation, Nicole picked up the phone and dialled Thomas's mobile. It was time to do her fraction of the evening.

Nicole spoke nervously. 'Sorry to disturb you, Tom. I'm not interrupting anything, am I?'

A pause. 'No. Not at all.'

'I'll be quick because I expect you want to get back to whatever it is you were just doing.' Her ear was tight to the receiver, desperately trying to gather where he might be. She continued. 'I was thinking of cooking an Indian meal tonight. I know it's late but I'm famished and I just feel like I need an Indian.' She took a deep breath. 'You must get that, Tom, when you feel like an Indian. I know you do.'

He chuckled. 'Keep away from the kitchen, Nicole. I'm not sure, but the firemen were talking about going on strike again.' He laughed again. 'Why don't I just collect one from Poppadom's on my way back? And, out of interest, what ingredients did you have in mind for this *Indian* you were going to cook? Apart from curry powder, that is.'

Nicole despised sarcasm in relation to her cooking, and in perfect rhythm to Strauss she waltzed quickly to the kitchen, yanked open a cupboard and pulled out a jar of hot mango pickle. 'Well, let me see.' She squinted her eyes at the small, oil-smudged label. 'Mangoes sixty per cent, vegetable oil, salt, chilli, mustard, fenugreek, spices, acetic acid and flavourings.'

'That's it?'

'Oh yes, there may be traces of nuts.'

'Right.' He refrained from laughing.

Nicole felt warm with success. Cooking was not

that hard at all. 'So, no need for Poppadom's. But, while you're offering to pick something up on your way back, I wouldn't mind a DVD. Erm, let me see. Oh, I know, *Bend It Like Beckham*. Stars that Indian woman. Quite pretty, isn't she?' Nicole waited for him to answer. And waited. And waited. It was a fairly simple question: was the Indian woman in *Bend It Like Beckham* pretty or not? Finally her anger erupted at his continuing silence. She yelled, 'Quite pretty, if you like that sort of thing, Thomas Harding!' Then she slammed the cordless phone down on its holder. Disconnected.

Back to being a Bond Girl. The last pair of trousers was tossed on to Mt Suit where it joined a huge pile of matching jackets and trousers now with creases and folds that would make Jean Paul Gaultier weep. Nicole shouted to the enormous wardrobe, 'Fill yourself back up with the suits!' But, alas, the wardrobe was not voice-activated, and a mechanical set of arms did not appear to help. There was only one thing for it, Nicole would have to sweat. Like the Tasmanian Devil on amphetamines, she scampered from the bed to the wardrobe restocking the suit rail as best her patience would allow. Her heart forming ideas quicker than her mind could dispel them. Scary voices in her head chanting, *He's with a woman right now. A beautiful woman who has taken your place.* The treachery of her own mind taunting. Nicole grabbed her wrist, the itchy scar now calling, *Why didn't you cut deeper, Nicole? You coward. You couldn't even kill yourself properly, could you? You can't do anything right, Nicole Newton-Harrington. YOU ARE A FAILURE!*

Nicole took a deep breath. Her mind was full of weeds; once an innocent flowerbed of colour, now an overgrown wilderness of madness. Where was the *Ground Force* team when you needed them? She decided to calm herself down with a drink before heading downstairs for part two of her snooping. If Thomas wasn't keeping his secrets in here, then he must be keeping them in his main office downstairs. The safe seemed like a good place to start.

With brandy-scented breath and a tummy filled with fire, Nicole collected the key from Reception, then entered Thomas's office, switched on the desk light, sat on the swivel chair and wallowed in the silent seclusion of his little hideaway. She had passed several guests on the stairs leading down, doing her best to avoid eye contact. Somehow she knew that this place would never agree with her. How could you call the Regency 'home', sharing it with strangers week in and week out? Daddy was right, the hotel life was no life for his baby.

The answerphone fired off a succession of blinks. Fifteen voice-mails for Mr Popular Thomas. Like a good Bond Girl, or more like a good Miss Money-penny, Nicole made notes on a piece of Regency writing paper as the messages were reeled off. After each message, Nicole wrote a descriptive word: 'Boring'. Each caller spoke on a first-name basis, some leaving witty messages about how fabulous it was staying here last time, some apologizing for how badly they behaved last time, but all had one thing in common – they were all special clients, big spenders, and looking for that deal which only the owner could offer, and the five-star treatment they were used to in this four-star establishment. But business was business, and when Thomas returned to listen to his voice-mail, his only interest would be in the bookings for rooms, cancellations for rooms and enquiries for rooms, nothing more than that – Mr Huxtable's latest fetish of having a daily bath filled with blackcurrant jelly was of no concern to Thomas. If Mr Huxtable was prepared to pay the extra cost of fifty bars of jelly a day then so be it. It was another room filled.

Rooms rooms rooms.

God, Nicole thought, looking on the bright side, if Thomas *was* straying, at least she wouldn't end up marrying a man who was obsessed with rooms. By message fourteen, Nicole was about to give up, when a woman's voice caught her attention.

> 'Mr Harding, sorry to ring so late, but I can't remember if you said you wanted me on Thursday. You know what happened the other time and I wouldn't want us to get caught out like that again. If I don't hear from you, I will see you tomorrow. My number is 8841971.'

The warmth in Nicole's face increased. The odd accent, the sneaky meetings, the obvious clue Nicole was looking for. Thomas Harding was having an affair with an Indian woman and when he came back this evening his ability to father children would be diminished considerably. She felt like smashing the place up, taking his stupid golf umbrella and releasing her pent-up anger on the electrical items. Like the DeLonghi coffee machine, or the blinking photocopier, or even the state of the art computer that he'd forgotten to switch off. Her vision focused hard on the monitor, and she almost laughed at Thomas's stupidity. The screen-saver glowed proudly. A picture of the Taj Mahal and two furiously ugly women dancing even more furiously in front. Racing across the bottom of the screen an advert from some travel agent: *Come to India the land of all your dreams and wake up in Eastern paradise.*

Nicole dropped to the floor and spun the dial of numbers on the safe. The safe door swung open and Nicole could feel the coldness of the heavy metal box. The chanting in her head returned. *He's with a woman right now. A beautiful woman who has taken your place.* Her hands groped inside, feeling for anything that could be inspected. Bundles of papers, two black velvet sacks of jewellery, five huge wads of notes, a red ledger with the words 'Not for Mr VAT'. And finally a box. A solid-silver metal box. No engravings, no abrasions, no dents. A near perfect container with Hobbs stamped on a brass plate by the keyhole. Nicole's curiosity picked a fight with her morals. Should she find a screwdriver and jimmy open the lock? Hardly a violation worth putting on *Crime Stoppers*. But the lock was barely a mystery to Nicole. Hobbs was a name that was not only stamped on the box but also stamped on her memory. On the night of the Cockneys' wedding she had found such a key hidden in a matchbox, which had been hidden in Thomas's suit jacket pocket. But where was the key now?

Nicole groaned with frustration. It was at times like this that she wished she wasn't a lady. The F word was a treat that she allowed herself from time to time, and right now, she let loose with a string of them. Unladylike in the extreme. Mary fucking Whitehouse it was not. Not to mention that her dress was riding halfway up her backside and her glittery G-string on view for all and sundry. The swearing felt good until a voice from above spoke her name.

'Nicole, is that you?'

Nicole winced. 'Yes, can I help you?' she croaked into the safe.

'Sorry, I did knock, I thought Mr Harding was here . . . I'll come back later.' Emma, one of the waitresses, turned to leave. She'd seen people in compromising positions before and it was normally she who ended up with scarlet fever.

'Wait!' Nicole sprung up, pulled her dress back down and smiled feebly. 'Come in and close the door. It's Emma, isn't it?' Emma nodded while shutting the door behind her. 'I'm in a bit of a pickle here. From where you're standing it must seem like I'm nosing in Thomas's office. It must look quite bad.' Nicole pointed to the chair.

Emma sat down, her eyes wide in awe of Nicole's amazing beauty. If only, even for just one day, she could leave the world of a waitress, step out of her plain black skirt and white shirt and set foot into Nicole's world. If only. Suddenly conscious of her gazing, Emma looked down at the carpet. She replied, 'It's your business what you do in Mr Harding's office. You are getting married, after all.'

Nicole found herself liking Emma. 'That's true. And married couples have no secrets, do they?' she said, closing the safe door.

'Some do. They get divorced in the end, though.'

Emma watched Nicole's face drop and felt bad. 'But not Mr Harding, everyone can see he loves you.'

Nicole sat on the edge of the desk. 'I'm going to be very truthful with you, Emma, and I would very much appreciate you doing the same in return for me.' Emma nodded. 'I know what this hotel is like, rumours spread and multiply like the plague here. One thing leads to another and before you know it, there *is* a plague here. I have heard something recently which needs confirming. It's about Thomas and an Indian woman. Do you know anything about this?'

She did. It seemed the whole of the Regency staff knew, thanks to Stuart. And the grocery delivery van man, the newspaper boy, the milkman and even Daisy and Maisy, the two large sisters. Emma explained all to a horrified Nicole, confirming most of Stuart's story. There were brief silences as Nicole brushed away tears, then asked Emma to continue. There was definitely a bond forming between the two women, but not quite the bond Emma would have hoped for. To bring bad tidings to a woman Emma idolized made her more than a little uncomfortable. But a true friend was an honest friend.

Emma resumed. 'I heard that Mr Harding was spitting mad when the Indian woman threw the Ganges water over him. He never swears in Reception, but, by all accounts, he swore like a trooper that day. Guests or no guests, he was *really* annoyed.' Emma felt like she was gaining ground in this friendship, not just the bad-tidings-bringer but the bringer of hope. 'When I was on my break last Sunday, I saw her get in the car with Mr Harding. Honestly, Nicole, I swear on my life, he doesn't have any feelings for her. He looked really pissed off. I think you should just ask him about her, it's probably not what you think at all.'

Nicole shook her head at Emma, she was quite a sweetie. 'You are being wonderful about this, I can see what you're trying to do, but . . . It's best you listen to this.' Nicole reached over and pressed the play button on the tape. Message fourteen, one above unlucky thirteen.

The message finished and Nicole raised her eyebrows. 'Well, what do you make of that?'

'You know who that is. She cleans Mr Harding's apartment. It's Josephine.'

'Josephine?' Nicole squeaked as a picture of the fifty-five-year-old chambermaid emerged. 'I was this close,' she held her finger and thumb apart, 'to phoning her back and calling her a silly little tart and telling her to stay away from my man.'

They both laughed until the door opened.

Thomas stood at the entrance. A DVD in his hand. A brown paper bag full of Indian takeaway in the other (just in case). What was the joke? He laughed anyway in case it was funny. After a quick winking match between Emma and Nicole, Emma departed leaving the two engagees together.

The smell of Indian food was overpowering and would put paid to any 'sniffing' plan Nicole had in mind. Her brain was thinking up ways to strip him naked as quickly as possible and then smell him. EVERYWHERE. If she found an apricot Haze air freshener in his boxers – he was guilty as charged. The quickest way she knew of getting a man to remove his clothes was to remove her own.

Following a tip she'd picked up from an old Kenny Rogers song, Nicole walked to the door and locked them in. No escape for the coward of this county. She then took the DVD and takeaway from his hands, dumping them on the floor in the corner by the photocopier. Nicole tried to think of ways to stretch out a striptease when she only had two items of clothing on: props. Good old-fashioned props. She eyed the golf umbrella in the corner. Before, an imaginary weapon for destruction, now a necessary accessory for erection. With a lunge, she grabbed the umbrella and began her routine.

Thomas sat back on the chair. One could never get enough of this type of thing. He smiled at the wild look in her eyes. She was amazing when she was this turned on. It just showed – leave a woman waiting a little bit longer than promised and hey presto, she's rubbing her pelvis up and down your thigh when you get back. It's their way of showing how much they've missed you. Her fingers began to roam and his pulse became erratic. People have been known to have heart attacks when using coke while having sex. And the morbid thought reminded Thomas of his chat with Terence earlier: 'You could have skied down the inside of Lester's nose with the amount of coke he'd shot up it.' The vision of Lester having his wicked way with Nicole, whispering sweet nothings (and they would be sweet nothings, pure bullshit) in her ear, promising the world, as his own mind took off to another planet, was enough to ruin Thomas's mood. Even the sensation of one of Nicole's hands on his cock bulge while the other spun the umbrella above her head, could not keep this moment alive. Thomas gently pushed her off. Her wandering hands were moving dangerously close to his stash of cocaine anyway.

He stood up. 'Could we continue this tomorrow?'

Apparently Nicole did not hear and drew herself in real close, her nose sniffing frantically at his chest. 'Let me undress you.' She tossed the umbrella to one side and dropped to her knees. Her fingers fumbled with his zipper. 'Let me.' Sniff sniff sniff. Her hands tugged on his jeans. 'I need you, Tom.' Sniff sniff sniff . . .

'Look,' he stepped backwards, yanking up his jeans. 'Tomorrow. I'm not in the mood. Anyway, it's pretty damn selfish of me to take pleasure from you when you've got such a miserable cold.' He plucked a tissue from a man-sized box and handed it to her. 'Blow your nose on that, you've got a terrible sinus problem. Maybe the Indian takeaway will help soothe it.'

Sniffing of a different kind now. Tears rolled down Nicole's cheeks. 'Yes, I bet Indians can soothe everything.' She sobbed. 'Not once in all the time we've been together have you pulled away from me unless the phone was ringing. Men only do that sort of thing for one reason. When they've already had their pudding. You don't know how much you're hurting me right now.' She climbed back into her dress. 'I can't bear your face any more. I'm going back home to Mummy.' And without any more ado, she opened the door and quietly closed it behind her.

Thomas was left confused. People took drugs to get this mixed up. He didn't need them. Ten minutes with Nicole would do the trick.

Running out of the room he followed Nicole up the

corridor while buttoning up his burgundy-coloured Fendi shirt. He found Reception deserted bar one receptionist, Hannah, and Stuart, a fag in his hand, a cheap grin on his powdery face.

'Well, well, well,' Stuart began. 'What have you done to the poor woman now, Mr Harding? She left here in a commotion of tears.' He then did a *Roadrunner* impression. 'Beep beep.'

Thomas turned to Stuart, who appeared to be covered in some sort of flour. 'Fuck off out of my sight and get right back to the kitchen or consider yourself sacked.'

Stuart looked to Hannah for some sort of moral eyeball support. But Hannah kept her head down, she'd never seen Mr Harding this upset before – and she had been there that awful evening when the thirty Germans cancelled their rooms. Thomas had thrown out anything German from the larder that night. Stuart's sausage swastika the following morning at breakfast had not been appreciated by Mr Harding. Especially when served by a commis chef with a drawn-on moustache, a German accent and a stiff walk. 'Brekvast is zerved, Herr Harding. Heil Hitler.' Jobs could fall by the wayside very easily when a boss was in a foul mood.

Stuart toddled back to the kitchen, smiling to himself. Thomas was ruffled, his cool exterior was crumbling. Swearing at staff. Well, well, whatever next? And now Nicole had run off, left him; the marriage would soon be called off, Stuart was sure of that. The plan was turning into a triumph, Thomas's landslide was on the move, the avalanche was just days away – he could feel it.

Outside in the car park, Thomas watched the rear lights of Nicole's Mercedes as it spat back gravel and lurched down the road and out through the hotel gates. There was only one thing for it. He returned inside, along the hall into the near-empty bar and added an entry in chalk to tomorrow's menu on the blackboard:

Wednesday's Lunch Special
Limited amounts so HURRY!
Poppadoms with anchovies
Cold samosas with tossed salad
Baked potatoes with chicken Rogan Josh

Thomas climbed the stairs to his apartment, ransacking his brain for clues to Nicole's odd behaviour. Being innovative with uneaten takeaway food was one thing – a good businessman uses the tools at his disposal – but figuring out the workings of a woman's mind from a few crumbs of information, well, just the thought of it was draining enough.

Upstairs, alone, after making countless attempts to get through on Nicole's mobile and on her Castle Cliff Manor bedroom answering machine, and even with Castle Cliff Manor's butler, he resigned himself. He didn't want anything more to do with today; and tomorrow couldn't come soon enough. He lay on the bed and waited for sleep to arrive.

But sleep that night must have been coming in a taxi, it was taking for ever, and so Thomas bunged in the DVD, dived back on his bed, and prayed a film about an Indian girl playing football would throw him over sleep's edge. *Bend It Like Beckham*. It was enjoyable, Nicole would have liked it. He found himself wondering if he would be up to managing a women's football team in Oxford. No, he'd stick to hotels. And Nicole was dead right about one thing, the Indian woman starring in the movie *was* pretty.

When she let her hair down, that is.

Thomas jumped off the bed and picked his jeans from off the floor. He pulled out the snappy bag from his back pocket. 'Fancy a party, Hal?' He shook the bag of cocaine in his hands. 'Imagine how alert your circuit boards would be.' He moved to the living area. 'All lights on, Hal. Thank you.' The apartment was immediately lit. Thomas walked to the bathroom and tipped the coke down the loo.

Even having the substance in his vicinity felt odd. A doorway to hell, although, to some, a temporary gateway to paradise. But Terence would have been less eager to discuss Lester and his habit if Thomas had not purchased the powder. Where coke was concerned, you were only in the need-to-know club if you were in the need-to-use club. And now, in Terence's eyes, Thomas's character had been marred for life. But if it helped Thomas find out more about Lester, then so be it.

Chapter Twenty-two

The biggest club in the world, the club with the most members, is Death. The fee is the same for everyone – your heart stops. The rules are simple: don't move and don't talk. Any objections, then see the manager – God. One other thing, and this confuses newcomers all the time, death-club membership is for life.

Except for Hindus.

Hindus are the Indian escapologists of death. By a clause added to their life agreement, they have stipulated that upon the heart stopping, reincarnation will take place. At no time in the proceedings will a Hindu join the death club. And, how well or how badly a Hindu has performed in this life, will determine how privileged a Hindu will be in the next. As easy as that? Well, not quite. In order for the Gods to agree on life displacement, certain criteria have to be met if a Hindu is to reincarnate to their next life.

Marina was worried about criteria today. In fact, she'd been worried about criteria for eighteen years. Since her gran had died, in fact. The consequences of a young girl's action back then had seemed so insignificant, so inconsequential, so . . . childish. But as Marina grew older, the consequences of that action seemed to become ever more ominous. How could any human being play God? She'd listened eagerly to a TV debate on abortion once, as the participants discussed whether aborting a child before a certain age constituted murder, whether not giving a child the chance to live was killing it. Marina had lain awake that night, ascertaining her predicament. Was she a murderer? If, in some way, she had prevented a life from being lived, would she, in the eyes of Shiva, be considered a killer?

Marina sat on her duvet, dressed in her Betty Boop jim-jams, wondering if she should open the dreaded case beneath her bed. It had been more than five years since she'd last set eyes on the contents. She slipped off the bed and knelt down, pulling out the small, tapestry suitcase. If her parents knew what lay hidden here, they would disown her in the blink of an eye. No judge, no jury, no stay of execution. Hindus did not do what Marina had done. There was no excuse that could possibly account for it.

Two combination locks blocked entry. Three numbers to both the left and the right of the brass handle. And one shaky hand hovering over them like a butterfly. How many people were responsible for killing their own grandmother? How many people on this Thursday evening were charging themselves with murder?

A knock at Marina's door and Emily barged in. 'Look at that, Marina.' She lobbed her mobile towards her. 'I'm beginning to wish I hadn't put my phone number on my Hit List letters.' A large piece of Emily's mud pack fell to the floor and collapsed to dust on impact. Emily watched it. 'Sorry about that.'

Marina, the murderer, shoved the suitcase back under the bed and looked at Emily's phone. A colour picture of a hairy arse stared back. A message followed: 'Stick your apology up your . . .' Marina hoped that the bottom in question belonged to a man. If not, why did the woman, to whom Emily had apologized, have a set of prickly testicles hanging between her legs?

'Emily, that's the third obscene picture this week. I bet you wish you hadn't stolen their boyfriends now.' Marina sat on her bed and handed Emily back her mobile. 'But it's their problem, Emily. If they want to hold a grudge, then let them.'

'So you don't recommend I—'

'No,' Marina interrupted. 'Don't retaliate. It will wreck your karma.'

Emily huffed and flopped down beside Marina. 'But there's a fresh one on the pavement.'

'No!' Marina repeated. 'No sending pictures of dog poo down the phone.'

In walked Hilda followed by two other people. No knock. No announcement. Just a charge of footsteps. Three different noises on the thinning carpet. The sliding sound of Hilda's slippers, the solid thump of men's boots and the gentle tapping of . . . stilettos.

'Run!' shouted Emily, scampering across the floor, pieces of mud pack falling en route. 'Bailiffs.' And

Emily was gone from the room – most likely hiding under the kitchen table.

But Marina was glued to the spot. A blonde woman of extreme beauty was standing but a few feet away. Class in its purist form. The sweet smell of a successful broad. A woman equipped with all the best tools. Marina never liked to stare too long at another female – unless in bitch mode – but she found her eye muscles wouldn't pull away. The sparkly, shell-pink beaded dress, with matching scarf was obviously designed by God. At least one thousand African miners must have risked life and limb to descend the South African mine shafts to gather all the diamonds that decorated her body. And her aura was that of a queen. It did Hilda, with her surgical mask and laddered stockings, no favours standing next to a woman this beautiful, for she now looked like something from *Steptoe and Son* – Steptoe's cart horse.

Nicole's eyes checked the small room. It was a hovel. Big dollops of Blu-Tack were flush to the rotting window frame (to keep the rain out, Nicole presumed) and the walls were cracked like eggshells. *Changing Rooms* would need a whole series to sort this place out. Alternatively, one match might do the trick.

Nicole spoke, relaxed and confident. 'Handsome, isn't he, my fiancé?' She nodded towards the poster of Thomas over Marina's bed. 'He never did like that picture. Although, at the size you managed to blow it up to, I'm slightly put off by it myself.' She turned to Ramone, her six-foot-seven, man-mountain bodyguard. 'Do you mind waiting outside, Ramone? I'll be just a little while.' Then to Hilda, 'Thank you, Hilda,

I will surely try that wartime recipe for cabbage soup sometime.'

Hilda quickly curtsied before being ushered out by Ramone, his walkie-talkie hissing in the background, the floorboards creaking like a rickety boat under his weight. The door was shut behind them, with Ramone standing outside, legs apart, arms crossed, on standby in case Nicole screamed for help. It had taken Ramone three charges of GBH before he realized that when Nicole was given presents by her friends she was in actual fact 'squealing' with delight and not 'screaming' for her life. Although once, when Nicole had been given a pair of genuine Elton John piano gloves, it was Ramone who screamed – Elton John was his idol, his English Rose.

Nicole had seen rooms like this on *EastEnders*, so it wasn't a total shock to the system. What was a shock, though, was the sight of Thomas staring at her from this woman's bedroom wall. With the amount of chin-wagging Hilda had subjected her to downstairs about the war, it was surprising that there weren't the words 'I WANT YOU' scrawled above his head, like some army recruitment poster from the forties. But, Nicole squinted her eyes, there was writing of some kind written down the side of his body. It made sense not to read it.

Marina swallowed her initial surprise and pulled herself together. She stood up and wrapped a plain blue dressing gown around her. 'What is it you want?'

'I want you to stay away from Thomas. I want you to forget whatever little plan you have up your sleeve and leave him alone. There are lines that you do not step over, Marina. This is one of them. Thomas is a very attractive man with many things going for him. I happen to be one of those things. And call this what you may, intuition, a sixth sense or even a pre-emptive strike, I will not let *anyone* interfere with what we have. No one.' She stared sternly into Marina's widened eyes. 'You're not the first woman to chase after him, you know? You are certainly not the first woman to chase after him for his money.'

Confusion bit hard. How did Nicole know about her intentions of stealing Thomas? Maybe she was possessed of alien powers. Marina glanced out of the window to see if a flying saucer was hovering outside. No, no flying saucer, just your run of the mill, top of the range Bentley with all the mod cons including a fully kitted-out chauffeur reading *The Times*. In this town, a Bentley *was* a flying saucer. God, how rich *was* this bitch? And soon rumour would be spreading through Fenworth that Stephen Hawking could walk again and was dressed up as a chauffeur, because anyone who could understand *The Times*, *had* to be him.

Marina bristled with embarrassment. 'There's absolutely nothing going on with me and your racist Thomas.' Between Nicole's two perfectly tanned, smooth legs stood a black briefcase, new and shiny. Marina crossed her fingers, hoping that there was not an Uzi inside waiting to pepper her with bullets. 'I don't know where you get your information from, but there's no little secret romance going on here.'

'Romance? Maybe not. Secret? Maybe not.' Nicole walked right up to the poster and slapped her hand against Thomas's face. 'But something weird is definitely going on. Whether it's in your mind or not.' Nicole stretched for the briefcase on the floor, leaving Marina wide-mouthed with respect. Nicole was one supple woman. The case landed on the bed and Nicole flicked it open. 'There is £70,000 in cash. It's my way of cushioning the fall.'

Greed rushed through Marina's veins like some sort of drug. 'Fall?' She glanced up. 'What fall?'

Nicole enjoyed the look of astonishment on Marina's face. 'Well, I say "fall" assuming you had some sort of feelings for my fiancé. If not, well, you have just landed yourself £70,000 for nothing.' Nicole grabbed a wad of fifties and flicked through the notes with her neat French-manicured nails. 'I never want your path to cross with Thomas's again. Use this money and make something of your life.'

A thud from next door. Either Emily had just lost the last of her mud pack to the floor, or she'd dropped the glass she'd been using to listen in with. This was a moment that Marina needed to share. And without Emily here to share it, without thinking, she leant across and gave Nicole a hug.

'Thank you so much,' Marina said, choking back tears of happiness. 'I hope you and Thomas are very happy together.'

'So, we have a deal?'

And they did. Nicole remembered the conversation with her sister, Arabella, yesterday, when they'd concocted this plan together. Arabella had dimmed the lights, told her to sit back while they listened to an ABBA song, *Money Money Money*. How money was funny in a rich man's world. But, in a poor man's world, where bills ruled people's lives, money was never anything to joke about. Arabella was sure that Marina would take the money. It could change her life.

Nicole declined the offer of a coffee. Instead, she set out to explain that if Marina reneged on the agreement, the Newton-Harrington family could not be held responsible for its actions. A deal was a deal. Nicole pulled an envelope from the top flap of the Gucci briefcase. Inside were pamphlets on how to invest large sums of money and gain maximum in return. Nicole didn't mind squandering the odd thousand herself, but when it came to other people, she wanted them to treat money with respect.

'You could even set yourself up in business. Two years from now you could be a roaring success.' Nicole held out her hand. 'Well, goodbye then.'

'Stay for a cup of soup. It's the least I can offer.'

And it was the least anyone *had* offered. Champagne and caviar was the norm.

After wishing farewell to Hilda and clarifying that there was no 'blue' blood in her family, Nicole left, following after Ramone, who was busy checking the high windows for stone-throwing snipers. He wondered if it was within the family's security protocol for him to ask Edmond Newton-Harrington for a Purple Heart re: Mission Fenworth when he returned his baby daughter unscathed.

Just as they were about to leave, a gigantic scream worthy of the film *Scream* threw itself from the top window. Instinctively Ramone went for his baton.

'At ease, Ramone, at ease,' Nicole said calmly. 'It's most likely the girls just discovering the Gucci catalogue I hid in with the money-saving advice. I've heard that, to a poor girl, a Gucci dress comes close to orgasm.'

Ramone wouldn't know about that. He was a professional bodyguard.

As Fenworth became distant, as the air became cleaner and the graffiti more legible, as Ramone sang along to 'Goodbye Yellow Brick Road', by Elton John, and the chauffeur joined in with his whistle, Nicole took a fly-on-the-wall look at her life. She was twenty-eight years old, wealthy in the extreme, about to marry the catch of the century, very lucky indeed. But was she, though? Every time it rained, she became a gibbering wreck, unable to escape the memories of her traumatic past. Memories of Lester struggling as the car skidded in the rain. That fucking rain. Why couldn't she have been less selfish and stopped him driving that night? If it wasn't for her, Lester would be alive today. If it wasn't for her stupid snobbery and spoilt behaviour, Lester would never have been in that car in the first place.

The Bentley drove through the gates of Castle Cliff Manor and swung round the roundabout in the centre. Nicole asked to be left alone for a few minutes. Leaving her in the car, the chauffeur and bodyguard headed for the staff quarters. The bloated moon, healthy and bright, hung low in the sky above. Nicole pressed a button and the side window lowered, letting in the sound of the water fountain. A huge marble sculpture of a stallion spewed foamy water from its mouth and down its saddle. Just one of the many presents from satisfied clients to Daddy, whose life was so measured and exact that he probably knew when his next sneeze was coming.

Nicole's, however, was turmoil. Each day she worried about her mortality. She worried that the day would come when she might slash her wrists again. There had been no warning last time. Just a sudden welling of emotion that shook her rigid and sent her down shit alley. She remembered the feeling as she held the blade tight to her vein all those nights ago in the Regency corridor. Could feel the blood getting excited beneath her skin, knowing it would soon be free. Her eyes blurring over with tears. Nicole looked at the stallion, its posture so solid and confident. The moonlight caught the stones set in its eyes and Nicole smiled. So steadfast, strong and still. And how still she would have been that night had Thomas not come charging down the corridor. The vein had buckled at the first stroke, her life leaking away as the blood squirted outwards. But, although her mind was cloudy and confused, she could still hear Thomas. His frantic shouts for help and his desperate cries for her to stay alive.

Without Thomas, life was not worth living. She picked up the car phone and dialled Thomas's mobile; it was time to make things right again. It was time to apologize.

Back in the Bank of England, or Hilda's house, the money was floating like a ticker-tape parade. No moon landing, no four more years for Kennedy, no fourth of July.

No, this ticker-tape parade was for the shops. The girls had never had so much fun with the Queen's head – apart from the time they smoked some skunk through a fiver. The once crisp money was now covered in dust, sweat, dribble and mud pack. They could presently be classed as 'used' notes. And tomorrow, at shop-opening time, they would be classed as 'spent'.

'Do you realize what this means, Emily?' Marina said, pulling out £1000 from her bra. 'We'll be in a tax bracket. Perv Bazzer can stick his job.'

They cracked open a can of Lucozade. 'To our karma,' they cheered and gulped the celebratory fizz. Hilda had already been turned away three times, asking questions, unhappy to be out of the loop. She wanted to know what her lodgers could possibly have in common with someone like Nicole who was obviously royalty but couldn't admit it for security reasons. Hilda was soon threatened with a bowl of leftover Garlic Balti if she continued to interrupt their celebrations. After stomping downstairs to her flat, Hilda fumed like a spoilt pensioner. As soon as the girls were off to work tomorrow, she would investigate their rooms.

The light stayed on late that night in Marina's room. Two best friends had been thrown a lifeline, saving them from drowning in the rough waters of Fenworth. Marina had always called Fenworth Rut City – a place from which no one escaped. Their whole life controlled by cheap price tags and discount foods and saving money for the catalogue man, Arnie, who came once a week. It was hardly the vision that the two girls had imagined when setting out on the road to Fenworth for the very first time. That vision was now stored away with many others under the heading 'naive'. And they had been so naive. For starters, the two young women had thought that Oxford and Oxfordshire were much of a muchness, two peas of the same pod. Fenworth in Oxfordshire must be an old town heaving with young and trendy student folk, they thought. Wrong! Fenworth was an old run-down town, mainly filled with people just heaving. The job that had been promised by Emily's cousin involved computers and hygiene management – that's all they knew. Computers were 'in', new wave, the technology of the future. It sounded good, until they arrived, full of ambition, at their new employment, Wacko Data Communications PLC, and were told to start de-fluffing the keyboards (the computer aspect of the job) and then scrub the toilets (the hygiene management side). They were now Fenworth cleaners. Two hours into the job, Emily resigned, after spotting someone else's job on the toilet seat. NO way! The girls left without saying goodbye. Next up was a small ad in the window of Napkins Sandwich Bar. It was either accept Perv Bazzer's sweaty handshake and begin their new career, or return to their parents shamefaced and losers. Too pretty to be losers, too gutsy to be shamefaced, they promised themselves to save as much money as they could, and leave Perv Bazzer, Fenworth and Hilda for Oxford within six months. Unfortunately, promises to oneself are the easiest to break. Four years later they still inhabited Rut City – and their bank accounts were infested with debts.

Not for much longer.

Snuggled up in Marina's bed the girls caressed the money. Being poor can feel like an illness sometimes. Walking around with an ailment that only one medicine known to man can cure.

MONEY.

Chapter Twenty-three

Oxford is famed for its three Bs. Brains, Booze and Bonking. Stuart was famed for just two. And traditionally, on Stuart's birthday, he tested his two Bs to the max.

It was early Friday evening in the busy Regency bar, Stuart was in the midst of celebrating his twenty-seventh birthday, along with five ex-lover waitresses and one ex-lover chambermaid. It was the girls' treat; Stuart had been feeling down lately and it was their duty to pamper him on this special day. And what better place than the hotel bar? Where people dumped their day-to-day problems at the entrance, and where affairs, like mushrooms, grew overnight. The hotel world really was a parallel universe.

Stuart, in his favourite Arsenal jersey, had been impressing the table with tales of his senile grandmother. How treating her 'normal' was imperative to her well-being, how keeping whatever was left of her mind occupied was crucial.

'Sounds to me like you're trying to send her even more round the bend,' said Barbie-doll Penny listening to Stuart's latest story. 'And how can you tell she enjoys chasing this loaf of bread around the room?'

'Penny, Penny, Penny, you think too much. Pound for pound my gran is the best gran in the world. I wouldn't do anything to harm her.' Stuart sipped his 'It's A Gusher' cocktail, then lit up a fag. 'How many grandkids these days would go to the trouble of hollowing out a bloomer loaf and fitting a remote-control car inside? I'm telling you, she loves it. Running around the floor on all fours, trying not to bash into things, you should see her little ol' face. Bless her.'

'You're sick, Stu-pot,' stated Holly, sucking off a cherry from a cocktail stick. 'You'll be old one day, too. She could really hurt herself.'

Stuart, now a little drunk, shouted, 'Well, next time I'll make her wear a flipping BMX helmet, then.' He huffed, placing his arm round Stephanie. 'In case you've forgotten, ladies, this is my birthday. Shall we all try a bit harder? I'm in a good mood today, don't miss out on this window of opportunity.'

The volume of noise in the bar increased until it reached maximum overload, a general buzz of chatting, laughing and the odd till-pinging filling the smoky room to capacity. Only one table became silent when the boss walked in. Thomas, dressed smartly in his Versace suit, walked across the floor towards birthday boy.

'Happy birthday, Stuart. The next round's on me.' Thomas shook Stuart's hand. 'I'll be over there for the next half hour or so, just ignore me – enjoy yourselves.' He smiled at the women. 'And, because it's your birthday, Stuart, I won't even remind you that it's bright and early tomorrow. Breakfast shift.' Thomas headed to the bar, pulled out a stool and talked away to some businessman. Casual meetings like this put the clients off guard. And when they were off guard, they spent more money.

'Wanker,' Stuart whispered into his creamy cocktail. 'Stuck up wanker!'

'Oh come on, Stu-pot. He's not bad for a boss,' Penny said, wishing the stuck-up Thomas would get stuck up her. Two years of flirting and not so much as a wink. 'He lets you get away with murder.'

Holly and Lauren had also given up on Thomas. He was a man who kept people at arm's length. It was at times like this that the girls wished Thomas had no arms. Although that vision was rather at odds with their dreams of him hugging them tightly at night. They watched him in discussion with his client as they swooned like love-struck teenagers. If only he knew they were even alive.

Lauren agreed with Penny. 'You could learn a lot from a man like Thomas, Stu-pot. Look how successful he is. A man that confident with himself has to be fantastic in bed. It's a shame his official engagement party is tomorrow, that's us definitely out of the picture, girls. And I hear it's going to be bigger than Jen and Brad's wedding.'

The girls chuckled, the cocktails were doing their job, and six sets of women's eyes became ever more transfixed to a money-making Thomas sitting at the bar counter. Nicole was the luckiest woman alive. The girls continued praising Thomas until Stuart's face turned a deeper shade of claret.

Pushing his drink away harshly, Stuart stared at them. 'I've just had about a fucking 'nough of this,' he shouted, his voice slightly slurred. 'Mr Fucking Harding is no gigolo. I'm the one who takes you silly cows to bed, I'm the one who satisfies you, I'm the one who comes up with the filthy ideas. But that bastard over there gets all the credit.' Stuart stood up, wobbled a bit, then headed towards small-dick Thomas. Wide eyes all round.

Thomas was in the middle of an important deal. A guaranteed three months' booking for fifteen rooms in the winter season. It was not a good time to be disturbed by a death in the family, let alone someone who was jealous of his bedroom skills. Stuart announced his arrival with a huge belch.

'You . . .' Stuart began, steadying himself on the client's shoulder. 'You, Mr Harding, are *crap* in bed. Useless. You don't know how to please your lover—'

Thomas could feel his client's embarrassment matching his own and broke in hurriedly. 'That's quite enough, Stuart. I'm busy here, I'll talk to you later.' He turned to his client. 'I'm sorry, Mr Tameche. It's the booze.'

'HA! It's my birthday. Nicole would understand.'

'Nicole?'

'Oh yes, Mr Harding, your beautiful *Nicole*. Didn't you know? Obviously not. Well, well, well. What do you know? Her and me will be in bed very soon.' Stuart sniggered. 'We have our secret chats together and . . . we have an understanding.' He paused to enjoy Thomas's shocked face. 'And, while we're on the topic of happenings inside your hotel, see those girls over at that table?' Stuart pointed and waved to the red-faced gang. 'I've slept with every one of them. In your best rooms, on your cleaned sheets.' He shouted, 'Ain't that right, girls? We've all slept together in this hotel. Tell him. You tell Mr Small Willy Harding how I shagged you all and satisfied you all. Go on.' He hollered, 'TELL HIM!'

Mr Tameche picked up his briefcase. 'I'm sorry, Mr Harding, but maybe booking in here would be a bad choice.' With that he left.

Left Mr Harding asking himself whether he could cope with a fifteen-year stint in prison. Whether he would avoid prison through the Mental Health Act. Could he pretend that he thought Stuart was a cat? Persuade the jury that taking away just one of his lives shouldn't be classed as murder considering he still had eight more left.

Ushering Stuart outside, Thomas dialled for a taxi, and waited for the poor taxi driver to take the disgraced chef away. Stuart's job was on the line. He would find out after breakfast tomorrow if he still had one. Thomas would take his birthday into consideration and also the fact that Stuart's grandmother was in hospital, having hit her head on a low table – chasing after a bloomer loaf of all things. He would also demand to know exactly what Stuart was implying when he mentioned Nicole. Stuart was prone to wind-ups, and this had *better* be one. The idea of Stuart making small talk with Nicole was enough for Thomas to drive blindfold at 100 m.p.h.

down Lamppost Lane – dragging Stuart by his testicles behind him.

And just as one taxi left, another one arrived. What was this, an airport?

The new arrival swept through the hotel entrance, giving Thomas a pitiful stare, then headed to Reception, her high heels clicking on the marble floor. The receptionist, Hannah, offered her complete assistance with an American smile.

'Good evening, madam. And how can I help you?'

Dropping her bag, Marina planted her elbows on the counter and rested her head in her hands. 'Hello, is it possible to speak to Nicole Newton-Harrington? I know it's late, but it's extremely important. Extremely.'

Hannah, who had been faking interest, now showed real interest – in spades. 'Oh my. Erm . . .' She nodded in Thomas's direction. 'Maybe Mr Harding can help, he owns the place. Nicole doesn't actually reside here.'

Marina snorted, raising her voice slightly. 'No, I don't deal with matters of this kind with racists. This is a completely private matter that can only be dealt with by Nicole and Nicole alone.'

Surprise surprise Thomas arrived. 'Would you care, Ms Dewan, to refrain from using such a tumultuous voice? I am not a "racist" *per se*; you are just a misinformed foreigner.' He paused, shaking his head – where the hell did that come from? 'I mean . . . I don't know what I mean. Would you care to walk to my office and we can discuss Nicole in there.' He took Marina by the arm and dragged her through, slamming the door shut behind him.

'Sit!' Thomas pointed to a seat. 'I'm finding your remarks about me being a racist rather tiresome, Ms Dewan. It's a cheap shot when things don't go your way. Now what's all this about Nicole? How do you even know her?'

'You look stressed; are you having a rough day?' If Marina had smoked, she would have lit up now, instead she played nervously with his stapler. 'I think you need to loosen up a little, may I suggest one of your Regency special massages? It did the trick for me.'

Thomas stalked the room, still annoyed at Stuart, his annoyance enhanced by this Indian woman. 'Could we stick to the reason why you're here? Now what's all this about Nicole?' A jarring thought occurred and his face twisted in concern. 'She hasn't invited you to our engagement party tomorrow, has she? Tell me she hasn't.'

Marina giggled. 'I wouldn't go if you paid me.' Clunk clunk clunk, the staples were making great border decorations on a piece of paper. 'Really, I can only discuss this with Nicole, so, if she's not here, then I shall be going.' She stood up. 'I have nothing further to say to you.'

Abruptly, Thomas sat himself opposite Marina. 'Sit down, *please*.' He waited for her to re-seat herself and softened his voice. 'Trust me, Nicole would want you to tell me.'

'No, you trust me, Nicole *definitely* wouldn't want me to tell you.'

Trust? Thomas knew all about Nicole and trust. Her daddy had been paying into one for years. But why should he trust this virtual stranger? He spoke.

'I'll ring Nicole and you speak to her.' He reached for the phone.

'I don't think that's a good idea. She wouldn't want me to be here when you phone her, or anywhere near here. Believe me.'

He dropped the receiver back in its cradle, confused. His speeding brain hit a Stinger. An equation in his head without an apparent solution. Marina was 'M', Nicole was 'N'. Now, how the F did M and N add up? What circumstances would bring these two women together? What was the common denominator? And then he smiled, thanking the boffin in his brain for solving the equation. This had nothing to do with 'What'. No, this was all about 'Who'. *Who* was the common denominator? But it was just a theory at the moment. Just a foetus of an idea.

Thomas asked, 'Nicole wouldn't want you anywhere near here? *Or* anywhere near *me*?'

Her eyes grew wide and excited. 'Near you.'

And now it was a proven. Who was the who? Thomas was the who. That's who.

He studied Marina. For the first time in his life he really saw her. There was no getting away from it: Marina was undeniably beautiful. He watched her stamping away with the stapler – her face intent on finishing the border. But how could Nicole ever believe that he would get mixed up with Marina? Well, that was obvious all of a sudden; his list of lies had caught him up. Or rather, tripped him up. The question was: who helped him trip? Who stuck their foot out? His staff of course. Nothing could be kept a secret for long in this place. From the Ganges water to the lipstick on his face. Then there was that business of giving her a lift home to Fenworth. The evidence was strong. Why lie unless you have something to hide? But she was Indian! Surely Nicole would have given him some credit? She knew how he felt about races mixing. However, most likely, all Nicole saw was a pretty Indian woman who had stolen some of Thomas's attention. Race never came into it.

'Correct me if I'm wrong, Ms Dewan, but does Nicole think you and I have,' he visibly shivered, '*shared* something?'

'Shared? I've never heard it put that way before. Does the word "fuck" embarrass you?' she said, feeling totally embarrassed. Clunk clunk clunk.

'Hardly.' He refrained from smiling. 'I'm not easily embarrassed, Ms Dewan.'

'Oh.' She dropped the stapler, pulled up her Head bag from the floor and, with a confident pull, unzipped it. 'Well, Mr Harding, would the fact that your fiancée thinks you're only worth £70,000 embarrass you?' She stood up and emptied the bag on to the desk. A mass of notes cascaded in front of stone-cold eyes. 'For a woman reported to be from a family worth billions, it seems a pittance.' She paused. 'Seventy thousand pounds to remove me from your life. HA! I would have taken a fiver.'

'Jesus!' Thomas managed to say before slumping into a thoughtful silence.

Clunk clunk clunk. Marina enjoyed the scene before her eyes. Clunk clunk clunk. He was quite cute sitting there all confused-looking. Clunk clunk clunk. If only he wasn't a racist, she would have jumped across the table, kissed him hard on the mouth and then suggested sharing each other. Clunk clunk . . .

'Will you stop that racket!' Thomas bellowed. 'For fuck's sake. Besides, it's illegal to deface the Queen's head with staples.'

Sor-rey. Marina waited for Thomas's temples to stop dancing before she began to explain yesterday evening. No, Nicole did not wear a contamination suit before she set foot in her Fenworth flat. No, Nicole did not bring a full tank of oxygen. But, yes, she did bring her bodyguard, Ramone. Marina watched various emotions change Thomas's expression as she explained the situation.

Thomas listened with different degrees of shock, his mouth opening and closing rapidly like a paparazzo's camera. Had Indians never heard of the saying, 'Never kick a gift horse in the mouth'? Why the hell hadn't Marina taken the money?

Marina explained morals to Thomas. How accepting the cash was wrong. How her whole life had been set free from the Indian restraining order. Her parents had taken a huge leap against their own kind to let Marina have the freedom of a 'Westerner'. It would be both unfair and unkind to snub that very same freedom. Marina had a saying herself, 'Never kick your parents in the mouth'. By taking Nicole's bribe, she would be throwing away her choice. Without choice, she would have no freedom. Without freedom – you are a slave.

Marina sipped posh coffee. 'Nicole had no right to tell me to keep away from you. That's my choice.' She watched his eyebrows raise. 'Not that I want you anyway. Because you wouldn't sleep with me if I was the last woman on earth. Would you?'

Thomas passed Marina a refill for the stapler, then

went on to explain that no, he would not sleep with Marina even if she was the last woman on earth. And, yes, he would be quite happy to let civilization cease – the end of the human race would not be through World War Three or a plummeting meteorite. No, the end of humanity would come about because Thomas could not sleep with a brown-skinned woman. He was sorry, it was not personal, or anything to do with racism, he just didn't believe in cultures mixing. And besides, he didn't fancy Marina anyway.

A look in Thomas's eye suggested he thought he'd explained himself pretty darn well. He said, 'Excuse me while I make a quick call.' He phoned through to Reception. 'Hannah, when you have a spare minute, bring in that parcel that arrived yesterday, would you? . . . Yes, that one. Thanks.' He returned his attention to Marina. 'I will prove just how serious I am when I say I am not racist.'

Clunk clunk clunk. 'I can't wait.'

The thought of Nicole handing over money in *that* condition didn't make sense – she was a mint girl, used notes gave her a rash – the pile of cash in front of him looked like it had been found in a dustbin, tossed in a tumble-dryer and thrown into a wrestling ring with John Prescott and one pork pie. Counterfeiters could learn a thing or two from Marina's laundering techniques.

'Ms Dewan?' Thomas questioned, picking up a few scrumpled £50 notes and examining them carefully. 'How come the money is in such a terrible condition?'

He should have seen it before it was starched and ironed this morning, thought Marina. She smiled, wondering about the strength of coffee Thomas had supplied her with, which was making it extremely hard for her mouth to stop talking and confessing all. 'Emily and I stripped naked and slept with it last night. Just for the thrill.' She visualized back to their rolling about the bed. 'We tried it with Monopoly money once – hasn't got the same feel as the genuine article. I suppose you don't do that sort of thing?'

As though the notes in Thomas's hand were covered in anthrax, he threw them across the room. 'No, you suppose correctly. So,' his blue eyes clamped on hers, 'if there is a shortfall in the total, where do you suggest I look?'

'Up Emily's . . . Use your imagination.' They both laughed and Marina wondered if, at last, Thomas was showing signs of flirting. Maybe the Ganges water was a patient servant. Maybe Gran's advice was finally paying off.

A knock at the door. Hannah was greeted at the entrance by Thomas. He thanked her for bringing the parcel, then sent her on her way.

'Right.' Thomas unwrapped the cellophane wrapper, pulled out the burnt-orange-coloured robe and tossed it at Marina. 'And you dare to call me a racist. Shame on you.'

Flummoxed, Marina felt the luxurious material and opened the garment out fully. Her eyes nearly shot off their stalks. This man was a moron. Embroidered in flowing gold writing on the fabric were the words *Monsoon Wedding*.

Before Marina could show her discontent, Thomas dropped another bombshell.

He spoke easily and confidently. 'And if that

doesn't prove my case, if I am such a notorious, atrocious racist, then why on earth would I stay up to the early hours of the morning watching a film called *Bend It Like Beckham*? Twice.' From his drawer he pulled out an envelope and threw it towards her. 'Please would you open that.' He flicked his VDU around to show his screen saver, still the Taj Mahal, still the dancing eunuchs. Thomas smiled brightly – still the moron.

Inside the envelope were five tickets for *Bombay Dreams*. What next? She waited for Thomas to don a turban. Maybe he would perform a *bhangra* dance for her? Or perhaps a quick recital of the 100,000 verses of the *Mahabharata* – in perfect Hindi.

'You are quite welcome to the tickets,' Thomas said, pleased with himself. 'Sorry there are only the five. I know you people breed like rabbits and five would hardly even cover your sisters, but the thought is there.' His smile faded as soon as he realized what was coming out of his mouth. 'My apologies. That's a bad analogy. Rabbits. I think you should go, Ms Dewan. I keep putting my foot in it. I really don't mean any disrespect. Your people are lovely people and . . .' He paused. 'Here I go again. If you stay much longer then, God forbid, I'm just going to end up calling you a Paki.'

And she didn't stay much longer. Just about the time it took for her to slap him hard around the face.

There was nothing worse than an ignorant toff.

Chapter Twenty-four

Sometimes one has to cry to save one's job. Stuart was due to meet Thomas for his appraisal at 9.00 a.m. in the bar. It was now 8.45 a.m. and not a tear in sight. Onions were a no-no – he was immune to them. Harry, the head chef, had offered to slap him around the face – and still no tears. There was only one solution.

Stuart pulled out the Arsenal/Chelsea programme for the 2001 FA Cup from his knife bag. The happiest day of his life was wrapped up in those pages. He could still remember the deafening roar as the ball hit the net, the ecstasy as the whistle blew at full time, and the train ride home from the Millennium Stadium in Cardiff where he had proposed to five women. No takers, mind, but plenty of groping and kissing.

He flicked open the brochure. One page in, and a lump had formed in Stuart's throat. Two pages in, and tears were developing in his eyes. Three pages in

– God he was *so* immensely proud of his team, Arsenal – he was completely bawling now and it was time to meet Thomas. He handed Harry the programme and made his way to the bar.

At a table looking out on the barbecue, Stuart sat snivelling in the empty bar. Outside the window, leaves and twigs danced on the lawn to a cross-country wind. Nature had a way of looking so beautiful to people when they were feeling down. As though it tried to cheer them up. But it would take more than a few crappy pirouettes from the twigs to cheer up Stu-pot. He loved his job and he might be losing it.

The door swung open, Thomas walked across the patterned carpet and sat on the facing chair. 'I haven't got time for games, Stuart. You're a good commis chef, I don't want to let you go, but your attitude stinks. From next week you will be sharing your job with a new commis. If your attitude doesn't improve he takes over fully. Simple as that. You're always complaining that you never get weekends off. Well, now you can. All of them. You can see Arsenal live again.'

Tears of joy rolled down Stuart's cheeks.

Thomas added a few new rules to Stuart's job plan. No drinking on the premises. No shagging on the premises. No shooting wildlife in gardens. And no spreading rumours to waitresses regarding their job security – it was cruel.

'And one more thing.' Thomas handed Stuart a napkin. 'No lies, Stuart. I don't care how much you drank yesterday; there is no excuse for what came out of your mouth. You embarrassed me, my client and the waitresses.' He coughed, now on to the serious matter. 'Nicole. What were you referring to last night? These chats you speak of, these cosy, friendly chats. I want to hear what you have to say. I'm particularly intrigued by this fantasy of yours of getting Nicole into bed. Would she be part of a gang-bang? Or would you give her special Stuart treatment?' Thomas stared sternly.

Stuart blew hard into the napkin, then gave the tissue a thorough visual autopsy. 'It was the drink and the girls winding me up.' He looked away from Thomas to the garden. 'It proves one thing, though. It proves to me that you and Nicole have a weak relationship. One drunk comment from me shouldn't have upset you so much, like I saw it in your face. Sign of a weak relationship, that is, when a man can't handle another man's jokes. And before you threaten to sack me again, just hear me out. I'm only telling you these things because I like you and respect you.'

'Go on,' Thomas said, showing a modicum of interest. 'I'm intrigued.'

And intrigue turned to anger as Stuart explained his pet theory. How Thomas was *not* in love with Nicole, had never been in love with Nicole, but, definitely, Thomas was in love. Stuart didn't need UN chemical inspectors to find out where Thomas was storing his 'love'. It was not hidden in some bunker out of eyeshot. It didn't need Hans Blix searching the herb gardens round the back. No, to anyone who saw Thomas on a daily basis, it was quite obvious where Thomas was keeping his love – right here, in the hotel. The Regency Hotel was Thomas's lover. And Nicole was just the beautiful woman; a status symbol in line with his Porsche, designer suits and posh apartment. No wonder the poor lass tried to top herself.

The table was quiet as Thomas considered this. Finally he opened his mouth: 'So, in your opinion, not that it really matters, or will make a blind bit of difference, but do you think that Nicole loves me? Or am I just a status symbol too?'

Stuart told Thomas to hold steady while he thought about this. He didn't want to upset their relationship with a snap answer. Stuart thought back to his favourite film, *Lethal Weapon Two*. Danny Glover sits on the toilet seat atop a bomb. To defuse the bomb it's either the red wire or the blue. Stuart eyed Thomas. This was one of those 'red' or 'blue' wire situations. If he said the wrong thing his job would explode, just like the toilet had. But he so wanted to say the wrong thing. He wanted to hurt Thomas badly.

With a jittery voice, Stuart opted for the truth. 'Nicole loves you. Fact! You're a very jammy man. Fact! How do I know this? Fact!' He scratched his cheek. 'No, that's not a fact. Erm, well, if you had to listen day in and day out to the waitresses explaining how much in love with you Nicole was, you would puke. It's a woman thing.'

'And this is a man thing,' Thomas said, grabbing Stuart round the neck. 'Go anywhere near her and I will kill you.' The gulping noise emanating from Stuart's throat suggested an agreement had been reached.

Fifteen minutes later, upstairs in his apartment, Thomas opened the safe and pulled out the letter he'd written to himself when he was fourteen. Stuart's ideas were duplicated on the sheets of paper. How packaging was the driving force in his life. If it looked good, then Thomas wanted it.

And by golly did Nicole look good.

Pinned on the tiles above the juice squeezer was a timetable. Its title: *Thomas's Engagement Day Schedule*. Splashed on the timetable was a smattering of kiwi fruit seeds, lemon pips, and cherry stalks. Nicole had stuck it there over a week ago, just before attempting her kiwi, lemon and cherry smoothie. The guide was brief but very helpful.

1. Get up, get dressed.
2. Don't be late for engagement party.
3. Oh yes, if you are late . . . leave the country.
   Love Nicole

Thomas smiled. The party preparations had taken over Nicole's life this week, leaving her with very little time to spare. Barely enough time to bribe Marina with the money. He thought about that for a second. Christ, that was a shocker, he didn't realize the extent a woman would go to, to keep the status quo. But he couldn't mention it to Nicole yet, he would have to let that one lie until after the engagement party. It was something that obviously needed discussing, but, to mention it now, when Nicole was so looking forward to tonight, well, he couldn't do it. Special days don't come around that often.

He'd already made arrangements for Nicole's seventy grand to be returned to her bank account. Not that she would realize. Only the other day she'd discovered another account that she'd completely forgotten about with over £200,000 in it. Thomas had unintentionally joked, 'Saving it for a rainy day?' and she had clouted him round the head with a French stick.

Sitting with his feet up, Thomas enjoyed a quiet moment. The letter lay on his lap begging to be read one more time. He checked the clock, 10.45 a.m. Only nine hours until the engagement party. Castle Cliff Manor waited to host its guests. The Gothic-style arched doorways perfect for their stuck-up noses. The huge echoing chambers ideal for their bumptious boasts. And, once inside, the party games would begin. I Spy Lester's Trophies. I Spy Lester's Photographs. I Spy Lester's Presence. Until Thomas's patience would snap. 'I Spy Lester's Ashes, up there on the fireplace. How did you manage to squeeze his big-head ashes into that little bowl?' Gasps all round. Wasn't Thomas a horrid man? Lester was buried not cremated. And the so-called 'ashes' were in fact a bowl of red and pink pot pourri.

Thomas was prepared for whatever the Newton-Harringtons & Co. threw at him tonight. He accepted that he would never fill Lester's gold-studded shoes in their eyes, but as long as he filled Nicole's dreams in her eyes, then *que sera sera*, what will be will be.

A bird squawking outside the window broke Thomas from his thoughts. He picked up the letter. Glaring up from the page was an unblinking passage. Written in the sturdy, confident hand of his youth, only to be read by the uncertain eyes of adulthood. Oh, what a jester he was.

Get rid of the leggy blonde. You know you don't love her.

DUMP HER!

Hitler missed Fenworth with his bombs, which, some would say, was a shame. Nevertheless, the Fenworth people were a proud people when sober and took a certain pride in their poverty. Forever boasting who claimed the most from Social Security or who lived off the least. Life had dealt them a crappy hand and they accepted it. But, if news got out that Marina had given back £70,000 – without a gun to her head – then fuck pride in poverty, this street was home to a mad woman, and she would be dutifully hissed, booed, then snubbed – for not giving the money to them.

Emily had been hissing and booing since yesterday when Marina had returned with the empty Head bag. It was now time to snub her. How could a best friend take away the chocolate cake after giving a taste? Why would Marina turn into Mother Teresa? Why? Oh sod why, now Emily couldn't afford that beautiful Gucci dress in the catalogue – not to mention the matching speedboat that went with it.

'Emily,' Marina knocked firmly on Emily's locked door, 'you can't stay in there all day. The money was poison. It would have turned bad on us, trust me. Our karma would have suffered and right now . . . Are you listening in there?'

'Go away! You took away my dream. We were supposed to go shopping yesterday but what did we do instead? We made sandwiches with Perv Bazzer. Fuck my karma. You kept me waiting all afternoon with your decision. I had to put up with his wet belly button rubbing against my thigh. Felt like a giant slug.'

'This is silly.' Marina took a deep breath and then in her best 'customer care' voice she continued. 'I'm sorry, Em, I'll be in my cell if you want to talk about this some more. If it's any consolation, you can have my choccie bar money this week.' Marina jumped as something smashed against the door, and she turned away feeling bad.

Emily shouted, 'Betrayer!' as Marina snuck into her room.

Today was supposed to be market day. The girls' weekly pilgrimage to Fenworth market, where they made their selection of fruit and vegetables freshly scrubbed of mildew and set out bruise-side-down on wooden trestles. Stocks were running low in the kitchen cupboards; Marina hoped that Emily's sulk ended soon, before the sun dropped.

And what a bad time to lose a friend – even if it was only temporary. Marina moved her view around the room. Wall to wall, floor to ceiling. Materially, all she owned was in this place. In this day and age, people would laugh at the meagre amount of goods she possessed. But she could remember seeing on TV families fleeing from floods, their whole life bundled into a blanket and tied with rope upon their heads. Who was laughing at them? Did it really matter what hi-fi you owned, or how fast your car went, or what carat of diamond sat neatly in your ring? Materialism was the curse of the modern age. The fun and games of real life surely lay in talk, cuddles, laughter – and sticking pins in Anne Robinson dolls.

Lately this world seemed alien to Marina. She

couldn't understand people's obsessive attitudes to excelling themselves through the addition of the latest DVD player. Belittling Mr and Mrs Shoestring because they lived their life on one. Strip it all away, and what are you left with? Human beings. We all come into the world with nothing and we all exit the world with nothing. Marina sat looking out on to her street. Oh boy, her mind was racing again.

But why live a life of drab when a comfortable existence sat staring you in the eye? Why turn your back on the world of make-believe? Marina thought of the woman who seemed to have free-fallen out of the pages of *Vanity Fair*. Nicole. An expensive woman with expensive tastes, that much was obvious. Nicole breathed with the disposition of a pedigree snoot. A very hard woman to please, no doubt.

And that's where Thomas came in. He was Nicole's pleasure. An engagement of the century lined up, a woman so obsessed with him that she resorted to bribery, and a man who was tarred with the same brush. Top suits, top car, top earnings. Money was their food of life, the pair of them, and nothing Marina could see would ever have them go hungry. She thought back to the parting slap in his office last night. He may never go hungry but his mouth would surely hurt from that. His eyes had bulged with adrenalin as the force of Marina's hand crunched against his cheek. There, she had thought, as he wobbled to one side, that's for all the idiots who go round saying the word 'Paki'. Enjoy the pain like we do.

A bus shot through Fairground Road careering around a discarded pushchair, fearful of Saturday violence in the district – possibly from the missing baby. One had to resort to playing dead in the road these days to get a bus to stop around here. Marina smiled then blinked across to the poster-picture of Thomas. 'I know, you shouldn't still be up there on the wall. But haven't you seen the film *Return Of The Jedi* where Hans Solo is frozen at the pleasure of Jabba the Hutt? I keep you up because I know at any time I can take you down. It's a power thing.' Despite herself, her heart still jumped at the sight of him. Maybe, if Marina got her kicks from a mild racist like Thomas, it was worth giving the National Front a go. Could be orgasmic. All those handsome skinheads, swastikas on their foreheads, missing teeth still imbedded in their last victim's thigh – ohh, heaven.

Lying back on her bed, Marina tapped her feet together in time to 'Mundian To Bach Ke' by Panjabi MC. A piece of music that crossed two cultures. English and Indian. Why couldn't people be as harmonious as music? Why all the barriers? This racist issue strolled around inside Marina's head, walking down avenues that she rarely visited. Different parts of her personality attacking the question from different angles. Even the word itself sounded rotten – racism.

Racism: a disease for the naive. Racists: experts in the art of nicknaming. Shallow, deprived people who would gladly let an Indian doctor save their child, but they wouldn't want their child mixing with one. Gladly eat Indian food at Indian restaurants while tipping only expletives with their forked tongue, mumbling 'Paki' behind the waiter's back, then tucking into their Chicken Tikka Masala with an attitude pickling in its own false sense of superiority. Gladly proclaim that Raj, the cheeky Pakistani chappy who owns the corner shop, is one of them. A white man in a brown body. 'You're one of us, Raj, you're okay. It's the other darky bastards I can't tolerate. Load of bludgers. Those foreigners are wrecking this country. But not you, Raj, you're one of us.'

No thanks.

Marina never wanted to be one of anyone. Just herself. Although, on occasion, being herself felt wrong. Her boat was adrift in life's ocean and sometimes the tide of India pulled her one way and at other times the tide of England pulled her the other way. But she was English; practically born, bred and fed in this country. Her loyalties varied depending upon how life was treating her. Today, life in England felt crap and India called with a loud voice. Tomorrow, life could be cool, and her ears would be deaf to India. Taking the best of both worlds was a juggling act all British-born Asians learned swiftly.

Shiva watched, his bronze-coloured skin dusty under the sun's glare. Marina rolled off the bed, collected a KFC wet-wipe from her drawer, and wiped the statue clean again. The spirits were potent today, and just the touch of the deity felt gratifying. As though it cleansed her smudged thoughts.

Marina uttered, 'Aum.' The sacred sound rang clear in the air. 'Aum.'

Kneeling upon the *puja* mat, Marina prayed to Shiva. A nonsensical garble of words and ideas in her mind came out as one solid sentence from her mouth. 'Tell me, Shiva, is racism a disease for life, or can it be cured?' Marina lit a juniper berry joss stick and returned to the window gazing. She knew Shiva might take some time getting back to her. Outside, the pushchair was still there, now filled with a cracked orange traffic cone, one car tyre and a bent bird cage, while two scruffy kids sat on a low wall across the road, fingers crossed, waiting for a mass pile-up in the road. They'd hit on the plan while watching CCTV footage of a group of boys laying a plank of wood on a railway line – *Crimewatch* gave them all the best ideas.

Marina knew in her heart that, just like the abandoned pushchair in the street, life had its obstacles. And bad karma was a huge obstacle at that. Emily and she had been busy, whittling away the corrupt vibes with letters of apology to old acquaintances they had wronged. The karma was getting better. Even so, Marina understood, the karma was still infected.

But maybe there was another reason why the Ganges water had not worked as Gran had said it would. Gran had mentioned something about it being vital to have her parents' blessings when decisions of the utmost importance were being considered. Finding a partner most definitely came under the category of 'utmost'. However, let's not forget reality here, thought Marina. Finding a partner was great, tip-top, it just so happened the partner who she'd chosen was getting married to someone else – he wasn't exactly on the market.

But her trust in Gran was huge. The Ganges water *would* work. It would ruin the wedding plans, it would turn Racist Thomas into Raunchy Thomas and her life would be a rip-roaring success.

Marina shouted, 'Aum!' triumphantly, then felt like crying. What a load of hopscotch. This was ridiculous. Eighteen years she'd saved that Ganges water for the man of her dreams and what does she do? She pours it over the first man who filled her exterior criteria. His gorgeous 'I want to have your babies' looks. His fabulous 'I want to lick you all over' body. And his fantastic 'Tie me up, do as you please' mouth. What a waste of Ganges water. A rapist can be good-looking, and so can a murderer, even a politician (actually, maybe not).

But so can a racist.

There was a huge screech outside, followed by a car horn, then an angry man yelling, 'You stupid little boy. You could have killed someone.' To which the kid replied, 'That's the point, moron.' Marina waited for calm before picking up her mobile. It was time to speak to her mum – watching a grown man being manhandled into a bird cage by five youths wasn't her cup of Darjeeling.

'*Namaste*,' Marina greeted.

'*Namaste*,' Mum replied. 'I had a feeling you were going to call . . . but that was three days ago. What took you?'

'I had a feeling you were going to be out. So, I didn't bother.'

'Very smart, Marina. I'm so glad you take after me and not your father. Thirty-three years we've been married and not once has he said anything clever like that. Although he once astounded everyone by solving the *Daily Mirror* crossword. Five letters, begins in B ends in D, carbohydrate food. How *ever* did he get that?'

Dad shouted in the background, 'The answer is bread.'

Marina and Mum laughed. Dad always bore the brunt of jokes. The conversation twisted and turned until it came full circle. And Marina came back to the topic of intelligence.

'Mum, you're clever, you have the wisdom of many years behind you. I have a moral question that needs the mind of a genius to answer it.'

'That will be me,' Mum agreed. 'Go on.'

'Am I, your daughter, good enough for *any* man?'

Mum changed ears. Left was best when discussing men. 'There is not a man on this planet who could honestly declare you are not good enough for him. But, and hear me very carefully, Marina, there are definitely men on this planet who are not good enough for *you*. Should I be asking why you ask?'

When to lay the trap, Marina wondered. 'Okay, so, I am good enough for all men, but some men are not good enough for me? Would you still say that if I married someone who was, how do I put this? Look, you and Dad married each other even though you were from different castes. Right?' Mum agreed. 'And you have a lovely life together – not to mention a lovely daughter. My point is this, how would you feel, and remember this is hypothetical, how would you feel if the man who I chose was not quite the man you had in mind? I mean, if he was not a Hindu.'

A pause, a sigh, a natter in the background, and then the voice. 'I would have to be happy for you. But I am convinced that you will find a good Hindu boy. And, Marina, in my heart, I feel that the time is coming very soon. I can feel it.'

Trap time. 'So, bearing in mind that my happiness is paramount to you as you have said countless times, and that you have no argument against me marrying someone who is not a Hindu, how would you feel, hypothetically of course, if I brought a white man home one day? Would I have your blessing? Your hypothetical blessing, that is.'

Silence. Followed by . . . silence.

'Mum?' Marina said. 'It's only a hypo—'

'Hypothetical, yes, I know. Look, there are many great white Englishmen, you know how much I love Hugh Grant, even your father looked a lot like him when he wore that Hugh Grant mask last *Diwali*, but—'

Marina interrupted. 'Hugh Grant slept with a prostitute, Mum. My hypothetical man wouldn't do that sort of thing. In fact, the hypothetical man who I am thinking about is a real charmer.'

'Hmm. A charmer? Well, in that case I would have to say "yes", you would have my blessing. But, in my heart . . .' She paused. 'In my heart, Marina, my dreams would be dampened – hypothetical dreams, that is.'

Marina gave Thomas on the wall the thumbs-up. The blessing had been delivered – it could not be undone now. Maybe the Ganges power would be allowed to flow at last. The support of her parents gave her bow the arrow.

Just one good shot would send it far into St Meridians, Oxfordshire, and deep into Thomas's heart.

A hairy spider crawled across Emily's ceiling, easily gripping the dirt. Haven't you got a web to go home to, thought Emily, who sat on her bed protecting herself with a pillow. The sexy voice of Dr Fritzgerald Guztelburg sounded from her cassette recorder. This was self-help tape number seventeen and his voice was becoming harsher, more affirmative, lacking the original softness he had displayed in the earlier tapes. And the animal noises now in the background were becoming a cause for concern.

'Conned' was a word that sprang to Emily's mind. Conned out of £70,000. Conned out of Thomas. Conned out of life. But, as Emily well knew, there were times in your life when you just had to put your trust in God. Take, for instance, Michael Johnson, the 400-metre man. God gave him speed, and Johnson won Gold. Or Einstein. God gave him brains and he helped the world to acquire the Atom Bomb. And even the Queen. God gave her a throne, and she gets licked on stamps. Emily glanced at the mirror opposite. Now what had God given her? She smiled: big breasts, blue eyes and blonde hair. And for what purpose would God give someone like Emily these, she contemplated, puckering up her lips, puffing up her chest and fluffing up her hair.

Well, *that* was entirely obvious. These gifts from God were to win men like Thomas. To make a play for him in full view of money-bags Nicole. And then . . . wait to be paid off. Marina had been given £70,000 and she wasn't *even* blonde. God knows how much Nicole would pay to keep a blonde minx like me out of their lives, Emily wondered. Could be millions. Low-cut dress, all-over tan, the highest heels, the sexiest walk. Every trick known to woman-kind would be utilized. Resistance would be futile.

Either Thomas would practically die choking on his own drool, or Nicole would get her chequebook out. It was a win-win situation. She got Thomas or she got the money. Maybe she would even get both. (Thomas came with an awful lot of money anyway.)

Emily tucked herself deep into her duvet. It was hard to relax with a 500-gram sumo-spider dangling above one's head. 'Piss off, Charlotte,' Emily ordered. 'Or I'll put you in Mr Redips's sandwich.'

Some customers were as rude as hell. Mr Redips had been eating dead insects for the last two weeks, since his remark regarding Marina and Al-Qaeda. If Marina knew where Bin Laden was hiding it was her duty, as a Muslim, to inform the correct authorities. Suffice to say, he preferred his sandwiches to be served by someone who didn't pray to Mecca – *comprende*? And so came the arthropod mix. Cheese and pickled silverfish. Ham and granary mustard insects. And his Tuesday special – cottage cheese, chives, beetle thoraxes and maggots. Yummy. Napkins Sandwich Bar floor had never been cleaner.

Emily thought of her friend next door. It was not Marina's fault her goody-two-shoes logic overtook her survival sensibilities sometimes. It was make-up time with Marina, and after that – Emily viewed her reflection in the mirror – it was make-up time with her face.

Within a few weeks, and Emily didn't need no crummy Ganges water to predict her own future, she would be with Thomas or she would have a healthy bank balance. Either way meant the same thing: she would be able to afford that amazing see-through Gucci dress from the winter collection.

Bring it on!

Chapter Twenty-five

In Britain alone one thousand men propose to one thousand women per day. Out of those one thousand men, possibly nine hundred change their minds the minute they ejaculate. Out of the nine hundred who have changed their minds, at least one hundred will forget to tell the woman underneath them. Men like these, this world could do without, thank you very much.

Thankfully, not all men are bastards.

Thomas stood beside his Porsche on the winding lane that led to Castle Cliff Manor half a mile up the road. It was 7.45 p.m. and his arrival was cutting it fine for the official 8.00 p.m. start. To be late for one's own engagement party gave out the wrong message; and his usual 'there was a problem at the hotel' excuse was wearing a bit thin these days. A Rolls Royce Silver Ghost drove smoothly by, but Thomas paid no heed. The last ten minutes had seen a convoy of collector's cars, Ferraris, Bentleys, Rollses, BMWs, Jags, Aston Martins and Porsches, sneak towards the manor. The sight would have hit Jeremy Clarkson's G-spot – somewhere in that mop of curly hair no doubt – but, to Thomas, each car brought with it a cargo of boasts. Who owned what, who knew whom, who earned the most. The who's who of the upper-class world. Circles within circles and wheels within wheels. The Dow Jones index would change as a result of this party.

And so would Thomas Harding.

No one stopped for Thomas, all of them oblivious to the handsome man in the smart tuxedo standing beside his red Porsche. But why would they? Most of them didn't even know what Nicole's fiancé looked like.

The sky was swept clean of clouds, a perfect night for a shooting star. From his pocket Thomas removed the letter he'd written to himself as a lad, and flicked through the pages one more time before flicking his lighter and setting the words to flame. It was unhealthy keeping a closed mind. Holding on to ideas and ideals just for the sake of history.

The burnt letter puffed with smoke as Thomas grated it to pieces with the sole of his shoe. Nothing quite like letting go. Nothing more wobbly than a mind confused by its youth. Now, with a steady heart and a happy mind, Thomas could walk into Castle Cliff Manor and do what he was supposed to do.

At the entrance to the manor gates, a security guard tapped on Thomas's window with his sovereign ring. No one was getting through without the required, unfakable, watermarked invitation. A few journalists stood waiting out of eyeshot, hoping that the security guard would soon need feeding. The rumbling noises they mistook for his belly earlier were, in actual fact, guard dogs heaving against their chains.

'No invite, no entry,' the guard said to Thomas. 'It's a private function. Just driving up in a posh car doesn't get you entry into this place, my son.'

'Well, tell Nicole Newton-Harrington that her fiancé cannot make it to the engagement party because' – Thomas looked up to King Kong's name tag – 'because Franco Colombo has taken an executive decision and barred him entry.'

A booming laugh, followed by, 'Nice try, son, you're the second fiancé I've barred today.' He waved to a cowering journalist, the bushes barely concealing his four-foot camera lens. 'That's the other idiot over there. Although at least you made the effort to dress accordingly.' A pause. 'And the accent wasn't too bad either. Now, on your way, or else I'll call for back-up.' He stood aside giving ample room for manoeuvre. 'And just in case you were thinking of ramming the gates – I'm an expert in special forces training, I've read everything Tom Clancy's done. So don't take me lightly.'

Five minutes later, after a brief conversation with Nicole on her mobile, the gates opened. Franco Colombo reassured Thomas that he was only doing his job and kissed Thomas's hand as a mark of respect. The journalist in the bushes was only doing his job as well when he snapped the photo of Franco's lips on Thomas's hand, which would head tomorrow's Sunday rag with the caption: *Gay affair at Castle Cliff Manor. Billionaire's daughter,*

Nicole Newton-Harrington, engaged to a rampant HOMOSEXUAL! It was a cruel world.

Ignoring Franco's 'popstars' bog-standard attempt at 'Uptown Girl' by Billy Joel, Thomas drove through the security gates and up the avenue lined with beefy oak trees, past the wide five-barred gate that led to the stables and further on into the heart of the Newton-Harrington empire. A helicopter chopped overhead; maybe it was a film crew scouting a location for the re-make of *Dynasty*.

Thomas jammed the handbrake and stared up at the side of the mansion; ivy crawling like arteries amongst the old brickwork. God, maybe that chopper was spraying the air with LSD, warping the guests' minds, turning their understanding to mush. Possibly then, with a bit of luck, the hallucinations would turn Thomas into Lester – the true son-in-law the Newton-Harringtons wanted.

The dead son-in-law they would never get.

A short walk from his car and Thomas stood at the main doorway, its huge Gothic presence almost alive with its history. A waitress appeared, handing Thomas a flute of champagne. Behind her stood another waitress holding a box of pink carnations for buttonholes; he picked one and popped it in.

And now for the fun and games, he guessed, standing in a hall big enough to land an aeroplane. Thomas often thought it a good idea at gatherings such as this that labels should be supplied to guests, on which they could scribble down their net worth and stick it to their shoulder. At least it might curtail some of the boasting that was already the meat of most conversations.

People lubricated the long corridors like top-grade oil, a mass of bodies mainly from the south; the few northern accents disguised by years of elocution lessons. Except the Liverpudlian accent, of course, which was undisguisable. Thomas did his thing, smiled on cue, hid his real feelings deep down inside. Most faces were a mystery to him, some he could vaguely recollect, and a few, a very few, were his own friends and family. Everyone had bothered to turn up. Two rooms had been put aside for gifts alone.

'Ah, Thomas, great to see you, old boy.' Smithy, Thomas's butterfly man in the four-by-one medley relay team at Oxford University, slapped Thomas on the back. 'Bloody great bash you've got here.' Smithy would be hard to shift. Once he found Thomas, he never let go. 'So, marrying into the Newton-Harringtons, eh? You always were a brave one. Nudge, nudge, wink, wink. Need a little collateral, go marry a Harrington.'

A woman's voice sounded. 'Thomas, darling.'

It was rare that Thomas's mother saved him, but, thankfully, she did right now. And Thomas received her warming hug with an even warmer smile – she looked ravishing for a mother. In fact, she looked ravishing full stop. Dressed, for all the world, as if this were her own engagement. Low-cut, cappuccino-coloured silk Chanel dress, elegant ankles balancing on high heels, and an all-over tan. If Pops wasn't careful, he'd have another heart attack.

'Mom, you look sensational. Where's Pops?' Thomas walked her away from Smithy and stood in front of a suit of armour.

'Grumpy is apologizing to blonde thingamajig's

father, Edmond, for later. In case he gets drunk he's apologizing in advance. Saves on embarrassment, don't you think?'

Thomas sniffed his mother's breath. 'Thought so. Stay off the sherry, Mom. It's an important night, don't show up the Hardings . . . and that goes for Pops too. And just for the record, Mom, her name is Nicole. My future wife.'

A balloon popped in the background, sending the hallway into fits of laughter. What the blazes was in the balloon, thought Thomas, laughing gas? This lot were easily pleased. Or were they?

From above, the sound of heavy shoes clomped down the elaborate staircase. Nicole's younger cousin, Stefan, purposefully walked towards Thomas and his mother. A grim expression tied his face in a knot. A dim view of Thomas seared his brain. Life was about winners and losers. Only the strongest survive. It wouldn't take much noddle to realize that this complete jerk was an army man – the full military uniform sort of gave the game away.

'Congratulations, Thomas.' He saluted Thomas with a stiff hand. 'You are an extremely lucky man marrying my cousin. Extremely.' He nodded towards Thomas's mother. 'You have raised a fine gentleman, Mrs Harding, a hard worker. We all hope that he fulfils his obligations to Nicole. Although,' he paused, 'I fear Nicole's dreams will never be quite fulfilled . . . Lester. How we all miss Lester.'

Before Victoria Harding had time to remove her Chanel shoe, Nathan, Thomas's best mate, arrived in the nick of time. Just like a best mate should.

'If you miss him so much, why not join him?'

Nathan said, staring towards the sword dangling by Stefan's side. 'Run yourself through. Serve your country.'

'I didn't mean any harm by it. My apologies,' Stefan replied. 'It's just that Lester set such a high standard, that's all. It's a compliment in itself to even be compared with him.' Stefan saluted again. 'I'm sorry if I've upset you. My mission was to fetch you for Nicole upstairs, Thomas. If you follow me, then I shall lead the way.'

But Thomas already knew the way. Up one set of winding stairs that led to an impressively large landing where huge Persian vases decorated the floor and an enormous oil painting of Lester and Edmond leaning against a hedge, shotguns at the ready, covered part of the facing wall; then up another small flight that fed into a well-lit corridor which smelled strongly of perfume. Thomas hoped in his soul that the photograph of Lester and Nicole, horseback-riding in the snowy meadows, would have been taken down from outside her bedroom door. Just as now, in a minor way, he was hoping that Lester himself was missing from inside her heart.

Hope faded. The smiling, red-cheeked faces of Nicole and Lester shone out of the frame. Never had he studied this snapshot before, never had this snapshot meant so much before. It said a lot that Nicole had thought to leave this photograph on the wall during her engagement party. It kicked Thomas to second place on the podium.

'Nicole.' Thomas knocked on her bedroom door; the women's voices within fell silent. 'It's me.'

A sudden squeal, a patter of feet, the door burst

open, two sets of lips hit his mouth. Greetings by way of Nicole's sisters. Thomas couldn't be sure but there might have been an invasion of privacy in his mouth just then. Arabella was a self-confessed kissaholic. Just the barest opening of a handsome man's mouth and she'd be there, tongue at the ready. Mummy and Daddy would go apeshit if they knew. And as for Holly, well, she was the quiet one, the one who read Brontë novels, one of those sad women who wished to marry a man just like Daddy. Then of course there was Nicole. Good point, *where* was Nicole?

'She's in her wardrobe,' Arabella said, lying back on the four-poster bed, crumpling her bright-red velvet Dior dress beneath her. 'I couldn't find her in the shoe section; maybe she wandered down to accessories and handbags.'

Thomas shook his head. The Bermuda Triangle wardrobe. Nicole might never return. If nothing was heard within fifteen minutes, he'd call Ramone and send in the search party. Ramone wasn't opposed to wandering through women's underwear anyway – it reminded him of Elton John – it was a 'Sacrifice' he was happy to make.

Holly stood facing the antique mirror, combing her long blonde hair, humming 'Greensleeves' to herself. She partially begrudged Thomas. Three sisters would soon become just two. Their power, like witches', would be diminished. Broken up by the most random element in the world. Love. As haphazard as the wind and sometimes just as destructive.

But Holly didn't like the random. It interfered with the uniformity of her life. Three virtually identical sisters, all blonde, all leggy, all *extremely* beautiful would be torn asunder by a man whom her parents despised. The thought brought an ugly frown to her forehead. She walked to the window and gazed at the tremendous view outside.

Only an act of God would separate Nicole and Thomas now.

Arabella meanwhile watched Thomas as he uneasily shifted from one foot to the other. A sign of nerves, perhaps? Or a sign of something else? Daddy detested a man who couldn't control his nerves. A sign of weakness. 'This country used to be "Great",' he would say. Now Daddy called it Weak Britain. But Arabella knew why Thomas appeared to have the collywobbles: he felt unwelcome here. Mummy and Daddy made sure of that. Which was why Arabella went out of her way to do the opposite.

Arabella smiled across at him. 'Imagine if you stayed over tonight, Thomas, and mixed up my room with Nicole's. You might end up sleeping with me.' She fluttered her eyelashes. 'You'd love that, wouldn't you? Two sisters, both shagged by you.'

'I can't say I've ever really . . .' Thomas began. 'Can we change the topic?'

But there was no need. Like someone being spat out of a huge cave, Nicole appeared holding a pair of Patrick Cox sandals above her head, tossing the new box to one side. 'Found them! The engagement is back on.' She spotted Thomas and her mouth grew huge. 'Yeeeeeeek!' Nicole squealed all the way across the floor in her underwear, wrapped her arms around him and covered him with kisses.

To stay would be rude; Holly and Arabella left. Their dates for the evening were being kept on ice downstairs. It was time for the Newton-Harrington babes to mingle. The party could now officially begin.

And so could this fairy tale.

Once upon a time a princess stood in front of her prince and slipped into her dress. Nicole redefined Thomas's idea of beauty that very moment. Elegance and happiness poured from her every fibre and it was quite incredible that she was his. A strapless, violet satin dress hugged her curves all the way down to her ankles. Her hair was pinned up with a few wispy curls dangling. She'd made a daring attempt at looking absolutely perfect – and pulled it off completely. To stare with one's mouth open would be impolite. Thomas stared impolitely.

'You look, oh my God, just beautiful.' Thomas stepped forward and held her tiny waist. 'Although, you have got lipstick on your teeth.' He kissed her passionately.

Nicole picked a violet carnation off her dresser and passed it to Thomas. 'I'll wipe my teeth, and you, Tom, must change your buttonhole. This one matches my dress. I picked it from the garden myself this morning,' she said.

Thomas swapped flowers, slightly nervous, but hopeful that all would go smoothly tonight. He watched as Nicole daintily removed the lipstick from her teeth using the barest of material from the handkerchief's corner. With clean teeth she smiled over at him, shaking out the hanky . . . Thomas's eyes suddenly jammed wide, staring at the silk material. Totally unprepared for the sick feeling that smothered him all of a sudden, he sat back on the bed, bitter, jealous, angry and betrayed at what he'd just witnessed. Of all the times, of all the days, of all the things.

Nicole set about topping up the lippy. Sometimes the finishing touches take the longest. Thomas reeled. His heartbeat seemed to be counting backwards like a ticking time bomb.

10 Ignore what you saw, Tom.
9 *Can't!*
8 She loves you.
7 *Does she really? After what I just saw on the hanky?*
6 But you love her!
5 *Do I? Or do I simply love her packaging?*
4 But that's shallow, Tom.
3 *That's me. Christ, what a bastard I am.*
2 Don't do anything stupid, Tom, you'll regret this.
1 *How can I regret it, I'll always be second-best to Lester.*
0 BOOOOOOM!

'I'm sorry, Nicole, but I can't marry you,' Thomas said. 'It would be totally wrong.'

There was an unhappiness in his voice that shook Nicole to the core. She pulled back from the mirror, turned round and stared at Thomas with fear in her eyes, her shaking hand still holding the hanky. 'What do you mean?'

'It would be a sham. I don't think you've let go of Lester yet. Besides that, I know this isn't the best of timing in the world, but I don't think I love you like I thought I did.' Thomas rubbed the back of his neck with his hand, sadness permeating through every pore. 'For God's sake, Nicole, look at what you're holding. You removed that from underneath your pillow – now you tell me that Lester is the furthest thing from your mind.'

Sullenly Nicole's eyes dipped. The white silk handkerchief, the smoking gun, felt light in weight but heavy in significance. Lester's famous embroidered words, *I'm a Winner*, guiltily sparkled from the gold glitter thread. A keepsake that shouldn't have been kept.

Especially under her pillow.

Panic pounded Nicole's heart. She could see how upset Thomas was; how was she going to deal with this? One thing for sure, she thought, it was fixable. She dropped the handkerchief, walked over to Thomas and knelt before him where he sat on the bed. Admittedly, she wasn't too sure what to say.

'I'm sorry, Tom, it's just a silly memento. I don't lie in bed thinking about him every night.' She placed her head on his lap. 'I blame myself for what happened to him, but I never wish I was still with him. I love you, and I have never loved anyone like I love you. It's a cliché, Tom, but it fits: you are my life.'

He gently stroked her neck. 'I'm trying to convince myself that you are sincere, Nicole. But there are clear signs that persuade me otherwise. Just outside in the hall, for example, there's a huge photograph of you and Lester; this may sound petty, but the least you could have done for me today was to have that photo taken down. It was an insult. It proves you were thinking little about me.' He paused. 'This is not all about Lester, though. Marriage is a total commitment, it's enough to bring me out in a cold sweat, I admit that. I have to be sure about this step and, to be truthful here, I don't think I love you enough to marry you, Nicole. It's a horrible thing to say, it really is. But, to be honest, I don't know if I will ever love anyone enough to marry them.'

Silently Nicole cried into his lap. She'd witnessed this scene a thousand times before in her mind, scared that her nightmare would come true. There were aspects of Thomas that hinted he might bail out, but even she didn't think he'd leave it until the eleventh hour. Warnings about him had come from all sides: family, friends and pets (even docile Pongo became rabid at the sight of Tom). Many people had expressed their concerns over Thomas's fascination with blondes. Beautiful blonde women who looked spectacular on his arm. 'You'll just be his toy, Nicole, nothing more than that.' A toy to look good, by his side, in his hotel. Always always always his hotel. She'd seen his grouchy face when the hotel had been compromised for romance. He'd rather sort out the plumbing in Room 36 than sort out the plumbing in Nicole's knickers. Hardly the telling signs of a man in love! Hardly the potential signs of a man eager for marriage.

Nicole peered up, her eyes a tangled mess of make-up and tears. 'I never asked you to marry me, Tom, it was *you* who asked me. Why? Why ask if you knew you didn't love me enough? That makes you a fraud. And it makes me . . .' She burst out crying again. '. . . *single*.'

It was a ruddy good question: why did he ask? There was one answer that seemed to solve everything nowadays, so he used it. 'It's 9/11. The terrorist attack made me see life differently. That's all.' He could hardly explain that it was her perfect packaging that had prompted him to pop the question. It seemed easier to blame Al-Qaeda. 'Seriously, I assumed it was what we both wanted. But today I realized it was only you who wanted it.' He handed her his hanky and waited while she wiped her eyes. 'I was dreading this engagement party. It all seems so plastic. So false.'

Nicole by now had slipped to his ankles. Her sobs pock-marked the white carpet. 'It's not plastic, it's Mummy and Daddy trying to welcome you into our family. The only thing plastic here is your honesty. Your lies. I know the reason why this engagement has been torn to pieces and it's got nothing to do with Bin Laden. It's that Indian woman you met, you've fallen in love with her,' she whispered. 'Haven't you, Thomas?'

Thomas laughed intensely – those laughing-gas balloons again. 'Indian? An Indian, Nicole. Now *come on*. That's all you credit me for, is it? I go from you, the top end of the scale, all the way down to an Indian at the bottom. You must be mad.'

'*And* she comes from Fenworth,' Nicole snivelled.

'Exactly. An Indian from Fenworth. Now stop all this.' He took her hand and pulled her up. 'It's no one, Nicole. It's the hardest thing I've ever had to tell anyone, but we can't be together any more. I can't give you what you want. I can't—'

She interrupted. 'If we love each other, then nothing else matters. You used to tell me that all the time. Forget everyone, you said, just think of us as the last two people on this planet. We can be happy, Tom, please don't throw it all away because of pre-wedding nerves.' Her eyes were wide open with expectancy – but in her heart, she knew it was hopeless. 'Don't leave me, Tom, I can't live without you.'

Thomas brushed his eyes – dust probably. He spoke harshly. 'This is hard for me to say, Nicole, but I don't love you enough to want to spend the rest of my life with you. And people will say I'm mad, and maybe one day I'll think I made a terrible mistake . . .' He stopped as she flopped down his legs and slumped by his shoes, crying with such sadness that his eyes watered up. He'd never seen her this way before. A lump grew in his throat. 'I hope that you will forgive me for this one day.'

A knock at the door was met with a warning by Thomas to stay out. Nicole's sobbing was clearly audible even through the thick door of the bedroom; Arabella pushed in anyway and froze at the sight which met her eyes. Nicole seemed so small and lost, grovelling at Thomas's feet. Such pain was never meant to be part of today. What the hell had just happened here?

Arabella ran to Nicole and knelt beside her. At a guess she knew this was serious. The fact that the floor was filled with so many tears that the bed had a high-tide mark more or less gave the game away. Only a man could bring a woman to the floor like this. And there was only one man in the room.

'What have you done, Thomas?' Arabella screamed, cradling Nicole in her arms. 'Why is she so upset?'

'He doesn't love me, Bella, he's called the whole thing off,' Nicole moaned. 'I want to die. I want to end it all.'

Thomas looked to Arabella, who stared daggers back at him. Thomas had come here to celebrate his engagement. Two rooms were filled with presents downstairs. Six of the guests had flown in from Australia. A large crowd awaited the happy couple to join them in the main hall.

'Nicole,' Thomas began, bending down on one knee, ignoring the spite directed at him by Arabella, 'come for a drive with me and we can discuss this further.'

'Is there a chance you might change your mind?' Nicole saw him shake his head. 'Well, bog off then.'

The two sisters whispered with each other. Various cutting remarks slipped out, like Bastard, Fake and Devil. It was decided that Thomas would have to pay a price. Quite a steep one at that.

Arabella spoke. 'You have to explain in person to all the guests downstairs why you are calling off the engagement. No slipping out of the back door for you. You owe it to Nicole.'

'No way!' he joked – but the timing was off.

Arabella rose from the ground, a dragon spitting fire. 'Thomas Harding, if you are not downstairs within fifteen minutes, then I will see to it that your precious hotel receives atrocious publicity – say goodbye to your four AA stars. Trust me, I mean it. It will be my personal vendetta.'

For some unknown reason Nicole burst out laughing at this. Thomas shook his head. Sisters. He hated it when sisters got together. He gave Nicole one last look. Hordes of guests awaited him on the ground floor.

He took a deep breath as he walked out to the

corridor where Lester smiled down at him from the photograph. Thomas sneered. 'I haven't finished with you yet. Just a few weeks and the truth will be known. Winner? I don't think so.'

There were thirty-five steps to the bottom. Each one seemed to take an hour to descend. Thomas entered the noisy hall filled with four hundred happy people chatting . . .

Which was nearly as noisy as Marina's parents' living room in Watford filled with just two Indian men chatting. Mum was in the kitchen – surprise surprise – while the men discussed Marina's love life. Palekji, Marina's and Zaine's adopted uncle, voiced his opinion in the only style he knew how. Bloody loud.

'It's all about fingers in pies, Sundeep, fingers in pies,' Palekji shouted, spreading out his ten fat digits and wiggling them like tentacles at Marina's dad. 'And you know I love my pies.'

The men laughed, guzzling Teachers whisky, determined to have a skeleton of a plan ready before the deep-fried *pakoras* were dished up. Marina's problem was her freedom. She'd been given too much of it. She was a glutton. Even so, Palekji's remedy was ruled out immediately.

Dad spoke. 'I'm not sending my daughter to India to instil discipline, Palekji, she's a good girl, it's just her age that's the problem. You know lots of people. I can rely on you to find her a good Hindu man but I need more than this from you.' He refilled Palekji's tumbler. 'I need tactics.'

Palekji nodded, scratching his bald patch, God he

missed hair at times like this. 'Tactics. Like a game of chess? You honour me with your confidence, Sundeep, and I shall prove my worth with my cunning. Do you have the blessings of your wife? Or is this between the men?'

'She knows. Our discussions have kept us up very late. It's time Marina was married. Her clock has now run out, I'm afraid. If we leave it any longer.' He stared up at Palekji. 'Well, you know what I mean.'

Palekji nodded. He knew. 'Her ovaries will pack up. Nasty business.'

Dad hadn't quite meant that. He was referring more to the market of arranged marriages. Where women, like fruit, are great when ripe, but when bruised and old, get left until last. Only the desperate and needy will buy old, bruised fruit. And Marina, so pretty and intelligent, was not about to be married to a desperate needy man. Her life had been free, she'd had her choices and chances, but sometimes a daughter of strong mind will not ask for help when she needs it most. Marina would never sink to her knees and ask for Mum and Dad's help in finding her a man, so, instead of her sinking to her knees, Mum and Dad would have one delivered. Right to her door if necessary.

'So,' Dad munched on *pakora* number six, while Mum sat hopeful that the men would find the solution. 'So, you say you have this list of bachelors? Suitable men who fit the criteria I laid out?'

'Tall, handsome, clever, rich, honest, hard-working and extremely Westernized. Rich pickings. Only the best for my good friends.'

'And you think this can be arranged soon?' Mum asked, concerned as always.

Palekji smiled. 'Let's just say, I'm mildly confident. I have this one man in mind who I think fits the bill perfectly. I would gamble a rupee or two that Marina falls in love with him on first viewing.'

Dad grinned to his wife. 'See, I told you he was good.'

'Tactics. That's me. Tactics.'

The men laughed.

Food filled bellies as the plan was sculpted. On this Saturday evening, on a warmish night in September, the Indian family tree machine steamed into action. Not just in this town, but in every town across the UK, Indian relatives planned and concocted the futures of their children. Weddings, engagements, first meetings and even first viewings via the Internet. The best interests of the children lay at the heart of most parents and sometimes being sneaky was part and parcel of arranged marriages.

Marina's parents and Palekji were not proud of their devious plan but it was necessary for success. Marina could be very stubborn and it was of the utmost importance that she felt any decisions regarding men were hers and hers alone. And that's why her Uncle Palekji was drafted in to help. He would set the whole thing up.

And to think Cilla Black thought she was the expert at blind dates. Ha!

Thomas felt like Daniel, but this den was filled with more aggressive lions. Nearly four hundred expectant sets of eyes watched with a certain amusement as he wobbled unsteady on the small platform that had been erected for tonight's speeches. One reason why Thomas wobbled so much was he was pissed. Nearly a whole bottle of champagne gurgled in his stomach popping bubbles of pure alcohol into his bloodstream. His hand was sore from the handshakes of congratulations as he'd walked to the podium. His back was numb from the pats. And his cheeks were a rainbow of lipstick colours. The mood was ripe for a happy end to the evening. But where was the beautiful Nicole?

'Good evening everyone,' Thomas began, his mouth spraying spit into the mike, his free hand clutching the champers bottle. 'Thank you all for coming. And thank you all for your wonderful gifts.' Thomas pointed to the huge ice sculpture of himself and Nicole, melting quietly at the rear of the hall. 'So sweet.' His eyes narrowed, hard to focus, lots of blur. 'For those of you who don't know who I am, I'm Thomas. Nicole's . . . I'm Tom.'

A door opened towards the back letting in a small group of people who settled quickly. Waitresses buzzed around like worker bees keeping the hive happy with drink and canapés. A few coughs, one drunken giggle and a young child being told to wait with his party popper. The celebrations would come soon enough. But where was Nicole?

Thomas continued. 'I'm sorry to bring bad tidings to this wonderful occasion. Many of you have travelled the length and breadth of Britain to be here. But, as you all know, I own the Regency Hotel in St Meridians, Oxfordshire. A four-star establishment of en-suite rooms with twenty-four-hour room service and a health and beauty salon that, to be honest, knocks socks off my competitors.'

His eyes were caught by someone waving from the audience. He strained hard and just about made out Nathan, his best mate, mouthing something like, 'This is not the time, Tom, no hotel advertising. Later.'

Thomas grew redder. 'Erm, sorry about that. Nerves. I always get nervous when I'm about to relay devastating news.' He took a huge swig from his champagne bottle, then with icy cool delivered the next sentence. 'Nicole and I have called off the engagement!' Silence. 'She's crying her heart out right now. God, I've screwed this up.' He staggered back a bit, steadying himself with nothing and fell over, the mike landing on top of him. From the floor he continued, 'I have hurt a very special woman, a true one-off and, as you all know, I think she deserves better than me. I am an unfit partner. One might say, a true cad.'

A frantic Nathan scrambled across the podium and helped Thomas to his feet. He whispered, 'I think this speech is over, Thomas,' as he tried to grab the microphone.

The upper class are well trained in the dramatic. Watching endless scenes of opera is where they fine-tune their poise. It's a rarity indeed when one is so shocked that one stares with one's mouth open.

Thomas viewed the four hundred open mouths. Mom, Pops, friends, the Newton-Harringtons, all of them. Enough tonsil meat to keep a pot-bellied pig happy for a week. More sets of perfect teeth than at an Oscar bash. It was the largest game of musical statues that Thomas had ever seen. And it was the first time that he'd witnessed Marion Newton-Harrington without something to say.

A snotty bloke's voice broke the silence, loud and clear. 'Shame on you, Thomas. This is a far cry from how Lester would have treated Nicole. A far cry indeed. I therefore repeat myself: shame on you.'

Nathan tried to plug Thomas's ears with his fingers but it was too late. Thomas had heard. It was just a matter of how long Thomas's drunk brain would take to make sense of the words. Certain things didn't go together. Black tights and white stilettos. Red wine and lager. Even *chapatti* and chips. Pissed Thomas and Lester was a no-no – don't go there – in fact, just hide.

'Lester?' Thomas yelled to the heckler. 'Born-to-be-Prime-Minister Lester? More like Snowy the Snow-man. What is wrong with you lot? Why this obsession with Lester? Have I missed something here? Did he get knighted when my head was turned? Could someone please enlighten me about this God you all revere?'

A female voice, Thomas's mother's, fought its way through the tutting. 'Thomas Harding, behave. Put a stop to all this. People are beginning to talk.'

Thomas, sobering rapidly, replied in Italian, something the two of them used to do to annoy his father. '*Non la amo.*'

Mom replied in Italian. '*Sei semplicemente nervoso. Non è troppo tardi per scusarti con gli Newton-Harringtons, e in qualche modo fare pace di nuovo.*'

Various eyes homed in on Thomas and his mother. Russell, one of the stable lads, was half Italian. He translated back in a whisper to the Newton-Harringtons as quickly as he could and was ordered by Edmond, Nicole's father, to keep the translation accurate. So far, Russell explained, Thomas had said he didn't love Nicole. And his mother had replied it was just nerves, telling Thomas to apologize to the Newton-Harringtons. Easy enough so far.

Then things got messy. The translation continued:

'I can't stand the family,' Thomas shouted in Italian. 'They make me sick.'

'You're not marrying the family, you're marrying Nicole.'

'Have you seen Nicole's mother this evening? She looks like an inbred.' Payback. For three years Marion Newton-Harrington had been insulting Thomas and words like these felt as refreshing on his tongue as sorbet.

Mom laughed. 'Now now, Thomas. Don't bitch like a girl. It's just her wrinkles, nothing plastic surgery won't repair.'

Russell sniggered. But Edmond wanted the truth. So, the truth was unleashed. Translating Italian to English had never been so much fun.

Thomas's mother continued. 'I know they have their faults, but this is a respectable family.' She pleaded, 'You and Nicole are perfect together. If you only listen to me once in your life, then let this be the time; marry her, Thomas. Make me proud.'

The crowd watched the event with eager eyes, hoping that all would be revealed soon. Was there an engagement? Or wasn't there? Was this a celebration or a split? Could their gifts be justifiably claimed back if the engagement was cancelled?

Bitter laughter escaped from Thomas. 'You call this family respectable? Edmond had an affair with that tart, Daphne Lillytwait-Potter,' he pointed her out at the back wearing her bright-pink feathered hat, 'that nearly led Marion to a nervous breakdown. It makes a good argument as to why I have doubts about the daughters' true parentage. I mean, the three beautiful daughters, Nicole, Arabella and Holly, couldn't have possibly come from an ugly toad like Marion. Surely not.'

Russell translated until he reached a stumbling block. He whispered in Edmond's ear: 'I'm too not sure, sir, I'm not that familiar with the word *"Rospo"*. I think it means toad. Your wife is as ugly as a toad? Make any sense?' He winced. 'If I might add before you sack me, sir, I think Mrs Newton-Harrington is extremely beautiful.'

But Edmond wasn't listening, he barged through the crowd, his face a tight grimace, his eyes nearly popping from his skull. Fifteen minutes ago Edmond had been smiling, now he was baring teeth. It was the greatest mood swing in the Newton-Harrington long family history. Standing just three feet from Thomas, Edmond pointed to the door.

'Leave now, or be escorted out by security. You're not welcome in our house any more.' Edmond raised his fist, waving it before Thomas's face. 'You will pay harshly for hurting my daughter. Make no mistake. I will squash you . . . I will . . .' He seemed not to know quite how to end the sentence.

So Holly did it for him. She jumped on the small stage, pushed Nathan out of the way, then slammed her hand around Thomas's face. SMACK! She hissed out, 'I hate you, Thomas. You'd just better hope that Nicole doesn't do anything stupid.'

And talking of stupid, Thomas made his response. A huge net of metallic balloons marked Thomas & Nicole waited above the disgusted people's heads. Now was not the moment. He pulled the string and it rained balloons.

This time they were not filled with laughing gas.

This time no one was laughing.

Chapter Twenty-six

Home became different places for different people over the next few weeks. Nicole was bundled off to Monte Carlo with her two sisters and bodyguards. Twenty-one days aboard Daddy's yacht, *Aurora Borealis*, seemed a bit drastic to keep her from Thomas but the advantage of Monte Carlo was in the climate – no rain. Both Holly and Arabella were convinced that Nicole was just a baby's push away from attempting suicide. One English storm could be the final storm of Nicole's life. Thomas talk was banned while on the high seas.

And Thomas talk was non-stop at Castle Cliff Manor. Revenge was high on Edmond Newton-Harrington's agenda. His calls to the hotel proved fruitless, however; no one seemed to know where Thomas had gone. He had, quite literally, vanished.

That's what the Regency staff had been told to tell callers. Truth was that Thomas was hidden away in his apartment. His home had become just four walls. Not hiding from anyone in particular – just grabbing some time to himself to think through his life and the consequences of his actions. His parents were completely disgusted at him – their hopes for a grandchild vanquished. All in all, everyone was appalled at Thomas for putting an end to Nicole's dreams.

Well, not quite everyone. Marina and Emily were thrilled: Thomas was back on the market. For the last three weeks, home to the two Fenworth girls had been in cloud-cuckoo-land. Straitjacket city. And they were as confused as ever. Too many questions with too few answers. Why did Thomas dump Nicole? Was the rumour true, did Thomas have a million-pound bounty on his head? If so, was it a milk chocolate bounty or dark chocolate? Was Nicole's party dress really see-through? The Oxford local papers and a few of the nationals had covered every angle.

Except one. Which one of the two Fenworth beauties would Thomas choose? Emily or Marina? The girls were in an emotional wind tunnel. Hope, happiness and security being tossed about by the turbulence of Thomas's failed engagement. It was so obvious to both of them that Thomas had cancelled his future with Nicole because his thoughts were with one of them. But which one?

It was clear-cut to Marina. Her Ganges water was being allowed to work now she had obtained the blessings of her mother. Emily could fantasize all she wanted about how Thomas would not be able to refuse her in her red rubber dress. But when it came down to it, Emily might well wear the rubber with Thomas, but it would be Thomas wearing the rubber with Marina. It was settled in her mind already.

Thomas checked the calendar. Thursday 15 October. He checked his watch. 11.00 a.m. He checked his appearance in the mirror. Rough. He checked his pulse . . . he checked his pulse . . . Jesus Christ. He was dead. With a smile he sank back down on to the bed. If he was dead, then there was no way he could clear up the mess on the floor. And if he was dead, then there was no way he could worry about Nicole. But if he wasn't worrying about Nicole, then why was he looking forward to getting drunk again – to take away the pain?

The vodka bottle lay on the pillow beside him. It would be a brief affair. Thomas would be on to his next bottle by tonight. Another day of stinking and drinking. He remembered Nicole's plans of having a family together, of settling down, of becoming closer. Each of her plans he had promised to fulfil. And each of his promises had been broken three weeks ago at the engagement party. Why did people have to become so attached to each other, thought Thomas, cuddling the bottle, praying that the Smirnoff would never leave him as he rubbed the cold glass against his forehead. He reached for the phone and re-dialled Nicole's mobile. For the thousandth time the answerphone clicked on and for the thousandth time he knew of only one thing to say: 'I'm sorry, Nicole. Ring me.'

But he knew she wouldn't.

Outside the window a tally of gardeners were in full swing, tidying up the grounds, pottering around

Thomas's gravestone, preparing the garden for winter. The weather had been odd this year, unreliable, untrustworthy. Flowers that should have been gone months ago still lingered. And Jack Frost had hardly called.

Looking down, Thomas examined the markings left by Ron and his sit-down mower. So straight and tidy was his lawn that Thomas expected to find Pete Sampras practising volleys there. Ron waved up to Thomas, and Thomas waved back, suddenly ashamed that he was still holding the bottle of vodka. A sign, maybe, that it was time to get back on with his life. There were many ways to beat depression, but booze wasn't one of them.

He dialled Josephine's mobile, hoping that his head chambermaid was up to the task. 'It's a complete state, Josie . . . No, no sick on the walls . . . Just bottles, takeaways, clothes, that sort of thing . . . The windows are open already . . . Yes, thank you, I'm feeling better . . . I'll pay triple time and a bonus if you find the TV . . . Three o'clock's fine. See you then.'

Shower time. Thomas viewed the werewolf growling back from the bathroom mirror. He was tempted to shout down to Ron in the garden for his shears. But the birds might see his massive beard protruding from the window and land in it. Five Gillettes later and Thomas was the best a man could get. Hair, designer messy, and suit, designer style, Thomas left his apartment and wandered down the stairs.

Since being holed-up inside, Thomas had left the running of the hotel to Charles, a close friend and ex-hotelier, whom Thomas had met on a business conference quite a few years back. Charles was an Oxford man through and through, and his knowledge of Oxford life was indispensable. Anything under Charles's control ran like clockwork. The rooms – immaculate. Bookings – up. Restaurant – full. Staff – in order. Stuart – worried. Thomas – happy.

'And now for the painful part, Thomas. My fee!' Charles handed Thomas a piece of paper. 'I've taken off fifteen per cent for our friendship. A further ten per cent deducted because you gave me my wedding reception free. Also, I have removed thirty-five per cent for my pity of you. And that leaves forty per cent, which if you look on the invoice is very fair indeed.' Charles snapped the lid on his laptop, pleased that Thomas was back to his normal self – women weren't worth moping over.

Thomas stared at the blank sheet. 'No fee?'

'I'm a friend. It's just a favour. Nothing more than you would have done for me.' Charles paused. 'You have two pads of messages. None from Nicole, I'm afraid. But plenty from a woman named Emily who lives in Fenworth. An ex-girlfriend of yours? You ate marshmallows together over a fire in Dorset she said. She ate the pink ones and you apparently ate all the white; and you were planning on adopting a dolphin together? Ring any bells? You were going to call it "Captain Stingray". She sounded rather common, if you don't mind me saying.'

Thomas grunted. 'Common? I know posher farm animals than her. She is *not* an ex of mine, but I would hazard a guess that she is an ex of about ten thousand other men.'

They both laughed. Charles needed a couple of

hours to tot up the books, leaving Thomas with a couple of hours to make amends with a list of people as long as a basketball player's arm. Mom and Pops were still waiting for a full explanation. The Newton-Harringtons would be needing a woolly mammoth apology for his despicable behaviour. Then there were the mates who had tried to calm him down that night who had been told to quite literally 'fuck off'. And that wasn't even the full list of people who needed his apology. There was still this Marina. His remarks to her had been totally rude and unfair. It was so easy to dismiss how hurt she must have been – she'd get over it, he couldn't have been the only man to have called her a Paki – but he'd seen the pain in her eyes, he'd heard the sadness in her voice, and he'd sure as hell felt the sting of her slap. Something was telling Thomas that, out of all his apologies, Marina's was going to be the hardest of them all today.

And in some ways the one he was most ashamed of.

Thomas stood in the car park and took in the beauty before his eyes. 'God, I've missed you,' he said, his eyes slightly wet. 'It's been the most difficult time of my life and sometimes, and I know it's hard to understand, but we men do the most shameful deeds.' He coughed, feeling an amount of rejection – his Porsche wasn't responding. Maybe it was even sulking. 'Look,' Thomas said jumping in, revving the engine, 'I'll make it up to you. We'll buy a new air freshener today. And if you're still upset, how about I book you in for a valet. How about that?'

The car shot down the road and away from the hotel, Thomas anxious to begin his grovelling as soon as possible. Marina, in Fenworth, would be first up:

apology, chocolates, then get out of there. Even now, Thomas seemed to be sitting in his Porsche with a large 'R' branded across his forehead. R for racist. He didn't want to be viewed this way and would think up a story that Marina would believe which would totally exonerate him. Now what was the name of that Indian girl who used to belong to the under-twelves' swimming club? Ah, yes, Amisha, extremely rich parents. Good freestyle, not bad breaststroke, backstroke okay, but butterfly – atrocious. Thomas smiled to himself at how he used to swim behind her worrying if she broke wind: would the water go curry colour? Maybe he wouldn't tell Marina that story. Maybe he wouldn't even mention curry at all.

Thomas parked behind the burned-out Cortina just outside Marina's place. A white and yellow note was fixed to its rusty bonnet: POLICE AWARE. To which someone had scribbled: AND! But it proved to Thomas the danger of leaving his brand new Porsche unattended. He looked up and down Fairground Road, scouting for teenage rebels. Within minutes word had spread that a Porsche was here and a group of three louts duly headed towards it; Christmas was early.

'Whose patch is this?' Thomas asked the tallest.

Just stares. Too tough to answer. All three lit up a fag.

So Thomas continued, 'I will give you fifty pounds to protect my car for half an hour.'

More stares. They shook on it. Still too tough to talk.

With a firm knock, Thomas waited for the door to be answered, his ears already becoming used to the sirens in the background. How could anyone live here with any kind of peace of mind? Thomas suspected even the ice-cream man wore a flak jacket.

Hilda appeared at the entrance and examined what she saw. 'My my, a smart handsome man at my door. Haven't had one of those since 1977 – Jubilee year. We had a street party just outside and this man, I think he was called Brett, wore a suit much the same as the one you're wearing there—'

'I . . . don't . . . *think* . . . so,' Thomas said. 'Anyway. To the formalities. Good afternoon, would it be possible to speak to Marina Dewan?'

'You mean Maryanna. The Indian. She's upstairs, if you would like to follow me up.' Hilda grabbed her surgical mask from a coat peg and snapped the elastic behind her ears. Her words were muffled now. 'You *do* have a well-spoken voice, I'm not a fan of it myself, reminds me of the war. Churchill spoke that way. And my late husband. Sends shivers down my arthritic spine.' She stomped up the stairs, two at a time and attempted her 'snobby' accent. ' "We will fight them on the beaches". Oh, dreadful times, dreadful. A posh voice didn't stop a Buzz Bomb from landing on my husband's head.'

On the small landing, Hilda paused at Marina's door. 'Are you decent, Maryanna? Thomas is here.' She spun round. 'I heard her say "Yes". This way. You'll find out why I wear this hospital mask any second.'

Thomas stared bemused, he couldn't recall saying his name to Hilda, but he followed her in nevertheless. A mixture of German voices and sounds came from the room next door. Either the walls were very thin or the voices were *very* loud. Thomas tried very *hard* to ignore what was being said, but it was at times like this he wished his understanding of European languages wasn't so advanced. *Scheissen!*

Inside the bedroom Thomas stood, wondering if Hilda was senile: Marina was nowhere to be seen. He thought of the Carlsberg Export advert where the old lady dumps the lorry drivers in the cellar.

'Stinks in here, doesn't it?' Hilda remarked. 'All that Indian food she cooks.'

'Erm. Where is she?'

'Oh, she must have popped out to the shops. Yes, that's right, to get me some custard creams. She'll only be five minutes. Good girl. I'm only her landlady but really she treats me more like a second mother.' She patted Marina's bed. 'You wait here and I'll fetch you a nice cup of tea. It will give you time to look over that.' Hilda pointed to the huuuge poster of Thomas on the wall. 'It's you, isn't it? It caused quite a stir, I can tell you, when your Nicole spotted it. It's a good job she didn't see what was written behind it. Anyway, see you in a bit.' Hilda smiled at Thomas's shocked face and slipped out of the door.

He was stranded. Left alone amongst a virtual stranger's belongings – something a hotelier should be easy with – something Thomas found slightly awkward. Hilda had said five minutes. This was an invasion of privacy if there ever was one. An infringement of a lodger's rights, surely. But, holy mackerel, she had a poster of him on the wall. Didn't that infringe on *his* rights?

He dropped the Milk Tray chocolates on the bed

and gave in to temptation. The purple writing down one side of the poster needed closer inspection.

Name: Thomas Harding.
Breed: Snob.
Age: 30.
Height: 6 ft 1 in.
Sex Appeal: Nine fully charged gold vibrators and a dildo.

Thomas winced. Did he even want to know what lay written behind? He paused to consider, then gently pulled the poster off the wall.

'Jesus . . . H . . . Christ!' Thomas ogled the masses of writing on the now visible wall, all relating to himself. Poems, sexual comments, sexual drawings (good artist), confessions, fantasies, hopes and dreams. 'Oh my God.' He ogled some more, his eyes drawn to a caption that read *Thomas and Marina, The Road to Their Happiness.* He cringed as he read the contents.

Our love grew steadily as we learned to touch each other in dangerous places. I grew ashamed as Thomas taught me things that made me scream out his name. People watched us together, jealous, wondering how we could be so in love. But Thomas could only ignore them. Ever since he saw me naked Thomas has been ignoring everyone. It felt so wrong to go down on my knees and suck him off. I moaned as he stroked my hair. Nothing could feel the same again. I'm so glad we found each other. I am so happy that he chose me over Nicole. Our lives have been sewn together by fate. I will have children with him, I am sure. Only last week he said he wanted my baby and he . . .

The door nearly burst off its hinges as Hilda barged in, banging down a chipped mug by the Shiva statue. 'Read it, then?' She scampered across the floor to join him, enjoying how red his face had become. 'I was a bit confused here.' Hilda pointed a bony finger to a passage. 'Would you know what a Bombay Roll is? Some sort of sandwich, I presume.'

'Bombay Roll? It is *sort* of a sandwich.' Thomas stuck the poster back up, annoyed at Hilda's personality. Her game plan was obvious: to cause maximum embarrassment for him and embarrassment for Marina. Well, if it was embarrassment she was after . . . 'The Bombay Roll, as I understand it, although traditionalists might now call it the Mumbai Roll, is when a man gets a hard-on, slams it between a woman's breasts and cums all over her. Quite pleasurable, I might add. Quite pleasurable indeed.' He paused, then said firmly, 'Marina isn't coming, pardon the pun, is she?'

Hilda, blushing, pulled up her mask to show Thomas her smirk, then pulled it back down again. 'No, silly me, she's at work. I told you I was senile. Or did I? That's senile for you, I can't remember.'

'Senility, I think you mean, "That's senility for you." Well, as you're senile you might have forgotten that you asked me to call you an old bag then.' Thomas stalled at the bedroom door, eyeing the mug which stood beside the multi-armed statue. 'One more thing, the tape that's playing in the room next door. Why?'

'Oh that. It's Emily's German self-help tape. She always leaves it playing when she goes out, keeps the burglars away, she says. It's all gobbledegook, though, no one here can understand a word.'

Thomas hovered at the top of the stairs, listening to the tape, understanding everything. Understanding how Dr Fritzgerald Guztelburg had taped his love-making while giving a running commentary, one sexual exploit after another, and then sold the recordings off as educational sex tapes. Only an oddball would buy such a tape. Why did Thomas get the feeling that he was standing in the house of the loonies? And yet, it wasn't even close to being called the White House.

He bid farewell to Hilda, then paid off the youths guarding his car. Still staring. Still too tough to speak. He couldn't bear it any longer and gave the tallest one an extra tenner just to say one word.

'Boyacasher!' the lad said, throwing his fag on the floor.

Ten pounds well spent, thought Thomas as he drove towards his parents' house on the outskirts of Oxford. If only the next transaction went as smoothly: his apology in return for his parents' forgiveness.

Somehow, as he parked his Porsche outside the huge barn converted to a mansion, amongst the two Mercs, one 4 × 4, one huge camper van and one tandem bike, just twenty yards away from a duck pond bobbing with ducks, he doubted 'smoothly' would be the operative word here. More like 'disgracefully'. Only Thomas could have mishandled his own engagement party so disgracefully. Pop's favourite anecdote from his own grandfather would be used over and over: 'Life was not meant to be easy. Our family accepted this years ago. That's why we have the word "Hard" in our surname. We are Hardings.' In his youth, Thomas had told a string of girlfriends that the 'Hard' had meant something else entirely; sometimes following it up with proof.

Mother opened the door, shaking her head despairingly. 'I love you from all four chambers of my heart, and this is how you treat me. I don't know what to make of you any more, Tom, it seems to me that you are a little on the weird side. How could you let a beautiful woman like Nicole go?'

'Pardon?'

'Weird, Tom. That's what you are. A weirdo.'

He kissed her on the cheek and handed her a colourful bunch of flowers. 'But I'm not the one who winds up her own son pretending she fancies him. Or who sends a recording to her son of his own birth. Am I?' He smiled. 'May I come in? I'm craving a Bombay Roll.'

'A what?' she said, letting Thomas pass.

'Ask Pops, he knows all about them.'

Ten minutes later, a shrill voice bounced off all four walls and even scared the ducks from their pond. 'Thomas Harding, you are a filthy, disgusting oik,' his mother said. 'I've never heard of such a revolting thing. I am sure Bombay is famous for more than that. And not that you need to know this, but your father has never had a Bombay Roll with me, young man.'

She was right, Thomas did not need to know this.

Chapter Twenty-seven

FREE KISS WITH EVERY SANDWICH
(and a bit more if you're lucky)

Emily stuck the sign to Napkins's window facing the street outside. Perv Bazzer had called a meeting during the week, explaining profits were down and if things didn't improve, one of the girls would have to go. The redundancy package for Napkins was a packet of Sainsbury's own-brand ready salted crisps.

'He wanted initiative, he got it,' Emily said, tidying away her felt-tip pens. 'I expect Perv Bazzer to have a rampage on his hands tomorrow.'

The girls giggled. They were on annual leave tomorrow, abandoning Perv Bazzer to hold the fort. They wouldn't leave their boss in the lurch if he wasn't such a leech, and anyway, it was good for Joe

Public to see ginger-haired people in employment from time to time – if he could do it, anyone could.

After shutting up shop and shuttering down the windows, the two made their way home, desperate to wash the smell of smoked fish out of their hair, keen to avoid gardens with cats. Dinner tonight was a charming meal of spam, beans and boiled spuds. No wonder they were rushing. Rushing home for dinner, but rushing away from thoughts of what they could have been eating had Marina kept the money. Seventy thousand pounds buys a lot of tasty takeaways. Indian, Chinese, Italian, Greek. Yum Yum. It also buys the tummy tucks and liposuction one might need if one indulged too much. All those stitches. Yuck Yuck.

Inside the house, Hilda sat on the bottom stair flicking through the pages of a *Reader's Digest* magazine; it was her way of hinting she wanted a chat. Something was obviously amiss in the house.

'Good evening, Maryanna, Emily. I expect you're wondering why I'm sitting here on the stairs.' Hilda closed the magazine and rolled it up.

Emily shrugged. 'No, not really.' She turned to Marina. 'Were you wondering?'

'No.' Marina unbuttoned her coat. 'But you can tell us if you want to, Hilda.'

Hilda put out her hands and wobbled them about a bit. 'I'm shaking from an experience I had today. A vision. The doctor gives me all these pills for my *senility*.' She smiled lamely. 'And sometimes I see things. Today, I swear I saw that man on Maryanna's bedroom wall. He seemed real enough to touch.'

'Who? Robert De Niro?' Emily exclaimed. 'My

God, the Raging Bull was in Fenworth.'

The girls laughed. Then apologized. Then encouraged Hilda to continue.

'Not Raging Bull, the other picture on your wall. The one of Thomas Harding.' Hilda watched their faces carefully. 'I saw him standing in Maryanna's bedroom today.' Using the rail she heaved herself up. 'I must go and lie down, the tablets are beginning to affect my balance.' She walked off into her den.

It was group-decision time. If Hilda was really as cracked as she appeared, she might forget to charge them rent this week. That was the positive side. The negative was that Hilda might accidentally leave the cooker on and the girls would be gassed in their sleep. Marina suggested they bought a canary. Kill two birds with one stone. Use the canary as a gas alarm for its main employment and for its subsidiary job it could be bait for Pinstripes the cat. Just until Hilda got her marbles back.

Closing her bedroom door, dropping her coat and *Charlie's Angels* bag on the chair, Marina felt the cold creep of an intruder's presence. Someone had been in *her* room and invaded *her* living space. Clues shouted from all corners. The poster of Thomas was wonky. A Regency Hotel mug had been left beside Shiva – a liquid stain like a gigantic snail's trailed from the doorway to where it sat. The bed covers were creased. A box of chocolates on the pillow. And topping the clues, something Colombo would only spot near the end of the episode, 'One more thing . . .', there was the distinct smell of men's aftershave stifling the room. Marina remained motionless with shock for what appeared minutes. Abruptly, she dropped to her knees and prayed as she did so. Her tapestry case! Her secret case! 'Please let it be there. Please let it be untouched.' And thankfully it was. Marina sighed deeply. Grateful that Shiva had protected it.

Within a short while, Marina had concluded that nothing was missing, nothing had been taken. Nothing to worry about? Yeah right. Just on the radiator alone was enough embarrassment never to leave the room again. Five pairs of what could only be described as 'poor-girls' knickers' hung drying. Another pair, standing innocuously on the window ledge, looked like Marina had messed herself. It had taken Marina fifteen minutes to explain to Hilda that the brown, crusty gunge on the panties was mildew from the windows, and she never wore them and didn't intend to. And then there was the poster, or rather, what lay behind it.

So, Hilda was telling the truth after all. Mr Harding, Thomas, had been here. The question was: why? Right on cue . . . a knock at her door. It couldn't be Emily, she was next door on the phone to her mother, her voice clearly audible. So, it had to be Hilda. In her mask, with a tray and three mugs of tea, Hilda crept across the carpet, eager to begin this woman-to-woman chat. Marina sneered at Hilda's transparency. She was sure Hilda had an answer or two. It was amazing how quickly a senile OAP could regain her balance when there was stirring to be done.

'What did Thomas want?' Marina asked, clenching her teeth, taking the tea tray from Hilda.

Hilda nodded towards the Milk Tray. 'Ooh, I would love a chocolate. Would you be opening them soon?' She pulled a plastic drinking straw from her dress pocket. Making a small hole in the mask she shoved the straw through and began to suck on her tea. 'Mmm. That's better, nothing like a cup of tea. A bit hot through a straw, though.' Hilda sat down on the bed, nearly doing a backwards tumble on the squashy mattress, then righted herself quickly without spilling a drop. She continued, 'This Thomas, you know, such a polite man. Lovely posh accent. Very well educated. Amazing how quickly he changed personality when he saw what was written behind that picture of him up there. He must have been reading it for, ooh, half an hour or so.'

A blanket of embarrassment enveloped Marina. Her relatives in India said life was hot out there, but that was nothing compared to the heat she felt right now. Blistering. If only she'd fancied an illiterate man and not an Oxford graduate, then it wouldn't have mattered what she'd written. She bet the First Lady Laura Bush didn't have to worry too much about what was written on her walls. Marina cast her thoughts back to a particular passage she'd scribbled hastily in a fit of sexual frustration. God, she hoped he hadn't read that.

There are many things that rhyme with sock
But what I want is Thomas's cock!

Marina blushed. 'I'm really confused here, Hilda. How did Thomas know to look behind the poster?'

Hilda ripped the cellophane off the chocolates and rummaged for a strawberry cream. She popped one under her surgical mask. 'He was so mad when he saw that picture of himself he wanted to dispose of it. He yanked it off the wall and then we both—' Hilda sighed despairingly. 'We were shocked and disgusted at your filth. Really, Maryanna, what were you thinking? Do you know how humiliating it was for me to listen to him explain what a Bombay Roll was? Or should I say, Mumbai Roll? In detail, Maryanna, in full detail!'

Three–two–one, Marina tried to control her breathing. She wanted to die. 'I'm missing something here, Hilda, and maybe it's because I'm stupid, but what was Thomas doing in my room in the first place? And why did he leave chocolates?'

'Germans!'

'Germans?' Marina had to hear this one.

'He can't stand them. His father had a grave experience with the Krauts in the war . . .'

Hilda went on to explain how Thomas was asking for Marina at the front door when his ears caught the sound of Germans coming from upstairs. Instinctively Thomas had run up, kicked open the nearest door, and was shocked to find, not a poster of Hitler staring back at him, but a poster of himself. As for the chocolates, he never explained why he brought them – for all she knew they were for someone else and, in his anger, he'd forgotten to take them back with him.

Marina wrestled the box away from Hilda. 'Well, if they are for someone else we shouldn't be eating them, should we?' She watched with amazement as Hilda stuffed in four quickly. 'And, if you will excuse me, I will be taking my bath now. I think that we should have those locks fitted after all, Hilda, it will save these awkward occurrences from happening again.'

A few minutes later, Marina poured in the last

kettle of water, then slipped into the bath. Their system of half a tank of hot water each, topped up by the kettle was primative but hygienic. Just like the bathroom, which was yet to be discovered by archaeologists, or decent plumbers, electricians or decorators, but its array of priceless artefacts would need an *Antiques Roadshow* special to do them justice: the bath ring itself predated Oliver Cromwell. Marina dipped her head beneath the soapy water and tried to cast away some concerns.

It seemed that her pathway was bewitched. A spell of misfortune had been set upon her road. Since reading of Thomas's split from Nicole, since spending two weeks' yoghurt money on a cheap bottle of wine to celebrate, since discussing into the wee hours with Emily how Thomas was now a free man, Marina had been convinced that the Ganges water was working. Slowly, mind, but working. Her gran's faith in having faith was being put to the test, leaving Marina's plan simpler and neater: wait for Thomas and the Ganges water would bring him.

Marina sipped some bath water, then squirted it out like a whale. Apparently, whales can hold their breath for forty-five minutes. Marina felt like giving it a try. Until she drowned. God, what must Thomas think of a grown woman having a poster of him on the wall? What must he have concluded when he read four thousand words of sexual fantasies about him? Indian girls didn't do this sort of thing, they were supposed to have fantasies about blending spices, not about being spicy with men. It was time to submerge. To the depths of the Sea of Embarrassment. Oh, Shiva, is there nothing you can do?

A knock on the bathroom door and Emily appeared. 'Mum sends you her love. Do you want me to boil another kettle?'

'Please, and then would you pour it over my head? Kill me, Emily, just do it. Or we move to Switzerland. Euthanasia. It's legal there.'

Emily dropped the toilet seat, sat down on it and asked for an explanation. If she was going to be killing her best mate, at least she wanted to know why. Ten minutes later, Emily was screaming with laughter and flapping around on the wet floor like a seal. It was worth being Marina's friend all these years for this moment alone.

'Tell me more, Marina, tell me more.' Emily was in heaven's heaven.

'There is no more. Thomas saw it all and now I have to confront him. I couldn't live with myself if I didn't put this right. I have to face my demons. I have to explain to him that when I wrote that I wanted to be strapped on a pottery wheel and massaged by him with wet clay, while his manhood stood firm and erect prodding my back, then front, alternately, as The Righteous Brothers played "Unchained Melody" in the background, I was referring to another Thomas Harding who owned another Regency Hotel in Oxfordshire. Oh, Emily, I'm doomed.'

Emily smiled. 'Yes, Marina. You *are* doomed. I would hate to be you at the moment.' It was clearer than vodka to Emily; Marina had blown any chance she might have had with racist Thomas. Oh shame, Emily pondered. With Marina out of the picture, didn't that leave the door open for a certain blonde girl from Fenworth? Now, what was her name again,

Emily wondered, oh yes, it's me. She hoped the door was left open wide enough for her huge bust to squeeze through. Emily smiled at a wicked thought. It was a good job busts were not filled with morals, or she would be as flat as a pancake. How could Emily contemplate a relationship with racist Thomas after all she had seen Marina go through when racism reared its ugly head? Easy, she cupped her bust and smiled from left to right; he was too good-looking and wealthy to give a shit.

It was decided then: Marina would face her demons within a few days. Time to adjust to the idea. Time to think up a story. Time to order a *hijaab* on the Internet.

In bed that night, Marina tossed and turned beneath the watchful eyes of Thomas still gazing down from above her head, her stubborn will still refusing to bring the poster down. Realizing, uncomfortably, that she might not be bringing the poster down, but it was surely bringing her down.

'Oh, Shiva.'

Chapter Twenty-eight

Thomas replaced the receiver knowing that what he had just set up was possibly the most corrupt plan of his life. He wanted something, money talked, and people were generally greedy. And what are people? They are cleaners and nurses, doctors and teachers, judges and policemen. Enough money, enough greed and anything could be bought. Things were coming together.

The morning sun was high in the sky, casting great shadows across the hotel's lawn. The marble gravestone near the gardener's shed looked as lonely as a lighthouse, the green waters crashing around it, no ships to be seen for miles. Thomas could feel his life piecing back, bit by bit. Routine, followed by more routine, was the key.

It had been four days since he'd apologized to his parents, friends and the Newton-Harringtons. Only the Newton-Harringtons refused to take his apology face to face; Thomas resorted to writing a letter, attaching it to a heap of expensive flowers and asking the Castle Cliff Manor security guard to smuggle it through. As Ramone had often said, 'Sorry seemed to be the hardest word.'

The apartment was spotless, Josephine had done a spectacular job, even packing and labelling some of Nicole's belongings. It was hard to focus on all the labels. Nicole's. Nicole's. Nicole's. Knowing that never again would he be *Nicole's*. Never would he be her apostrophe s.

He was dwelling again. A hotelier doesn't dwell, he runs a dwelling. A top-class one at that, thought Thomas, walking out of his apartment and down the corridor. A cleaner's trolley squeaked up ahead and Thomas noted that the wheel needed oiling. Shipshape. That's what a good hotel thrives on, a boss who is in complete control and knows every aspect of his business. Thomas smiled. Back at the helm of his ship, navigating the waters of success. He wouldn't allow his personal life to interfere with his profession again. Not a chance.

Down in Reception, a group of Japanese tourists stood huddled by their interpreter, smiling at everyone, cameras at the ready. Thomas waved gleefully; what a start to the day, what a day to be part of.

'Good morning, Cheryl, and how are you?' Thomas leant over, grabbed the booking book and began to whistle his way down the entries. 'Excellent, Cheryl, excelllllllent! Fully booked. My favourite words in life.'

Cheryl worried about her boss. Too cheerful. Too un-boss like. Like a small earthquake, the hotel had been shaken by the news of Thomas and Nicole's separation. All bets were off. No one knew how this might affect him. He could sell up, have a breakdown, sack them all. No one could understand Thomas's new found happiness. There would have to be an aftershock, surely.

A multitude of Japanese voices broke into some sort of commotion and Thomas could almost taste the buzz in the air. One of the Japanese shouted out, '*Basic Instinct*. Yes, *Basic*, she in *Basic Instinct*.' Another voice, 'No, no, *Nine and Half Weeks*, she Kim Basinger.' A cheer rang out as at least ten voices shouted, 'No, she Sharon Stone.' Flashes popped off like fireworks. 'Hollywood star. Hollywood star.'

Thomas turned to see a mass of heads crowding the 'Hollywood star'. His eyes scanned the booking book quickly, checking to see which guests could be kicked out of which rooms, if the star had been double-booked. But no movie star *was* booked. Maybe a look-alike? He peered across, hard to make out with the bobbing black-haired heads shoving pads of paper in the star's face, but . . . if Thomas didn't have such expensive trousers on, his knees would have buckled. Given way to the beauty who now stared him straight in the eye like a bull would to a red sheet. Nicole was back. Sexier than ever. Smothered from head to toe in a perfect tan, wearing a daring dress that must have weighed all of one gram, the delicate material showing quite clearly that Nicole sun-bathed naked. In fact, she might as well be naked right now, thought Thomas, as the book dropped out of his hands and onto the floor, bouncing off his hard-on en route. His pupils grew tenfold in size and his heart beat like maracas. There was not a star in the whole of Hollywood who could raise Thomas's blood pressure this quickly. If he hadn't already fallen in love with this woman once before, he would have fallen in love with her now. Love at first sight.

But how to get rid of the Japanese? Thomas shouted, 'Jean-Claude Van Damme in the bar now!'

Frantic feet across the floor and cameras at the ready. 'He better than Bruce Lee,' they said as they ran. 'He better than Bruce Lee.' But deep down they knew no one was better than Bruce Lee – everyone understood that!

Nicole held Thomas's eyes. The word 'why' fluttered about her like a butterfly. Why did you hurt me, Tom? Do you know how I live now, knowing I've lost you? I only wanted us to be together and now we are apart. I wish I'd died before I met you. And now I have met you, you have left me to die. Why?

Before Thomas could realize what was happening, Nicole was upon him, arms tight round his waist, lips jammed against his. She kissed him, enjoying how easily he surrendered, amazed at how Arabella was so right. 'Trust me, Nicole, if you seduce him, you'll get what you want.' Arabella had a way of knowing things. Men things. Nicole whispered filth in Thomas's ear, feeling his bulge pushing forcefully against her thin dress. And Arabella had been so right about the clothing as well. 'You must wear the most sluttish dress you own and the highest heels. A glimpse of suspenders would do no harm, either. Men are weak in this respect.' Nicole guided his hand up her leg, moaning freely, enjoying her power. Thomas groaned. This feeling was priceless.

'Er hum,' Cheryl coughed as she watched the porn show. 'Er, Mr Harding, the conference room is free. I mean, erm, hello, Nicole.' But the porn show continued, unabashed, unhearing. 'ER HUM!!! MR HARDING. Guests are here.'

'Guests,' Nicole whispered in his ear. 'Let's finish this upstairs.'

The two departed hastily.

Then, from nowhere, Stuart appeared at Reception with his bloody machete. 'Will someone tell these sodding Japs that I am not Jean-Claude Van Damme.' His eyes spotted Thomas and Nicole, kissing each other passionately as they stumbled up the stairs. 'I thought I split you two up!' He stamped his foot. 'Cheryl, a Nurofen if you please! Actually make that a Nurofen Plus. I feel a migraine coming. Why does nothing ever go my way?'

Cheryl threw the Nurofen box at Stuart's head. 'You're a horrible person, Stu-pot. Is it really so bad when two people love each other? Some of us girls are beginning to wonder if you really have got a gentle side like you say you have.'

He stared at her, bewildered. 'God, you bore. All my women moan, Cheryl, but you're the only one who does it out of bed.'

'Oh go away, Stu-pot, go and bake a cake. And remember, what goes around comes around,' she said, picking up the ringing phone. 'Good morning, Regency Hotel.'

Like an unstoppable fire, Thomas and Nicole swept up the stairs, down the corridor and into Thomas's apartment. This was an emergency. Thomas closed the door behind them, wishing in some ways that the flat had been left untidy, wishing that Nicole could have seen for herself the pain their split had caused. Then he remembered the beard. And the stink of booze. And the breath that smelled like a Glastonbury toilet. If he recalled correctly, Nicole had never shown any inclination to snog a drunk David Bellamy.

'I told myself that if you had taken this down, I'd never speak to you again.' Nicole stood looking at a framed photo of herself on the wall. 'But photographs are just snaps of the past.' She turned round smiling. 'It's the future that matters.'

He nodded. No one can change the past (except maybe history teachers) and the future is blank – waiting for us to catch up. 'To get to the future, Nicole, we have got to pass through *now* first. And right now, I only want you.'

He took her hand and led her to the bedroom. The fresh smell of cut grass mingled with Mr Sheen and a large vase of flowers took centre spot on his desk by the open window. The bed looked like a swimming pool of comfort, ready to dive into, ready to splash around in. But one thought! One horrible thought that was recoiling through his brain like a misfired dumdum bullet: what if Nicole had slept with someone else in the last four weeks? Offers would have been aplenty, he was sure. It was a harrowing vision for a husband, or a boyfriend, or fiancé, to contemplate – but why was it such a terrible thought for him? After all, he was only an ex. An ex who had dumped her. At her engagement party. In front of all her friends and family. After promising her a baby. After promising her that their future was as secure as

Fort Knox. After . . . Oh sweet Lord, what a bastard, he admitted, for the umpteenth time, what a complete . . . His eyes were now loaded with lust as Nicole planted her high heels by the bed and dropped her dress to the floor. The sun skimmed across her smooth, perfect, tanned skin, washing away Thomas's envious thoughts as easily as a wave erodes writing in the sand. A word had been invented for this moment. Paradise. And it was. With a capital P for Pornography. Nicole stood there, wearing just black suspenders, high heels and a sultry smile; her eyes sparkled mischievously, giving out one clear message. Fuck me, Tom.

Within one second the hotel's poltergeist had arrived to send Thomas's clothes flying across the room; jacket, tie, shirt, shoes, belt, trousers, boxers and plonk . . . clink . . . clink . . . clank. Objects freed from pockets landed on the wooden floor with a tuneless tune. Nicole's eyes flicked from object to object like a digital camera, storing info, ready to download after sex. A credit card. Two pound coins. A mobile phone. A penknife. A calculator. A bunch of keys. And . . . a key without a bunch. Nicole knew immediately which lock was home to this key. Downstairs, in the office, a box sat waiting in the safe. The Hobbs key had once again made its presence known. Nicole made a determined reach for the key on the floor, plucking it quickly, palming it in her hand.

Before coming to the hotel, Arabella had told Nicole to keep things simple. 'I want your mind to be pure,' she had said, checking Nicole's nails were long enough and sharp enough for later, if needed. 'As pure as the Garden of Eden.' And now, on this summery day in autumn, a snake had entered the garden – in the shape of a key.

Thomas pressed himself up to Nicole, kissed her open mouth, deftly prising the key from her fingers. There were plenty of other things she could be grabbing apart from keys and he guided her hand down to his cock, watching her eyes widen, feeling that unbeatable sensation of sexual expectation. Nicole was a filthy lover, naughty beyond the norm, nothing was too sordid or low for her to try – unless it involved kilts. So used to the etiquette of upper-class life was she that in the bedroom it was a free-for-all. Anything went.

Except kilts.

Lying back on the bed, Thomas watched as Nicole knelt over him, a fearless expression on her beautiful face. She ordered Thomas to shuffle on a condom. It was a very important part of today's plan. Arabella would be most annoyed if she forgot.

'Right,' Nicole said, unclipping her suspenders, then tossing them over her shoulder. 'I am going to do something that would have been impossible a few weeks ago, Tom. This is to show you how much I love you.' She giggled. 'And don't worry, I'm not going to pour acid in your face or anything like that.'

Thomas flinched, both hands automatically covering his privates. 'Oh, good!'

'It's a simple matter of me' – Nicole began to unfasten the buckle on her diamond bracelet – 'undoing this.' She slipped the bracelet off, shivering at the inscribed words: *Light My Flame. End This Pain*, and walked over to the desk, gently placed it down, then returned. 'This is Nicole Newton-Harrington, warts and all. Except in my case, it's scars and all.' She held out her wrist to Thomas; the ugly four-inch slash mark had lain hidden for a long time. Finally unmasked. 'Utterly horrible, isn't it? I'm not so perfect in your eyes now, am I, Tom?'

Thomas knew the right thing to do was to kiss her on the scar and say it didn't matter. But that was Hollywood, this was Oxfordshire. People just didn't go round kissing each other's scars in Oxfordshire. Then he thought of his circumcision. Nicole had kissed that over and over. Fair's fair. He pulled her down on the bed and, oh, sod it . . .

'You make too much of this, Nicole,' he said, kissing the scar. 'It's part of you. It's a bookmark for a chapter in your life. It's nothing to be ashamed of, or regretful of. As you said earlier, like the photographs, scars are just snapshots of the past.'

Relieved, Nicole smiled. So far so good, Thomas's performance had been exemplary. Her confidence was strengthening with each minute; Arabella's intuition was to be admired. Without any further ado, Nicole pushed herself on to Thomas, feeling him deep inside, enjoying the breathlessness that followed. Always Thomas was gorgeous, especially up close, always always always. Couldn't he at least show an ugly frown from time to time, or an off-putting sneer to his mouth? Even with his messy hair he was A1 perfect. The bastard. Women would always look back when he walked by, married women, single women, even, for God's sake, lesbian women. He was the male equivalent of a super babe.

And a super stud when having sex. Nicole was sure

there would never be an energy crisis with men like Thomas around – he could go at it for hours. Their most romantic occasion to date was when they had shagged their way through the solar eclipse – cumming together at totality. To be on the safe side they had worn their Armani sunglasses. But being blinded by the sun was different from being blinded by passion.

Nicole admired Thomas's firm muscular body as she moved her hips up and down, riding him, feeling another total eclipse coming. Their eyes fused together, daring, shameless, happy. Watching him enjoy fucking her was best of all. Knowing that at that very moment he was thinking only about her. Not his hotel, or his customers, or his Porsche, but just what was sitting on top of him, staring into his eyes. And those eyes, she loved how he never closed them, always paying her attention, never wandering off to some fantasy woman in his mind. Nicole bent down, feeling her breasts press against his warm chest. She kissed him and breathed the whole moment inside, always listening very carefully, always ready to punish him severely, always afraid that one day in a fit of orgasmic splendour he might yell out the name of an ex. Knowing that soon it might be her name that another woman would pray he didn't yell out.

'I love you, Tom,' she whispered in his ear. 'And I don't want to know your reply.' She kissed him again. 'Lie on top of me.'

'Stereo!' He stated firmly as they swapped over. 'CD track four. Curtains closed! Air-conditioning full! Thank you, Hal.'

Nicole giggled. Men and their gadgets. Track four

began as the curtains quietly shut. She felt the goose bumps invading, an army of memories taking hold of her skin. Their song – 'Whenever I'm Alone With You (The Love Song)' by The Cure – was arousing powerful feelings.

With the lights down, and the music a welcome guest, Thomas and Nicole took turns in giving each other pleasure. Nicole's blood sugar was creeping dangerously low, her sweats and shakes now quite off-putting for Thomas.

'I can't go on, Tom, please can we have a break?' Nicole was panting as she sat up in bed, her once silky hair now a bedraggled mop of nylon. 'I only had a small breakfast.'

'Stay there, I'll get you some chocolate,' he said, chucking the used condom across the room. He popped to the kitchen, returning with a cold bottle of Lucozade and a Snickers bar. 'Refresh yourself. Half time.'

Five minutes later, the two were at it again. Nicole wriggling with pleasure underneath him, anxious that she choose her moment correctly. 'Premature action is nearly as bad as premature ejaculation,' Arabella had said when discussing the final details of their plan.

Thomas appeared as if he was about to cum. His face, still handsome for God's sake, had a certain detached look about it. Sportsmen would describe it as 'in the zone'. Ten seconds later, Thomas would be out of the zone and his sperm would be in her zone. It was time to flash her jewellery. She knew her engagement ring would come in handy one day.

Some people sniff amyl nitrite when they are about

to orgasm. To intensify the feeling. Nicole wondered if having one's back scratched by a diamond would do the same. One way to find out. Thomas pushed deeper and harder, his enjoyment clear, as Nicole scraped the diamond ring down his back; the pain and ecstasy becoming one. If only she had some ink, then Thomas could have his first tattoo. A tiny amount of blood, not even a snack's worth for Dracula, seeped on to Nicole's fingers from the razor-thin wound. She giggled quietly. Thomas had cum, his blood was dripping, strewth . . . he was leaking everywhere.

They lay in each other's arms until 'their song' on repeat began to piss them off. 'Stereo off, Hal. Thank you.' Thomas lifted himself on to his side and stared into Nicole's eyes. 'I do love you, Nicole, but—'

Nicole jumped up from the bed. 'I know, Tom, but you don't love me enough to marry me. Doesn't matter. More importantly, I seem to have scratched you in my frenzy.'

Quickly, Nicole whipped out a cotton handkerchief from her Prada handbag and gently wiped the blood away. Collecting the two condoms from the floor, smiling, she walked to the bathroom to impregnate herself with Thomas's sperm via a syringe, and instructed him to make coffee. They needed a little chat.

A little chat? Thomas was foxed. Why did women always need to talk the talk when it was quite obvious here that the man had just walked the walk? He pulled on his boxers then, like a fully domesticated man, followed his orders and made the coffee in the kitchen, confused why one foot was cold on the floor and the other warm. With a certain horror he looked down to see he had one sock on and one off. Oh, what a total spamhead! What modern-day man makes love with just one sock on?

'Nicole!' he yelled. 'Why didn't you tell me about the sock?'

Nicole, now fully dressed, appeared in the kitchen. 'Forget your socks, we've got much more important matters to discuss.' They headed into the living area, and sat beside each other on the sofa. 'You need to know how much you've hurt me.'

The chat became a talk, which became a lecture, but never an argument. How could Thomas argue with Nicole about her sadness? She explained to him how just a few weeks away from the rat race of normality had given her a new view on life. How she'd become more honest with herself. She had expected him to follow the road she'd laid out for the pair of them without asking him if he wished to come along too. The engagement – his proposal, her idea. Babies – his sperm, her idea. Their future – all her ideas. Never stopping to ask Tom his. No wonder, come engagement day, he panicked.

'I love you, Tom. You're the only man I want and I will wait for you, but I won't wait for ever.' A tear trickled down her cheek. 'And if you do decide to be with me, then I want marriage. I couldn't settle for us being lovers again. Your mother might say the heart has four chambers, Tom, and she's most likely right, because it feels like all mine are broken.'

Thomas wiped her tears away with the back of his hand, and with a lump blocking his throat he spoke, 'Somehow, I can't believe this is the end of us. I just wish I could give you what you want. I can't believe after all we've been through, we'll just end up as friends.'

She stood up and forced out a smile. 'I don't do friends, Tom, I've got enough of them to last me this life. So,' she picked up her handbag, 'I guess this is the goodbye I always dreaded would happen.'

A quick hug extended for fifteen minutes. Both silent, both afraid to let go. This would be the last time that they embraced each other and neither wanted to throw away the moment so easily.

Finally, Nicole brushed her fingers through his hair. '*Que sera sera.*'

'What will be will be.'

In the hallway outside, Nicole couldn't hold it together, her tears falling heavily, her strength all but gone, her mind a complete wasteland. Why did love hurt so much? Fearful of being seen in such a state, she walked quickly to the end of the hall. All was not lost, though. Like a shot of morphine to the unbearable pain of her broken heart was the thought of what she had just collected from Thomas. His blood, hair and semen. Enough DNA to grow a thousand Thomases in the future, which would be stored with Nicole's DNA. Arabella's idea was far-fetched and based on science fiction, but if it helped Nicole accept that she might have lost Thomas in this life but would gain him in the next, then what the hell. Nicole just hoped that, when they made the new Nicole from the old Nicole's DNA, and when they made the new Thomas from the old Thomas's DNA, the future still had lots of shops – and that Thomas and she became a married couple.

With her tears now dry, Nicole regained her breath,

then headed to the stairs. Arabella's idea was a nice thought, it would mean couples would never have to lose each other, but it was a long time to wait to have Thomas back again. Nicole tapped her stomach. Maybe, she smiled to herself, just maybe she might not have to wait that long. In nine months' time, she wouldn't have the whole of Thomas, but she might have at least a part of him.

Inside, Thomas flopped back on the bed where the smell of Nicole's perfume still lingered. Angrily he yelled, 'CD track four. NOW! HAL!' but Hal only responded to kindness. 'Sorry, Hal,' he said softly. 'Stereo. CD track four. Thank you, Hal.'

And Thomas drifted away in a sea of tranquillity. A hundred images of Nicole and himself washed up on the shore. Each grain of sand a heartbeat missed for the woman he loved so much – even if it was only for her packaging. And hiding amongst the grains of sand a solitary conch shell from another sea. Shipwrecked amid the dunes. But what was so interesting about this shell, from another land, from another life?

Thomas scrambled out of bed as if he'd wet it. A frightening idea had sunk its evil talons into his senses. The shell? From another land? Thomas knew damn well what it meant. It explained why he had let Nicole go. Why he *had* to let her go.

'Shotgun, please, Hal. Make it look like a suicide. Shoot my brains out!' Thomas picked up his light sabre and swished it around the room, sound effects on full, lights on max. He could feel his Jedi Knight force weakening daily. The women were draining him of his power.

Chapter Twenty-nine

The millennium year 2000 was a huge year for rubber. Condom sales had been up. Sports equipment sales up. Car tyre sales up. Even bounced cheques had been up. It was hardly surprising with all that rubber bouncing around that some went missing.

'I am not walking into the Regency Hotel with you when you are wearing that,' Marina stated outside the hotel gates. It was a shivering Thursday even though the sun was out. 'You remind me of a slag. You said you'd wear something that blended in and you would remain inconspicuous. This is embarrassing enough as it is, without having to walk through the entrance with an Amsterdam hooker on heat in tow behind me.' Marina's nerves were spinning now. 'How can I pretend to Thomas that I'm not obsessed with his lunchbox when I walk around with someone who looks like they nibble on them all day long? Hey, Emily, it's not on.'

Emily stood proud in her bright-red rubber dress. Her knee-length red leather boots climbed her slim legs. Her puckered lips were smothered in a ruby-red lipstick. And if she had been wearing any underwear, that would have been red too. The taxi driver had had to repeat himself three times for his fee because of the noises her rubber made when she stepped out of the cab. Sounded like two toilet plungers kissing.

'Just chill, will you? I am the peacemaker.' Emily crunched up the gravel towards the main entrance, mumbling to herself, 'Thomas won't be able to resist me in this. Face it, Marina, you've blown your chance.'

'Pardon?'

'Nothing.'

It was hard to upstage Emily. A pair of Jimmy Saville's now then, now then, now then, marathon jogging bottoms would have done the trick. But Marina had worked magic today. Two hours of hocus pocus. She'd added a few curls to her straight hair, anguished over her make-up until it was as perfect as Superdrug's own could make it, then slipped into a neat, short black skirt, slit down one side, with a tight, black lacy top, and the highest strappy sandals she owned (complete with safety net in case she fell) to finish. Sophisticated and sexy. Out of place at an Indian wedding perhaps, but totally at home in a four-star hotel.

Cringing, Marina crossed the marble floor in Reception with Emily. Each step, each pull on the toilet plunger, brought a titter of laughter from a group of businessmen sitting in the corner. Marina felt like picking Emily up in a fireman's lift and depositing her in the nearest chair. But, no knickers, no thanks.

Cheryl pretended that red rubberized women walked into the hotel every day. 'Good morning.' Cheryl pointed her nose towards the men in the corner, who quietened down immediately, then turned back to the girls. 'And how can I help you?'

'Good morning,' Marina said, cheerful and bright. 'Is it possible to speak to Mr Harding? I know he's a busy man, but this is very urgent.'

'I'm sorry, but Mr Harding is not available.'

'Oh. It's just that . . . It's very important that I see him today,' Marina said, disappointed but relieved at the same time.

'Like I said, he is not to be disturbed today unless it's of the—'

Emily interrupted, nearly shouting, 'Look, Cheryl, my friend here is pregnant with Mr Harding's child. Now could you bring him out here immediately? I expect he would like to know that, yet again, he has got someone up the duff.'

Cheryl crossed her arms in defiance. 'I don't think so somehow. Now, is there anything else?'

There was no secret to the whereabouts of Mr Harding. Ever since Nicole left the hotel three days ago, his body had been in the garden by the headstone and his mind had been . . . No one knew where his mind had gone. Mr Harding was acting very peculiar. Venting his anger by way of a foul mood. It was a testing time for everyone. When a boss becomes unstable his staff tend to become jittery, followed shortly by the customers. Stuart had made a small fortune selling his granny's Valium tablets to the most nervous of the staff. That was the plus side for Stuart. The negative was his granny had been in a state of paranoia and sleeplessness ever since.

The two Fenworth girls continued to be instructed by Cheryl that Mr Harding was not to be disturbed. He is too busy to be interrupted. He is too snowed under with work for social meetings. He is . . .

'He is in the garden round the back,' said a trouble-making Daisy. Never did like young, pretty, SLIM receptionists. 'Right out the back by that tomb.' Daisy turned to Tweedledee. 'We're getting a bit worried about him, aren't we, Maisy? He needs a little TLC, if you really must know.'

'We are *so* worried about him, it's playing havoc with our diets. Both of us have put a sliver around the tummy.' Maisy patted her drum belly. 'We gain weight when we worry, don't we, Daisy?'

Emily leant towards Marina and whispered, 'Fuck me, they must worry a lot.' She was kicked by Marina's shoe. 'Tragic,' Emily said, 'most tragic. Maybe we can pop round and cheer him up. I wouldn't want you two babes to worry any more.' You might just explode!

Rubber Girl agreed to give Marina a five-minute head start. The dress chafed if she walked too fast. Besides, Marina needed all the time in the world to get the initial embarrassment out of the way. How was she going to explain the writing on the wall?

A short stroll had Marina standing on the edge of a huge lawn surrounded by trees and bushes. In the shadows she made a quick survey for watchers, then did a trial faint on the ground. The mossy mattress made a great cushion for her fall and her hopes began to lift slightly. If things became too embarrassing by the tombstone, she needed to know that she could bail out at any time, hit the dirt, fall at Thomas's feet.

Never to be underestimated 'the faint' had a great reputation, even in the far reaches of the East. Indian women were known to faint in India – when their husbands made a cup of tea, or washed the dishes, it was a great way to show their surprise. Marina wondered if Thomas himself had fainted when he read the passage that began: *My body is a temple, my mind an open fire, now get your clothes off, Thomas Harding, and fill me with desire . . .*

Keeping close to the fence, Marina edged her way towards a huge wall of conifer trees that barred her vision any further. No doubt the cobblestone pathway that bisected the pines would lead to where Mr Harding was stationed. She stealthily crept up and peered round the prickly branches. About fifty yards ahead, sitting on a wooden bench, a sight so lonely that it would live with Marina for ever. Men were never meant to look this sad.

Fishing for tissues in her handbag, Marina prepared herself for tears. Thomas, with his bowed head, was in complete contrast to the confident Thomas Marina had witnessed last time. No wonder Cheryl was keen for people to stay away. Quickly Marina pulled her head back from the branches and began the hunt for flowers. No flowers. What then? Just by an empty patch of soil, ready for seedlings, was a medium-sized gnome. She picked it up. It was the best she could do.

'Heavy little bugger, aren't you?' Marina said to the gnome as she heaved it across the grass, towards Thomas. Marina took a breather, shaking her head at poor Mr Harding. He must have loved that person so badly. How many people bury their loved ones in their own garden? What a lovely thing to do. She picked the gnome back up and struggled the granite beast across the grass. Puffing and blowing and f-ing, she arrived a few metres away from Thomas, whose eyes were closed, in prayer no doubt, she guessed. It was such a private moment that Marina decided to share it with him, standing as near as she dared, closing her own eyes, staring into the darkness of her mind. Such peace.

Moments passed until Thomas realized he had company. 'What are you doing, Ms Dewan?' Thomas said. Baffled at what she was doing, but not totally surprised that she had turned up to cause trouble again. He waited for Marina to open her eyes. 'Who are you praying for?'

Marina unclasped her hands. 'For the poor soul who was taken from you, Mr Harding.' Marina bent down, picked up the stone ornament and placed him by the grave's flowerbed. 'It's a garden gnome. It's not my place to bring flowers, I mean, I don't even know the person under there. Flowers would be inappropriate at a time like this.'

'But a gnome is appropriate?' Thomas patted the bench for her to sit down next to him. 'Thank you. It was kind.' He paused. 'I'm just musing, not grieving as such. I like it down this end. It's too far for staff to come unless it's an emergency.'

'Or a crisis?' Marina sat down close, extremely close, any closer and she would be in his pockets.

He glanced across at her. 'Or a crisis.'

Here goes, thought Marina, it's now or never. She

focused on a blade of grass in front of her. 'Well, I have a crisis. It's about what I wrote on my bedroom wall. I feel pretty foolish that I wrote all that stuff about you. Actually, I feel even more foolish now talking about it. Maybe I should just shut up.' She paused. 'It's the sort of thing I used to do as a teenager.'

'You were *one* filthy teenager.'

'Anyway, what I did was shameful, but what you did was unforgivable. You read my private words. Okay, so they didn't have "Diary" written above them, but they were hidden behind a poster . . .' She cringed. 'A poster of you.'

'Ms Dewan, please leave it there. I apologize for my actions. We don't need to go into the nitty gritty. That would be positively mean and childish. Although I am intrigued by the live sex-show story, "Thomas And His Tank Engine Enters Marina's Tunnel"; what *was* the ending to that one?'

'You died!' she half whispered.

'In your tunnel?'

She giggled. 'So, you haven't explained why you came round. Or why you brought the chocolates.'

And he began. On a bench, in the hotel gardens, just a stone's throw away from a huge black and gold speckled headstone, Thomas quietly confessed to Marina his reasons for turning up at her flat. How, as shallow as he appeared, he didn't want to be mistaken for something that he wasn't, i.e. a racist. The trip to Fenworth was about apologizing for any embarrassment or hurt he had caused with his ungainly mouth.

'So, you're not a racist then?' Marina asked.

'Absolutely not, Ms Dewan.'

'And if you were in need of the kiss of life, it wouldn't matter what colour the person was who revived you?'

'Of course not. And it is here where I think I can prove my point. Not only would the colour of skin have no bearing on my choice of life saver, but I would even let a man do it.' He grinned – for about one second. 'As long as he was pretty, and he didn't take the kiss as a come-on.'

'So you *would* let me do it, then?' Marina waited for him to answer, his dark-blue eyes connecting with hers, sharing a moment. There was flickering behind those large pupils of his, she could feel it. They were trying to tell her something. Which was more than his mouth was doing right now. 'Well, would you let me kiss you?'

'Ms Dewan, are you aware that the kiss of life does not involve tongues? It's a simple blowing of air into another person's mouth. It's not sexual. One does not wait until one sees another dying of asphyxiation to get one's kicks.'

Marina thought back to the nicotine-stained moustache of the St John's Ambulance man on duty at her school fêtes. No girl dared to faint with him there. Now, if he had looked like Thomas, well, they'd have been dropping like flies. A whole crop of giggling girls cut down by his fantastic smile. And here was a good point: Thomas was a man who would have seen countless women begging to be noticed. Why on earth would a man like him notice a woman like her? Even more importantly, if he did notice her, how would she keep his attention? Talk of sandwich fillings? Mobile phone tunes? Or even Indian spices? They hardly pushed the envelope of highbrow chitter-chatter now, did they? She would hate to be thought of as dim. Maybe if Marina were to know what interested Thomas, she would feel a whole lot better.

'So, how do you get your kicks? What interests you?' she asked casually.

He pondered for a second. 'Erm, I'm pretty obsessed with the Maastricht Treaty, if you must know, and all its ramifications. Also, and you'll just die when you hear this one – I love anything to do with the Caro-Kann defence. It leaves most players in a zugzwang.' He watched her face drop despairingly, amused at the confused frown left upon her forehead. Then his amusement turned to guilt. A bit of a bastard thing to do, really, poncing up his sentences for a quick thrill, picking two of the most boring topics in the world; the Maastricht Treaty and a chess opening called the Caro-Kann defence were pretty anorak at the best of times. He looked with dismay as Marina's hand reached for her handbag. She was about to go. He'd scared her off. Without thinking, almost in a panic, Thomas leant across and kissed her on the lips. ZUGZWANG!

The kiss grew to a snog; the bench creaking in harmony with their moans. This was a moment that belonged in her dreams. Except in her dreams the kiss had never been this pleasurable. She'd never experienced this kind of voltage before. Boyfriends had come and gone, none leaving much of a footprint in her life so far. Any spark of romance was normally quelled by their inadequacies. Too immature. Too selfish. Too small. But out here in the garden of plants and trees, under the breath of a cool breeze, everything felt as everything should: wonderful and romantic. To stop and wonder what her relatives would think, to worry whether she was good enough for Thomas, to question herself how far she would take this kiss if given the chance, would be bowing down to her insecurity. This was her life and if it flowed one way towards happiness – then why paddle upstream?

Thomas had amazing hands, Marina thought, enjoying his subtle touch, surrendering her body as he caressed her. Like dowsing rods he could tell where her energy lay and focused his own energy there. Divine divination. A whole party of excitement sweeping her chakras into mayhem. She just hoped that Thomas didn't think of her as too forward when she went looking for his chakras under his shirt and in his boxer shorts. And by golly did she find them!

As always in situations like this for Thomas, his phone began to ring. He pulled away from Marina and retrieved his mobile from under the bench. It was Reception calling. And when Reception called, Thomas answered. 'Hello, what's the problem?'

Cheryl's voice was heavy with guilt. 'Sorry to disturb you, Mr Harding, but we have a situation here. We have a loud tart in a red rubber dress getting very drunk and extremely vocal. I have tried to persuade her to leave but she insists on waiting for her friend.' She paused. 'The Indian woman who came out to see you, Mr Harding. She's waiting for her.'

'Okay, Cheryl. Give me two minutes.' Thomas shook his head, then stared over at Marina. 'Your friend is causing a scene. I would guess that we have something in common here.'

Marina grimaced. 'We both wish she was dead?'

'More or less. Yes.' He buttoned up his shirt.

Just before setting off, Thomas took another loving look at the headstone. Nicole had ordered the huge slab of marble and had it set in the grounds over a year ago. Its significance quite deep. Its effect on their relationship quite dramatic. So sick was she of coming second place to the Regency Hotel that she murdered the deeds. Set fire to Thomas's paperwork. Killed off his VAT books, his PAYE books and any receipts. For all intents and purposes the hotel was dead. And that's why she buried it, in the back garden. The words, just like the lady who had them inscribed, were loopy.

THE REGENCY HOTEL
Murdered by a jealous lover Valentine's Day 2003.
Sorry, Regency, but heaven was fully booked.
A Harvest Of Tears
Sing a song of sixpence
A bucket full of pain.
Four-and-twenty razor blades
Slashing through my vein.
And when the flower opens
And when the song begins
Four-and-twenty razor blades
Are slicing through my sins.
R.I.P.

They made their way back to Reception in awkward silence, taking the short cut through the kitchen.

Hurrying down the corridor that led to the lobby, with Marina in her high heels trying hard to keep up,

Thomas told himself to remain calm, adhere to the rules of professionalism, and defuse any situation that confronted him. Rarely is there anything so off-putting to a guest than an owner who loses his cool.

He entered, his coolness evaporating immediately. Nothing prepared Thomas for what he saw in his hotel lobby that day.

Emily sat in the corner sharing a table with a man, sharing her conversation with everyone. In her excitement at being chatted up by a good-looking guest, Emily had become extremely loud.

'And so,' Emily shouted, caressing the businessman with her eyes, sitting on his lap, stroking his face, 'she asks me if the banana was big enough. I said, "Big enough?" I'm telling you it was about the size of an elephant's . . .'

Einstein was wrong. Thomas Harding could travel faster than light. Across the floor he scurried like a loose streak of lightning, past the flurries of red-faced people all suddenly finding the ceiling of great interest, all afraid to glance Emily's way, and skidded to a halt beside Emily & Co.

'Bouncy bouncy bouncy bouncy,' Emily shouted, squealing with delight at the rubber noises her dress made, ignoring the severe black look from Thomas. 'Bouncy bouncy . . .'

Thomas spoke. 'Please, Emily, I implore you.' He appealed to Mr Cartwright, one of his top-paying guests, who seemed to be enjoying himself. 'Take it from me, if a woman does this in public, just imagine what fun she'll be in the bedroom. Go on, Mr Cartwright, take her to your room. Have a bottle of champagne on the Regency. Just go.'

Emily jumped off the lap. 'I beg your pardon, Mr Harding. Are you implying that I'm nothing but a two-bit slag? Well, I'll tell you something you . . . you guttersnipe, I have standards. I never—'

Marina grabbed Emily's arm and yanked her towards the door. Just before departing, Marina spun round to make eye contact with Thomas, but he was already gone, and so, in her mind, was her last chance.

'Thanks a bunch, Emily, you've just completely blown it for me with Thomas,' Marina fumed.

Within the office, Thomas flicked open his mobile. With a steady hand he dialled his best mate, Nathan, and with an unsteady voice he explained he needed to meet today, stressing the fact that he thought his mind was cracking. 'Honestly, Nathe, I have made the biggest mistake of my life. We were all over each other. I feel like a fraud. If the phone hadn't rung when it had . . . God, it doesn't bear thinking about. I'll put it another way, I am right up the Ganges river without a paddle . . .'

Inside Samson and Delilah's Fitness Centre in Watford, three sweaty Indian men with Nike headbands and bandannas, gasping for breath, were racing each other on the running machines, each fighting for the right to be the first Hindu man Marina would view as a prospective husband.

Palekji, Marina's adopted uncle, was overseeing the race. Marina's parents had entrusted him to find their daughter the best Hindu man in Britain and from an initial list of thirty asylum seekers, he'd whittled it down to four. The fourth man, Bipin Karoki

Ratnakar, also known as the Rajasthani Rat, narrowly escaped 'Palekji's Fitness Appraisal' by order of his doctor. An inherited heart problem left Bipin short of breath from the slightest exertion. His dream of competing in the London Marathon earlier that year went out the window when he realized he couldn't jog more than three metres without turning purple – and although he begged Palekji to allow him to meet Marina with a full canister of oxygen and a selection of pre-loaded adrenalin injections, the idea was ruled out immediately.

'Looks like we've got a winner.' Palekji checked Boy Number Two's LCD display. 'Ten kilometres. Without trainers. Well done.'

The humming noise from the treadmills diminished, only to be replaced by the heavy panting of all three bachelors. Palekji had assured them that the woman they were fighting to meet was worth every drop of sweat. Worth all the tests he had made them do. The maths test. The English test. The cooking test. The finance test. The manners test. And now the fitness test. Only the best for Marina. And to keep things simple, Palekji had made sure all of the Hindu men had no relatives in this country. No one to criticize his way of handling things.

In the upstairs bar, fruit juice and milkshakes were on offer. Palekji ordered all three men to sit with him at the corner table, overlooking a badminton match. Four frothy strawberry smoothies, topped with a sprinkling of Palekji's wife's home-made garam masala powder, stood ready.

'As I keep explaining, Marina is a good girl, extremely beautiful, like a princess.' Palekji slurped his smoothie, then continued talking with a pink and brown speckled moustache. 'She talks non-stop about having children. She says she doesn't regret making a go of her life with her career, but now the time has come to put her career to one side and settle down to bring up a family and provide for her husband. You three are what's left of my list of one thousand Hindu men. Feel privileged that you got this far. Unfortunately, only one of you can come away the winner.' He eyed Boy Number Two. 'Massoud, as you won five out of the six tests, it is only fair that you have first go at her. You will not be disappointed, you will not be—'

Massoud interrupted. 'When can I meet her, Uncle?'

Palekji shook his head disapprovingly. 'You interrupted me, Massoud, and you wonder why you came third in the manners test.' He slurped again, then belched aggressively. 'This Sunday you and I are going to surprise Marina with a visit. A small trip to a quaint village. Fenworth, very picturesque I am told, very picturesque indeed.'

But inside Palekji's head the view was far from picturesque. His brain bubbled with fiendish ideas. It was his duty to uphold at least some of the Indian virtues that his ancestors had fought to instil. All this business of giving girls like Marina her own freedom was making a mockery of tradition. If her own parents couldn't see it, then the onus was on him. And if that meant the odd little brown lie, then so be it. It was up to him to inculcate the strong wholesome Hindu values back into Marina. Rewire her mind and undo some of the Western ways that, no doubt, had clogged her Eastern thinking. Goodbye, Marina, the bad Indian girl with Western ideas and values. Hello, Marina, the good Indian girl with impeccable Eastern promise.

Palekji rubbed his hands together and blew on them like a craps player wishing on a dice. Sometimes all it took was a little bit of luck and a little bit of discipline. If things went to plan, this time next year Marina would be married to Boy Number Two, Massoud, and Marina's parents would be able to sleep at night.

Chapter Thirty

Most people can count their true friends on one hand. Shortlists of people who are friends, not just when you're swimming, but when you're sinking also. Right now, Thomas felt like he was sinking – but he could rely on Nathan to throw him a lifeline.

Parking in guest bay number fifteen outside Nathan's enormous house built in the depths of the countryside, Thomas smiled at the sight of the new heliport set to one side of the garages. Luxury lived here. Envy lived just outside. Most people of the well-to-do club had to go back to the drawing board when they'd visited Nathan's far from humble abode. It was the be-all and end-all of modern-day living. Even the toilets were the flashiest of flushers. Weighing each sitter and analysing the stools, then sending the information to the printer next to the gold-leafed toilet-roll holder, and advising them on their dietary habits. Money to *waste* – literally.

Inside the hall Thomas was greeted first, as always, by Liberty Cap, Nathan's rascal Jack Russell. Flying through the air, the dog landed in Thomas's arms, then licked his face clean. Thomas was quite sure that he had interrupted Liberty Cap's dinner. Pedigree Chum breath.

'Fancy a game of snooker before you explain this "problem" of yours?' Nathan said, in his prominent upper-class accent. He stood there in long shorts, flip-flops and a Hawaiian shirt. A tall, handsome man who was never short of a girlfriend (or two). 'Pot a few balls before we discuss saving yours?'

Thomas followed Nathan down the hall, up a long electric-blue neon-lit passageway and into the latest extension, the Games Room, covered in framed pictures of Marilyn Monroe. The room boasted a snooker table in the middle, a pool table next door, a selection of eighties arcade machines: Missile Command, Space Invaders, Galaxian, Frogger and, of course, Pac-Man. A minibar. And a jukebox bristling with lights in the corner.

They sat in luxurious burgundy-leather armchairs across a carved wooden table, signed by Hollywood greats and Arnold Schwarzenegger. Various alcoholic beverages were at their disposal.

'Did you end up cleaning the dress?' Thomas pointed to a white dress hanging on a mannequin, encased in a glass tomb, a fan blowing beneath the material in tribute to *The Seven Year Itch*.

Nathan appeared horrified. 'And wash away Marilyn's wonderful fragrance. Do behave, Tom, not a chance. Even you must agree she was the queen of blondes.'

Thomas sipped his whisky. 'To be honest, I don't know what I agree with these days.'

'Which brings us neatly to the Indian woman. I take it she isn't blonde?'

'Well, if blonde is the new "black", yes, she's jet blonde.' Thomas chortled, then became serious. 'I nearly slept with an Indian woman.' He glared. 'An *Indian* woman, Nathan.'

'Yes, yes, I'm assessing the situation. What was her name again?'

'Marina.' Thomas thought back to how turned on he'd been in the hotel gardens, how amazing Marina felt, how beautiful she was. 'You have to help me, Nathe, this is pretty serious.'

Nathan put down his drink. Measured responses required measured drinking. Thomas was having a mid-life crisis twenty years too early. It would be most unfortunate if Thomas suffered a heart attack like his father just because he'd taken to a woman who wasn't blonde. Most unfortunate indeed.

'What exactly is your problem with Marina, Tom, is it her hair colour or her skin colour?' Nathan pressed 09 on the jukebox, the record flipped across and 'Here Comes The Rain Again' by Eurythmics, came to life. 'Or is it something else?'

Thomas tried to explain. It was about values. It was about class. It was about ideologies. It was about . . .

'*Colour*, Tom, just admit it. It's about skin colour. Additionally, you cannot handle the fact that you've fallen for a woman who is not blonde and not upper class and who doesn't fit into your neat little package of what a woman should be.'

Thomas frowned. 'No. It's not that. I just don't think cultures should mix.'

'And why is that?'

'Because it would be like gatecrashing their religion, Nathan,' Thomas replied weakly, as he scratched the ears of Liberty Cap who was sleeping by his feet. 'Why rock the boat? They're brought up completely differently to us, their values are so old they're fossils. And what you and I might call backwards, they call culture. For two people of two different cultures to be a couple, something has to give.'

'This is my house and I shall swear in my house. What a fucking load of CRAP. It's feeble, Tom, and you know it, I expected better from you. I can see what scares you, it's as plain as day. You cannot admit that you are not in control of your own life. You don't like the fact that this Indian woman, who is beautiful but lower class, has taken you by surprise. She has made you call off your engagement – subconsciously – and sprung on you a whole load of feelings you cannot cope with.' He paused. 'You know what, Tom, I think you are in love with this Marina. I don't think you know what to do about that.'

'I know it's not my house, but BOLLOCKS! I hardly know her.'

'But, aha, I think I'm right. And I will tell you why. Out of all the women you've dated, not one has managed to change you. They were, as I think you often said yourself, "brilliant packaging". Blonde, beautiful, leggy and moulded to what you wanted.

This one woman comes along, nothing like you expect, and she breaks the mould. She's got you, Tom. Maybe you don't love her now, but it's definitely coming. Trust me.'

This time a very feeble 'Bollocks.'

But was it?

Thomas walked towards the Pac-Man machine. It always bothered him, if Pac-Man ate so much, where was all the poo? But games didn't always make sense. A bit like love. Although at least Pac-Man had rules. Unlike love. Thomas grabbed the joystick and wiggled and wobbled it about until he'd cleared a sheet, his mind resolute on solving at least some of his problems today. Nathan was fully aware of his role as a friend right now: to keep quiet; his best mate's sanity was a just cause for silence. And talking of just, Thomas had a few justs of his own:

Just because he let Marina grope in his boxers. *Just* because he admired her for not keeping the seventy thousand pounds when it was blatantly obvious she was hard up. *Just* because he saw the real intelligence and depth of Marina's character hidden beneath some of her 'cleaner' poetry on her bedroom wall. *Just* because he apologized to Marina first over his racist remarks before he apologized to his parents, friends and the Newton-Harringtons over the engagement fiasco. *Just* because he had been sitting before the gravestone in the hotel gardens thinking of nothing but her for three days. *Just* because of all that . . . surely it didn't mean he was falling for her? Where was the just justice in that?

Pac-Man died again. Thomas turned to speak to Nathan. 'I'm at a low ebb, Nathe, I think the split with Nicole has dragged me down. If you really want to psychoanalyse this, then it's quite obvious what's happening with me. I'm gorging myself on feelings that would otherwise revolt me. It's a rebellion of sorts. I'm not in control. It won't be long before I'm back to my normal self.'

Both Liberty Cap and Nathan stared sympathetically. 'I see. It sounds like a good theory if, indeed, you did love Nicole and you are, indeed, missing her as much as you imply you are. But I fear Nicole was more for decoration than love. Your love was entirely of the superficial kind.' He paused. 'Although I will grant you this: your blondes are not of the dumb variety.'

Thomas looked sheepish. 'Honestly, that's how you think my mind operates?'

Nathan nodded, gave Liberty Cap a good belly rub, then suggested Thomas take a swim to think things through while he ordered in a couple of Indian waiters and a top-class Indian chef to cook lunch.

The full-size heated pool, with Jacuzzi add-on, was a marvel to look at. A huge mural of Marilyn Monroe, with the words *I Wanna Be Loved By You*, was cast in the swimming-pool floor's tiles. And high above was a glass-structured dome which let the sunlight gush through, spraying a rainbow of colours on the rippled water. Thomas checked the huge wooden trophy cabinet near the shallow end. Empty. Maybe he might lend Nathan a few of his own. In Male Guest Locker Four, Thomas found a pair of black trunks and a monster towel. Five minutes later, he was tearing up and down the pool, his perfect style eating up the water like a dolphin.

As clear as the water he swam in, Thomas's mind was gradually purifying. Viscous ideas once thought unthinkable were solidifying in his head. The conch shell amongst a zillion grains of sand. The red poppy in a field of white. Marina, the pauper Indian woman, amongst the multitude of rich blonde babes. Could she really have stolen his heart? Thomas sped on for a few more lengths, tumble-turning at each end, racing over Marilyn Monroe's face. Thomas knew of theft before, women who had nearly stolen his heart. He was also aware of how he behaved when his feelings for a woman became strong. One word: embarrassing. His mouth acted like a complete jerk.

He thought back to a blonde he'd once dated, Janeane, who had been adopted by rich folk. Without fail, and without realizing, Thomas would have sensitive Janeane in tears most nights by bringing up the topic 'Family blood-ties'. Another ex, blonde, sensitive Belinda, had lost a brother in the Gulf War. Without realizing it, Thomas would talk about GWS, Gulf War Syndrome, constantly. Even ex, blonde, sensitive Vanessa, whose father was in prison for fraud, would have Thomas unknowingly mentioning the TV show *Porridge* on every date.

Now, he'd topped the lot. Marina, the non-blonde, the proud Indian, had been subjected to a Thomas special. Almost every time he saw her, his conversation would steer towards India, racism, and Paki talk. Even when she'd had her hand in his trousers earlier today, it had taken him every ounce of discipline not to mention Kashmir. A sure sign, if ever there was one, that his mind was being guided by his heart. Marina, like it or lump it, was now taking up an awful amount of his thoughts.

A shadow appeared at the deep end. Then a splash beside him. If Thomas wasn't mistaken, Liberty Cap was swimming next to him in the pool. This was the second true meaning of the words 'doggy style'.

'Out, Mushroom, out!' shouted Nathan, calling the dog by its pet name. 'Liberty, there's chlorine in the pool.' Nathan stood with a towel in one hand and with the other he held out Thomas's mobile. 'Nicole's father is on the phone. Sorry, I thought it might be important.'

Thomas thrust a soaked Liberty into Nathan's towel then heaved himself out. With his legs dangling over the pool side, he took the call.

Edmond spoke harshly. 'I am going to be blunt with you, Thomas. I never liked you and I never will. But we seem to be stuck with a problem. Nicole, my baby daughter, is crying every day because of you. It needs to be sorted, Thomas, and it needs to be done ASAP.'

'Look, I—'

'I have the VAT and Inland Revenue ready to go on a minute's notice. Friends in high places, Thomas. Good friends in very high places. I expect that like all successful businessmen, your books may well be full of holes. On top of these unwelcome guests, I have set in motion a planning proposal to build a huge, luxury hotel on that beautiful piece of land I have acquired directly behind your hotel. If all goes well, I expect the building work to begin in one month. Tractors, dump trucks, goodness knows what will have to travel up that narrow lane and pass by your hotel, blocking the guests' only way of entry into your Regency.' Edmond

Newton-Harrington paused as long as it took to say his name. 'Or, you marry Nicole, as you promised. Think about it, not too long. The wolves are scratching at the door, Thomas.' And he hung up.

Thomas looked up to Nathan, who was drying Liberty Cap. 'He's threatened to take away my baby, Nathe. My hotel.' Thomas flopped into the pool and dived to the bottom. Five seconds later, a mobile phone was seen flying out of the water.

Chapter Thirty-one

It was Sunday breakfast in the Fenworth girls' kitchen, three days since Marina had made a slut of herself with Thomas. A bowl of worms in milk waited to be scoffed. Vermicelli literally means 'little worms' in Italian – and the slimy, threadlike pasta treats floated in the bowl of warm milk, as if treading water. Marina could remember the day, as a teenager, when she chose Crunchy Nut Cornflakes over the traditional Indian breakfast; her parents' faces had dropped, their eyes stating, 'I think we're losing her.' And Marina's guilt had followed her around the house like a lovesick puppy.

Now, whenever Marina felt guilty, she gave herself a temporary Eastern make-over. Acting the way she'd done with Thomas, in front of a gravestone of all things, was disgraceful behaviour for a good Hindu girl. The guilt factor was high. If she continued at this rate, she'd be reincarnated as a slug. Something had possessed her mind since she'd first set eyes on Thomas. Some of the values instilled by her parents, once so steady, had now become shaky; and as far as she knew, only one force encouraged such behaviour: the force of love. Either that or Hilda's senility was catching. Marina thought about her clothes lying on the bed. Today's Eastern make-over would have to be a sensational one.

And it was.

Today, anyone would imagine that Marina was the perfect Indian housewife. Dressed to the hilt in traditional Indian clothes, with a silk marshmallow-coloured *shalwar kameez* clinging tightly to her curves and a matching pair of *chappals*, plastered in diamantes, on her feet. Her face dolled-up Indian-Bollywood style, heavy on the eye-liner, thick on the lipstick, her shoulder-length black hair flowing about her freely. Who said tradition couldn't be sexy?

Dr Fritzgerald Guztelburg was angrily shouting at two women in German. Self-help-tape number eighteen was quite a boisterous affair, but Marina, like Emily, had now become addicted to his soothing voice. Marina closed her eyes and swallowed the last disgusting mouthful of vermicelli, wishing Emily would come home, needing the ear of a good friend.

Marina clomped around in her *chappals*, noise the least of her worries: Hilda was at the car boot sale; Emily was at the Regency Hotel – Mr Cartwright, her new man, had become smitten with Emily and the rubber dress, inviting her to spend the weekend in his hotel room. Marina had received just two texts since Friday from Emily. One explained he was gorgeous, rich, single, wanting and waiting. The other explained that Emily may have fallen in love and not to expect her back in the near future and to tell Perv Bazzer to stuff his job right up his fat ginger arse – her karma had obviously improved. And, thus, Marina was all alone.

She stared towards the gardens round the back. Four houses down, a smoking bonfire was being tended by a gangly, scruffy youth called Kelvin. A pile of broken furniture from last night's parent row waited to be incinerated following another lottery fight. Apparently, Kelvin's mother, the stupid, thick cow, had chosen the wrong six numbers AGAIN! Marina had heard the crashing and swearing through her window, an unpleasant sound, something she couldn't wait to be away from. As always the blue lights of the police van and the barking of police dogs had put an end to it.

A knock on the front door made Marina jump. She was dressed perfectly for bible bashers and legged it down the stairs to confront them. Normally asking them if they wanted to convert to Hinduism had them running back up the path, clinging on to their *Watchtower* booklets, muttering the Lord's Prayer under their breath.

This time, it was Marina muttering a prayer under her breath. Thomas was at the door. She snatched her head away from the peephole, already hot and extremely bothered under her *shalwar kameez*. Even through a distorting lens he looked magnificent. As he hadn't phoned her since that business with Emily and Mr Cartwright in the hotel lobby, she'd assumed their future was null and void, she'd guessed their time together was finished. And yet – Marina fluffed up her hair, smoothed down her *kameez* – here he was. Oh, thank you, Shiva.

With the 'astonished' look in place, Marina opened the door. 'Oh, what a fabulous surprise, Thomas.' She smiled joyfully, her head to one side imagining him standing there naked. 'If I'd known you were coming I would have tidied the street.'

Thomas seemed taken back, his eyes scanning up and down Marina's body. 'You *really* are an Indian, aren't you?' Cringing at his remark, he turned his head to check on his car, then back to face her. 'Sorry, I mean, dressed that way you look more Indian. Authentic.' His ears picked up the German tape that seemed far more intense than last time. Dr Fritzgerald Guztelburg was now commentating on having sex with four women at once. A Frankfurt orgy. 'Look, Marina, the reason I came round . . . God, I don't quite know how to put this. I'm normally articulate with words, but all I can say this time is I'm really sorry—'

The garden gate flew open and banged against the hedge. Thomas and Marina jumped out of their skins.

'Surprise!' Palekji appeared at the gate entrance, another Indian man, dressed in a shiny suit, following behind. 'What a shitty neighbourhood you live in, Marina.'

Palekji stormed down the path, leaving the other man where he was. Marina stood rooted to the spot, flabbergasted; what the hell was *he* doing here? Shoving aside Thomas, Palekji walked to the front door and hugged Marina, commenting on how touched he was with her choice of clothes.

'Really, Marina, this means so much to me.' Palekji

ushered Massoud over with an angry wave. 'Come and meet your future wife, Massoud. This is Marina. And Marina, this is Massoud.' Palekji glanced at Thomas, noting the designer suit. 'What are you doing here? She's not interested in your double-glazing, it's not even her house, so, if you please, leave us be.' He turned back to Massoud. 'Well, what do you think? Pretty isn't she?'

'Very. Everything you promised me, Uncle.' Massoud smiled at Marina.

'And don't worry about her vagina, Massoud, I've already made preparations to have it checked out. I've got a good doctor who will probe every angle and channel. Make no mistake, if she is not a virgin, Doctor Habashi will know.' He sneered at Marina. 'You'd better not have slept with any men, Marina, not after the effort I have put in here to find you a husband.'

Thomas coughed. 'Erm. I must dash.'

'Go on, get out of here,' Palekji shouted, as he watched Thomas walk to his car. 'Take your double-glazing sales tactics away. Can't you see how tacky you look in a Porsche?' He returned to Marina. 'Can we come in?' He barged through with Massoud, still smiling, behind.

Marina slammed the door in a fit of temper, *hoping* that Thomas hadn't picked up on any of that.

And a mile outside Fenworth, Thomas sat in his car *wishing* he hadn't picked up on any of that. Golly gosh indeed. It just proved what wankers men could be sometimes. Which reminded him of one particular wanker he needed to sort out. From the glove compartment he pulled out a business card. After being threatened by Edmond the other day, his mind had been calculating the risks of doing nothing. Of ignoring the Newton-Harrington threat. Of always looking over his shoulder. Only wimps dance to the tune of someone else's flute.

Thomas lifted up the car phone, dialled and waited for an answer. If Edmond wasn't careful he'd have that flute shoved right up his . . . 'Hello, Frank, it's Thomas Harding. I need some information.'

'Go on.'

'I need you to find me a skeleton in Edmond Newton-Harrington's closet. It must be full of them. It would be a huge favour for me if you did and I would certainly pay handsomely.'

'Zombies. Vampires. Ghouls. Skeletons. His closet is stuffed, leave it with me.' Frank paused. 'That other business you asked me to check into, it's nearly done. We just need a mutually agreed time to meet and then I should be able to rush it over to you.'

They arranged to get together in a week's time.

There were certain elements of life that left a bad taste in your mouth. Blackmail was one. But in order to blackmail someone efficiently, especially a bully like Edmond, it helped to have something or someone to barter with.

Thomas dialled Nicole's number, awkwardly spoke about how awkward he felt, rambling on and on about the unfairness of it all, love, life and let-downs. He apologized once again for wrecking her life.

'My life is not wrecked,' Nicole said, dabbing her eyes with a tissue. 'It just feels empty not having you in it any more. Holly says you're a murderer.'

'A what?'

Nicole almost laughed. 'She says that you have murdered the children we would have had together. She says—' Nicole burst her tear banks. 'I miss you, Tom.'

Thomas gave Nicole a phone hug (talking her through the hug he would have given her, had she been there with him), calming her down, soothing her sadness, trying desperately to stem a weeping wound. Maybe Holly was right, maybe he was a murderer. Thomas Harding, you stand accused of murdering the happiness of Nicole Newton-Harrington. Have you anything to say? How do you plead?

'Guilty,' Thomas repeated to Nicole. 'I feel as guilty as hell.'

They chatted for a little while longer, then made arrangements for the collection of Nicole's belongings from his apartment. Nicole preferred it if Thomas would be absent from the Regency Hotel when she arrived tomorrow evening at seven. She wanted to make the break as clean and swift as possible. Ramone would be on hand to help with the heavier items, and Thomas agreed to make himself scarce for a good few hours. They said their goodbyes.

Nicole replaced the receiver and lay back on her four-poster bed. Three large laundry bags waited by her bedroom door to be collected. Anything she owned relating to Lester was in those bags and was to be burned by the gardener this afternoon. It was as good a time as any to straighten out her life. Before she could begin with her new life, the old one had to be extinguished.

Her veins filled with trepidation, liquid fear for what lay ahead tomorrow on Hallowe'en. When she asked Ramone to jam open the Hobbs box in Thomas's safe, she knew an answer awaited her. The real Thomas would finally be revealed.

What had he been hiding from her all this time?

'I love the smell of garlic in the morning, it smells like victory,' Palekji said, ribbing Massoud, laughing loudly, as Marina boiled tea and cardamoms in the saucepan. His *Apocalypse Now* joke always a winner with his cronies.

Being introduced to your future husband in a poky kitchen was hardly romantic. After switching off the German self-help tape, Marina hovered over the bubbling water, fully aware that she was being scrutinized from behind. Her mind was yelling, 'Get out of here!' But inside she knew her parents were a party to this meeting. That hint her mother had dished out – 'I am convinced that you will find a good Hindu boy. And, Marina, in my heart, I feel that the time is coming very soon. I can feel it' – had been a shot across the bow, a warning that an 'occurrence' was in the making. And in an Indian family, an occurrence usually involves an arranged marriage. If ever there was a day not to be wearing traditional clothes then this was it.

Marina stirred the anaemic-looking tea bags with a wooden spoon, then added milk to turn the liquid a murky yellow. Along with tea brewing in this kitchen there was also irony brewing. Indians grow the finest tea leaves, yet they sometimes make the yuckiest tea. There was also another tea in the house today – the audacity. Marina was still aghast at what had just happened. One minute the man she wanted to marry was standing at her doorstep, the next minute he was replaced by the man her parents wished her to marry. One second she was staring at a prime hunk, the next, she was faced with . . .

Marina snuck another look at Massoud. Good God alive . . . she was faced with a primate. The wildest head of hair and sideburns she'd seen since *Gorillas In The Mist*. Zoology wasn't her specialist topic but this monkey was a rare breed and she worried that there weren't any bananas in the house. Although for some reason, Massoud, sitting there on the chair with his legs so far apart, seemed to want Marina to look at his banana.

Palekji elbowed Massoud to speak. 'Go on. Sell yourself. I can't do everything for you.'

Massoud cleared his throat, then spoke in broken English. 'Six foot one, thirty-two, no criminal record. Full English passport. Very fertile family.' He counted fingers. 'Eight brothers and two sisters. My hobbies include dowsing for water wells. And you?'

Bringing over the teas, Marina sat with them at the table. 'I haven't got a hobby. You could say, my hobby is trying to find a hobby.' She felt Palekji kick her under the table. 'Sorry, only joking. Erm, hobbies? Oh, all the usual things that good Hindu girls love. I love praying and slaving over a hot stove. I get a buzz knowing that there aren't enough hours in the day to complete my chores. I just love waking up knowing I have the whole day ahead of me full of shitty little—'

'She is so funny, isn't she?' Palekji pinched Marina's cheek and gave it a good tug. 'Hindu girl with a sense of humour. So hard to find these days.' Palekji turned to Massoud. 'Go to the toilet.' He then shouted, 'Make sure if you're wiping then you're flushing. And wash those hands of germs afterwards.'

As soon as the kitchen door closed, Palekji became threatening.

'I know all about your lies, Marina. I've been checking on you. Not quite the good girl your parents think you are, are you? It would break their hearts if they knew the truth. All this talk of working for a top estate agents, saving a bundle of money, when all the time you fill sandwiches like a servant in a dingy shop on wages that even my paper boy surpasses.' He grabbed her hand and held it in both of his, his shining bald head blinding her eyes. 'Massoud is a nice boy and you could do a lot worse. You will marry him if he agrees to marry you. No objections, I won't hear of it. Is that understood?' He kissed her forehead. 'Good girl. The last thing we need is for your parents to know what you've been up to. Good girl, Marina.' He walked to the door and shouted down the corridor. 'Massoud, back in here now!'

Massoud returned in a jiffy and sat down, hoping beautiful Marina, his future wife, wouldn't mind that he had used her toothbrush while he was in the bathroom. Palekji had warned him about hygiene. Girls detested smelly men. Hence the half bottle of Blue Stratos under his armpits. In India, a smelly man is a hard-working man with many friends and family. In England, a smelly man lives alone.

With a peppermint smile, Massoud reached across and held Marina's hand. 'Tell me your dreams, Marina. Let me into your heart.'

Palekji folded his arms and smirked at Marina. 'He *is* good, isn't he? So sensitive. Go on, tell him your dreams.'

He is very creepy, thought Marina, withdrawing her hand to the safety of her lap. This was a delicate matter requiring subtle diplomacy. Massoud was the innocent party here and she wanted to avoid hurting his feelings if she possibly could. It was obvious a certain amount of duplicity was behind this sudden introduction. Palekji, who often called himself the Wandering Temple, was a through and through advocate of the Indian way. There was no doubt in Marina's eyes that Palekji had been a major influence in organizing today. Possibly twisting her parents' arms, tying their minds in knots, and reiterating the proven advantages of marrying Marina off to a good Hindu man. Especially before Marina reached that past-it age of thirty.

But what to do? Her mother had always encouraged honesty no matter how hard it seemed. This was one of those moments when honesty was her only real ally. And now, Massoud wanted to know her dreams – none of which would have made it past Mary Whitehouse's front porch.

She looked into Massoud's expectant eyes, trying desperately hard to ignore his Bruce Springsteen *Born to Run* sideburns. 'I'm sorry, Massoud, you seem a really nice man. Extremely nice. But my thoughts are with another man and it wouldn't be fair on you if I didn't mention this.'

'She is joking, Massoud,' Palekji exclaimed, confidently.

'It's not a joke, Uncle Palekji,' said Marina.

'She is joking, Massoud. Ho ho very funny,' Palekji confirmed.

'It's not a joke. He is English, you saw him as you came up the path.'

Palekji and Massoud swapped a look, then Palekji continued. 'The double-glazing salesman? You are having sex with a double-glazing salesman?' A yellow globule of phlegm shot across the table and landed by the sugar bowl. 'I spit on him.'

'You promised me a virgin, Uncle,' Massoud said, raising his voice. 'You said if I pressed the top of her head, it wouldn't pop, because she had not been tampered with. Just like a new jar of blackberry jam.' Massoud stood above Marina and pressed his hands down on her head, making a popping noise with his mouth. 'Dirty girl. You have brought me to the house of a dirty girl, Uncle. I paid you one thousand pounds and I ran ten kilometres for *you* to find *me* a wife who was pure. And what have I got? A dirty girl.' He pretended to retch. 'And to think I used her toothbrush.'

Marina retched for real.

Another globule of phlegm landed by the sugar bowl. Palekji spoke. 'I spit on you, Marina. You shame me and you shame your parents. Come on, Massoud, let us go. I will find you another wife. You're my Number One Boy and trust me, the next woman *will* be pure.' He turned to Marina. 'I'll check she is a virgin myself if I have to.'

Marina didn't even have the time or the satisfaction of yelling, 'Get out!' They were gone. If a lesson was to be learned here, it was this: hide your toothbrush when guests come calling. The astonishment turned to anger turned to guilt turned to sadness. A mish-mash of emotions that needed the temperate and wise voice of Shiva to calm her. Mum and Dad had let her down. Their promise of a free life without the tug-a-tug tugging of Indian ropes had been snapped like string today. Did they honestly think that by using a go-between to arrange her marriage, she would succumb to the idea? Had all their liberal ideas vanished up their Khyber Pass?

Later that evening . . .

Kneeling on her *puja* mat, Marina lit the seven candles surrounding Shiva. Sometimes she felt guilty about the way she used her god. Only calling upon him when in times of need and strife. Not once could she remember dropping to the floor and making small talk just for the sake of it. It was always always when she felt low.

'Aum.' Her hands were held together in prayer as she closed her eyes.

Drifting towards the darkness of peace, Marina let free her mind. Thoughts all clammy with fear were dispersed by Shiva like unwanted pests until her head was as silent as an empty church. Her mood relaxed as her heartbeat slowed and soon the soft voice of reason called quietly. It was time to accept some truths. So hell-bent on achieving perfect karma peace, Marina had foolishly hidden away the one significant item which needed to be solved if *ever* true karma could be fulfilled.

The tapestry case under her bed. The monster nightmare that sometimes went bump in the night. All her fears and tears were wrapped up inside that suitcase. Her life could never be settled until she'd made the journey of ten thousand miles and finalized the deal with Shiva in India. It had to be India. And India, more than ever right now, seemed so far away.

'Aum. Please, Shiva, find me a way to get to India soon. Let me put my wrong to right. For the sake of my family if not myself.'

Opening her eyes, Marina stretched across and touched Shiva's head, thanking him for being there, for listening, for understanding. She blew on the candles, snuffing out the flames. And as the last flame died, her loneliness returned . . . bringing the cost of denial thundering down around her.

Today had been about truths and honesty. Thomas's last words to her this morning – 'God, I don't quite know how to put this. I'm normally articulate with words, but all I can say this time is I'm really sorry' – had left Marina in a tizzle. It would be easy to imagine that Thomas had come round this morning to apologize for his hair style, or for being so good-looking. Or even for kissing her so perfectly in his hotel gardens. But the truth of the matter was, if she didn't live in denial, Thomas had come round to apologize for not wanting to be with her. It was blatantly obvious. How amazing was the swing of events sometimes. One minute she was sure her Ganges water was working and had thrown Thomas into a spin of lust, and today: dump time. Goodbye, Indian girl, you were not to my taste after all, maybe you're an 'acquired' taste – unfortunately I haven't got time to find out.

Suddenly an alarm bell sounded in her head. EMERGENCY. Quicker than an antelope on Nandrolone, Marina hurtled down the hall and into the bathroom, fished out her toothbrush, then threw it in the pedal bin with the look of 'Yuck' on her face. A minute later, after convincing herself that it was safe to do so, she risked a peep at the brush in the bin. Yep, thought as much, she shivered.

Staring up from the bristles was a clump of spinach. Some men leave red roses, others it's choccies, but this man had left a masticated lump of *sag* on her toothbrush. What class!

Chapter Thirty-two

After collecting one hundred packets of sparklers, which Daddy had forgotten, from Trick or Treats party shop, Nicole asked Ramone, her bodyguard-cum-chauffeur-cum-friend-cum in his pants when he hears Elton John, to proceed towards the Regency Hotel. It was 6.46 p.m. Judgement Day. A rusty crowbar and hacksaw wrapped in a clean towel sat on the back seat of Nicole's Mercedes: Ramone's tools for opening the metal box in Thomas's office safe. It also happened to be 31 October, Hallowe'en, the night of goblins and witches, *when nightmares come out to play*.

The Newton-Harringtons were hosting their annual Hallowe'en and fireworks fancy-dress ball in the grounds of Castle Cliff Manor from 9.00 p.m. It would be the first party in three years where she and Thomas would not be a couple and as such Nicole's depression had left her feeling sick. She swigged from a flask of brandy, then, without thinking, offered it across to Ramone.

'I'm driving, Nicole.' Ramone watched the narrow road. 'Anyway, Frankenstein doesn't drink. It rusts his neck bolts.'

Nicole giggled. Ramone's face and huge hands were the colour of frozen peas. His wig was a dusty blue and his ripped suit jacket, two sizes too small, was caked in fake blood. Two near-misses had occurred already when the drivers of oncoming cars had spotted a zombie creature thing and his sidekick driving towards them at speed.

Parking in Thomas's spot, Ramone collected the tools and a sports bag, then followed Nicole into Reception, slightly anxious at the droplets of rain now falling. Even though he was paid to protect Nicole from evil, he couldn't protect her from herself. Tonight, he feared, was going to be eventful – it had that nasty, crack-of-lightning feel about it.

Hannah manned the Reception desk with her usual 'I'm so busy you'll just have to wait', eyes-down attitude. A move of a pad here, a touch of her pen there, one minute later she was ready to be of service.

'Oh, hi, Nicole. I didn't recognize you dressed as a—'

'Witch.' Nicole stood back and let Hannah admire.

It was the flooziest witch this side of the Yellow Brick Road. Black stockings and suspenders, black high-heeled leather boots, black ripped satin dress, a black cloak tied round her shoulders and one witch's hat. Even with the collection of black, hairy moles stuck on her face, Nicole somehow managed to pull off beautiful, although she had drawn a line when

Ramone had suggested she blacken out her teeth.

'Undo your zip, Ramone, and give me your package,' Nicole said laughing.

Ramone undid the zip on the sports bag and handed Nicole two gift-wrapped parcels. Nicole asked Hannah to give one to Cheryl, the main receptionist, and the other to Emma, the waitress who didn't know left from right. But no present for Stuart, the commis chef, who didn't know right from wrong. The expensive gifts were just a little something for being nice to her. And being nice was a commodity that seemed rarer and rarer nowadays.

'Righty-oh, all set, Ramone?' Nicole nodded at her jolly green giant, then back to Hannah. 'Thomas should have left me the key to his apartment?'

Hannah handed Nicole the key. 'He said you can have anything except his light sabre and his *Rumble in the Jungle* and *Thriller in Manila* Mohammed Ali boxing tapes.' She watched the pair of them head for the lifts, then returned to her 'I'm so busy you'll just have to wait', eyes-down attitude.

'Nicky!' Stuart appeared from nowhere and kissed Nicole on the cheek. For some reason he wasn't covered in blood today. 'How's my tasty sausage?'

'If you are referring to me, Stuart, then I am fine.' She thumped the lift button, knowing her civility was on a short fuse this evening. 'And yourself?'

'Me? Tops.' Stuart grinned. 'So, how are you coping with the split? What that bastard Thomas did to you, I don't know. I'm surprised you haven't taken an overdose or cut your wrists.'

A dirty great six-foot-seven shadow appeared in the shape of Ramone. If Stuart had been wearing underpants they would have changed colour. As it was, his underpants were boiling away in his mum's kitchen at the moment and it was the inside of his trousers that now had a new lining.

Stuart stepped back as he spoke. 'Horrible business, suicide. I wouldn't have known what to do if you had killed yourself, Nicky. I would always be asking, "Stu-pot, was there anything you could have done to prevent this? Anything?"' He grabbed Nicole's hand, fumbling for her diamond bracelet, desperate to see the scar – this could be his last chance. 'I want you to look in my eyes and promise me that you will never, ever try anything like that—'

SLAP! Nicole whacked his face. 'How dare you! You worthless little weasel. Is nothing sacred to you? Suicide is never a laughing matter, Stuart. How you get your rocks off on someone else's misery is totally beyond me. Now, I suggest you go before I set Ramone on you.'

One look at rabid Ramone was enough to have dirty pants running towards the kitchen. Nicole shook her head and Ramone placed a consoling arm around her. This was too much for anyone to shoulder, to keep their boat afloat. The lift pinged and the two stepped inside. A short climb up and the lift pinged again. This time, as Nicole stepped into the corridor, Stuart's words drilled holes in her boat. The memories of that awful night flooding through like sea water.

The rain that day had been enough to sink Noah's Ark. Relentless and daunting, ruthless and cruel. Memories of Lester had come crashing into Nicole's guilty mind as each brutal flash of lightning struck. To know you caused another person's death is to stare the Devil in the eyes. A baby to a boy to a man. Meet Nicole, now meet your coffin. No getting old, no having grandchildren, just the still of the dark and the cold of eternity. Nicole knew her life was forever scarred by Lester's death. And that night, more than any other night, she had needed the arms of Thomas around her. She had craved the reassurance of the only man she ever loved.

But where was he that night?

Where was Thomas on the night that Nicole couldn't get Lester's lifeless body out of her mind? Where all she saw was the ambulance crew screaming through the deafening rain that Lester was gone. He was DOA. Dead On Arrival. Where was Thomas when Nicole needed someone to explain that the crash was an accident, a heartless trick of nature? Where the hell was Thomas?

Busy. Always busy with his hotel. A string of customers with an even longer string of demands. Busy making money, too busy to find the time for Nicole.

'Look, Nicole, babe, we'll talk later, I promise. I'm under-staffed tonight and if I don't do it, who will?'

'But, Tom—'

'Later, Nicole.' And after a peck on the cheek he was back to being busy.

And the rest . . . was bloody history.

Walking into the apartment with Ramone, Nicole squeezed back tears, thanking God that Thomas had not removed the photograph of her. She gave herself an hour to pack her books, clothes and shoes, leaving another hour to investigate the secret, sealed box downstairs. Already her heart was hurting.

'Curtains closed, Hal,' Nicole said clearly.

Ramone gave a Frankenstein nod of approval when the curtains did as they were told. This was the first time he'd been in Thomas's apartment. He'd always liked Tom. Fair, honest and with plenty of time for the hired help. Unlike Lester, who had treated servants with contempt. Most likely, if Lester could have, he would have looked down his nose at the grave diggers who buried him. As it turned out, he ended up looking up the noses of the grave diggers who buried him.

Just about to head to the bedroom, Nicole spotted a red rose and an envelope with the words 'Dear Nicole' lying on the coffee table. Two easy words on the outside, but would there be hard-hitting and difficult words on the inside? If only she had X-ray vision, she could see what was written, *then* decide if she wanted to open it or not. But she didn't. Just an X-rated mind.

Sitting down on the sofa, Nicole sniffed the rose as she called out, 'Open envelope, Hal.'

Ramone waited with his mouth open – amazed.

'Just a joke, Ramone.' And gently she ran her French-manicured nails under the envelope seal.

Parked on Fairground Road outside Marina's flat, Thomas waited in his Porsche for the rain to subside. From the downstairs window a torch light was flicking on and off. Three short blinks, followed by three longs blinks, followed again by three short blinks. If he was not mistaken, the landlady downstairs was calling for help. SOS. He hoped she was okay – because there was no fucking way he was getting his hair wet for her. It had cost £100 to give it the designer mess and he wasn't having it neatened up by a Fenworth downpour.

A few minutes later: 'Oh, sod the hair.' He ran to the front door and arrived drenched. Before he had time to knock, Hilda was facing him, scorn in her eyes.

'Didn't you see me calling for help?' Hilda held the shining torch up to Thomas's pupils, nearly blinding him. 'In my day men would help an old lady sort out her TV aerial when the picture went screwy on *Corrie*. That's the problem with men today. Active service for all of you, I say. Three years of hard graft in the army would make men of you. Now, what do you want from me?'

'Sorry, I'm not that clued up with Morse code, I thought your torch-light message read "old bag in distress". Is Marina home?'

'You mean Maryanna. Follow me, she's in her room.'

He decided to stay put. Last time he'd followed Hilda to see Marina he'd come face to face with his own face on the wall. He couldn't face it again.

'Suit yourself,' growled Hilda, then mumbled something about Bombay/Mumbai Rolls as she clambered up the stairs, snapping on her surgical mask, exaggerating her arthritis, stooping like she had a donkey on her back, moaning each time her knees cracked.

Minutes passed, leaving Thomas, standing by the open door, wondering what the hell was going on. More minutes, more wondering, more minutes, more wondering. What on earth could be keeping her? He looked worriedly towards a streak of lightning jig-sawing across the black sky. He wouldn't put it past the landlady to have Marina on the roof holding a metal coat hanger as an aerial for *Coronation Street*. Rod Hull should have been a lesson to everyone. Just because he had Rod in his name didn't automatically make him one – a lightning rod.

The rain was ceaseless, a swarm of anger. Thomas watched nature do its worst, wondering why he felt something was amiss. This moment didn't feel right. Voices grabbed his attention; Marina and Hilda appeared in the doorway. Nothing too shocking about that. But when Thomas saw what Marina was wearing, he was shell-shocked, or rather, shell-suit-shocked. Marina was wearing an eighties shell suit. Pink and yellow, worn and torn, old and out-dated. The badges on her chest, 'Fame' and 'Who Shot JR?', were the killer punches.

Marina hated Hilda.

Hilda had successfully explained to Marina that Arnie, the catalogue man, was downstairs waiting for his money, and suggested that she dress in her worst possible clothes if she wanted Arnie to waive this week's payment out of sympathy. The twenty-five-pence jumble-sale shell suit was a joint decision. No man in his right mind would take anything off a woman wearing that. What was worse, other than the socks with sandals she was wearing, was the manky mildew shower cap on her head. For all intents and purposes Marina looked like a mental person.

She *really* hated Hilda.

Marina could sense Thomas was trying not to laugh. She looked blankly at him, wondering how he managed it. God, he must be thinking about funerals and cancer, she thought. She turned her attention to a smiling Hilda.

'Where's the catalogue man?' Marina spat, sliding off the mouldy shower cap and crunching it up tight.

'He *is* the catalogue man.' Hilda crept towards Thomas and gave his chest a hard prod with her forefinger. 'Oh, no, silly me. That's that man you've got up on your wall. It's my senility again. Those blasted doctors.' She whispered loudly to Thomas, 'Horrible tracksuit Maryanna is wearing, isn't it?'

Marina gave Hilda a precision-guided bitch stare. 'If you want this week's rent, Hilda, I suggest you give me and the *catalogue* man some privacy.'

Hilda tutted herself back to *Corrie*, leaving Marina to justify to Thomas why she was wearing a shell suit. And just because she appeared like a retard didn't mean she was one. Thomas explained that he wanted to have a chat with her. And he disagreed: anyone who wears a shell suit *is* a retard, whatever the reason. Marina then, very quickly, tried to clear up who Palekji and Massoud were, to which Thomas raised his hand and said, 'It's really none of my business.'

And more to the point, it really was none of her parents' business either. It had taken until today before Marina was calm enough to speak to her mum and dad regarding Palekji and Massoud. How dare they interfere with her life this way? She had blown off steam down the phone, totally angry, totally let down. Her parents had lamely tried to justify their incursion into Marina's life but Marina was having none of it. If it happened again, Marina would lose all respect for them. And once respect has gone, it rarely returns.

With her parents on the defensive, the opportunity was too good to pass up; Marina had come clean about her job. She'd explained how pride had kept her from telling them the truth. In Indian culture, as with many cultures, status begins with your job description. A sandwich filler to an Indian parent was equal to a road sweeper. Selling property was much a easier sell. They had been disappointed, but at least their daughter wasn't a pole dancer.

After much reassurance, Mum and Dad had promised Marina that her life was her own. She was free to do whatever she chose, with whom she chose. And that included white men.

An hour later, Thomas and Marina were sitting at a table in Pixies, an exclusive bar on the outskirts of Oxfordshire, Marina now dressed in her one and only designer dress, Thomas as he was, in his one of four million designer suits.

Thomas had found out about Pixies through a guest. Hidden away in the rural countryside, Pixies lived off the self-circulating referrals of satisfied customers. No advertising was necessary for the establishment which proudly didn't boast of such customers as Richard Gere, Kevin Spacey, Halle Berry, Julianne Moore, to name but a few. They didn't boast of them because they never ate there. But it was *extremely* posh. Full of loaded wallets and enough plastic to build another Millennium Dome out of . . . plastic? Some might liken it to a Swiss cottage in the Alps, open fires and plenty of wooden beams. Although yodelling was banned, unless specifically requested by a customer.

Left with a chilled bottle of costly wine for company, Marina took in the warm surroundings as Thomas popped to the loo. Many small and medium tables, each with a pumpkin lantern in the centre, were scattered across a dark wooden floor. Most were occupied by loving couples or groups of designer-clad women, knocking back high-priced cocktails and over-priced wine. A constant babble of upper-class chit-chat hung above the swooning jazz music, the price of stocks, the cost of yachts, the Milan fashion show, thoroughbred horses, and tallyho. All snobs, except for Marina, the only customer in Pixies who knew the cost of a loaf of bread. At a push she could even calculate the cost of a slice.

Running out of things to make with the complimentary cocktail sticks and book of matches, Marina sighed with relief upon sighting Thomas returning from the Gents'. The relief was short-lived as his journey back to Marina was thwarted by a pretty brunette grabbing his arm and smiling up at him from her table of girlfriends. Thomas obviously knew the woman, thought Marina sourly, as he failed to yell out, 'Sexual harassment'. Seconds passed, a few comments were made, then Thomas yanked his arm away from the harasser and aimed her a cold look. Just before departing, Thomas leant into their table and said something that turned all four faces beetroot. He returned to Marina, who was suddenly engrossed in the Pixies beverage menu.

'A Quick Hard Fuck,' Marina said, reading out the name of one of the cocktails. 'Sounds good.'

'Trust me, it's a let-down,' Thomas said smiling. He removed his suit jacket, then sat on the extremely comfortable chair. 'I won't beat around the bush. I've brought you here for a reason and the last thing you need is to be kept hanging on, so I shall commence with my speech. Look, Marina, I'm sorry if this sounds outrageous, but I seem to have come across some feelings for you that I find very discouraging.' He gave up on the idea of this speech being perfect and poured them both some wine. 'Have you ever heard of the expression "Diamond in the rough?"'

'No.'

'It implies that beneath the roughly hewn rock lies a beautiful diamond. And—'

'Hewn?' Marina interrupted, not familiar with the word.

'Yes, hewn.' He paused. 'Marina, I will be frank. You and I come from very different backgrounds. It would be almost impossible for you and I to see eye to eye on anything. As though we view life through different lenses. And yet, I find myself profoundly attracted to you. Knowing full well that what I see when I see you is the diamond, ignoring the rough, ignoring all the differences our upbringings entail.' His mobile blipped, a quick check of his texts, then he continued. 'You and I can gloss this up as much as we like, but we speak differently, we mix in different circles, we even—'

'So, what shall I do about it?' Marina said defensively, upset at his attitude. 'If you think I'm going to take electrocution lessons, you can forget it.'

'Elocution lessons,' he corrected. 'Anyway, my

point is this: you and I can never be an item. I am sorry. The gap between us is insurmountable. A chasm so broad the whole of India could float though it. A mountain so high even the top Sherpa would fail. Our duty to each other is to forget what happened in the garden the other day. To forget what is written on your wall. To forget how much I think about you every night. To forget . . .' Thomas stopped. Marina's head was downcast and he took her hand. And it was here, at this moment, that his crowded mind emptied. Leaving just one thought. Leaving just one idea: he couldn't lie to Marina any more.

And more importantly, he couldn't lie to himself.

Here she sat, Marina, a world apart and yet only one seat away. Who sets life's standards? Who follows other people's principles? What right did anyone have to say a man and a woman of different backgrounds couldn't be happy together, shouldn't be happy together, wouldn't be happy together? Surely people didn't fall in love because both knew which fork to use with which course? Or who pronounced the Ps and Qs correctly. Love is more brutal than that. If ever there was something without manners it was love. Barging into people's lives and kicking down the doors. Waking them up in the middle of the night. Turning flesh and bone to gibbering jelly.

And what did other people know anyway? thought Thomas. His hotel project was a classic example of negativity. A whole host of friends, relatives, professionals, all slamming the hotel idea before he'd even laid a brick. 'What if?' 'How can you be so sure?' 'Bankrupt in two years!' 'What a waste of an Oxford education.' One month after opening, those same friends, those same relatives, all had different comments: 'Can we stay for free, Tom?' 'We knew you would succeed, Tom, with our moral support.' 'We are so proud of you, Thomas.'

It was all about risks.

Thomas surveyed the crowded Pixie bar. A place chock-a-block with his type of people. A gathering of full wallets and empty smiles. But how many of them had taken just one risk in their lives? Who could honestly say they were in a happy relationship? Which ones would, if they could, swap the cars, luxury house, holidays abroad for that one true love they knew was missing from their hearts? Thomas knew human beings were explorers. It was natural to search outwards. However, how many humans explored inside themselves? How many really took stock of their lives before it was too late?

A waiter arrived and unloaded a blue drink, giving it to Thomas. 'From the blonde lady by the aquarium. The cocktail is called "For Old Times".'

Thomas glanced at the blonde, grimaced, then placed the drink back on the tray. 'Send it back. Have you by any chance got a drink called "For The Crappy Times We Had"?' The waiter laughed as he hurriedly walked back to the blonde's table.

Marina giggled, but her eyes were still sad. 'Ex?'

'Ex-crement. Yes.' Thomas swigged his wine. 'I've been very unfair on you, Marina. Some would say cowardly. I'm not being truthful when I say I don't think we could make a go of this. Because I do. Sincerely, I do. If we try hard enough, then anything is possible. That's of course if you haven't changed your mind.' He raised his eyebrows. 'The fact of the matter is, when I truly give the idea deep consideration, I would hate *not* to give us a try.'

Blimey. The Ganges water bloody worked. 'You would regret it if you didn't give us a try.'

'I know.'

'You'd spend the rest of your life wondering if I was the one. The rest of your life wondering what I was up to. What sort of Hoover I own. How many—'

'Point taken.'

The waiter returned and unloaded a pink drink. 'From the blonde lady again. Would you like to know what the cocktail is called?' Thomas nodded. 'It's called, "I Faked It!"'

'Thank you, kind waiter. Please would you take it back to her.'

Even with the music and chat, the rain could be heard pummelling the roof as Thomas and Marina took trips down each other's memory lane. Views of his life, views of hers, careers, dreams and pastimes. It was the quickest get-to-know-each-other on record. Marina explained the reason behind the Ganges water, why she had thrown the stagnant, ageing sacred liquid over him.

'I did it to seduce you. Indians aren't just about spice, you know,' Marina said.

'A spicy seduction,' Thomas mused, then laughed. 'What utter codswallop.'

'Not quite. You're here with me now, aren't you?'

And he most certainly was. A fact that was noted not only by himself, but also by any table within shouting distance. Love may be blind but love sure as hell ain't deaf. Marina's common voice had ground most conversations to a halt. Most improper. And if this performance seemed outlandish to the other customers, then it would worry them to know she was currently on her absolute best behaviour. Normally saved for interviews with the bank manager.

An indoor firecracker exploded on a table at the other end of the bar. Thomas jumped, then turned to watch a barrage of party poppers being burst over a birthday cake. Marina studied his profile. Why watch a cake when you can watch this, she thought. What a complete hunk! She made a quick prayer to Shiva: please hurry this along. I need to be in Thomas's bed tonight. Please arrange for our sex life to be so full that I have bed sores! Aum.

Marina took a sip of her wine. It was time Emily was updated on the Marina Love Roundabout. She grabbed her handbag, made her excuses to Thomas, then headed across the floor and into the Ladies'.

POSH TOILET ALERT!

Marina hadn't seen anything like it and she wanted to move in right away. No wonder posh people didn't think their poo smelled, it never stood a chance in here. The ventilation system was designed to suck out farty smells and pump in Opium perfume. It was toilet heaven. Even the marble sinks were big enough to take a bath in.

After playing with the bidet for a minute, Marina pulled out her mobile and phoned Emily.

Marina's place at the table was filled by another woman quicker than a football substitution. Charlotte, an ex of Thomas's, had arrived. This time, instead of sending the cocktail via a waiter, she brought one with her.

'It's called "Stringless Sex", Tom, always a great way to have a relationship, I think, without strings.' She passed him the green-coloured drink.

Charlotte was blonde, leggy, beautiful. Her packaging was perfect. It had taken Thomas a full month to realize what a total bitch she was.

'Take the drink away, Charlotte,' Thomas said firmly. 'As you well know, I am here with company, so, please, would you mind?' He gestured with his eyes towards her table. 'I would be most grateful.'

'Always the nice Thomas, never could say what you really meant, could you?'

'Charlotte, fuck off!'

She twiddled her long, blonde hair. 'With pleasure, Tom, but first let me give you some advice. People are beginning to talk about you. Some are saying they think you've lost it. Especially after finishing with Nicole. I mean, a Newton-Harrington. HELLO. Are you mad? And then today you turn up with her.' Her face creased and folded. 'I am struggling with this one, Tom. I thought I knew you. Can you imagine how hurt Nicole will be to find she has been replaced by a commoner . . . Argh, I swear I would be sick if you had dropped me for that. And,' she squared right up to his face, 'I don't know if you are aware, but that dress she's wearing was on the Versace catwalk over ten years ago. That's ten, Tom, ten years out of date.' Charlotte was nearly crying with frustration and sipped the Stringless Sex to calm herself down.

'My my, I'll inform my lawyer first thing in the morning. Surely wearing a dress that old is illegal. It has to be.'

His eyes searched towards the Ladies'. Judging by

the behaviour of most of the women in this place tonight, the title above the toilet entrance should read: Bitches. It was hard to believe that some of these women, all of them from wealthy backgrounds, should have such a low opinion of people less financially fortunate than themselves. Take, for instance, Sophie, the brunette who had grabbed his arm earlier. The upper-class cow team leader. Her greeting to him today – 'Are you going colour-blind, Thomas? She's not a blonde' – had provoked sniggers from the other three cows. Then, 'We all thought that one day you might change your obsession with hair colour, Tom, darling. But skin colour? We nearly died when we saw you walk in with her.' More sniggers, until Thomas had retorted viciously, 'Why don't I bring her over, Sophie, and you can repeat what you just told me.' Ironically, it was the four girls' skins that had changed colour then, to a sore-looking red. And he'd added, 'Thought not,' as he walked away.

Thomas wondered how he would feel, how he would react, if, during a trip to India, he was greeted with a barrage of racial abuse. What defence mechanism would he have in place to appear oblivious? Because he would have to appear oblivious – to let people know that their racist comments bothered you was to feed their fire. So much better to shrug, smile and walk away. He wondered how much shrugging and smiling Marina had done in her life; how many people she'd walked away from feeling upset.

And he'd seen the upset that racial hatred can bring. Even at university, the clashing of great wit and mind, he'd witnessed for himself the low punches dished out to those of colour. Sometimes the racial abuse would be stealthy, hidden within a sly sentence. Other times in the turn of the head when the victim wasn't paying attention. Some would be blatant. Some would be skilled. But none would go unnoticed by the recipient.

No racist can fool another race.

But what about those people, like himself, accused of one thing but guilty of another? Thomas wasn't racist, just ignorant. Blurting out comments quite dazzling in their stupidity. Who in their right mind says to an Indian, 'If you stay much longer then, God forbid, I'm just going to end up calling you a Paki'? Toe-curling stuff. Shameful stuff. Ignorant stuff. But, thankfully, never racist stuff.

Charlotte was still here, still talking; Thomas not managing to get a word in edgeways.

'I mean, Tom, have you heard her speak? She is so common. Her diction isn't exactly top form, is it? Are you not embarrassed sitting here with her?' Charlotte crossed her long legs. 'I can see men being attracted to her, she's stunning, but why you? I thought you were much more traditional than this.' She used the menu for a fan. 'I am just going to say it right out: Thomas Harding, I thought you had more class, I really did. You do realize that by being with her you are making a mockery of all the other beautiful women in this bar, don't you? You are choosing a woman – now how can I say this nicely? – you are choosing a woman who is far, far inferior to us. She hasn't even got a French manicure for God's sake. It's pretty low, Tom, everyone thinks so. I find it hard to—'

Marina grabbed the green Stringless Sex cocktail from the table, with her Collection 2000 nail-polished hand, and casually poured it over Charlotte's head.

Thomas had the presence of mind to push himself out of harm's way and watched with a smile as the radioactive-looking drink dripped downwards from Charlotte's £500 haircut, over her £3000 dress, then finally onto her £1000 shoes. It was a good job she was wearing her cheap outfit tonight. Which, some might add, went very well with her cheap mouth.

The first scream was too high pitched for human ears. The second scream sounded like she was sending out a fax – businessmen instinctively looked to their laptops. But the third scream was the real deal, recognizable to anyone with precocious, spoilt, two-year-old children, a lengthy squawk that had all customers staring and sniggering.

'You will be hearing from my solicitor,' Charlotte said to Marina finally. 'That will be the most expensive drink you ever paid for. You just can't behave like civilized people, can you? This is why your sort is not wanted in our country.' Charlotte dabbed her head with a tissue. She couldn't wait to ring her top-notch solicitor, Mr Sanjeev Tunjar Bharadwaj – he would know what to do. 'I will collect your information from Thomas at a later date.' She marched off, nearly slipping on the Stringless Sex.

'As you know, that was Charlotte, my ex, I'm embarrassed to say,' Thomas explained, as they were moved to another table. 'Although most people who get to meet her know her as Sue.'

Marina sat down. 'Sue?'

'She threatens to sue everyone. She thinks she's an American.' He smiled. 'I wouldn't worry: nothing ever comes of it.'

And the two were soon back to chatting.

Chapter Thirty-three

Ramone was the quintessential professional pretending earnestly not to notice the huge pink and veiny dildo that fell out of Nicole's bag on to the floorboards. It landed with a loud clunk on Thomas's apartment floor sending Duracell batteries cascading down towards Ramone's size seventeen feet.

'Whoops.' Nicole bent down to retrieve the pleasure tool, fumbling for the slippery batteries. 'I hope it's not broken, Ramone.'

And so did Ramone. For it would be he who would be sent out to buy a new one if it was. Not one to shirk his duties – even if it did involve buying substitute penises for his boss.

Two hours had passed since they'd begun packing Nicole's belongings, leaving the car nearly full with posh frocks and designer shoes. Bored guests had watched from Reception as a beautiful witch and a frightening Frankenstein had loaded up the Mercedes in the incessant rain. For once, Nicole had forgotten the weather, deep in thought over the words in Thomas's letter, lost in a storm as to their meaning.

Dear Nicole,

You said I had a heart of gold
More like iron pyrites I'm told.
You said I caught you when you fell
But missed the time you fell to Hell.
You said when all is said and done
Of all I am, I am the one.

Nicole, I only wish I was the one, I am so sorry I am not.

Love, Tom XXX
What we had is ours to keep.

Carefully zipping the penis in her Louis Vuitton handbag, Nicole grabbed a last look at the apartment, then told Hal to switch off the lights. This place was crowded with memories. A colourful catalogue of happy and sad snapshots. They say every hotel has a ghost. Well, the Regency now had one. The dead ghost of Nicole and Thomas's relationship.

Locking the door behind her, Nicole walked down the corridor with Ramone. At this moment Nicole's insatiable curiosity was that of a one-month-old grey fluffy kitten. The electric atmosphere in her head was palpable. It just *had* to be snoop time.

'Synchronize heartbeats, Ramone,' Nicole said, just outside the downstairs office.

Ramone patted his chest. 'Heartbeats synchronized.'

With a guilty look behind her, Nicole unlocked the door, switched on the light, then ushered in Ramone. Time was on their side, as Mick Jagger might say, but how much time? Nicole smiled across to Ramone, who had been having some doubts about the impetus behind Nicole's logic. He was normally paid to stop things like this happening.

'It will be fine, Ramone. I *am* within my rights here. Now get your tools ready.' Nicole bent down, swivelled the dial, unlocked the safe door, then with a nervy grin lifted up the metal tin and placed it on the desk. 'Do it, before I change my mind.'

Nicole turned her face away as she heard Ramone crunching and grinding with his tools. A few choice swearwords, a few huffs and puffs, then BOOM! The box cracked open. And Nicole's heart swam into her stomach.

'I want you to look inside, Ramone. Please. Tell me if it's good or if it's bad.' Nicole held her breath while she heard the sound of his fingers frisking the box. 'Hurry hurry.'

More rummaging by Ramone with an endless rustling of paper. Nicole felt so hot she thought she might melt like the Wicked Witch Of The West. Her nerves on fire, her mind champing at the bit, and enough tension in here to split a coconut. Nicole could only take so much of this before she . . .

'Oh fucking hell, Nicole.' Ramone slammed everything back in the tin. 'There is no way you can see this. NO way!' He grabbed the box and held it above his head way out of her reach. 'If Thomas was here right now, I would . . . I don't know what I would do. He's a weirdo.'

'Give me the box, Ramone. It's an order.'

Ramone stood on tiptoes. 'NO! I'm here to protect you and that is what I will do. I cannot have you see what is in this box. I am very sorry, Ms Newton-Harrington, but—'

One finger was all it took for Ramone to drop the container. One finger on his ticklish body. A big man like that with tickle problems.

The sound of Ramone laughing soon died down, leaving Nicole sitting on the floor with the box between her legs. No wonder Thomas had kept this secret. Or rather, tried to keep this secret. And in many ways, as Nicole sorted through the contents, she could understand why he didn't want her to know about it. Tears slowly rolled down her cheeks. This was worse than anything she could have expected. This was something sick. Her hands shook as she lifted out the items one by one. With a throat as dry as hers, she wondered if she would ever talk again. How could Thomas have done this? How could she have been so wrong about him?

Never would she have guessed that love could turn to hate so quickly. Never did she believe that she could ever hate Thomas. But she did now. And he would pay for this.

'Ramone,' Nicole croaked out, 'what does Thomas hold dearest to his heart?'

He fidgeted. 'This, I suppose. His hotel.'

She jumped to her feet, anger the emotion controlling her actions. 'Take the box and wait for me in Reception, please, Ramone.'

Reluctantly Ramone left, carrying the tin of evidence in his hands. Nicole locked the door and leant back against it, a feeling of uselessness combined with her sadness. She switched off the light and stood sobbing in the dark. Thomas had used her like an unpaid hooker. Fucked her life until it was dry. It was time that Thomas was introduced to the world of regret.

And on this stormy Hallowe'en night, when the screams were not real, and the monsters drunk beer, Nicole switched the office lights back on, walked to Thomas's desk, then pulled out a pair of gleaming scissors. The pain would have to stop soon. She needed to unburden the hurt.

It took just two minutes for Nicole to destroy the leather chair and cheese plant with the scissors. Methodically she went about building a pile of electrical goods in the centre of the room. Computer, VDU, printer, fax machine, photocopier, coffee machine and phone. With the fire extinguisher, Nicole beat the living crap out of the entire pile – sparks flying, silicon chips ricocheting off the walls and glass smashing. Two framed pictures, one from the film *The Big Blue*, the other from *The Abyss* were punctured with the golf umbrella, which in turn was slashed to ribbons with the faithful scissors. Books, files, bills, invoices and computer disks were tossed out of the window into the rain, soon to be followed by the contents of his drawers. After spraying the entire room with foam from the extinguisher, Nicole headed to Reception in a frenzy. In the words of Maggie Thatcher, 'The lady is not for turning.'

Screaming to the half-filled lobby, 'Get out, all of you!' she ran behind Reception and picked up the bookings book, chucking it across the floor. 'I said GET OUT!'

Many eyes stared at the mad witch. Two huge streaks of lightning crucified the black sky outside; the immense cracks of thunder that followed rattled even the sturdiest nerves. Nicole's pupils were wide and fearful, her one-track mind steering towards destruction.

Hannah, the receptionist, stood like a waxwork, frozen and petrified. She would tell her friends later that if only she could have snapped out of it, unplugged her feet from their spot, then she could have prevented Nicole from disconnecting her laptop and hurling it through the front glass window. A pane the size of a garage door shattered into shards, scattering the frightened guests to all corners.

Ramone watched. Thomas deserved everything. And he pointed Nicole in the direction of the grandfather clock. A family heirloom. Nicole strode towards it and, with a massive injection of strength, toppled it to the floor. Just like in a cartoon, springs and cogs popped and sprung out at random angles – but, not like in a cartoon, 'That wasn't all folks!' not by a long shot.

'Does anyone have the time?' Nicole shouted, now in a state of delusion. 'This clock has stopped.' Her cackling laughter was a cause for concern to Ramone. Maybe Nicole had finally flipped.

Hiding below the counter, Hannah phoned Thomas. She winced at each crash, wondering why Thomas had insisted on decorating the Reception with antiques. Please pick up, she prayed, please please please pick up.

Eventually, her prayers were answered . . .

Half an hour later, Thomas entered the *Scrapheap Challenge* lobby. Nicole, still dressed in her costume, was sitting on a chair surrounded by Regency staff, a small mountain of used tissues on the table in front of her. Stuart was doing his best to cover the window frame with a tablecloth. Thomas wished Stuart had used a cloth without gravy stains. So classless.

But look at all the mess! Jesus. Thomas despaired as he took it all in. Thousands and thousands of pounds' worth of damage. A once-proud Reception area now cowering under the shadow of Nicole's tantrum. At least one good thing had come about from all this, he thought lamely, staring at the now legless piano, at least he could advertise that the Regency catered for midget pianists. As long as they didn't mind reading music off the music stand that was somehow lodged in the ceiling plaster. What had possessed Nicole to do all this?

He walked towards her, his anger as heated as a blowtorch. 'I would like to book a building site for one please!' Thomas ground his teeth. 'What the fucking hell happened here?' He glared at Nicole, the witch! 'Please, I'm begging you, don't tell me that the rain made you do this.' He kicked a piano key across the floor, his anger enflamed by her lack of response. 'Will you please speak to me? What happened?'

Rising from her seat, Nicole faced Thomas, dust and debris falling off her. The two stood motionless, like musical statues. Silent and cold. Then, as if the music had restarted, Nicole slapped Thomas hard around the face. And again. And again. Vicious shots meant to hurt, just as she was hurting inside.

And, boy, did they hurt. Thomas grabbed her wrists, surprised at the determined strength coiled up in her arms. Her eyes were bulging, her limbs thrashing like a shark out of water, the panic, anger and pain on her face was unbearable. She reminded him of a boy he'd once known at school waiting in line for his BCG injection. But why was Nicole so upset?

Thomas eyed his staff. 'Anyone who doesn't need to be here, can you please leave,' he requested, still holding on to Nicole's wrists. No one budged. 'Okay, anyone who still wants a job in the morning, can you please leave.' It was as if someone had dropped one. The staff were gone, leaving only Hannah, Ramone and his wrestling partner, Nicole. By now, most of the startled guests were cowering in their rooms.

'And, Hannah, could you phone the glazier, please?' Thomas turned his attention to Ramone. 'I'm taking Nicole to my apartment. Feel free to have a waitress bring you a drink.' Ramone showed his contempt by refusing to acknowledge Thomas.

Without further ado, Thomas walked Nicole to the lift. He turned to her as he pressed the button. 'I take it the lift still works?'

Three minutes later, they were sitting on the sofa, just like old times. Thomas instructed Hal to dim the lights, and increase the room temperature. He usually imagined Hal whistling at this command, because sex was what normally followed it. But not today; sex was furthest from Thomas's mind. Although, not quite the furthest thing from Nicole's.

'I have never told you this before, Tom, but Lester

was better in bed than you. Much better. He was a real man.' Nicole could feel Thomas stiffen. 'He made it impossible for you to be anything other than second best. At night, when you and I would talk openly to each other, I would close my eyes and dream you were him. Every time you touched me I would try to imagine his hands.' Nicole smiled, pretended she was reminiscing. 'There was this one time, I had been thinking about Lester all day long. I just couldn't get his wonderful handsome face out of my mind. You and I made love madly that night, if I remember rightly you said I was "hot", but I was really making love to Lester. I was always making love to Lester. Do you honestly think if he were still alive I would ever have chosen you over him? Honestly, Tom, do you really think I would?'

'Why did you smash up my hotel?' Thomas asked, ignoring her words.

'You just cannot handle me talking about Lester, can you? Anyone might think you were obsessed with him. TOM!'

He stood up. 'You want to hurt me for hurting you. I understand that.' His voice was angry but controlled. 'And this talk of obsession, Nicole; I fear the inescapable fact is quite the opposite: I think it is *you* who is obsessed. Myself, I couldn't abide the guy. I loathed him. And it's wrong to speak ill of the dead but if—'

'You're a liar, Thomas,' Nicole snarled. 'Do you want to know what drove me to smash up your baby, this hotel?' She shook her head, tears forming. 'I could not believe my eyes when I saw what you keep in that safe downstairs.'

Thomas looked surprised. 'Safe?'

'I saw what you hid in that box you keep locked up, Tom. Your secret box of sickness. I asked Ramone to open it, and even he agrees with me: you are depraved.' Nicole glared at him, then broke down crying. 'It's weird, Tom, really weird.' After a few sobs she phoned Ramone and asked him to bring the container up. She would not listen to another word Thomas said until the box had been brought up.

Minutes later it arrived and Nicole, with an amount of unease, emptied the contents on the coffee table. Her eyes shied away as her bad dream spilled on to the polished surface.

Pictures of Nicole and Lester together at charity balls, Ascot, weddings, posh bashes. Newspaper cuttings of Lester. A wad of clippings in relation to Lester's fatal car accident. Copies of Lester's death certificate, birth certificate, passport, even his degree certificate. Bank statements, credit-card statements, a list of his stocks and shares, endowment policies. Everything about Lester was in this pile. Even a copy of Lester's will.

Weird? Most definitely.

Nicole's impression of Thomas had been recast. He had never loved her, she was just his prize. The first-prize trophy in a competition between himself and a dead man. But the competition didn't stop at women. Oh no. Financial comparisons were just as important. She imagined Thomas in the wee hours comparing details with Lester. Setting up his bank statement beside Lester's, admiring his lists of flourishing shares against Lester's declining shares. What next? Who had the finest coffin?

She picked up a picture of Lester playing polo and held it out for Thomas to see. 'You, Thomas, are more obsessed with Lester than Lester was with you. Are all men this insecure?'

As a general rule of thumb, Thomas liked cats. Except when they were out of the bag. He tore across to the kitchen, poured himself a large brandy, then gulped it down quicker than an alcoholic. With his throat on fire, Thomas assessed his predicament: not good. Nicole now knew his secret. It was just a surprise that she hadn't torched the hotel. She was supposed to have found out this information on his terms. Now, as she had said, this whole matter appeared 'weird'.

He watched the kamikaze raindrops smash into the pane, mesmerized by their ferocity, then turned towards the living area, noting that the mood in the room was as if someone had died. The onus was on him to sort this mess out. There were many things to explain but so many wrong ways in which to explain them.

'Nicole.' Thomas sat beside her on the sofa, head bowed, and took her limp hand. 'I want you to listen to everything I say. Some of what you hear will seem ridiculous. To be frank, I had trouble digesting it myself. But, and you must remember this, I did what I did because I care about you.' He breathed in deeply as she squeezed his hand, a sign to continue. 'Lester was a man of many layers. A man with more than one life, each with myriad facades. He . . .'

Thomas took Nicole on a journey. A trip without LSD but one which involved plenty of drugs nonetheless.

Lester was a coke head. A man ruled by the white demon. Some people drank, others smoked, Lester snorted. People had died climbing smaller mountains than the one Lester had sniffed up his nose. Thomas explained that it was Lester's lifestyle that had killed him, not the car crash that Nicole had blamed herself for since the accident. But how would one go about proving that?

Money talks. Simple as that. If something is hidden deep, then money is a JCB. Thomas had hired Frank to unearth anything that could take the accusing finger away from Nicole and point it in the direction of Lester. 'I need a starting point,' Frank had said. And Thomas had replied, 'Coke, and not as in the real thing.'

From coke, to medical records, to doctors' reports, to police files. The collection increased weekly. All Thomas needed now was a copy of the autopsy report, which Frank had promised him in the next few days. The reason Lester had died that night had nothing to do with fashion, as Nicole had always presumed. It had nothing to do with her selfishly demanding that Lester drive them both out in the torrential rain to her fashion guru to order a pair of yellow Prada sandals she had just spotted in *Vogue*. No. It had everything to do with Lester sniffing twenty lines of coke, taking three Es, and washing them down with two vodka oranges. That's what had killed Lester.

'Because of him, you nearly died, Nicole. There's no way in a million years that Lester should have been behind the wheel of a car that night. Or any night for that matter. You don't find men any more selfish than that. And if he had lived and you had died, would we find him here today worrying about having killed you?' Thomas shook his head. 'I doubt it very much.'

Nicole's mind was a maypole, her multicoloured emotions weaving in and out among each other. Guilt for smashing up the hotel, happiness for the burden being lifted regarding Lester's death, anger at Lester for being a fraud, and sadness for Thomas, realizing that if anything she now loved him even more than before. What a tangled mess. Why couldn't she have left that box alone? She kicked it with her foot.

'I was planning on explaining this to you as soon as the autopsy report came through,' Thomas began. 'I'm not one for interfering with the past – you cannot change it, what's done is done – but when you attempted to take your own life, I had to do something. To carry the guilt you do is an awesome weight and I know how you struggle with your memories, but it hurt me to see you in such pain when I had my suspicions of what might have *really* happened that night.' He kissed her forehead. 'Try and put this behind you, Nicole.'

They hugged while the wind shouted hoarsely outside, Nicole whispering her apologies over and over and Thomas requesting her to shush. She felt awful. A sickening, stomach-turning, how-can-I-make-it-up-to-you awful. After forcing Thomas to admit that nothing could be worse than witnessing his hotel Reception in such a state, she told him about the mess in the downstairs office.

'I'll pay for it with Daddy's money,' Nicole offered sheepishly.

Thomas declined. 'But there's something that you could help me with involving your father.'

He went on to explain the predicament involving the land at the rear of the hotel. How Nicole's father was threatening to build a rival hotel there unless he took Nicole's hand in marriage. How Edmond was preparing to wage a war on him using the tax man and VAT man as his infantry. How he was going to squash Thomas unless he appeased him. How . . .

'Leave Daddy to me,' Nicole declared, not even slightly shocked at Daddy's behaviour. 'I know things about my father that would have his life more screwed than the corks in his wine bottles. It's the least I can do.'

The two chatted for a while until Nicole could feel those tell-tale signs of hope slipping past her defences. Maybe there was still life yet in this relationship. Only one way to find out. She leant in to kiss Thomas on the mouth and felt foolish as he sharply pulled away. Who bloody well invented hope? Her eyes glistened with tears as the look on his face said it all. It was over.

Chapter Thirty-four

Marina poked her nose through the car window and sniffed the delightful smell of petrol as she waited for Thomas to pay the lady at the BP garage. She had just eaten a starter that cost as much as a week's food bill, a main course that cost as much as her last holiday, and a pudding that cost more than the clothes she was wearing. Scallops Point, Thomas had informed her, was a run-of-the-mill three Michelin stars restaurant. Nothing too fancy. 'Just leave the ordering to me,' Thomas had said, when Marina had enquired whether Scallops Point served her favourite dessert – the Knickerbocker Glory. 'I love it when they shove a flake down the middle,' she had explained excitedly.

But the meal was a disaster from Marina's standpoint. The huge gap in their upbringing manifesting itself in a hundred different ways. Dunking her bread roll in the lemon-scented finger wash bowl was a bad start. Thomas had just smiled, teething problems, that's all. Then one of her scallops had skidded off her plate and landed on her lap. More teething problems. It was left to the dessert for Marina to make amends. No such luck. She'd made a complete fool of herself by screaming, 'Fire!' at the top of her voice as the waiter tried to blow-torch the surface of her crème brûlée. It was all so very cringe-worthy. Teething problems? More like first-degree toothache.

But at least it wasn't interrupted like last time when, four nights ago, Thomas had deserted her in the middle of Pixies after receiving his emergency phone call. Well, not quite deserted, but it felt that way. He had left her with £50 for a taxi, an IOU for an evening out, and a rather scrummy smoochy kiss on the lips. And God, what a kiss; if a man could kiss that well in the middle of a crisis, then bring on Armageddon.

Marina watched Thomas paying the cashier at the BP garage. For some reason it had never occurred to her that a Porsche used normal petrol; she'd thought it was filled up with blessed petrol. Holy Petrol sanctified by Juan Pablo Montoya himself. Through the garage kiosk window Thomas held up a box of Roses and pointed to them, miming 'Would you like some chocolates?' Does the Pope pray? Does Pavarotti enjoy Eat All You Like buffets? Of course she would like chocolates. Did he know nothing about women? Marina smiled back, hoping that the next thing he held up at the window would be a packet of condoms. Alas, just chocolates.

Since Pixies, the pair of them had spent many hours talking on the phone. Learning small details about each other, filling in the gaps that a new romance is always full of. Marina was so different to Thomas's previous girlfriends, so unique, so true to herself. To look for pretence in Marina, one would be looking in vain, Thomas concluded. She was more than a breath of fresh air, a change for the better; she was a woman with such a fantastic inner self that her packaging never came into it.

Although, if the proof of the pudding was in the erection, he'd had many puddings lately. She was beautiful. And he hoped that things worked out. It was all up to the two of them in the days ahead.

Tonight was supposed to be about maturity. Two adults discussing whether they had a future together, considering all the obstacles in their way. Thomas had made it clear that he was at a slight advantage in the mind-game stakes as he already knew most of Marina's private thoughts, courtesy of her bedroom wall. Today, this evening, he was going to lay himself bare. If Marina still wanted to make a go of it with him after that, then 'fuck everyone'.

The Porsche huffed as it was forced to drive at 20 m.p.h. behind an extremely old couple in a bright-green Citroën Dyane, which had a label on the back window: Honk Twice If You Take It Up The Exhaust.

Marina giggled as she viewed the tailback behind them. 'This proves my point, Thomas,' she stated. 'Sometimes it takes just one person to do things differently and others have to follow.'

Thomas nodded in agreement. Marina had already explained to him the difficulties for Indian families in accepting change. They had already seen their roots dug up and sprayed with weed killer back in the forties when India was under partition. It had left a bad taste in everyone's mouth, leaving in its wake a moral justification in clinging on to *everything* that was Indian when one moved abroad.

And arranged marriage was Indian. Marrying in the same caste was Indian. Letting your parents choose who you spend the rest of your life with was Indian. What Marina and Thomas were doing now . . . most definitely was *not* Indian. Two cultures mixing. It was a bad example. Just like the two biddies driving ahead. But, just like the two biddies driving ahead, it forced everyone to stop and see. Maybe, just maybe, mixing ain't that bad.

Thomas guessed, at the rate they were travelling, by the time they arrived at the Regency he would find heavily bearded archaeologists in multicoloured jumpers playing with trowels trying to discover where the walls to the hotel lay. Thomas hooted twice, watched the Citroën wobble over in shock, then took his chance overtaking on full thrust and sped down the country lane towards St Meridians. As he parked up in the hotel car park, a comment Marina had made regenerated itself in his mind: 'Sorry, Thomas, but I didn't enjoy myself tonight. I just felt so out of place in that posh restaurant.' Maybe he might have said something similar had they eaten in a Beefeater. But the point was clear. In order for this relationship to stand a chance, they would have to give a little, take a little. And, amusing as it had been to watch Marina this evening, her monkey manners would soon become embarrassing. He'd never seen, at first-hand, a woman eat with her elbows on the table before. He'd never had the privilege of someone rummaging around *his* plate searching for mange touts with *their* fork before, either. But, Christ, all this was fixable. Nothing to worry about. Just teething problems.

They headed into Reception. Apart from the absent grandfather clock, still in intensive care waiting for a donor spring, the place was spick and span, not a clue remaining as to Nicole's outburst the other night. Thomas spotted Stuart crouched by a guest's table looking terribly suspicious. He asked Marina to wait a moment, motioned to the receptionist, Cheryl, to keep quiet, then crept across the marble floor and sat himself snugly behind him. Thomas could not shed the potent feeling that something untoward was transpiring. He listened in.

'So that we understand each other,' Stuart continued, 'you pay me £50 and come Sunday at noon I will make sure that all the churches in the surrounding hills ring out in tribute to— Whose birthday did you say it was?'

The large man answered in his New York accent, 'Jeannie, my fiancée's.'

'Right. Jeannie, your fiancée, will wake up on Sunday morning to the beautiful sound of the Oxford bells. All at the princely price of £50.' Stuart coughed. 'It's so moving. Make sure before you listen you take a huge mouthful of air in your lungs, because, Chad, I'll be honest with you, mate, it sure takes your breath away. And, just in case you want to smuggle a little slice of Oxford back to Uncle Sam's with you, for an extra £10 you can purchase the Oxford Bells tape that—'

Thomas had heard enough. He stood up, tapped Stuart on the shoulder, then ushered him over to the fixed piano. 'Right, you little bastard, you are sacked! How long has this been going on?'

'He's my first customer, Mr Harding, I swear,' Stuart said, glaring at Cheryl, who was meant to have warned him when Thomas came in. 'The money was going to go to charity.'

'So, let me get this straight. You were going to charge my guests for the privilege of having the bells ring on a Sunday. Even though, without fail, the bells ring every Sunday anyway?'

'Yes.'

'And they are taken in by this, are they?'

'Honestly, Mr Harding, you wouldn't believe how dumb some of your customers are. Last week this bloke paid £200 . . . Erm. Like I said, he was my first and only customer.' Stuart buried his head in his hands. 'Don't sack me, my granny needs me to support her. You don't pay me enough.'

'That is correct. From now on, Stuart, I will be paying you nothing. Now collect your belongings and leave.'

Stuart was toast.

Marina felt like she was stepping into a palace. Thomas's apartment. She wasn't too sure, but if her memory served her well, Debenhams was just a bit bigger than this place. Moving into a luxury apartment had been on her 'To Do' list for years. And this flat dunked the biscuit. Even if she fell out of love with Thomas, she would never tell him. To lose this after having it would be insane. But should she take off her shoes?

'Make yourself at home, I'll just check my

messages,' Thomas said, heading into his office.

Trying not to be too nosy, Marina ordered herself to stay put and relaxed back into the mighty sofa, placing the choccies beside her. Talk talk talk. Thomas wanted to talk. What about sex? Her brand new underwear had cost this week's rent. From accommodation to accommodating. The lady in the shop had told her that the lingerie was their best seller and they had had hardly any returns. It was now up to Thomas. As far as Marina could see, there was no excuse for him not making love to her tonight. He had the woman, she had the knickers, he had the body, and they were in the venue. This was a huge apartment, with no doubt a huge bedroom, and a huge bed; she hoped and prayed Thomas had a huge . . . duvet.

'Right, Marina, let's talk,' Thomas announced, as he joined her on the sofa. 'Let's see if you and I are going anywhere.'

Marina rolled her eyes. 'So you want to talk.' She slouched back, sighed for England, then said, 'Let's talk, then.'

Thomas began. 'You do realize that the path we are treading will lead us to an awful amount of rejection, Marina. I think we both witnessed what I am talking about the other night with Charlotte. To her, and as awful as this sounds, you were beneath me. And unless I keep away from all my old haunts, this will inevitably happen again.' Thomas opened the Roses and handed her the fudge, by coincidence her favourite, or according to Marina, just another reason why the two of them were destined to be together. He continued. 'My point is this: people will talk behind your back. Can you handle it? They will snigger at your accent, laugh at your manners, and take pity when you mix up your pronouns with your adjectives. I cannot say I am agog with enthusiasm at this kind of behaviour, but unfortunately it's something I have been brought up with. Snobbery, like white blood cells, is built into the very marrow of their bones.'

'Sounds like cancer. Is there a cure?' She smiled. 'Look. Do you honestly think that an Indian woman hasn't had her fair share of verbal abuse before? Do you really think there is even one Indian woman in this country who's spared the odd derogatory racial comment? The words don't sting after a while. It's like – have you heard that record by Pink Floyd "Comfortably Numb"? Well, that's what most Indians are, comfortably numb to it all. The point is, Thomas, does it bother *you*? Can you walk proudly beside me knowing I am, in the words of a rather wet Charlotte, "inferior"? Could you look forward to going out to a party with me, an Indian woman, by your side? My brown skin, my common accent, my rough ways. And not forgetting my appalling manners. Is this what *you* want?'

And the ball was back in his court.

Thomas could feel the magnetism of Marina's self-belief. Completely happy in her own skin. A rare energy flowed about her that was so enchanting, he wondered if he'd ever come across it before. Even though it shouldn't have to be this way, to stand up for who you are is sometimes gutsy. And Thomas just loved gutsy. In fact, the notion of Marina bawling tears over a bitch's remark seemed laughable now. She was more than capable of standing on her own two, very brown, very sexy legs.

So the question was: is this what he wanted? And the answer was a resounding yes. He was attracted to her *just* the way she was. If she changed to suit others, then she would become someone else. A fake. She would be no better than some MPs.

Time kicked on as big talk gave way to small talk. Thomas determined to act like a gentleman and respect Marina. Marina hoping that Thomas would stop acting like a gentleman and start behaving like a savage. She was bled dry of innuendoes. How many more times could she bend over in her short skirt, exposing her rear, and pick up her purposely dropped Tic Tac box before she appeared too obvious? How many more times could she say, 'I bet you have a lovely bedroom,' before he took the bloody hint?

Marina dropped the Tic Tacs as she returned from the toilet. Here we go again, she thought, bending over. For God's sake, Thomas, will you please . . .

'I got the hint about six drops ago, Marina. I was just hoping you would have changed your tac tics from Tic Tacs, that's all.' He looked at Marina's flushed face. 'I always think sex is better when at least one party is in a foul mood, don't you?'

'Oh for sure. I have the best sex when the bank manager turns me down for a loan. Or when I find that the neighbourhood stray moggy has pissed on my washing. You should have seen me perform when I heard that there might be a Spice Girls reunion concert. I was on fire. I grabbed the nearest willing bloke and said, "Shag me. Take away my anger."'

Thomas laughed as he pulled her down to join him on the sofa. They studied each other with affection, sharing that look once again. A sudden connection which hot-wired their brains together. The very same look had passed between them all those weeks ago when Thomas had helped Marina to her feet after she had slipped in the beauty salon. Back then, Thomas subconsciously had chosen to ignore it. Right now, there was nothing about her he could ignore. He kissed her mouth, savouring the moment, enjoying her soft lips pressed tightly against his. Enjoying even more the teasing of her finger just above his belt. He hoped that Hal had the sense to switch off the emergency smoke alarms from the fire currently materializing in his boxers. Even though, in reality, there was only one *real* emergency present: to get to the bedroom.

'It's wonderful,' Marina stated, on entering the bedroom. 'Can I take a look around?'

'Later.'

He threw her on the bed and began to remove her clothes, straddling her hips, each button undone giving a further glimpse of her perfect brown skin. The top flew across the room and Thomas stared down at Marina in wonder. As she lay there in just her white lace bra and panties, Thomas was awestruck by her beauty. A purple gemstone lay against her pierced navel, and a small sexy tattoo of a dolphin on her bikini-line seemed to splash out of her knickers.

'Marina, I hate to be crude, but you are fucking beautiful,' he said, dropping tiny kisses on her stomach. 'So beautiful.'

She sighed with relief. One, because she was pleased he hadn't told her she had a crap body, and two, because she was sucking in her stomach to look slimmer. Not that she had a beer gut, but Nicole's boots would be hard to fill – or, rather, Nicole's Prada stilettos would be.

'And if I was the last woman on earth, would you still not shag me?'

He glanced up. 'I would join the long queue,' he chuckled. 'Of course I would. Twice.'

'And would you do it in your clothes, or out of your clothes?'

Thomas got the point and, more importantly, got naked. Marina was pleased to bits with her new toy. He was utterly gorgeous. It was almost like a dream.

And all she needed to make things perfect was Thomas's intimacy.

Thomas pushed himself deep inside Marina, enjoying each moan, their eyes locked together as she raised her hips slowly up and down. She was a worker, he liked that, not afraid of a bit of hard graft.

Marina looked into Thomas's blue eyes, feeling him inside her, delighting in his forcefulness, welcoming his ungentleman-like behaviour. Not one to bother with all that nonsense of waiting for the man to cum, Marina took her orgasms when and where she could. A deafening scream shot through Thomas's eardrums, causing him to stop momentarily. Was he hurting her? Was he THAT good? Do behave.

His muscles glistened under the dim ceiling lights as shadows danced across his bod. He was *the* bona fide hunky seismic shock wave sexy man and if she had a white flag she would have held it up: I surrender, as a feeling of submission washed through her. Just do what you want with me. But make me feel special. Marina could feel Thomas was about to cum, her nerves so hot they tingled, and she pushed herself towards him. His breathing was heavier and she couldn't wait to have him totally. Deeper and harder. Harder and deeper. Finally he climaxed.

He rolled over and said, 'The End.'

It was around this time that Marina realized how unfit she was. Thomas was ready to go again while she was in need of a medic. She didn't remember sex being this strenuous before. Any romantic evening in the future looked set to involve an oxygen canister and a litre of Red Bull. Then it dawned on her – Thomas was a swimmer. This was just a warm-up lap for him. It wasn't her fault that . . .

BANG! BANG! BANG! The apartment's front door sounded. Thomas and Marina exchanged glances.

'Do you get much "knock-down ginger" in this corridor?' Marina asked, innocently. 'Or dog poo in burning paper bags?'

'This is a four-star hotel, Marina, not Fenworth,' he replied, grabbing his boxers and stumbling into them as he crossed the floor. 'I'll be just a minute. Stay put.'

Semi-dressed, semi-hard, Thomas answered the door. It was his mother.

'Mom, do you know what time it is?' Thomas looked up and down the deserted hallway. 'It's gone midnight.'

'Time has no boundary, Thomas, when one is about to divorce one's partner. Your father and I have decided to call it a day.' Victoria Harding shook her blonde hair, gently pushed him to one side and walked straight in. 'I am at my wit's end. No one to turn to, no one to talk to. I need you now, Thomas. You're my only son.'

Closing the door, he followed her to the kitchen. 'Really? You and Pops? No.' He hadn't had a clue. 'You seemed so happy together. Are you sure about this?'

She leant back against the kitchen cupboards using her hands for support, her bust straining to escape the tight designer dress. 'We passed through the seven-year itch without a hitch, we had you and that was a bloody struggle I can say, you were a terrible child, and then the menopause, the mid-life crisis, then his heart attack, his rehabilitation. And now . . . divorce. What an end.'

Thomas was holding a tea towel. He couldn't even remember picking it up. 'But why, Mom? This is really terrible. Come here.' He walked towards her and cradled her while she snivelled. 'I can't believe this. This is so out of the blue.'

'I know, I know.' She talked to the ceiling. 'Some soft music please, Hal.'

'But you still love him, right?' Thomas reached for the Bacardi, poured a large measure into a crystal tumbler and handed it to her neat. 'Well?'

She sipped the drink and ignored him. 'Annette tells me that Nicole sabotaged your Reception on Hallowe'en. You might have told me rather than I find out from a gossipmonger like her . . .' Yackety yackety yack.

Thomas let her unwind, aware that soon he would have to explain that he had company. Hopefully, once Mom had the chance to let off some steam here, she would go back to Pops and sort this matter out amicably. He hated to see her in this state. He suggested they move to the sofa and she could explain where she thought it had all gone wrong – without using Thomas's conception as a scapegoat.

But the sofa talk never got started. Before she'd even sat down, Mom had noticed Marina's handbag on the floor. Charming, her own son hadn't the decency to inform her he was busy entertaining. What a way to treat your own mother!

'I should have put you up for adoption, Thomas Harding. Since when have your bedroom antics been top-secret in our family?' With a kitten-heeled mule she pointed to the satin handbag. 'Is she in your bed right now?'

'Erm. I thought we were discussing you and your divorce.'

'Oh that. Don't read too much into it. I was joking.' She walked across the floor towards the bedroom. 'Okay if I take a peek?'

'Joking? JOKING? You're sick.'

Thomas grabbed her arm. How could his own mother jest about something like divorce? What next? A death in the family? Half her friends were still sulking from the time she pretended to have served them with foot-and-mouth-flavoured beef at a dinner party a few months back. His parents' pranks were getting worse and he couldn't wait for the day that they were locked away in an old people's home.

'Mom, have some respect. Don't you think it might be somewhat embarrassing for her to meet you under these circumstances? No, I want you to go.' He removed the glass from her hand. 'Maybe next time we see each other my own mother might act like . . . a mother?' He kissed her on the cheek. 'Goodbye.'

Her ears picked up movement in the bedroom; if

she could just keep Thomas talking for a few more minutes . . . 'Let me guess: blonde, beautiful, long long legs, the usual? A bit like myself a few years back.' She sighed as she spoke. 'Another Barbie doll.'

'That's right, the usual, now off you go.' He shoved her towards the door with his hand, saying anything to get rid of her. 'Blonde, long legs, beautiful, you guessed it. Goodbye.'

A long winding creak interrupted proceedings. Thomas's bedroom door announcing it had just been opened. To avoid humiliation Thomas shouted out for Hal to turn out the lights immediately. Maybe in the dark, black hair could be blonde. Dirty blonde. But it was too late.

'Lights on, Hal,' said Victoria.

'Lights off, Hal,' ordered Thomas.

For some reason Hal malfunctioned, the CD came to life with *'Daisy, Daisy, give me your answer do. I'm half crazy over my love of you'* . . . Thomas hadn't heard that song since 2001. The lights remained on.

And Thomas's mother stared transfixed at the pretty Indian woman, dressed in black, who had just walked out of her son's bedroom. Her pet theory regarding Thomas suddenly debunked. Some men's bedrooms were like beaches washing up all sorts of women. Victoria had always assumed that Thomas's beach was Swedish and full of blonde waves.

'I thought I asked you to stay in the bedroom,' Thomas said, avoiding the two raised eyebrows of his mother. 'Music off, Hal.'

Marina gave Thomas a long, hard look. 'Sorry, I didn't realize this was Camp X-Ray. Anyway, I've got to be making a move, I've got work in the morning.'

She picked up her handbag, aware that her movements were being monitored by the tarty, blonde woman. Unable to keep her mouth shut, Marina continued, 'Don't tell me, another ex?'

He would have laughed if he wasn't so insulted. 'Don't be ludicrous! Do you really think I could lower myself to pick up something like that?' Thomas viewed his mum with contempt. 'She's my mother, for God's sake.'

Victoria seized her chance, floating in happiness to be considered young enough to be an ex of her son's. She spoke confidently. 'Will you please tell the truth for once, Tom, darling, honeysuckle. Our secret love affair cannot go on like this.' She ran her fingers through his hair. 'Mother? I don't think so.'

In frustration Thomas grabbed his mother's head and pulled it down, locking it under his armpit in a wrestler's hold, both of them facing Marina. 'Check the noses. Check the noses. How can she deny it?' Thomas let go of her head in disgust. 'I should *not* have had to do that, Mom.'

'Okay, okay, calm down. I am, unfortunately, his mother. The ugliest baby in the ward, he was.' She smiled at Marina, fluffing up her dishevelled hair. 'Very testy, isn't he?'

Marina liked slapstick humour, she watched *PM's Question Time* for Pete's sake, but these two were a joke. Her vision of Thomas's mother had been way off target. She'd expected a snooty, conservatively dressed, slightly old-fashioned lady. Instead – INSTEAD – Victoria was a beautiful woman still worthy of some catwalks, with a carefree nature that would put many youngsters to shame. Already Marina liked her.

After formal introductions, Thomas left them to chat, while he dressed in his room. His mother was likely to show off more if he stayed around. Besides, the frisky mood she was in tonight would have her pulling down his boxers before he knew it and uttering, 'Come on, Thomas, I've seen it all before. After all, I used to watch your nanny change your soiled nappies.'

Thomas returned fifteen minutes later to see that an alliance between the two had formed. Both smiling at him knowingly. What had Mom being telling Marina now? At least the atmosphere was warm and friendly, though, unlike many girlfriend encounters Thomas could remember. Mom either liked someone or didn't, but she would always try to get to know the person before she made that decision. Nicole, however, never gave Mom the chance to get to know her; she couldn't even be bothered to remember Thomas's mother's name. Hence the reason Nicole was labelled 'Thingamajig' by Victoria in retaliation.

But Marina was brought up to respect her elders, to be polite, to give them more leeway than she would people of her own age. Victoria liked that. In fact, there were many things she liked about Marina. She wasn't stuck-up like most of Thomas's exes but down-to-earth and genuine. The only thing plastic about her was her hair clip, and Victoria could see why Thomas would have fallen for her. In fact, it was impossible not to like Marina, and that was a gift that money couldn't buy.

Thomas flopped in the sofa chair. 'So what brings thee to these 'ere parts, Ma?'

'Your father and I have just eaten in your restaurant. And before you offer, we have already charged the bill to you.' She popped a hazelnut whirl into her mouth. 'You know what your father's like, making friends with anyone; he met a golf freak like himself and I thought while he chatted about balls, I would pop up and see my breast-fed son.' She stood up and turned to Marina, who was now giggling. 'It was so lovely to meet you, Marina. You really must come over sometime and we can continue that chat about Thomas and his magazines.' She winked.

A minute later Thomas was bidding farewell to his mother at the door.

'I love it when you surprise me, Thomas. All that time you have been searching for the perfect white pearl and then you come up with an even rarer black one. Remember, Thomas, there are many shades of skin colour but only one shade of kindness. And another thing, the brown sunset—'

'I get the message, Mom, you like her.' He kissed her on the cheek and closed the door.

Thomas tried to encourage Marina to forget about work in the morning and stay the night. She insisted that even though she only filled sandwiches, it was her job, and one that she couldn't afford to lose. Thomas said he understood and would pay her a year's wage if she stayed the night.

'You don't understand, then. It's not just about money, Thomas,' she said, undoing his trouser zip with one hand.

'I don't think you understand, Marina, I *really* want you to stay the night. What about two years' wages?'

'Money for sex, isn't that prostitution?'

'I think so,' he said, unbuttoning her top.

'Sounds whore-ible.'

Chapter Thirty-five

It had been two weeks since Nicole had said goodbye to Thomas, two weeks since she'd realized their future together was not going to happen, and two days since she'd realized she wasn't pregnant with Thomas's child. Today she stood amongst an army of dead bodies, watching with a slight amount of discomfort as a young girl ate some of her ex-boyfriend, Lester. Lester's gravestone (considering its size, it should have been called a grave throne) was surrounded by apple trees, their roots clambering in the earth below. Nicole grimaced as the young girl crunched into her frost-bitten, rotten apple, no doubt fed from water that had seeped through Lester's bones. Her morbid mind even surprised herself sometimes. Maybe because she'd once stared death in the face, she could look it in the eye now without blinking.

The sun was just light without heat, the perfect cold

mid-November morning, and Nicole was covered from head to toe in a warm cashmere coat. This was the end of the book as far as she and Lester were concerned. Her watery eyes flitted over the engraving on the massive gold-edged marble headstone, registering just a few of the words.

Lester Leonard Carradine III
Born A Winner.
Died A Winner.

It was a wonder his grave wasn't sponsored by Interflora, she thought, standing ankle-deep in flowers. The memory of Lester would live on. Which in some ways was the only thing Lester had really wanted in life – to be remembered when he was dead. He'd often confided to Nicole that if he reached the grand age of seventy without making a name for himself, he would glue his wrinkled scrotum to a passing rhino and have it stampede through Parliament Square at speed. He would be remembered then.

From her Gucci handbag, Nicole removed a bottle of cleaning liquid and a cotton cloth, then set about polishing the headstone. She ignored the urge to ask the spirit of Lester whether the build-up of white dust on the cleaning cloth had anything to do with him. She didn't give herself a ghost of a chance he would answer. Humming softly, she found the harmony she had come here for; it was probably as good a time as any to explain to Lester her current thoughts.

'Lester, there was a time when I couldn't wait to join you,' Nicole began. 'There have been many,

many days when I refused to enjoy my life, knowing that yours had been cut short by my hands. I felt as if I would never come to terms with your loss. I even wrote a will that asked for me to be buried right here, next to you.' She breathed in the crisp air, enjoying the release of burden as if it were carbon dioxide. 'I'm not here to blame you for anything, you had your reasons for keeping your drug habit a secret from me. Instead I'm here to say goodbye, because, Lester, I feel I never really knew you. I only knew the bit you wanted me to see.' Tears seeped from her eyes on to a ground that was surely soaked from them. 'Before we part, I want you to know that I never went looking for love in Thomas Harding. I knew how much you hated him. But he was there for me when no one else was. Nothing would have been able to stop me from falling for that man.' An apple fell from the tree and landed on Nicole's head. 'Ouch!' She stared up at the apple tree, then back to Lester's headstone. 'Okay, sorry, I won't mention him any more. Goodbye, Lester. You were a winner, whatever anyone says.'

As Nicole returned to her Mercedes, she smiled over to Ramone. A CD blasted from the car window, 'Candle In The Wind'.

Thomas had met many sets of girlfriends' parents over time. Never the most enjoyable of events to look forward to, nevertheless he found they always got off to a cracking start when he arrived with a present. Over the years the presents had ranged from flowers, chocolates, champagne, paintings, even to a tray of quail eggs once. Today, on this cold Sunday morning in November, Thomas was due to meet Marina's parents at their home in Watford, and the gift that Marina had suggested gave him cause for concern. 'They'll love it. Trust me,' Marina had said.

Parking on the empty driveway, Thomas hoped they might be out. He couldn't remember the last time he'd actually prayed for vacancies. But what was there to worry about? Marina had said herself that her parents were just your typical ultra-strict traditional Indian family who had come to this country and had their values vilified, desires discriminated against and their traditions trampled on. It should be a cake walk. Besides, it had been just over a week since Marina had been subjected to his mom in his apartment; maybe he deserved payback.

'And one more thing,' Marina said, helping lift the present from the boot. 'If my dad shouts, it's not because he's angry, that's just him. Okay?'

Thomas heaved the huge, wrapped parcel on to his shoulder and followed Marina up the short neat path, glad to be wearing casual jeans, jersey and trainers. The doorbell rang to the joyous welcome of *bhangra* drums and *sitars*. An Indian sound which was soon accompanied by an Indian smell when the door opened.

'*Namaste*,' greeted Marina to her mum.

'*Namaste*,' she replied, staring suspiciously past Marina to the white man standing behind her.

'This is Thomas, the man I told you about on the phone.'

Her eyes said, 'Is he indeed?'

All three entered in silence; Thomas parked the present beside a small table in the hall. An angry voice could be heard shouting at the TV in Hindi. An overwhelming sense of bad timing landed in the pit of Thomas's stomach. Marina really should have told her parents that she was bringing him today, but for some reason she thought it was a good idea to surprise them. This felt, in some ways, more like an ambush. Thomas reminded himself of the importance of not saying anything racist today, even writing the word 'Paki' on his hand to warn himself not to say it.

They introduced themselves, then Marina handed Dad a folded piece of pink paper. This was a first for all of them: Thomas had never been in an Indian household before, Marina had never brought home a boyfriend before, and her parents had never had anyone bring them a huge bag of *chapatti* flour as a gift before. The clue to the gift was the trail on the carpet. Small talk stayed small with everyone too polite to be political. Marina's dad decided that, after tea and coffee, it might be a good idea for Thomas and he to have a chat alone. But first a few words for all to hear.

'I'm interested in seeing if you live up to your CV.' Dad patted his pocket.

'CV?' Thomas appeared puzzled, then peered at Marina, who was busy looking out of the window, avoiding his eyes. 'What CV?'

'This!' Dad produced the pink paper and unfolded it, working his eyes down the entries. 'It says you studied at Oxford. Good good. And what's this?' He squinted his eyes at Marina's small handwriting. 'You own a four-star hotel in Oxfordshire.' He stared at Thomas. 'This I find *very* hard to believe. How old are you, thirty? It's not possible, I'm sorry. Someone your age is often in lots of debt. Have you money problems? Is that why you like my daughter? Hey?

Those scruffy jeans you wear, are these your best clothes?' He pointed to Thomas's head. 'Could you not afford a hair cut? Five pounds is not much to sort out that mess on your head.' He smiled and placed the CV beside him. 'I know what you are doing, I can see right through you. You hire a Porsche for £200, then you ask my daughter for a bank loan. It's an old trick. And like an idiot, she's fallen for it.'

Marina closed her hands together like a clapper-board. 'Cut. Cut. His jeans cost more than the bloody telly. His hair is IN. And sorry, Dad, but Thomas doesn't need loans, he's loaded.'

Dad gave a knowing nod to himself. 'If that's what you want to believe, my gullible daughter.'

Mum remained quiet, just staring, just watching. She knew it wasn't always what a man said that showed his character – good grief, if that were the case she would have been shot of her husband years ago – but how he acted. There was a confidence in Thomas that she found highly appealing.

'Why don't you two have *this* chat?' Mum began. 'Marina and I will amuse ourselves somehow.' The women left.

Barely had the door shut, when Dad bowled one straight for the middle wicket. 'Have you had sex with her?' His excitable eyes widened and focused on Thomas. 'Well?'

'*That* is an extremely impertinent question! Quite troubling, in fact, that you feel it's your given right to even pose this question to me.' Thomas eyed Marina's father coldly. 'It's none of your business and frankly quite insulting to both Marina and myself that you dare ask.'

Dad pawed the CV, turning it over and over in his hands. 'Maybe, maybe not. I will tell you what I see. I see a man who is a con artist. He preys on young girls and fools them with his clever tongue. A deceiver.' He nodded. 'Yes, you will get my daughter pregnant and leave her with bills to pay. What kind of a man does this? Are you not ashamed? A Hindu man would never do this.' He tutted. 'And what kind of gift is *chapatti* flour?'

Thomas looked at the far wall covered with colourful paintings of Hindu gods. So much faith in their religion, surely they could spare some faith for their daughter. Marina had explained that her parents had taken the road of their choice, wouldn't it be wrong if they were to block the road of Marina's?

Suddenly Thomas could feel himself drawn into a fight. 'And now I know how you feel when someone discriminates against you on the basis of colour. Not pleasant. Because this is what you're doing to me today. You're judging me on my skin colour. A layer of approximately five millimetres in thickness. You are not judging me on my morals, my personality, my sense of reason, or even on what music I enjoy. You sit there, with a self-satisfied manner, presuming you understand me, because I am a white man. Well, sorry to bring you back down to earth with a bump, but you are utterly wrong. *That* is the irrational behaviour of a racist.' Thomas gripped the armchair, fuming, as if he might take off. 'You don't want to believe what is written on that CV because I am white. Maybe if I was a Hindu you might decide to believe it.'

'Maybe if you were Hindu, you would give me respect in my own house.'

'Respect you will have from me once you have earned it.'

Dad pretended to sulk. He wanted to despise Thomas and yet he too found the man attractive in a father–son kind of way. His argument technique was superb, polite, without the use of swearing. This man had heart. Maybe he had Hindu blood in him from his ancestors. Marina had made a good choice.

'Okay, Mr Oxford University Man, tell me this, if you know so much about what is right and what is wrong tell me how the Indian flag came about.' Dad rubbed his hands together in premature triumph.

Thomas smiled. 'The Indian flag is made up of three colours. Orange, green and white. Orange represents the Hindus of India, green, the Muslims and white represents the other religions.' He paused, then continued to humour Marina's father. 'If I am not mistaken, the white stripe was an addition that was suggested by Mahatma Gandhi in 1921. And I may be wrong here, but I think the *charka* wheel that centralizes the white stripe is in reference to the Swadeshi movement. It's a truly lovely flag. You know of the Swadeshi movement? Of course you must.'

Dad nodded, impressed. 'This is great news. I like you. You have made a good showing for the white people.'

'Thank you.'

'Not a problem. And I insist that you teach Marina what you know about India. She knows nothing.' They both laughed. 'I bloody mean it.' He examined Thomas. 'I now feel comfortable enough in your presence to switch the television back on and continue watching the cricket without the slightest sense of guilt. Is this okay with you, my friend? India *is* the best cricket team in the world.'

Thomas agreed and looked on in amusement at how aggressive Marina's father became in front of the TV. Soon enough, thank goodness, Thomas's phone rang and he excused himself to take the call in the hall. Marina's father didn't even realize he had left.

Just about to speak to Reception at the hotel, Thomas noticed, through a crack in the door, Marina sitting on a kitchen stool crying steadily with her mother's arm around her. He told Cheryl he would call her back later as a fiery panic knotted itself inside his stomach.

He knocked on the door and poked his head round. 'Are you okay?'

'I'm okay.' Marina's eyes were fused with tears.

Mum shook her head at Thomas. 'She's not okay. Talk to her. She should be over this by now. The mourning period is long since passed.' She kissed Marina on the forehead. 'You silly samosa. Your gran died eighteen years ago, Marina. You make me so sad, I'm afraid to mention her without you falling to bits.' Mum touched Thomas on the shoulder and left them alone.

Marina jumped off the stool and wiped her eyes. Thomas was not supposed to have witnessed this. Now he knew what she had looked like when Take That had split up. It was all Robbie's fault.

'It's just the onions,' Marina stated, pointing to a huge orange netting bag of onions resting against the wall. 'Mum gets them from Sardau's Cash and Carry.' She sniffed. 'So, how are you and Dad getting along? Has he grilled you yet?'

'Fine, I think; I'm just waiting for him to mark my exam papers. I'm not too sure how well I did on India, his specialist subject, a subject he shows an immense interest in.' Thomas took hold of her hand. 'Why were you really crying?'

Marina led Thomas into the back garden where they sat on a damp wooden bench. A pitchfork was jammed into the hard soil near the garlic patch, Dad's one attempt at gardening for the year over. She took in the chilly air. What she was about to tell Thomas was not for her parents' ears. The words had been poisoning her for too long and it was time the infection was lanced. She would be letting Thomas down if she stalled with her honesty today. After all, from day one they had promised to be open with each other. It was a far cry from any boyfriends she'd had before where the object was to lie through her teeth, create as much hype about herself as she could, then blow the man out with a wave of her used Durex box. A far cry indeed. But Thomas *was* different and she knew all she needed to know about him to trust him. Just the other night his confession about Nicole had sent shivers down her spine, when he'd told her how he'd been an inch away from marrying Nicole for her looks. And looks alone. Thomas explained how low he was and Marina had agreed. Today, Thomas deserved to know how low she could be.

'I was crying because of my gran. It sounds funny now, but when Mum opened the jar of cumin powder, the powder reminded me of my gran's ashes.'

Thomas tried to contain himself. 'Sorry, I shouldn't laugh. Go on.'

'Anyway. When I was ten, I murdered my gran. I

killed the woman who gave birth to my dad.'

Suddenly Thomas was not laughing. Not this again, please. What were the odds of finding another woman who had killed someone? Was it the aftershave he wore? Did he have 'Murderess Sympathizer' stamped on his forehead?

He spoke. 'When you say murdered, in which context are you using the word? Also, have you disposed of the murder weapon? Are there any witnesses still alive? Did you enjoy it? And if so, can I recommend that the next victim is none other than David Blunkett. Obviously the guide dog gets a reprieve.' A thump on his arm silenced the sarcasm.

Giggling like schoolkids at the back of class at Thomas's last comment, the two soon settled down as Marina went on to explain the torment that had haunted her for eighteen years. She described as best she could the feelings of a young girl of ten in India.

Marina was at her gran's bedside when she passed away. Even though Nan looked peacefully asleep, Marina could tell she was dead by the way people were moving her around. Like a sack of old clothes, she was shunted off the hospital bed and on to a waiting stretcher. Marina had watched from the hallway as women howled their grief like wolves, a plan already forming in her young mind. Nan would be proud of her.

Outside on the dusty road a truck waited to transport Nan to the River Ganges. It was imperative that Nan was set on fire before the day was out. Her journey from this Hindu life to another depended on it. Cremation was the key that unlocked the door.

After Nan was washed and wrapped, her body was

laid on a pile of sandalwood then set alight by the riverside. Marina couldn't bear to look as the flames danced around her nan's body, and so she faced towards the mighty river instead, watching a boat dither past, and two sadhus, holy men, with their knobs out, washing each other. She heard prayers being uttered by relatives as Nan was basted with ghee, and the ghastly smell was intoxicating. Death may be senseless sometimes but it sure hit the senses. Marina was glad when the cremation was over and joined her family in solemn despair.

Three days later the family returned. It was the job of the eldest son to scatter the ashes on the River Ganges to complete the reincarnation ceremony. Marina waited until her uncle was talking to her parents, then took her chance. Quickly she pulled from her rucksack a small Tupperware container and filled it with a small amount of her nan's ashes, then hid it back in her bag. Nan was always ranting on about going to England, and finally that dream would be realized. It would be Marina's and Nan's secret.

Marina looked at Thomas then continued. 'It was only years later that it dawned on me that I might have only parts of Nan in my container.'

'You mean an arm or a leg? An earlobe, or even a hip bone? Or you might even, if you are really lucky, have the complete spinal column.'

She sneered. 'I'm sussing how your mind works, Thomas. It's not healthy. What I mean is this: because I stole some of her ashes, her entire body did not get released into the Ganges. Because of me, her soul is in limbo. Can you see why I am a murderer now? I have prevented my grandmother, the woman who cared about me so much, from enjoying her new life.'

Thomas dug deep for a comprehensive answer, bearing in mind that religion was rarely logical. 'My understanding of reincarnation, Marina, would have me believe that your grandmother did, indeed, pass on to her new life. Her soul would have moved on the minute she left this world, because the soul is immortal – unlike the body. I think that the ritual of casting the ashes into the Ganges is just that, *a ritual*. It's neither here nor there whether you held on to a handful of ashes, trust me.'

'And if you're wrong?' She raised her eyebrows. 'Hidden away in my suitcase under my bed is the container filled with her remains, what good are they there? They should be in the Ganges. Not a week goes past without me feeling sick with guilt. I really feel like I have let her down.' And Marina began to cry again, leaning into his chest. 'I had no right to interfere. I'm not a very nice person, Thomas. Nice people don't do that sort of thing.'

Thomas tried to calm her. Many a time in the past he'd spent consoling girlfriends, rubbing their backs, cheering them up. Whether it be that a zit had appeared overnight, or a dress suddenly didn't fit, or their hairdresser was out of town, the mantra he used was always the same: 'There there.' With Marina 'there there' wasn't enough.

He brushed her hair away, so he could see into her eyes. 'It's impossible to change what you did all those years ago, Marina, but you can make amends. Why don't we hop on a plane to India, book ourselves into a luxury hotel, then shoot down to the River Ganges?

At least after you have cast your grandmother's ashes on the river, you will be free of guilt.' He kissed her on the lips.

Interrupted by the sound of footsteps, they quickly pulled away from their embrace. Marina's father arrived with a huge smile.

He spoke directly to Thomas. 'I thought I would let you know that India just thrashed England at cricket. It was embarrassing to watch, they slaughtered them. You would have been ashamed of England.' And he walked away chuckling to himself.

Chapter Thirty-six

Thomas's mobile phone blared out its tune, the theme to *Jaws*, and he fumbled to answer it swiftly – his caller display showed it was the Regency. Quickly spinning around to improve the signal, Thomas spoke loudly into the phone. 'Hello . . . Hot . . . I normally give the Cliffords an extra ten per cent discount . . . Yes . . . And a bottle of champagne . . . Say again . . . SAY AGAIN . . . PROSTITUTES? . . . Jesus, *Charles*, how many were there? . . . Well, who let the camera crew in? . . . But you're not sure? . . . Well, you either are or you're not, Charles. I would bloody know if a porno film was being filmed under my nose . . . "Ramming in the Regency", that is *bloody* crude, Charles . . . Condoms?' he shouted, 'CONDOMS! Get rid of the porn stars and film crew immediately . . . Okay, thanks, Charles. Talk soon. Bye.' And Thomas switched off the phone, sweat dripping from his brow, and turned to an angry-looking Marina. 'Sorry about that.'

Marina was sitting amongst the shocked and embarrassed crowd of tourists, both Indian and foreign, who had heard *every* word. The same crowd of people whom Thomas and Marina had joined on an excursion to see the Taj Mahal. The same crowd of people who were still patiently sitting in place waiting for Thomas to rejoin them for the group photograph in front of the sacred monument.

This trip was one of many that Thomas and Marina had arranged for their month in India. Time had moved swiftly on since Thomas had suggested they visit Marina's homeland, its turbo-charged pendulum rushing past November, December and January like nobody's business. Marina chose February for the trip as this was the month in which her gran had passed away nineteen years ago.

And in the months leading up to this moment, Marina and Thomas had grown ever closer. Love was never mentioned but it was never far from their minds either. Life was changing rapidly. Not quite willing to surrender her independence entirely, Marina still rented her flat in Fenworth, although the lion's share of her time was spent with Thomas in his apartment. And her job? She clung on to it until Christmas, when Thomas gave her a credit card stamped with her name. Perv Bazzer would have to find another sandwich filler, Marina had her ambitions to follow. Thomas coaxed the dreams from her, never laughing, always encouraging. She sheepishly told him her fantasy of being a writer and he urged her to go for it. Underneath the filth on her wall, he'd seen some talent. It was just a matter of harnessing it.

The scariest part was the realization that her friendship with Emily would never be the same. Since that day with the red rubber dress, Emily had fallen head over eight-inch heels in love with Mr Cartwright, Andrew, and her eyes were misty with romance. Friendships like these never really die, Marina knew that, they just went into comas. But if either had a choice between men or friendship, men won every time. Emily proposed to Andrew after just a month and the white-rubber-dress wedding was due in April.

A text one day from Emily had Marina smiling:

Our Karma Is Fixed.
We Got Wot We Wanted.
Rich Gorgeous Men.
Now Let's Try Kama Sutra.
Love You Always – Emily XXX
PS I now own FIVE Gucci dresses.
Beat that!

And in many ways Emily was correct, their karma did appear to be fixed. Even Marina's parents and brother had taken to Thomas. Dad had begun boasting to all and sundry, his relatives included, that his future son-in-law was a multimillionaire. A white multimillionaire. Not that his skin colour *ever* mattered. How could it? He was a multimillionaire!

'Say *chapattis*,' the photographer requested, still in awe of the Taj Mahal before him.

'*Chapattis*,' the tourists said in unison, and the camera fired off another flash.

Marina and Thomas had been in India for a week, their lives most likely changed already. Yet India didn't even know they were there. Just another two bodies to scorch, another two minds to cleanse, another two . . . Hang on just one minute. A white man holding the hand of an Indian woman? What the *onion bhajis* was going on? Suddenly India *did* know they were here. In fact, Thomas and Marina had been shocked at the abuse they received from some of the locals upon arrival. It had been a while since Marina could remember being sworn at in Hindi, Punjabi, Gujerati and Urdu all at once. Holding hands in India was treated the same way as a couple having sex in public, although Thomas doubted the film makers in his hotel would make much money from a porn film of two people holding hands. Still, the lesson was learned and Thomas and Marina walked apart from that moment on.

And walking was the best transport at times. Through the bustling sun-scorched labyrinth of corridors, roads and passageways that swallowed up the visitors whole, Marina and Thomas uncovered the India that was hidden from the guide books. A world that *Going Places* never went to. Colourful, flimsy saris hanging to dry across narrow walkways where kids bathed naked in metal tubs. And smells that were either sickening or satisfying. Thomas and Marina struggled with the giggles when a dehydrated man of about seventy pulled down his *kachchas* and pooed in the drain before them. He smiled his gums at Thomas and Marina as they scampered by.

But life in India is a contrast of speeds. Either the mad sprint of the rickshaw man's muscular legs as he peddled to transport his customer, or the lumbering pace of the sacred cows which were reluctant to move from the hooting traffic. Hectic or humdrum, desperate or deliberate, speedy or sluggish. Just to watch the chaos was enough to need a huge smoke on a monster bong.

Thomas had already seen a man nearly killed by a runaway washing machine on a skateboard. He saw another man jump from a second-floor window, brush himself down, then carry on walking as if nothing had happened – with a limp. He'd watched with horror as two builders on opposite roofs threw breeze blocks across the busy road below. And he had witnessed his first Bollywood movie. Three hours of pain in a packed cinema; all the time Marina translating the plot and apologizing for the plot, Thomas impressed by the level of involvement the cinemagoers showed. Some wincing in anguish when the swords lashed the enemy, others cheering and stamping their feet on the floor when the heroine was won, and others crying, literally bawling their eyes out, when the hero died . . . But applauding loudly when he came back to life. Thomas was bewildered to hear Marina cheer the loudest.

And here they were, a must-see place in a must-see country. The Taj Mahal, which translates as the Crown of the Palace. Arguably the greatest building in the world. Thomas and Marina broke away from their guide and found a spot on the grass from which they could truly appreciate its magnificence. The white marble monolith was born from love. A grief-stricken emperor called Shah Jahan devoted twenty-two years of his life to building the monument in a tribute to the passing of his wife, Mumtaz Mahal, and just to be in its presence under the heat of the sun brings a sense of well-being to many.

'Do you feel India pulling you back, Marina?' Thomas asked, lying flat on the grass. 'Do you feel like it wants all its children to come back home?'

It was a powerful statement, but Marina *could* feel something. This was her true birth land, her life had begun in India's cradle. She had felt a sense of belonging the second she stepped off the British Airways plane and smelled the pungent air. As though a beacon shines in India to all those lost in other lands. A light that calls upon its children to come back if they need to. Do all Indian emigrants feel like she did, Marina wondered, as though they had turned their backs on the land that gave them a home?

'In my mind I have snubbed India. I have shunned the very place that was good enough for every other generation of my family. But we,' she glanced across at him quite sadly, 'we thought we deserved better and skidded off to England. It's pretty shameful really.'

Thomas tried to make her feel better, explaining about choice and how she'd had none. How her parents were not snubbing but branching out. An Indian is still an Indian whatever country he or she ends up in. He described how lucky she was to have roots in this wonderful country that was bubbling with personality and tradition. India would always be in her heart no matter how many miles separated them. She didn't snub India, she had just gone, as the Aussies would say, 'walkabout'.

They lay talking as others must have done in the

past, but, alas, even in India the sun goes down and soon sent them on their way. Thomas and Marina left the Taj Mahal grounds with a full quota of memories but empty bellies. Their luxurious hotel awaited them with a quality of service that made Thomas green with envy. Servants at their beck and call with generous smiles and genuine contentment. A food menu that had taste buds whimpering. Chinese. Indian. Japanese. Spanish. Italian. And after you had stuffed your face, a Jacuzzi, or a swim, or a night in watching satellite TV.

Or even a night out watching the biggest satellite of them all. The moon. Thomas and Marina ate, showered, changed, then headed on down to the River Yamuna, where they hoped to catch a last glimpse of the Taj Mahal before they headed off towards Kanpur tomorrow. The laid-back nature of most native Indians was in complete contrast to the stressed-out foreigners madly trying to fit in as much of India as they could before they returned to . . . more stress back home.

At the water's edge Marina and Thomas stared across the choppy river, the bold face of the nearly full moon reflected in the ripples. The distant Taj Mahal seemed to float above the water, an illusion that would defeat most magicians. To miss out on this moment would be sacrilege. Thomas stood behind Marina, wrapping his arms around her as they peered outwards in total silence.

Do I deserve all this? Marina wondered. To be standing with the man she loved in her motherland, to be looking forward to her future rather than dreading it, to have both her parents happy for her, in her choices, in her life. Maybe this was karma, this was the way of Shiva, this was what happened when you tried to do the right thing. What goes around comes around. The carousel of yin and yang. She squeezed Thomas's hand. To think that not even a year ago she hadn't even known Thomas existed, and now, she couldn't exist without him. She turned and kissed him on the mouth. Sod the sex police.

A tugging on Thomas's T-shirt broke the cuddle. Thomas stared down at a girl of about four. The pretty smile and wide eyes did nothing to hide the bleeding on her tiny bare feet. This was far from the first time Thomas and Marina had been approached by beggars this week. The girl stood there with her hand out, urging Thomas by widening her eyes even more.

'Please,' she said. 'Please.'

Thomas shook his head at Marina. 'I know what you said, but I can't ignore this any more.' He reached into his back pocket and produced a bundle of rupees – the equivalent of a hundred quid – and gently placed the notes in her grubby mitt. The girl looked hard at her hand, gave Thomas her best smile and legged it into the darkness.

'You say this every time, Tom. You can't change the world. I know it's hard but you have to ignore it.' Marina sensed her words would have little impact. 'How much have you given away this week? Two thousand? Three?'

'Five. I'm addicted. It's worse than gambling.' He took Marina's hand again. 'I think I might need to have a substantial amount of money wired over by next week if I continue at this rate.'

She laughed, but his explanation hit home. Thomas could afford to change lives. So what if by the time they headed home Thomas was the new Pied Piper of Punjab. So what if he couldn't help everyone. So what if the money didn't always find its way into the beggars' mouths. So what! At least he tried.

Thomas felt a tugging on his T-shirt – the little girl was back, this time with a friend.

Three weeks into the pilgrimage, Marina's and Thomas's journey brought them to Varanasi, the holiest of Indian cities. The learning curve for Thomas had been a steep one over the last twenty-one days, getting to grips with the different what-cans and what-cannots of India. No wearing shorts in temples. No eating beef. No public displays of nudity – learned the hard way when an old woman hit his bare back with a stick. No shaking hands with women. No photographs of military installations. Thomas even had to ask Marina if it was impolite to stare when they came across a holy man with his head buried in the sand – literally. Apparently he was punishing himself for some sin and would remain buried for a day. Marina had replied, 'It hardly matters if you stare, Tom, because he can't see you.' She'd pointed to the holy man's feet wriggling in the air. 'His head is buried in the sand. Dur! Are you sure you went to Oxford University?'

And as they walked around the city paved with prayers and trodden with heavy, guilty feet, Marina could tell why they called this place Shiva's City. They passed clans of people bewitched by soothsayers and tiny gatherings where sermons were being preached.

A queue of sadhus snaked its way through the streets, and the strong sense of belief was omnipresent in the air. Marina and Thomas kept close as they drove their bodies through the masses of worshippers heading towards the sacred river. The Oxford Street sales had nothing on this. And Thomas had to smile when he thought of the advice given by the old man selling whistles: 'If you get lost, just blow on one of these. Two hundred rupees.' The air was filled with whistles.

At last an opening with space. Thomas and Marina filtered away from the main crowd and lodged themselves under a small canopy made from woven coconut hair. The River Ganges was just half a mile down from this point and could be clearly seen down the shallow hill. From as far left as one could see to as far right, temples lined the water's edge. It would be almost inconceivable not to be religious here. Some Hindus say this place is *the* place to be born and *the* place to die. No doubt some Hindus live up to that saying or, rather, die up to it.

It was midday, oven hot and sticky wet. Marina watched Thomas, who watched the river, the sun bouncing off the whistle round his neck. He was as brown as an Indian now. A blue-eyed Indian. And like her he'd also shed a few pounds of weight. Much to her delight, Thomas had enjoyed every minute here. Showing off her country had been a pleasure when he took so much interest. It made it that much easier when the time came to tell him that she had misplaced the passports and plane tickets.

'So, do you need some quiet time alone before you do this, Marina?' Thomas asked, referring to her gran's ashes. She nodded yes. 'I'll just be over here, then.' He moved a few feet to one side and sat in the dust, contemplating.

If ever there was a place to contemplate his existence then this had to be it. Marina was the woman he had been fearing all his life. The woman he would fall in love with. Before Marina he had always carried a set of imaginary scales, balancing the woman against his hotel. Sometimes the hotel won, sometimes the woman won. Sometimes it was too close to call so he gave it to the hotel anyway. But with Marina there could be no scales. No comparisons. No afterthoughts. No regrets. No . . . God, he had fallen for her massively. And it wasn't just he who had been taken in by her charm. Mom and Pops thought the world of her, his friends found her amusing entertainment, although his exes despised her, and he – Thomas glanced over to Marina deep in meditation – he loved her.

Love used to mean 'fully booked' or 'a new Porsche', even 'Ultra Stay Hold gel for *extra* messy hair' but it was a word he never felt comfortable with around women. He had tried it out on Nicole a few times, telling her he loved her, although he really meant he loved the way she looked. How shallow was that? Nicole used to call him Superman, but really he was Superficial. Showering Nicole with watered-down versions of the word 'love' was a bastard thing to do and something he'd promised himself he would never do again. Love was a dangerous word in the wrong mouth.

'I'm ready.' Marina stood up and held the Tupperware container in her hands. 'I have made my peace with Shiva. Let's do it!'

They began their descent into the mayhem below, joining a trickle of people that soon became a stream. A hundred dialects gabbled excitedly, punctuated by the odd shout when someone lost their footing. The crowd forever swelling, continuous, unstoppable. Thomas was overwhelmed by it all. This was a zillion miles from Oxford. This was raw life. A lone cow decided to lie down in the masses' path, causing the people to steer around it. If a camel had tried the same thing, Thomas and Marina would have been wearing camel slippers by the time they hit the bottom. It would have given them the right hump. Onwards they went, an army of colour, a sweaty rabble of worshippers. The pushing and shoving, the dogs barking and children crying, in some ways it was utter chaos, in others it was pure harmony. The only practice that Thomas had had for this was a Guns n' Roses concert at Milton Keynes Bowl. Finally, FINALLY, the River Ganges was at their feet. It was a glorious sight.

A dead goat with its hooves turned up drifted past. Obviously not the swimmer it thought it was. Thomas was about to comment when he saw a man without any testicles bathing in the sacred water. Marina explained he was a holy man, devoid of any pleasure, proving his allegiance to God. They edged their way down the shore, past the wet sari competition, bypassing a family carrying a dead body to its last rites, then on to a fairly isolated patch of water which was populated with a few heavily bearded men on their knees praying and a couple of flower sellers with baskets of orange marigolds.

Thomas stepped back and watched as Marina walked into the River Ganges, the murky brown water rising up her sarong. She smiled back at him, a huge weight about to be lifted from her shoulders.

Marina took a deep breath then spoke very quietly in Hindi. 'I am sorry I ever took your ashes, Gran . . . nineteen years ago to this very day. Please forgive me and I hope that your new life is less hard than the one I know you had this time round. I love you, Gran.' Marina swished the container under the water, letting the Ganges wash the ashes away. She delicately scattered a handful of flower petals on to the surface and watched the waxy leaves gently drift with the current as her tears of happiness and relief fell to the river below.

About to join Thomas on the shore, Marina couldn't help but notice three things. One, he was the only white man there. Two, Thomas had, by far, the messiest haircut – he would be chuffed. And three, he was on his knees praying. She approached him warily, afraid to disturb his peace, and stood just a foot away. Even knee-deep in the Ganges, with the muddy water splattered all over his once-white Armani T-shirt, the man still looked gorgeous. It was here that Marina reflected on the cycle of events that had set her life spinning in the right direction. Gran's advice with the Ganges water had given her Thomas. Which in turn had brought them back to the River Ganges. Nineteen years to complete a full circle. Who knew what the next nineteen years might bring? Thomas was mumbling something under his breath which sounded like 'saveloy', maybe he was missing his sausages. A minute passed before his eyes opened.

'I should have done that years ago,' Marina began, 'it's like someone has taken the stone out of my shoe and I can walk normal again. I can't thank you enough for this.' She paused, a lump in her throat. 'This means so much to me, Tom, and you've been great. I really don't know how—'

'Marina, not this again. For the last time, it's been my absolute pleasure.'

'I just wanted you to know.' She viewed the throngs of people up and down the water's edge, splashing and bathing, frolicking and crying, their purpose a simple one: to wash away their sins. She returned her attention to Thomas. Marina wasn't going to ask, but couldn't help herself. 'What were you doing just then? You looked like you were praying. Somehow I never took you as a believer.'

Thomas smiled. 'I was praying on a star. The greatest star of them all. If I can't clasp my hands together here, amongst all this belief, then where can I?'

She squinted her eyes and looked towards the sky. 'You were praying on a star? Which one?' She *really* was confused.

'The only star. The fifth star.'

'Fifth?'

'The fifth AA star that I require to make the Regency a five-star hotel.' He laughed. 'It might work, who knows?'

'But, I thought I heard you say something about a saveloy?'

'Saveloy?' Thomas cracked up. 'No, I was saying I want my hotel to be better than the Savoy. Not saveloy. Dur!'

He placed his arm around her, people too busy in their own worlds to take notice of theirs, and helped her over to the bank. A swarm of mosquitoes fleeing from a nearby burning pyre whizzed by, momentarily side-tracking Thomas's unplanned speech. Then he waited until a group of destitute mourners had passed; the moment had to be right. As soon as their wails of sadness became distant, Thomas took hold of Marina's hand, gazed into her deep-brown eyes and told her that he loved her.

Marina giggled. 'Tom, I don't understand. What does it mean? You know I don't speak Italian. It's so unfair when you do this.'

Then he told her in French, German, Spanish, Russian, Japanese. He even told her he loved her in Hobbit language. Finally, after some arm twisting, Thomas declared in full Queen's English, that he truly loved her.

And this time the word 'love' was not watered down.

Also by Nisha Minhas

Chapatti or Chips?

For twenty-three years, Naina has saved herself for the man her parents have chosen for her to marry. They've chosen well: Ashok is handsome, kind and considerate. Although she's met him only twice, Naina knows he would make a good husband.

Dave, on the other hand, would not. Although, like Ashok, he's goodlooking and charming, he's also unreliable, thoughtless – and an incorrigible womaniser.

Dave is Trouble with a capital 'T'. And with six months to go until her wedding day, Naina knows she should keep well away from him. So why can't she stop herself . . .?

ISBN 0 7434-3045 X

PRICE £6.99

Also by Nisha Minhas

Sari & Sins

It's Kareena's wedding night and she's understandably nervous. Tonight, for the first time, she will make love to her husband, a man she's met only a few times, a man she barely knows. But everything will be all right. Her parents have chosen well – and Kareena is confident she will grow to love Samir, in time.

But Samir has a secret. A secret in the shapely form of Cloey, whom he's been dating for the past six years. Cloey isn't prepared to give up her man – or, more importantly, his bank balance – without a fight. And she's prepared to fight very dirty indeed.

Kareena, however, is not the timid little Indian bride Cloey had expected her to be. In fact, Cloey might just have met her match . . .

ISBN 0 7434-3046 8

PRICE £6.99